The Claws are Showing

Richard Stour

The Claws are Showing

St. Martin's Press New York

Library of Congress Cataloging in Publication Data

Stour, Richard.
    The claws are showing.

    I. Title.
PZ4.S8884Cl5   [PS3569.T657]   813'.5'4   76-28060

The Claws are Showing

Gerard Garvin Steele

THE corridor was carpeted in plum and panelled in ornately-speckled woods. It was wide and high, with a ceiling elaborately worked in moulded plaster and crystal. When the décor of the thirties becomes fashionable again, its contents will be worth almost what they cost, but meanwhile they are over-ornate relics. The man's feet moved along a line bisecting the length of the corridor; on anything less aborbent of sound than the plum carpet, they would have clumped. The walk was slightly forward-leaning, a little spring-heeled. Like the rest of him it was aggressive; he marched down the middle of the corridor, head down, brooding; a man so immersed in deep and penetrating thought that anybody approaching would instantly sense its importance and stand aside to let him pass.

A woman did this. She came out of one of the doors and, seeing his approach, stood against the wall.

'Good afternoon, Mr. Steele.'

She watched him walk past her. He did not acknowledge her greeting or even her presence and she wondered idly what was happening inside that shaggy and leonine head.

If the human brain made noises indicative of its emotions, the woman would have heard a sharp hiss of simmering resentment. Steele had been summoned. He was walking along the corridor to the managing director's office. Nor did he know why. All three facts offended him. He was, after all, the editor of an important journal of news and comment, wielder of influence, dispenser of patronage, arbiter of style and taste. People should and did come to him.

He opened the speckled door and Marion Fisher looked up pleasantly. 'Oh, Mr. Steele. He won't keep you a moment.'

Steele said, 'For Christ's Sake, it's press day tomorrow!'

'I know it is. But the Chairman telephoned *him*, Mr. Steele.' Her tone was mollifying but her manner was no-nonsense. Steele walked across to the window, wishing he could

7

ignore Miss Fisher and go straight into Fienburgh's office. He looked out over the streets that ran up to the Strand, simmering still, but feeling the satisfaction he always felt when his feet were on thick carpets in a high place.

'Would you like a cup of tea, Mr. Steele?'

He didn't reply and after a moment, Marion Fisher repeated, 'Tea?'

Steele turned. 'I'm sorry, I was . . .'

'Yes. Tea?'

Steele smiled at her. 'That would be marvellous. Thanks awfully.' He returned to the window and stared out and down as she rose from her desk and vanished into the little kitchen off Fienburgh's office. When she was gone, he crossed to her desk, picked up an early edition of the Evening Standard and began to handle it noisily, while his eyes searched her desk top for morsels of information. Miss Fisher, however, was securely tidy and everything was neat and out of sight, in folders or baskets. Damn it, why did he still think of her as Miss Fisher? She was his master's secretary, that was all. Fienburgh called her Marion, so why the hell shouldn't *he*? But he didn't. There was nothing to stop him; she could hardly object. But if he did, she would look at him in a way he did not wish to be looked at. So he called her nothing at all, neither the Marion of familiarity, nor the Miss Fisher of habit and formality.

She came back into the room, the cup in her hand. 'Here you are. Sugar?'

'Thanks.' Steele put in two large teaspoonfuls, stirred and sipped. 'He's having a long natter with God.'

'I suppose so.' She sat down and swivelled her chair to face the IBM Executive electric typewriter on the short side of her L-shaped desk. 'Would you mind if I went on. I have to get this done.'

'Not at all, not at all. Please carry on.'

'Thank you.' Marion Fisher's fingers moved fast and efficiently over the keys while Steele sipped noisily at the scalding tea and watched her. She must be sixty now; near it, anyway. When she had started work, it was probably on those old Remingtons and Underwoods whose keys had had to be thumped hard and accurately and which produced well-typed

8

letters only for typists whose touch was even. Yet here she was, forty-odd years later, mistress of this elaborate electric gadget many younger women hated because its feather-lightness demanded of them a level of skill they were not prepared to acquire. Miss Fisher . . . Marion Fisher! . . . was one of the women who, for half a century or so, have braced the backbone of British management. 'Braced the backbone of British Management', Steele liked the phrase and filed it in his mind. He began, mentally, to write the article '. . . Grey-haired, bespectacled, faintly disapproving; capable, meticulous, strong . . . often they, not their employers, were the real management . . . a generation going now, replaced by the smartly expensive young . . .' A light flashed on one of the telephones and she turned.

'Please go on in, Mr. Steele.'

Steele laughed, 'God has spoken, then.' He put down his cup, crossed to the door, opened it wide and went into Fienburgh's office. 'You wanted me?'

Fienburgh's head was down. He looked up. 'Hello, Gerard. Sit down,' and he pushed the scrap pad he'd been staring at to one side.

Steele said, 'God, what a day! All hell's breaking loose downstairs.'

'Why?' Fienburgh was, as always, interested, inquiring.

'The Chancellor. He's mucking about with the regulator. It means our leading article is nonsense.' Behind him he heard the soft click as Miss Fisher closed the door.

'That's his job.'

'What's it all about, then?' Steele's tone held a trace of resignation, a little world-weariness, a willingness to break off the mighty struggle and deal with pettifogging detail.

Fienburgh said, 'You, Gerard.'

Throb! Steele felt and heard the drum bang in his chest, felt the skin tighten across his forehead and at his temples. He said, 'Oh?' as casually as he could.

'Like a drink?' Fienburgh rose and walked to the walnut sideboard without waiting for the answer. Steele waited, fear expanding inside him.

Fienburgh returned with a crystal whisky glass containing

9

about two fluid ounces of pale malt whisky. His own was smaller.

'Thanks. Cheers!' Steele sipped at the whisky, feeling the smooth-harsh tingle spread through mouth and throat and across his chest.

Fienburgh said, 'You need a change.'

'Do I?' He had difficulty saying the two words: And as the sheep before his bloody shearers is dumb! He sipped the Scotch again.

'Cigarette?' The china box was pushed across the table towards him. Steele took one of the Sobranie Virginias and lit it.

'Thanks. Why do I need a change?' Bull by the horns!

'We all do. As often as possible and as total as we can make it. Don't you think?'

'If you're generalizing. *Dauer im Wechsel.*'

'Nature's mighty law is change,' Fienburgh quoted back.

Steele had to ask. 'Surely not Burns?'

Fienburgh grinned. 'Like Shakespeare and the Bible, he has something for all occasions. And easier than your Goethe for those of us born in Scotland.'

'What's the change to be?' Steele asked. Burns was the weakness in his armoury of quotation, and Fienburgh slid his phrases through the chink with irritating ease and frequency. Any other poet and he'd have set about mastering him, but with Burns there was another language to learn first.

'You're going on a course.'

Steele stared. After a moment, he said, 'A course? That's stupid!'

'Thanks.'

'Oh, I didn't mean you!' Steele said quickly. 'But what sort of course would—'

'A management course.'

'Christ! But why?'

'Because the group is running courses and certain people are going on them. You're nominated for the first one.' He corrected himself, 'The second, I should say.'

'Who nominated me?'

'Don't glare at me,' Fienburgh said. 'I'm not your target.'

'Well, I'm not going!' Steele said. 'And that's that!'

'The names have been selected by Mr. Philips, Gerard.'

'I'm still not going. It's bloody silly.'

'Philips says there will be no backing out,' Ficnburgh went on gently. 'Those selected will be present for the kick-off.'

'For Christ's sake!'

'If it's any consolation to you; one, you're not the only person who feels like that. And, two, the course is quite fun.'

'Fun!'

'Fun.'

Steele said, 'And if I refuse?'

'It's orders. Philips is, after all, the group managing director. He knows hardly anybody ever wants to go. That's why the instruction is so firm.'

'But I've got a paper to get out. Christ, what hapens to *Viewpoint* in the meantime?'

Fienburgh smiled. 'One of the things they'll tell you on the course is that nobody is vital.'

'That has always been the way one fool reassures another. That paper needs every ounce of effort that can be put into it.'

'It does indeed.'

'Well, then?'

'It's a resigning matter. Philips' own words.'

Steele said, 'He expected me to refuse, then?'

'Sorry. About somebody who didn't want to go on the first one, the one I went on.'

'I'm bloody well tempted!'

'Think what life would be like without a platform of your own. Then think again.'

'A course, though. It's like the army!'

'Oddly enough, it is,' Fienburgh said. 'Exactly like the army. "Morning gentlemen" and that kind of thing. But a touch more luxurious.'

'That settles it. I'm not going.'

'We had one or two fascinating sessions, you know. Lynd was there. I sat next to him at lunch.'

'Rupert Lynd?'

'Yes. He talked about the way the social structure would develop. Fascinating. What a man!'

'Oh, Lynd's all right. That would be tolerable.' Steele awarded a tattered accolade:

'It was more than tolerable, Gerard.'

'Great men and all that sort of thing?'

'Yes.'

'I don't believe in great men,' Steele said. 'Just men. If you prick us do we not bleed?'

'Have it your own way,' Fienburgh said. 'But I thought you'd better be aware of the alternatives.'

'Go – or go.'

'Just that.'

Steele grimaced, tipped the whisky down his throat and rose. 'Well, if this is to be my last edition of *Viewpoint*, I'd better make it a good one.'

'Yes.' Fienburgh rose too, picked up the glass from the desk and returned it to the sideboard. 'I didn't want to go, either. But I went and I enjoyed it. So will you.'

'Unlikely,' Steel said. He went to the door, opened it and walked into Miss Fisher's room.

She gave him a small smile. 'This came from Mr. Philips' office.' She was holding out a large manilla envelope.

'I don't think I shall be needing it.' Steele's smile held a sad defiance.

Miss Fisher pushed it into his hand. 'Better take it, all the same.' Then she turned and closed the door.

Back in his own office, Steele opened the envelope and pulled out a handful of paper. The top sheet was headed, 'Please complete immediately and return to the Managing Director's office.' He ran his eyes down the little questionnaire. Did he want a room with a bath or one with a shower? Steele grinned and wrote 'Both.' Did he require a special diet? The smart answer came into his mind, but he suppressed it easily and wrote 'No.' The other questions were much the same: minor matters of administration. He pressed the buzzer and his secretary came in, slim, long-legged, a calm blonde.

'Send this crap back for me, Sue.'

'To whom?'

'The managing director's office.'

He watched her make a note on her pad. 'No, not that twit upstairs. The other twit. Philips. At Euromob House.'

'With a letter?'

'No. No need. Oh, and look Sue, I'm going on a course.'

'A course?' She looked puzzled.

'Some management thing,' Steele said. 'Bloody silly, but Philips insists I go.'

'You'll hate it, won't you?' Sue asked.

'Oh God, yes! But it's one of the penalties. I'll be away three weeks starting on October the fourth.'

'Where is it?'

'The Princess. Bloody glass and steel barbarity.'

She said, 'Oh, but it's super! I went there to dinner the other night. You'll love it.'

She would! Steele nodded, dismissing her. As she walked to the door he admired the long legs and trim swaying bottom. One of the penalties of employing lissom girls with double-barrelled names was that they were always one-upping you. Sue had, from childhood, regarded as normal what he saw as wild extravagance. Take her to dinner at some posh restaurant and the head waiter would know her but not you. The other and better side of the coin was the pleasure of employing the upper classes, or at least the upper middles, sending for them, dismissing them with a nod.

He rang for her again and began to read the papers from the manilla envelope.

'Yes, Mr. Steele?'

He looked up. Quite slowly. She glanced away as he did so and Steele looked at her admiringly: her capacity to ignore, rather than resent or blush at a deliberately lecherous stare, was one of the things he envied.

'I'll do the critique,' he said.

'Very well.' She sat down, the long legs carefully on display, pen poised for his weekly 'Viewpoint on *Viewpoint*,' which was stuck on the paper's noticeboards.

'Teilhard de Chardin once said . . .' he began. 'Oh – er – can you spell that?'

13

Sue looked up at him apologetically. 'No, I'm sorry.'

He smiled at her in satisfaction and began to spell it . . .

Steele climbed out of the taxi outside the Princess Hotel, picked up his suitcase and briefcase and went inside. The electrically-operated doors opened and closed and he was in the air-conditioned lobby. A porter hurried to take his bags.

'I don't know the room number,' Steele said. 'Euromob booked it.'

'Yes sir. Mr. — ?'

'Steele.'

The porter returned a moment later from the reception desk with a key. 'Number one four oh three, sir.'

'Thank you.'

'I'll take the bags up, sir, if you're going to the meeting.' The porter pointed to the stairs. 'The Novello Room.'

Steele tipped him and walked across to the staircase, where a discreet sign pointed downward. The carpet beneath his feet was pleasantly soft, the air cool, the lighting gentle. At the bottom, he glanced around and saw the lettered artist's board which proclaimed, 'European Communications Ltd.' He opened the door and went in. The room was empty, but a long table was covered with a baize cloth and surrounded by chairs.

A minute or two later a girl came in; a neutral sort of girl who might, he thought, have brains, but had precious little else.

'Oh, hello. You're early.'

'Either that, or everybody else is late,' Steele said with quiet savagery.

She was unconcerned. 'I was chasing up the coffee. Mr. Longbottom's had to pop up to get something. You're the first, anyway. You're Mr. — ?'

'Steele.'

'Oh, yes. I'm Diana Hughes, Mr. Longbottom's secretary, dogsbody, p.a. general assistant. Ah, here it is—' A waiter came in, pushing a trolley. 'Cup of coffee, Mr. Steele?'

'Thank you. Did you say Longbottom?'

The girl turned. 'Yes?'

14

'That *must* be a joke. Nobody's called Longbottom outside funny books.'

'Oh, but they are,' said a voice behind him. 'I am, for one.'

'I'm sorry.' Steele looked at him. 'Gerard Steele.' He held out his hand.

'Of *Viewpoint*?' Longbottom said. 'It's a great pleasure to meet you. I started reading it at school.'

Steele said, 'I doubt if I edited it then.'

'No, of course.' Longbottom laughed. 'Coffee?'

'The girl asked me.'

'Diana?'

'If that's her name.'

Steele took the cup to the table, picked up a cigarette from the box of a hundred beside his chair and lit it. The table was T-shaped: room for three at the top; six chairs on each side of the descender. Immediately behind the top table stood an easel on which a big pad of paper hung, each sheet the size of a broadsheet newspaper.

This, Steele thought, was the schoolroom. Coffee instead of milk; cigarettes on the desk instead of in the lavatories. But school. The chair was plain wood and upright, the surroundings plain, too. For a room named after Ivor, the Novello Room was a bit bleak.

'Would you mind wearing this?'

Steele looked up. Longbottom was holding out a piece of black plastic upon which, in white letters, was the name Gerard Steele. He said, 'For one thing, I don't wear bloody labels. For another, it's not my name.'

'But—' Longbottom hesitated, 'You are Mr. Steele, of *Viewpoint.*'

'I'm Gerard *Garvin* Steele.'

'I see. Well, for the time being . . .?'

'No.'

Longbottom said patiently, 'The badges really are a big help. People get to know one another more quickly—'

'I will not be labelled like a piece of cheese,' Steele said. 'In any case, I'd have thought it was up to somebody to get the names right. It's easy enough. I expect some silly little bitch just cut it out—'

15

'I'll get another done for you,' Longbottom was almost deferential

'There's not a lot of point, I won't—'

'Good morning.' Another man had arrived. His voice was hard, flat somehow.

'Ah, you're Mr. — ?'

'Verity. Tommy Verity.' He was a big man, hard-looking, big-faced, with prominent features. His voice was flat and hard, too, its accent unmistakably Northern.

Introductions were made and then other voices were heard as more course members arrived. Steele stayed where he was, looking at them, noting the way they obediently pinned badges to their lapels, took their coffee cups and chatted politely. He didn't know one of them, and from what he could see, didn't want to. Brief, potted biographies of each had been supplied in the course documentation, but a quick glance had told him they were accountants and salesmen. Directors of major Euromob subsidiaries they might be, but they remained clerks and salesmen. The women, of course, might be more interesting, but they were doubtless going to make late and effective entrances.

He lit another cigarette and in doing so, missed Jane Roper's entrance.

'Lovely bit of crackling, that,' a voice said softly.

Steele looked round. The man beside him was small, fat, genial-looking. He wore spectacles with big brown frames and his hair, what remained of it, was lank and scruffy.

'Who—' he began irritably.

The fat man bent so that his badge came level with Steele's eyes.

'Malcolm Templeton. I'm the psychologist. And I said she's a smashing dollop of custard. Look at her, you fathead. There's little enough pleasure in life.'

Steele began angrily. 'Don't—'

'Over there, man. With the legs. Look!'

Steele turned and looked. She was all that Templeton had promised: an extremely attractive girl who stood with confident elegance talking to Longbottom's dowdy assistant.

16

'That's better than a drop in the market valuation, eh?' Templeton said, nudging.

Steele shuffled and stood up, hating the nudge, hating the assumed male alliance, resenting the intimacy.

'I wonder who she is?' Templeton mused. 'Still, we'll know in a minute.'

John Michael Longbottom

HE looked at his watch: five past ten. No more grace. He rapped the top of the table with his knuckles. 'Take your seats, please. You'll find name cards on the table.' He watched Steele get up and move, sit down moodily, then rise quickly to help Jane Roper into her seat. Apart from the presence of three women – unusual on senior management courses – they looked the usual bunch: the customary mixture of toughness and talent, glitter and grit, courtesy and callousness that characterized any similar assembly.

They looked down the table at him, expectantly.

Longbottom pointed to his badge. 'I'm John Michael Longbottom and I'm leader of this course. I'm responsible for the way it goes. I'm not a teacher, though I do some teaching. More than anything, I'm here to be talked to.' He looked round. 'Anybody been on a course before?'

A hand moved affirmatively on the right. There were one or two yesses.

'What?'

'Decision-making. Keppner Tregoe.'

'Would you give your name, please.'

'Sinclair, s—'

Longbottom smiled inwardly at the suppressed 'sir'. It was always astonishing how quickly the schoolroom patterns came back to the surface. 'Thank you. What else?'

'Graphic controls. Oh, sorry – Keller.'

'Thanks, Mr. Keller. Where?'

'U.C.L.A.'

Longbottom grinned. 'Big stuff. Will *you* give *me* a lecture, please! Anybody else?'

'I did one on creating productivity agreements – oh, sorry, Verity, Tommy Verity – but it was more a council of war.'

'Thanks. At least some of you know how we carry on. All this rigmarole of ours. The names and so on. Have you all got these

18

plastic badges, by the way? You have? Good. All except Mr. Steele. We got his wrong. Missed out his middle name. Still, we find after a while that everybody uses Christian names anyway. Now, we find the best way to start is to get people to introduce themselves. A brief, spoken biography. Just so that everybody gets to know everybody else. I'll start off; give you the idea . . .

'I'm John Michael Longbottom, which may be an unusual name to you, but isn't to me. There were two others in my year at school and we weren't related. I come from Yorkshire, near Cleckheaton, as a matter of fact, so comic names seem to surround me. I went to the local grammar school, then to Cambridge. I read classics, then I joined the marketing department of Unilever and stayed there three years after which I got involved in the manufacturing process at Metal Box. I'm a partner in MUNP, the organization which is running this course for European Communications Ltd.' He paused. 'Anybody mind if I call it Euromob? Everybody seems to say it nowadays. Good. MUNP is Müller, Urquhart, Nostell and Partners. Müller died two years ago and left a million. Urquhart and Nostell are retired now and live in the Argentine and Jamaica respectively. The partners hold courses like this, advise companies, solve problems, et cetera, et cetera. I, by the way, am married and I have two kids, both girls. They are the reason for all this white hair at the age of thirty-five.'

Longbottom sat down. 'That's all. Okay?'

They stared back at him and he let his eyes look from one to the other, round the table.

Eleven of them, averaging what? Seven thousand, eight maybe. Large cars, large houses. There was a lot of money in this room. A lot of pride too, and ability, venom and jealousy.

'You're sitting in alphabetical order, so perhaps you would care to start off, Mr. Farmer.'

'Me?' Mike Farmer looked up, anxiously. This, obviously, was a man whose nerves were near the surface.

'If you would, Mr. Farmer.' Unbelievable, almost, that this was one of the top computer men in the country, and one of the most experienced. Farmer could, and sometimes did, fill university lecture halls to talk about 'The Social Mission of the

Computer' or 'Autonomics – Basing Computer use on the Human Miracle.'

'Well, I dunno,' Farmer said. 'I started off in Statistics—'

'Where?' Longbottom prompted gently.

'Eh? Oh, evening classes at Goldsmith's. I was apprenticed to a carpenter, then. After that, I went into the Air Force and they helped and then I got a degree in maths. That was by correspondence course, you see. External degree from London. And then I went to the Foreign Office to work on their first computer. That's all, really.'

Farmer was sweating and stuttering. 'Family,' Longbottom prompted again.

'Yes. Well, no. Well, we're separated you see. Married to computers, I suppose.' Longbottom knew that if Farmer left Euromob, he could name his own salary at any of a hundred places in Britain or America, but it was hard to believe that now, looking at the pale face with its old-fashioned glasses and the ragged fair hair. Still, in the nineteen-seventies, computer wizards didn't need polish or grace. First-class honours in maths by correspondence!

Longbottom said, 'Thanks Mr. Farmer,' and looked at Farmer's neighbour. 'Mrs. Fazackerley? Will you carry on?'

Clare Fazackerley looked coolly back at him. 'I don't know about that, but I'll tell you what there is to tell.'

'If you would—' Longbottom stopped as he felt a nudge from his left.

'Forgetting me, aren't you?'

'Sorry, Malcolm.' Longbottom smiled at Clare Fazackerley. 'Mrs. Fazackerley, I shouldn't have started this yet. The custom is that *we* introduce ourselves to *you*, first. Do you mind?'

'Not in the slightest.' Clare Fazackerley was, he thought, one of those cool, brainy women who can't ever be wrong-footed.

'Now then, prepare for a sordid tale,' Templeton said. 'My name is Malcolm Templeton and I'm an industrial psychologist. I select people for jobs, I analyse the psychological problems work can produce. And best of all I attend courses like this because I like the free gin and lovely ladies. I'm thirty and I look forty because I lead a shocking life, what with all the gin

20

and all the ladies. I also collect Jewish stories. Did you hear about the Jewish fella, he was knocked dahn inna street—' Templeton slid smoothly into a stagy East End Jewish accent '—an' 'e's lying there sec. So one woman, she puts something under his head. And this other fella, 'e takes off his Crombie overcoat and covers him. Somebody else is away calling the ambulance. So the police arrive and one of them leans over this fella in the road and he says, "Are you comfortable?" And this Jewish fella, 'e looks up and says, "Comfortable?" 'e says, "Comfortable? Well, I make a living." '

Longbottom watched them laugh. There were two Jews, at a guess, round the table and they laughed, too. Only one man didn't. Why? Longbottom looked at the name card on the table: Giesing.

'. . . And that's about all there is to it. Except that you'll be wondering why I'm here. You don't believe it's just for the gin and you're right. I'm here to chip in my two cents' worth whenever the occasion arises. If any of you suspect I'm making out reports on you, forget it. I'm going to be the first to say this: *There is no reporting back.* You come on this course to be exposed to new ideas and techniques. Nobody's checking on you! Okay?'

Longbottom watched Templeton resume his seat, then cued him. 'Job evaluation.'

'Oh yes. Well, we do this job evaluation caper and some psychological tests. Just for fun, so you can see what they're like. That's how I picked my wife.'

'With psychological tests?'

'Yeah,' Templeton laughed. 'She could see me in every ink blot. It lasted eight glorious months, so you'll see how valuable these tests are.'

'Right. Mrs. Fazackerley?'

'I'm afraid I don't know any Jewish stories.' Her voice was cool, well-modulated, familiar as a result of all the television appearances. 'I'm an accountant and a solicitor by training, which may seem unusual. The reason is, simply, that my father was an accountant and he let me help him from the time I was about fourteen. I qualified and then did law and was admitted. Since then I've worked. The two professions are in demand and people qualified in both are rare, women particularly so. That's my contribution.'

'Oh dear me, no,' Longbottom said. 'You also appear on T.V., you have a family. Go on.'

'Very well. I appeared first on radio in *Woman's Hour*, talking about my job, and I just kept being invited back. The panel games and all the nonsense just followed. My husband is an accountant too, and he's with one of the insurance companies, in investments. We have two children and we live in Blackheath.' She raised her eyebrows a little, inquiringly.

Longbottom nodded, wondering what it would be like being *Mr*. Fazackerley. She was smooth and tough and efficient, and she'd spin you into a web of domestic legal and financial controls, like a spider with a fly. Would it, he asked himself, be worse being married to Clare Fazackerley than to Pat? He glanced at his watch, wondering whether she'd had a drink yet. But of course she had. Probably two by now. The sheer weary weight of arriving home night after night to an increasingly sozzled wife was ... Determinedly he stopped the train of thought. 'Mr. – er – Gaunt.'

Eyes switched to John Gaunt, who licked his lips nervously. He looked almost Indian, his skin several shades darker than any other in the room; but he was also extraordinarily handsome, in a gentle way. Longbottom glanced at the women to watch their reaction to him.

'I was born,' Gaunt said with an apologetic smile, 'in what is now Pakistan. My father is English, my mother – is now English, too. I was born in Karachi, but came to England as a child after the partition of India. I went to a grammar school in Suffolk, then to Manchester University, where I read psychology. I like to play cricket and hockey. I am not married. That's all.'

Longbottom said, 'Your job?'

'I am a member of the Development Group which reports to Mr. Philips.'

'Thank you.'

'Half a minute. What development group?' It was Verity.

'It's a little group – you could call it a think-tank,' Gaunt said.

22

'I've never heard of it,' Verity said. 'I'm not being rude, but what do you think about?'

Gaunt grinned in slight embarrassment. 'Various problems. Operating philosophy, attitudes to employees on various questions like pensions. That kind of thing. You see?'

'I don't really see at all. You just sit at desks and think.'

Gaunt said, 'Not even at desks, Mr. Verity. On the floor. On chairs. Wherever it's easiest to think.'

'Bugger me!' Verity's tough face showed the depth of his surprise.

'That comes under the heading of action, I'm afraid,' Gaunt said. 'Our function is purely advisory.'

Verity grinned at the quick laugh that spread round the table. 'I'm not used to this kind of thing,' he said. 'If I catch any of my lot lying down, I kick 'em to their feet. Still, I suppose it's sense. You think things through, I take it? Right through?'

'Right.' Gaunt's strange pale grey eyes smiled gratitude at Verity's instant appreciation.

'There's a bunch of us, from various disciplines.'

Verity said, 'What do you mean, disciplines?'

'I'm sorry, that's jargon. People trained in various areas: law, actuarial matters, finance, psychology.'

'I thought for a minute you were Miss Whiplash, the firm disciplinarian,' Verity said, 'but I see it now. Damn' good idea, too. So any problem gets looked at from every point of view?'

'Yes.'

'And your think tank advises Harry Philips?'

'We give him a paper setting out possibilities and probable consequences.'

'So everything gets a damn sight more thought than he could give it himself. What a beautiful idea!'

Longbottom watched the exchange with interest. Verity was a classic managerial toughie; Gaunt a pure intellectual. The natural thing would have been instant resentment, even contempt, from Verity. Instead he'd shown remarkable insight and appreciation. He looked at Verity with respect. This was a formidable man.

Judy Kernon

JUDY KERNON watched, too, thinking much the same thought as Longbottom: that a swift mind hopped merrily about behind Verity's craggy face. Furthermore, it was a swift mind with easy humour and a tough charm that enabled him to push hard and not be resented. Then she smiled to herself. 'Knock it off. Sure he's attractive. Remember he's just talent on the hoof.' All the same, she kept looking up the table at Verity, remembering Philips' words. The Group managing director had sent for her a few days earlier.

'Judy. A chore.' Quickly, in that metallic voice.

'I'm away, you know—'

'The course. I know. Man on it called Verity. Know him?'

'No.'

'Have a good look.'

'All right. You mean an assessment?'

'He's good. I want to know how good.'

'Anything in particular?'

Philips had blinked at her. Not a nervous blink; rather an interrupted stare while his mind worked on it. 'Possibly my deputy.'

'Blimey!'

Philips' smile, as usual, had touched only his eyes, but she knew it was there. 'Talk to him. Listen. Men talk to women. Tell me, when you're ready.'

Sitting now in the basement room at the Princess Hotel, she wondered if Verity had any idea. He'd referred to Philips as Harry, but so did many other people.

She heard Longbottom say, 'Thanks, Mr. Giesing,' and knew she'd been daydreaming. Damn! She'd missed the German. 'Steady, girl,' she told herself, 'keep your eyes off Verity. He's business!'

'Mr. Keller?'

Judy turned. Keller sat beside her, which was odd, because

24

they were both Jewish. Still, it *was* alphabetical order. Suspicion, suspicion!

Keller said, 'I'm an accountant, too. Terrible, isn't it?'

'It bloody well is.' Judy's eyes, like everybody else's, swivelled in Steele's direction. You truculent little bastard, she thought, and found herself speaking, saying: 'Why?'

And Steele replied. 'Because the whole bloody world is becoming dominated by figures and the people who can manoeuvre them. Kids don't learn the fiddle any more. They learn to fiddle the books. A painting isn't a good painting any more, it's a good investment.'

Keller said, 'I'm wholly responsible, Mr. Steele. I created this situation entirely alone. I also burn books.'

'Christ, I'm not getting at you,' Steele said. 'But look at this table! The criterion for sitting round it is, by and large, figures. Cleverness with figures.'

'Gentlemen, gentlemen,' Longbottom said. 'Order, please.'

Steele blew his nose loudly into a Macclesfield silk handkerchief a yard square and then there was silence.

'I hold one hundred and fifty-six directorships,' Keller went on, 'none of them of public companies. As company secretary of Euromob I am a director of every subsidiary, though not of Euromob itself.'

Judy listened to the constructed sentences, the pleasantly low voice, wishing the argument could have gone on: that Steele the intellectual Miura bull could have gone on charging Keller, the intellectual torero. Would horn or sword have won? With luck, they'd find out before the course was over.

'I was born in Golders Green, educated at Merchant Taylor's and Downing College, Cambridge. I am married—' Judy, knowing what was coming, felt her lips twitch and watched Steele to see his reaction '—to a musician and outside work, my principal interest is music. My wife and I founded a string quartet.'

Steele looked up, scowled, looked down again, and Judy was suddenly angry. 'Okay, Mr. Steele?'

He looked across at her. 'Spare me these feminine vapours, Miss – whatever your name is. Music is, in any case, the mathematician's art. The relationship is known.'

25

'I live in Hampstead,' Keller said, and somehow the flat statement cleared the air.

Judy looked towards Longbottom in time to see Templeton wink at him, and realized suddenly that, far from disapproving Steele's catalytic cussedness, the two of them welcomed it as a rapid way of breaking down barriers.

'Miss Kernon?'

So be it, she thought, let's see what we can contribute. 'I'm Judy Kernon. As you can probably tell, I'm American. New Yorker. You may also be able to tell that I'm Jewish. So what am I doing here? Well, I'm an Anglophile, and that's Kosher. I came here ten years ago and didn't go back. Mr. Steele ought to like me because I can't count past ten without slipping my shoes off. Everybody, including me, wonders why I've got the job I have.'

She looked round at the faces. Some of the men were eyeing her, the women examining. Clare Fazackerly seemed to be counting the stitches in Judy's dress; Steele glanced disapprovingly at her. Verity said, 'Which is?'

'I thought you'd never ask. Executive selection.'

Steele said, 'That's like accountancy. The hell with the spirit – fly the bloody flag of analysis.'

Gotcha! Judy thought. 'Listen toots, I couldn't analyse nuthin'. I go on vibrations. I can tell most of the time, anyway.'

'What can you tell?'

'If a man's good.'

'At *what*?' Steele's tone was cutting, contemptuous, insulting.

Right, Judy thought. 'I can tell if he's good at drinking, Mr. Steele. Or bullying. But mostly if he's good at his work.'

A rhythmic banging. Longbottom was hitting the table top demanding order. 'Miss Kernon has the floor.'

She went on, 'I don't make appointments and I only advise. Nor is my word *ever* the sole criterion. But sometimes it can tip the balance. Furthermore, I'm the best damn' cook in this room. Which makes it a mystery why I'm still a spinster.'

'Thank you, Miss Kernon. Management selection by instinct

has a long and honourable history,' Longbottom said. 'Now, Mr. Keyes, I think.'

Judy found a folded piece of paper in front of her. Keller, who had placed it there, shrugged and pointed towards Steele. She opened the paper. There were two words to the message: NO MYSTERY. – and when she looked towards Steele he was looking away.

Keyes, though, was speaking. 'I'm afraid I'm a terribly conventional chap, really. I was at Harrow and then I left the Brigade.'

Steele said, 'Why?'

Keyes smiled. 'It was a private matter.'

'Private matters,' Steele said, 'are usually something to do with boy soldiers, colonel's wives or gambling.'

'You are a perceptive man,' Keyes looked benevolently at Steele, 'and may go far. If you're careful.'

'I'm never careful.'

'But there are ladies present.' Keyes was urbane, amused, unembarrassed. 'We must be protective of their finer susceptibilities.'

'Don't mind us,' Clare Fazackerly said. 'We're riveted.'

'If you insist, then, it was the adjutant's wife. She was also the daughter of a Deputy Director of Military Intelligence. It was, of course, a long time ago. *Folie de jeunesse*. I am now married. No children, unfortunately. I play fives and scull a little.'

'Doncha know,' said Steele.

Judy looked from one man to the other in mixed amazement and amusement. Keyes was the smoothest thing she'd seen on two legs, Steele almost certainly the rudest. It was as though the editor of *Viewpoint* were trying to make an enemy of everybody in the room.

'My job,' Keyes continued, 'is marketing, particularly in the travel field.'

He sat down.

'Now, Miss Roper?'

Jane Roper looked round. She, too, Judy thought, had a high-gloss polish.

'I'm afraid there's remarkably little to tell,' Jane Roper said.

27

'I was born in London, taken to Rhodesia when I was very small. I went to Blackheath High School, then learned short-hand and typing, got a job as a secretary in public relations and simply stayed there. I joined the group four years ago and I'm now responsible for corporate public relations. Oh, and I'm unmarried.'

Longbottom said, 'Other interests?'

'I suppose a generally civilized life. Books, music. That sort of thing.'

As Jane Roper spoke, Judy looked at the others, watching the men's faces narrow with sudden lust and resenting it on the girl's behalf. Why could she not be heard rather than inspected? Keyes' languid gaze ran over her as though she were an object in a shop window; Farmer's jaw gaped as he stared at the kind of girl he could never begin to approach; Giesing sat very still, but in his neck a muscle twitched. And Steele *intended* – looking at him she could almost hear the words echoing in his mind – 'I'll have her.'

She was still watching him as Jane Roper finished. Momentarily Steele's eyes flicked in Judy's direction and she saw his lip curl before he swung his attention back.

'Thank you, Miss Roper. Mister Sinclair?'

The voice was soft, Scottish and almost inaudible. Around the table little ordinary sounds ceased because they had to if Sinclair was to be heard. It was an old and effective way of compelling attention, but one that only worked, Judy reflected, if the man who used it had quality. Sinclair had. He sat there, slim and dark, staring at the table through heavy, dark-rimmed glasses.

'I was born in Inverness and educated there and at St. Andrews. I then trained in accountancy, became interested in management accountancy and joined the group after doing the audit. As it happens I am interested in mechanical engineering, though I am not qualified in any way. I am now managing director of European Packaging Ltd., one of the subsidiaries of the group.'

Longbottom said, 'How old?'

'Thirty-eight.'

'Interests.'

'I should have said. I play golf and dabble in engineering projects. I am married.'

Keyes said, 'You play at The Warren?'

'Yes.'

'Then play no golf with this man.' Keyes looked round the table. 'He is genuine scratch. He has played for Scotland, beaten Bonallack and is a very stripey tiger indeed. I know his reputation.'

There was a brief flash of a smile from Sinclair. 'You flatter me.'

'I describe.'

Verity said, 'Off scratch, are you?' Judy was surprised he should be impressed. It was uncharacteristic.

'For Christ's sake, what's all the bloody reverence about. Just because a man hits a ball with a stick!'

Sinclair smiled briefly. 'I agree with Mr. Steele. It's a private pleasure, that's all.'

Verity said, 'Yes. Except that he doesn't understand.'

Longbottom came in smoothly: 'Keep talking, Mr. Verity. Take your turn.'

'All right. I'm a lorry driver. Or I was. They put me in charge of a few lorries. Then a few more. That's all there is to it.'

Keller said, 'That is a magnificent understatement.'

Verity grinned at him. 'It's very simple, really. I organize the group's transport. And I play golf off eighteen, only it's damn near twenty. I'm a bachelor. I've been with Euromob two years. Harry Philips brought me over. I used to know him when I was a lad. I was at Road-Rail containers before.'

Steele said, 'I'm disappointed. I thought it just might be merit and it turns out to be nepotism all the time.'

Judy had wondered whether Steele would take on Verity, challenge the unmistakable toughness of this big hard man; wondered, too, how Verity would react, because there was something else, violence perhaps, or temper, lurking somewhere not too far below the surface. Verity turned slowly in his seat, looking at Steele. 'When I was a lad,' he said, 'in the pit villages round Rotherham, they used to play a game. The miners, this was. Two fellers'd hold one another's shoulders and kick each other's ankles till one gave in. Very violent, that

29

was.' He paused. 'You get a lot of violence in lorry fleets, too. Specially if there's piece work. What I mean, Mr. Steele, is that we both know about violence, you and I. Know our way round it, so to speak. Only yours is mental violence and mine's the other kind.'

Steele said, 'Oh, I agree – the sword is mightier than the pen.'

'It's just that I've never been afraid of violence.' Verity grinned suddenly at Longbottom. 'Another slice of auto-biography.'

The threat hung in the air like thick smoke for a moment or two. Steele grinned back at Verity, but there was slackness at the corners of his mouth. Then he said, 'Hands that throw punches will never hold mine.'

'Keep talking, Mr. Steele.' Longbottom came in quickly. 'It's confession time.'

'This thing is patently absurd,' Steele said. 'We're shoved together in a room. We've nothing in common, nothing of value to give one another. And it's all in the name of some stupid piece of half-baked management nonsense that likes to think it's philosophy. It's pretentious rubbish! That man drives lorries, that man flogs package holidays, this man counts bloody bawbees and I deal in literature and politics. The whole thing reeks of monumental incompetence. You can't even keep to alphabetical order – S comes before V.'

Longbottom smiled. 'Just a brief résumé of your career.'

Steele said, 'Local newspapers. National newspapers. *Viewpoint*. That's it.'

'Education?'

'I am self-educated. I was on my back for years as a child. I have R.S.A. certificates in English and arithmatic. But then, I have never thought education had much to do with examinations.'

'Perhaps you've proof of it,' Longbottom said smoothly. 'Now,' he looked at his watch, 'Let's have a ten minute break.'

Judy was last to the powder room, where Clare Fazackerly and Jane Roper were being formidably polite to one another.

As she entered both smiled formally, and Clare Fazackerly said, 'Talk about smoke-filled rooms!'

The hell with you! Judy thought. I'm damned if I'll spend the next two weeks making that kind of polite pointless remark. 'C'mon,' she said. 'Tell me, which is the sexy man in there?'

Clare Fazackerly was applying lipstick. She straightened, pressing her lips together, then blotted them with a Kleenex. 'They all seem to be in rut.'

'Don't like?'

'Not much. There's a time and a place.'

Judy sighed. 'Must be nice when there is. I was taken with Verity, myself. All that controlled power!'

Jane Roper laughed. 'It's a good thing it was controlled.'

'He frightened Steele.'

'Oh. Did you think so?' Jane said. 'I thought he tried and failed.'

'What did you think, Mrs. Fazackerly?'

'I thought,' Clare brushed flecks of dust from her jacket, 'that it was very even indeed.'

She saw him standing alone finishing a cigarette.

'Mr. Giesing, I'm sorry but I was miles away when you were talking and I missed it.'

He smiled stiffly down at her. 'Was not very interesting.'

'Please tell me.'

Giesing shrugged. 'Am chemical engineer. Director of paper and printing companies in Germany, also of research. Am married. No children.'

She said, 'Thanks. I'm sorry.'

'Is all right.'

From the other end of the room, Longbottom called, 'Can we start again, please!'

Judy said, 'I'll buy you a drink to make up.'

'But all drinks are free, are they not?' Giesing seemed puzzled.

'It's a matter of intent,' she said.

Reinhard Giesing

HE watched her turn and walk away, suppressing a tremble that flickered in his cheek. It was the first break, the very first, in this meeting, and she came to him, directly. There was no pretence. She did not talk to others first; did not attempt to disguise what she was doing; she came to him, asking him to repeat what he had said. She knew, therefore *they* knew, therefore *they* would act. He wondered how long they had known, whether they were sure? After a moment he realized that the others were all back at the table and moved his own reluctant legs towards it.

'We're going to kick off with a general outline of what management *is*,' Longbottom said. 'Just that. Some of you will know a lot more about this than I do, so I'll ask them to bear with me, because others won't. You'll find the whole course is like that and the general principle applies. Now, I'm going to start with a question: What is the first duty of a business?'

Giesing half listened as the argument began. 'To make a profit, of course,' Steele said. And Clare Fazackerly: 'To develop.'

He smiled a little wearily deep inside his own mind. The first principle of business was the same as the first principle of anything else. It was to survive. Survive and you could make profit, develop, anything. But these people didn't put survival high on the list because they had never needed to think about it. They were sophisticates; not content to live, they wanted their lives to be elaborate.

He glanced to his right, with careful casualness, and instantly the woman's eyes switched from the speaker to meet his own, then flicked away again. Damned Jewess! His mind shouted at him: No! Don't say it! Don't think it! You don't even believe it! That's true, isn't it? Certainly it's true. You have deliberately cultivated acquaintance with many Jewish people. You like them; you admire their culture, their humour.

It's just that when you were eleven years old some damned racialist started poisoning your mind and went on and on for more than twelve years. You're a civilized, middle-aged man who works hard and responsibly but there's that damned bit of scar tissue that Hitler made and Streicher nourished.

'A matter of intent.' That was what she had said, this Kernon. Judy Kernon. Judy, *Jude*. They were implacable, these Israeli hunters. But who, after all, could blame them? It was not personal, except that it was always centred upon a person. It was a racial memory still demanding racial vengeance.

He had always known that it would happen; always known, but never known how; never known by what means they would know him, identify him, find him. Often he had sought to convince himself that his own sense of guilt was manufacturing the spectre, but deep within he had *known* otherwise.

They had him now. He glanced at the door and sensed that the woman was looking at him. But if he ran, where would he go? They'd find him; sooner or later they'd find him again. It would always be so.

On the fringes of his consciousness, Longbottom's voice went on '. . . management by objectives . . . The structural necessities . . .' He had had all that before; could recite chunks of Drucker and the rest. But what to do? Would they be merciful? Understanding? Would they know that he had carried this guilt for thirty years, or would they think he'd walked away whistling and never thought about it again?

He would never forget her face; he could see it now . . .

He was eighteen, newly out of the gymnasium at Baden-Baden; into uniform; into Poland. And indoctrinated. The German people needed space, expansion, *lebensraum* for the *volk*. On the flood tide of victory it was easy to believe, easy to say that this was progress. Easy to march and sing and drink and listen when they said that gods wore field grey and Jews were animals.

She ran, or tried to run, a farm, but she was losing the battle because she was alone. Her husband was dead, killed in the Panzer advance last September and she was not a country girl.

33

He was engaged upon a livestock census, one of the dreary duties of victory: counting pigs and cattle and chickens and keeping the count, making sure that they didn't die, that they were being tended. There were dozens of farms and he went from one to the next, counting. In the beginning they had gone in twos, or even threes, but there was little danger, now.

He had counted the sheep and the cattle, the geese and the chickens, noting the totals. The space under pigs was blank.

It was a pleasant day and she was a pretty woman and he had said, 'Funny, this is the only farm hereabouts with no pigs.'

She had blanched, hands flying to her face. And then, after a pause, said quickly – too quickly – 'My husband sold them all last year.' In that moment he had known and his heart had pounded.

'The sties. The pigsties. Where are they?'

She stared at him. Then, 'They were knocked down. Over there.'

He looked where she pointed to the ruin of a tiny hut. It could never have been a pigsty.

'You're Jewish.'

'No!' But she was; he knew it now. It was an attractive face and now that he looked more closely, a face that could be Jewish, dark-eyed.

'Don't lie. You're Jewish.'

'I'm not. Please!'

There was fear, the beginning of terror in her face.

'Jewish!' Suddenly he felt powerful, important; excitement flooded through his veins. They were required to report evidence of Jewish blood.

'I shall have to report this.'

'No! Please!'

'My duty.'

Her face was no longer mobile with the play of emotion; it had set in the stillness of fear. And she was right to be afraid. Had the Führer himself not damned all Jews? He felt the blood in his face, his hands trembled. He put the notebook in his pocket.

'Do not do this thing,' she said. He began to turn away, and suddenly she was on her knees.

34

In that moment all the excitement inside him seemed to come to a point, to harden. He looked down at her, listening as his blood pounded. He had never had a woman.

'Inside. I'll see your papers.'

Her identity papers said nothing about her Jewishness, but there was a desk with documents in the drawers and he turned it out and went through them until he found a wedding picture, the Star of David on the synagogue wall. Warsaw, 1938.

'No,' she said. 'No.'

'Stand facing the wall. It is necessary to search you.'

'I have no gun.'

'Stand still. Palms flat on the wall.'

He moved behind her, sliding his hands over her back, then to her armpits and round to her breasts and the space between.

She said, 'I have nothing.'

'Silence.' As his hands searched her body, she trembled but made no sound. He trembled, too, but with excitement rather than fear. And then, as his hands fumbled and she shrank instinctively back, her rump touched him.

It was like being set on fire.

'Your clothes. Remove them.'

She hesitated for only a second, and began to obey, her back turned to him. When she had finished, she stood still, hands at her sides and he touched her buttocks with his hands.

'Turn round.'

She obeyed and he stood looking at her, then reached his right hand forward to cup her breast.

She said, 'I will do anything. Anything. Anything at all.'

He was going to have a woman! His first woman! His heart thundered.

He was young and strong. He stayed an hour, potent with excitement, rejoicing in his power. When he had done the first time, there was a second, even a third.

As he left, she said, 'You will not tell?'

'I'll be back.' He pocketed the photograph.

'But you will not tell?'

He was late and the feldwebel was demanding explanations.

35

The man in front was also late, pushing a bicycle with a flat tyre; he could hardly offer the same excuse. It would mean hours of extra drill and he was tired.

'I have found a Jew.' He produced the picture.

Next day he was in the party that went to pick her up; three men in a small truck. She saw them coming and ran to hide but they found her. She stared at him in mute hatred all the way back.

Across the years he could still feel the intensity of that hate, the depth of her contempt. He was, he knew, as much of a war criminal as Eichmann, as deserving of retribution. In his mind he was certain that *somebody* knew, that *somebody* would inform. The weight of his guilt was too great for him to believe his crime might not be remembered.

It was to escape it that he had become Giesing, taking the papers of a dead soldier in the last confused days of war and leaving his own on the body. He had been Giesing, now, for a quarter of a century, but still he knew that one day he would be made to pay . . .

He returned to the present, to Longbottom's introduction to elementary management techniques, with his hands clasped tightly together and his brow wet with sweat. He glanced again at the girl, the Jewish woman, Judy Kernon. She smiled as their eyes met. Giesing throught it a strange smile.

There were drinks before lunch and though he badly wanted a cognac he managed not to ask for it, conscious that one country's normal drink was another's indicator of incipient alcoholism. Instead he sipped whisky as he watched, glad to be alone for a moment or two. The woman was talking now to the big man from the North, Verity. *In Verity veritas?* Probably. The man was strong and hard and looked honest. Might even be clever, though lack of education would be against him. Or would it, here in Britain? In Germany, certainly, but the British were . . .

'We have something in common,' a voice said, and Giesing turned. Keller was standing beside him.

'We have?'

Keller said, 'I was born in Berlin.'

'You are German?'

'My parents were. They left in 1936. I'm British.'

And Jewish, Giesing thought. Two of them and they're round me like wasps. He said politely, 'To be British, I think, is no bad thing.'

'Or to be German, now.'

'You believe that?'

'I think so,' Keller said. 'I go sometimes. On holiday, you know.'

'But this is your homeland?'

'Oh, yes.' Keller smiled suddenly. 'Do you like it?'

'I never see it. I fly Frankfurt to London six times a year, then I fly back.'

'You should try.'

Giesing nodded. 'But I do not think I shall. Not enough time.'

'Never enough. Maybe less than one thinks.'

Giesing felt the ting of fear in his chest. They were toying with him! Beneath the civilized surface, the pretended community of interest, the polite exchanges, were the mechanisms of retribution. Well, damn them. He might as well confront them now as later. He said, 'Do you hate us, Mr. Keller.'

Keller's eyes swung at him, widened a little in surprise at this directness. 'Hate?'

'I wore the uniform.'

'Did you? I was too young for anything but a school uniform.'

'Ladies and gentlemen, luncheon is served.'

'Excuse me,' Keller said. 'I must—' He moved quickly across the floor and Giesing saw that Harry Philips had arrived, that Keller was now talking to him quietly. What was he saying? 'We've got a war criminal among us'? No, they would keep that knowledge to themselves until they were ready. Meanwhile he must speak to Philips himself in the next day or two. He had news; news of a process, developed in the research lab in Frankfurt, that might be worth a lot of money to Euromob.

He walked towards the table, looking for the card which would indicate his seat.

John Gaunt

'MY eyes are simply a fluke; an accident, a genetic nonsense. It's a matter of pigmentation, that's all, like my skin.'

Judy Kernon said, 'I'll bet they've cut a pretty damn big swathe through the women of this world.'

It was a few minutes after midnight in the common-room on the fourteenth floor and she was talking to him because Philips had instructed her to do so. He knew that; he had seen Philips speak to her, seen her quick glance at him. A few moments later, pretending to stare into his glass, he had watched her feet cross the room towards him.

'Oh why so whatnot knight-at-arms?' she said.

He looked up and began to rise. 'Oh, Miss Kernon.'

'Don't.' She sat in the armchair beside his. 'You're slacking on your social obligations.'

He grinned. 'They end at midnight. These hours belong to me, not to the shareholders. It's shut-eye time but I'm being generous and hanging around.'

It was then that she asked him about his eyes. Sooner or later, women usually did. Men less often, but then women set more store by eyes.

She said, 'It's like standing in the beams of a pair of search-lights.'

'Why?' It was a long time since he'd patted the ball back. As a rule he allowed people to make their comments, made a joke of some kind, and let it drop. 'Why? They're just eyes.'

They weren't though, and he knew it very well. His father's eyes were blue, his mother's the deep brown of India; somehow or other, the mixture had produced irises of a pale blue-grey, brilliantly flecked with gold. The almost blue white of the whites of his eyes gave the colouration extra emphasis.

She laughed. 'No. To say those are just eyes is like saying the Koh-i-noor's just a rock. Do you mind talking about them?'

Do I? he thought. 'No. Or at least, not in the sense that I feel

38

embarrassed. They can be a nuisance sometimes.'

'Why?'

'Because you talk to someone and you suddenly realize they are not listening, they're staring.'

'They're not staring, they're hypnotized.'

'If I get something in them, do they not water? If I drink too much are they not bloodshot?'

She said, 'Everybody on this damn course is crawling with literary illusions.'

'Like?'

'Like that snipe Steele over there. Every word he speaks ought to have quotation marks around it.'

Gaunt said, 'The eccentric English literary figure.'

'He's no eccentric.'

'It's a licence to be rude, they get it and they indulge in it, like Shaw and Wilde. I think it's very enviable.'

'Why?'

'It's nice to be rude sometimes.'

She said, 'You? You've never been rude in your life. You're nice and you're not aggressive.'

'Haven't you ever wanted to be really devastating? Like Wilde to the customs man, "I have nothing to declare but my genius".'

He was delighted to see that she looked puzzled. And sounded it. 'Sure. It's one of those dreams-of-grandeur things. But why slaughter shop assistants.'

'Not shop assistants. Items like Steele.'

Judy Kernon grinned. 'This is getting nice and cosy. You can't stand him either?'

Gaunt said, 'At some point on this course, he'll seek to ridicule me for the colour of my skin.'

'Now how d'you know that?'

'I know the type. Lofty and intellectual. They go directly for the throat.'

'They don't in my case.'

'Oh, I see. No, but that's chemistry.'

She laughed. 'You know, it's funny, but I kind of know he'll slap me down too.'

'You mean, he'll try.'

'I mean he'll do it. He's a winner in any word battle: I'm a loser.'

'Coffee or a drink?'

'Thanks. Coffee.' He went across to the bar where the coffee machine bubbled and filled her cup, then his own, listening idly to the chatter around him, surprised that he should feel so at ease. A few years ago he'd have been terrified of people like these; his own precarious social assurance would have evaporated the moment it came face to face with theirs. Now, they sometimes made him angry, but no more. He picked up the two cups and glanced across the room towards the corner where Judy Kernon sat. Then, his direction charted, he set off.

Six feet away, he knew it would happen. Keyes and Steele were with Jane Roper and he had to pass them. Moving carefully, to avoid spilling coffee into the saucers, he began to skirt the little group, but then Keyes stepped back abruptly, almost colliding with him and the coffee tilted into the saucer.

Judy said, 'Bad luck,' and took her cup.

'It was deliberate.'

'No. He just didn't see you.'

'He'd have seen Philips or Mrs. Fazackerly.'

'You're overstating.'

'He's my racial superior and my social superior. Or so he believes. This is just about the only way he's got left of showing it.'

'Are you serious?'

Gaunt grinned and sipped his coffee. 'I knew he'd do it before it happened. One can tell. You notice he didn't apologize?'

'He didn't notice.'

'That's what I mean.'

'Listen, I'm Jewish,' she said. 'I've heard of racial put-downs. You just don't like his upper-upper polish.'

'On the contrary, I preserved it. I could have spilled the coffee over him. But there was time to decide and I decided against it. I'd hate to spoil those beautiful trousers.'

'Very generous.'

'Passive. A la Ghandi, you know? Weakness is strength.'

She said, 'That sounds like Nineteen Eighty Four.'

Time to detach himself. 'Nineteen eighty-four is getting a lot nearer, like bedtime. Will you excuse me?'

Nobody saw him go. Or if they did, like Keyes they pretended not to. He was, in a way, relieved. In there they were all plastering each other with good will of a forced and spurious kind. If anybody *wanted* to talk to him, he was prepared to wait until all the labels had dissolved and the people were visible as what they were, rather than as what they said they were.

With his key in the lock at his own room, he changed his mind and decided to walk. Twenty minutes in the cool, night air to breathe the smoke and staleness away. And, he thought wryly, to take in some more diesel fumes. He walked to the lift and punched the button.

As he crossed the lobby, heading for the door, a woman's voice said, 'Did you see those extraordinary eyes?' Gaunt kept moving and outside the wet pavements glittered and the chill sent a shudder across his shoulders. He took a deep breath and strode towards the park, enjoying the metronomic thrusting of his leather heels. Taxis slid by, taking people home after theatres and late suppers; businessmen with a drink too many inside them pushed their shiny cars a little too fast along the rain-slicked roads. They would get home, or most of them would, without understanding the danger they had been in, and tomorrow would be hung over, a little more arrogant, a little more tetchy.

And a little more intolerant.

Like Winstanley. Remembering Winstanley, letting the scene play itself again in his mind, he pushed his heels harder at the pavement, pounding along, letting the inevitable and unvarying anger dissipate itself in the violence of this stride.

Whoever had slung Winstanley out of West Africa had had a sharp eye, which was more than the headmaster who appointed him possessed. The Colonial Service had not wanted him either after independence, and Winstanley had used his golden handshake to add a year of teacher-training to his pre-war English degree. He'd been Gaunt's form master two unlucky years running: a petty tyrant with a racial chip on his shoulder, fond of telling his classes about 'the mess those black monkeys are making out there', imparting prejudice and intolerance with venomous skill, but less able to impart knowledge.

Naturally, he hated Gaunt. The boy's skin was little more than well sunburned, but it *was* colour and Winstanley hated it. He hated it more as it began to be clear that Gaunt was exceptionally bright.

'Bloody wogs,' he'd say to the grinning class. 'Running around in Rolls-Royces with bones through their noses.' That would be Kaunda or Nyerere.

'Half-naked bloody little savage,' was Ghandi. Nehru was 'a half-educated wog, always aping his betters'.

Consistently he humiliated the young Gaunt. 'There's a boy not washed this morning,' he'd say, then pretend a mistake. 'Oh, it's Gaunt. And that *won't* wash off, eh?' And when they were doing *Othello*, 'We can't let Gaunt play him, can we? That would be giving him a head start!' The pinpricks were endless. If others among his teachers had behaved like Winstanley, he'd never have made it through the school; fortunately they didn't and the unfairly low marks he was always awarded in English were not matched elsewhere. So he grew up hating a man, but not people. His parents loved one another and were liked, by and large, in the district. John Gaunt grew up with only one chip on his shoulder, but that was a big one. With every insult he endured, he vowed to get back; every time he was compelled to sit silent at his desk seething with rage as Winstanley belittled him, he swore he'd kill him one day. But killing was impossible. As he grew older he began to think in terms of humiliation: the same kind of deep and deliberate humiliation Winstanley delighted in heaping upon him, but he could never find a way. It is difficult for schoolboys to strike at schoolmasters short of accusations of homosexuality, and that was not the kind of revenge Gaunt wanted. It was important that the triumph, when it came, should be private; that he should know and Winstanley should know. When the opportunity came, it was almost accidental.

Gradually he built up a small store of information about Winstanley and his family. The wife was a faded blonde who constantly bemoaned the passing of the colonial life with its ease and its servants. There was a plain daughter, nine years old at a local school. And there was a sister, whose name he saw in the local paper one day, who was an artist. He kept that cutting and the others which appeared from time to time. She had a cottage seven or eight miles out of town and there she ran a small art gallery and had her own studio. She was, he discovered, at the seventy-five guinea level of portraiture, which meant suburban housewives and small local companies and clubs, and one or two of her portraits invariably hung in the Spring Exhibition at the Town Hall.

He was seventeen when he went to the gallery. An elaborately hand-lettered notice on the door said, 'Please come in and look at the pictures', and as he pushed open the door, a bell rang. Nobody appeared, but Gaunt sensed he was being watched. On the plain, whitewashed walls hung a few meticulous watercolours and some pretentious oils, all by local artists, and he went from one to another inspecting them slowly.

Eventually he heard the slap of slippers on the stone floor and a woman's voice said, 'Do you like them?'

He glanced at her with interest. 'They're quite good.'

She was a small dark woman in, he thought, the early thirties, wearing a blue sweater and dark slacks. She said, 'I think this one's especially nice, don't you?'

He looked. It was one of the watercolours, a factory in a valley painted neatly and faithfully.

'Yes,' he said politely. 'It's got the – the feeling.'

'But you're not keen?'

'I was just passing. I remembered seeing some of your portraits at the Town Hall. I wondered if there were others here.'

She said, 'How nice of you! Which ones did you see?'

'It was a chap with a cup, a silver cup. And there was another of a mayor or somebody.'

'I know. Oh, I'm so glad you remembered them. I feel very flattered.'

He was surprised at her enthusiasm. Surely artists *expected* people to take notice of their work.

'Well, I thought they were quite good.'

'Quite good means approval in this part of the world, I know that. So thank you. Would you like a cup of tea?'

43

A few minutes later, cup in hand, he was being shown the half-finished portrait of the president of the Rotary Club. 'Why don't you paint interesting people?'

She sighed, smiling wryly. 'The artist's job is to make people interesting. Rembrandt's portraits were just of the locals, most of them. But look what *he* could do!'

Gaunt found himself liking her, in spite of her brother. 'You're very good. I think so, anyway.'

She laughed. 'Thank you. I often wonder whether Rembrandt felt the same way. All I ever paint are local businessmen and do you know, they all look like frogs. I have a terrible temptation, every time, to paint a frog sitting on a lily pad.'

'Why do you do it, then?'

'To keep the wolf from the door. When you're a professional, unfortunately, you can only paint for pleasure part of the time.'

He was leaving when she said, 'Would you let me paint you?'

'Why?' But he knew.

'You have most remarkable eyes, and your face is . . . well, the lines are clean and straight. I'd like to. Very much.'

Suddenly, he had to tell her: 'I'm in your brother's form. I . . . I don't like him.'

She said, very softly, 'You mean, he doesn't like you.'

He nodded.

She said, 'Keith's so stupid about this. I don't know why. He's just got a bee in his bonnet. I apologize on his behalf since he's obviously got neither the sense nor the manners to do it himself.'

He was embarrassed. 'It's all right.'

'It's far from all right, but there's nothing I can do about it, I'm afraid. Except paint you. May I?'

The portrait went into the Spring Exhibition and he knew the day following the opening, that Winstanley had seen it because the remarks were brutal. 'Our friends from over the ocean like to lounge around as artists' models instead of working.' And later, 'Effeminate brown boys mincing about like girls.' There was no triumph; the insults went deep, but he could

44

have stood that. But the boys in his form, taking their cue from Winstanley, were rude as only schoolboys can be. Gaunt was a queer, a pouf and a pansy; he ought to be transferred to St. Mary's, the girls' school down the road. Boys of seventeen don't weep, but he was near to it when he got on his bike at four o'clock and pedalled hard and punishingly out to the gallery.

'John! What's the matter?'

He didn't know where to look, or what to say; he just stood, shaking his head slowly in helpless rage.

'John, tell me!'

Finally he exploded: 'Take it out of the show. Get it off the wall. Please.'

He expected her to refuse, to argue, but all she did was to say, 'All right.'

He stared at her. 'You don't mind?'

'The point, John, is that *you* do. I didn't put that picture there to hurt you.'

She made him sit on a couch and sat beside him. 'Was Keith awful to you?'

'It wasn't just him.'

'What then?'

'The others. They said—' he stopped. How could he tell her what they said? 'Never mind.'

He felt her hand on his shoulder. 'I know what they said. It's what they always say. Sooner or later artists get it. So do actors. Lots of people.'

'But I'm not! Why should they think I am when I'm not?'

She put her arm round his shoulder and he felt himself being turned, comforted. She said gently, 'Part of it's jealousy. Anybody who dares to be different. You mustn't let it worry you.'

His face was against her breast and he felt the warmth through the wool of her sweater.

'Honestly, I'm not.'

Her hand stroked his cheek and his neck and he pressed his face close against her. He raised his eyes to look at her face. It was important that she believe him.

She said, 'I know,' then bent her head and kissed him gently on the lips. It was a brief kiss, but as their lips parted their eyes locked and after a moment he saw her face come towards him

45

again and this kiss was longer and warmer and gentler, and suddenly his hand was on her breast and he was holding her tightly.

Then she pulled away. 'John!'

'Please,' he said, 'Oh, please!' His hand still held the weight of her breast and after a moment she looked down at it, almost surprised. Then she gave him a strange small smile.

'Is it *so* wrong?' she murmured.

He stared at her for a moment, uncomprehending and then at least it was clear to him that he could kiss her again if he wanted to, and he wanted to and heard a small sound in his throat as he moved. Now, somehow, he was not a boy being comforted; the hand on her breast was not tentative but urgent: he felt himself tighten as she brought her body against his. When her lips parted and her tongue touched his he felt his head was splitting with sensation and he thrust his own tongue forward in wild exploration. Awkwardly, she detached her mouth from his.

'No!' he protested, grasping her again. She was going to stop and he wouldn't let her. He wouldn't!

But she was smiling. 'Not here,' she whispered and took his hand. He followed her, bent almost double as he walked to try to hide his embarrassment and she stopped and brushed his lips. 'You don't have to do that, John. I *know*. Just be patient for a moment.'

She led him up the stairs to a room with chintz curtains, small, old, oak furniture and a bed, and there she turned and came into his arms and he felt suddenly as strong as Samson and crushed her to him, feeling her breasts against his chest, her groin against his.

She said, 'Take of your clothes and climb into bed,' and then slipped out of the room. He was lying there, naked, when she returned a moment later and his eyes widened as he saw her body. He felt the warmth as she came to him, his hands explored her in wonder; he felt shock when she touched him.

Then, almost without his knowing how, it was happening and he was pounding at her.

Her voice stopped him. 'John.'

He was impatient, barely comprehending.

46

She said, 'Let that hatred come out of you now. After all, he is my brother.'

Winstanley! He began pounding again, and pounding, and then it was all over and he was collapsing and she held him in her arms, soothing him.

When he could speak, he gasped, 'I'm sorry!'

'Why, John?'

'Because I *was* thinking of him.'

'I know. I was thinking of you. It's better that it should be over.'

He felt desperately guilty. 'But—'

She interrupted him. 'Rest. After a while you can begin to think of me.'

He was almost back at the hotel when heavy rain began again and he broke into a long easy sprint to the doorway. Two women, Americans, one elderly, the other young, scurried towards it, too, from a taxi at the kerb. Gaunt stood back to let them pass. The older woman stopped suddenly, swaying slightly, clearly a little drunk.

'Young man,' she said, 'you got beautiful manners.'

'Thank you,' he bowed.

'Gee – and such beautiful eyes.'

Gaunt grinned. 'I'll bet you've been quite a girl yourself.'

Harry Philips

THE faces stared back at him. After an hour and a half they were still lively, interested. There wasn't much doodling: he had seen little in the way of suppressed yawns or other indications of boredom. Nor was the reason entirely that he was the big boss. Rather was it because he was talking about the organization and its plans and these people had ideas about it. They were of it; they lived within it, thought about it, planned for its future.

'Questions,' he said. Not, are there any? but, I'll answer them now. This kind of audience understood. All the same there was a short pause. Even here, nobody quite wanted to be first.

Steele said, 'They told us yesterday that survival is the first duty. I'm taking survival for granted. What about profit?'

Trust him! Alex Hodder had said, 'Send Steele on the course. Stop it being dry and academic', and the chairman had agreed and they'd both been amused and there'd been no alternative.

'Profit is the product of an efficient company,' Philips said.

'All right, then. When will it become efficient?'

'As soon as possible. As soon as everybody in this room gets into profit. As soon as we have the structure right. If you like, when *Viewpoint* makes a bit more money. I've been explaining the problems, or some of them.'

'Meanwhile, you'll continue to run it?'

Philips smiled, not feeling like smiling. 'I'd hate ever to shut it. *Viewpoint*'s a national institution. But for every one who lives up there in the ivory towers, we've got to have a few in the cellars digging gold.' Digest that for a minute, he thought, and let somebody else in.

Ironside – Keyes came in smoothly. 'Obviously in a corporation like this, some things are done well, some badly. It

48

seems to me, however, that we have assets that aren't marketed properly, if they're marketed at all.'

'Go on.' Philips sipped at the glass of water. Curious how much better water tasted in committee rooms than anywhere else.

'Well, look at the information we have. All kinds of information, if we could get at it.'

'We do get at a lot of it,' Philips said. 'Don't we, Mike?'

Farmer grinned. 'Tell me more, Mr. Keyes.'

'Yes, tell him. If it's collectable and retrievable, Mike's boys will collect and retrieve.'

'All right,' Keyes said. 'Lists for a start. I mean, my lists of holidaymakers are the basis of next year's operations. We send them direct mail shots. Now why shouldn't the books end of the business use that list. Flog them guide books.'

Philips enjoyed saying it: 'Under way, I believe. Right, Mike?'

'Right,' Farmer agreed.

Keyes said, 'My point is unaffected. My lists would be valuable to others in this corporation. It's a case of knowing who.'

Clare Fazackerly said, 'Presumably half of them are women?'

Keyes said, 'Fractionally more than that.'

She began to tick off on her fingers: 'Clothes, cosmetics, magazines, electrical products, de-da de-da de-da.'

Farmer said, 'Already abstracted.'

'It occurs to me that our customers might be rather ignored,' Sinclair said softly. 'I don't want to destroy my own business, you understand.'

Philips said, 'But?'

'If they buy paper and board packaging they probably buy plastics too.'

'You wouldn't mind?'

'Not a bit.'

'Good. I'll tell Lawrence Draper. Maybe the two of you could get together.'

Sinclair said, 'I'll strip him naked by Christmas,' and grinned to show he only half meant it.

49

'Look,' Philips said, 'all this *does* matter. We've got computers and they cost the earth. If we can dream up new and profitable functions for them, it's pretty well pure bunce.'

Steele said, 'You're all tough businessmen. I'm just a simple lover of poesy. But is anybody interested in what the press says?'

'What do you mean?'

'Well, take the City papers for a start. The office library is full of cuttings. Would they be useful to anybody else?'

Philips said, 'You mean we should package cuttings and market an information service.'

'If that's the jargon. And if it has any value.'

'I haven't the slightest doubt,' Keller said, 'that that service will be universally snapped up. Computerized it's potentially a world service.'

'What do you think, George?' Philips asked.

Sinclair said, 'It's transmutation. Base Steele into real gold. No question about it.'

'Get on to it, Mike. And talk to the editorial libraries about their stuff. Thanks, Gerard.'

Steele said, 'For Christ's Sake try to press all those electronic tits without screwing up the libraries.'

'For a lover of poesy,' Keyes murmured, 'you express yourself with a tremulous shy delicacy.'

Philips said, 'We'll double the profit by Friday afternoon if we go on like this.' On occasion, even non-business people like Steele had valuable ideas. But the truth was that the profit situation was bad and getting worse. Euromob simply didn't seem able to get consistent growth. When Salt put it together in the early sixties, combining several highly profitable organizations, the potential seemed enormous, *was* enormous. But it hadn't happened. Other top companies had doubled their size, trebled it even, in the intervening years, but Euromob's leaden feet seemed unable to move. The question now, Philips was afraid, was whether the whole thing was not too complicated, its ramifications too wide for efficient operation. The American conglomerate giants, market high-fliers and glamour stocks like Ling and Litton had been clouted harder by the recession than anybody else. In Britain I.P.C., similarly placed to Euromob

50

though smaller, had galloped for safety into the embrace of the Reed Group.

He, as managing director had the pistol at his temple and there wasn't just one finger on the trigger, but dozens. The investing institutions with their money in Euromob, would move it out like magic if the profits showed another dip. Then the price of the shares would plummet and Slater or somebody like him would step in, bid, buy, and bust apart and make a killing. He flexed his shoulders instinctively, shedding the load perhaps, easing the pressure.

If they could only persuade old Salt to retire, things might be easier. But even that was doubtful. The old man had unquestionably done a brilliant job in the development of Europac, the company on which the whole vast empire was built and which George Sinclair now managed. The forests in Scandinavia were wonderful assets giving marvellous advantage in the paper and board markets. Salt had bought, on a whim, in the thirties, just as he'd bought Amalgamated Plastics on a whim in the forties. What the old man wouldn't realize was that the days of whims were over; that this was the time of the slide rule and the evaluation of facts and evidence. Even if Salt were to retire, Alex Hodder would move into his chair and there was no guarantee that things would be any better. Hodder was, after all, a devotee of the master-stroke, a hater of patient accumulation. Furthermore, he was the nominated heir. 'When I go,' Salt had once said, 'Alex Hodder will succeed me.' And so he would.

'I'm sorry Mrs. Fazackerly, would you mind saying that again?' Thinking about Salt and Hodder, he'd missed the question. They'd think his mind was wandering.

'Of course.' She smiled politely. 'I was asking, if the question's not presumptuous, whether it might not have been a mistake to buy Women's Press.'

'A mistake?' The decision to buy Women's Press Ltd. had been Salt's own. It was never put to the board; neither Hodder nor himself was consulted. Salt had simply bought in his Olympian way.

'I'm thinking of the trend of women's publishing. From what I can gather, it's downward.'

51

Philips smiled, feeling hunted. He was being invited to criticize the chairman in public and everybody in the room was aware of it; it was odd that his thoughts of a moment or two earlier should be followed so quickly by this. But what was the right answer? Candour? Discretion? He thought the old man had been a bloody fool over Women's Press, but to say so wasn't exactly wise. On the other hand, to approve something so apparently pointless would make *him* look a fool.

'Can we afford to be out of it?' he asked her.

Clare Fazackerly said, 'If it's losing money, I should think so.'

'It isn't.'

'No?' She had that irritating air of superiority clever women so frequently have. 'But that's the long-term trend.'

'Perhaps.' He was damned if he'd defend it. He said, 'It's the chairman's baby really. He says he smells success there.'

'Do you?' She was really trying to pin him down. Why?

'To be truthful, no. But he's smelled success a lot of times before.'

'Thank you.' Surprisingly she seemed willing to leave it there. He glanced at her again, met her cool eyes and looked away quickly, wishing he hadn't.

She came at him again over cocktails.

There was to be dinner for the course members in a small dining room and two Euromob directors were guests: himself and James Thornley, the director responsible for finance.

'Mister Philips, I'm still interested in Women's Press.'

He said, 'I'm afraid I've told you all there is to tell.'

'Yes, I know.' She took a glass of sherry from the waiter's proffered tray and sipped it reflectively.

Philips said, 'That really is a very stunning dress. Or gown? Should I say gown?'

'Thank you. I think my couturier would be distressed if you didn't. They have to be striking, you know, now the programmes are in colour.'

'It's nice to know there's money in television. They do nothing but moan to me over at Westminster T.V.'

She came back with a snap. 'Oh yes, the same problem as Women's Press. To get the money out as profit.'

52

'Waiter. Whisky, please. Black Label.'

He looked at her. 'I told you. They're in profit. Why are you so worried about Women's Press? It's not the worst outfit in Euromob.'

'No,' she said. 'But it's the worst *new* one. I'd have thought that if you were buying businesses, you'd buy things with a big future, not a big past.' She was looking at him steadily, inquiringly, wanting to know. And suddenly he remembered and realized why.

He allowed his face to relax a little.

'The economic climate's pushed everything down. Not just Euromob and not just Women's Press.'

'The best of them will bounce back.' Her eyes glittered.

He was right! Philips smiled. 'There'll be money to be made then. In the right places.'

He counter-attacked gently. 'Your husband's in investment, isn't he? Does he think we're in trouble?'

'I don't think he's buying Euromob, no. Are you?'

'I have a few.'

'Three thousand eight hundred and twenty-eight,' she said. 'And you've had them seven years, in which time they've lost half their value.'

'I'd have done better in Tesco, certainly,' he said. 'So?'

'Julian thinks Women's Press is rather crucial.'

'And you're gathering information for him. Isn't that rather. . . .'

'It's not exactly secret.'

'Nor is it exactly public.'

'All right.' She seemed to have considered something. She said, 'It's not a conflict of loyalties, really. You know where Julian is?'

'Prudential, isn't it?' He'd heard, somewhere.

She shook her head. 'He's now investment director at the Sapphire.'

'I see.' His heart thumped. Sapphire Providential Insurance had a big holding in Euromob and a lot of investment influence; capital followed its leads.

'I was on the phone to him tonight.' She held a cigarette and

53

waited confidently for him to light it. 'We wanted to invite you to dinner. But this course. . . .'

Philips said, 'Perhaps after it's over.'

She looked at him squarely. 'Julian would so like to meet you. He asked me if you could possibly manage to lunch tomorrow.'

Skin prickled on his neck. He was damned if he'd let her give him orders! 'I'm sorry,' he said. 'I have an engagement.'

'Such a—' she seemed to be searching for a word. 'Such a – pity.' He watched the flame of interest being turned down in her face. She said carelessly, 'Of course, if you do find you're free. . . .'

'Naturally.' With relief he saw Verity come into the room, look round and then march towards them. 'Hello, Tommy.' They shook hands. 'You know Mrs. Fazackerly.'

Verity grinned. 'I have to call her Clare, which is nice, isn't it? And she has to call me Tommy. Right, love?'

She said, 'Extraordinary, isn't it!'

'Is it?' Philips said. 'Surely it's a world of Christian names now. Especially your world.'

Clare smiled. 'The Telly?'

Verity said, 'If the second coming happened on David Frost's programme, there'd be no Mr. Christ. It'd be Hello Jesus and Welcome.' He turned to Philips. 'Madge well?'

'Very well, thanks.' And so she was; fit as the proverbial flea, and just about as efficient a bloodsucker.

'I knew his wife – Harry, too, for that matter – when we were lads in Leeds.'

'In Leeds?' she said. 'How interesting.'

'Aye. Harry lived a bit further up the hill than I did, mind.'

Tommy Verity

THEY watched him walk away towards the telephone in the corner.

'I'll tell thee summat,' Verity said. 'Yon's gotten himself a reet 'un.'

'Which means?'

'Where are you from, love?'

'I'm a Londoner.'

'Then you should understand bad English,' Verity said. 'Let's see if you can guess. You're good at guessing games.'

'Well, I take it you mean he married well.'

'Two points to your side, love.'

'Do you always call people "love"?'

'Only if they look as though they won't like it.'

She was looking at him with amusement: composure and amusement. 'It doesn't offend me, particularly.'

'Now if I were from Leicester instead of Leeds, I'd call you "me duck".'

'Me duck!'

'That's what they say.'

'You seem to know an awful lot about these things.'

'Aye, lass, I do.'

She said, 'He's an able man.'

'Harry? He was a clever lad to start with.'

'Tell me about him.'

Verity looked at her. 'Why? Are you bothered?'

'I'm not bothered? Just interested. After all, he *is* my boss.'

She remained cool and amused but fractionally less so. Curious, Verity thought, how people give themselves away, how intensity is instantly detectable. 'You don't fancy him, or anything.'

'Not even "or anything". Why? Would Madge scratch my eyes out?'

'Only if the account at Harrods was closed.'

'And they say women are cats!'

'Tabbies,' he said. 'Me – I'm a tom from t'backs.'

'I believe you.'

'Ladies and gentlemen, dinner is served.'

Verity looked down at her, smiling. 'Shame, that. I was enjoying it.'

She smiled back. 'Thank you. Perhaps you'll tell me some other time.'

'Only if you're wearing that dress.'

She had half turned away. Now she turned back. 'Why?'

'It's smashing, that's all.'

She wouldn't understand, though. She'd never occupied the kind of world they'd lived in: Yorkshire in the thirties with the slump and after-the-slump and then the war. They'd gone to the same junior school, but their homes had been different: Philips had lived in a semi-detached on the fringes of Moortown and he in a mean and run-down mill street down the hill in Chapeltown. Harry Philips was a respectable, reasonable, able boy. He worked fairly hard and lived within the rules most of the time because living within the rules was instinctive and he'd been brought up to it.

Verity wasn't. His father had died when he was eight and from what little he'd ever learned, it was no great loss. His own memories of his father consisted largely of the smell of beer, the swish of his belt and noisy explosions of temper. His mother had applied herself wearily to the task of supporting and bringing up her family. Tommy, as the eldest, a big boy already, had had to fend for himself, and earn, too. There was the paper round and the butcher's deliveries and the fire-wood chopping, and endless errands run for a ha'penny a time.

Fighting, too. Not the ankle-tapping he'd described to the other members of the course; that had been just to sober Steele; but fist-fighting and wrestling, boy against boy, before school, in the playground and after school. Although, come to think of it, he'd fought less as he grew bigger, because by that time he almost always won. Sheeny Mannheim won, too, and they had never fought each other because of some mutual respect or liking. Sheeny Mannheim who at fourteen was the terror of

Clayton Lane, at eighteen played at wing forward for Hunslet and at twenty was suddenly missing-believed-dead somewhere on the road back to Dunkirk. How many had he taken with him, old Sheeny?

They'd called themselves the Scouts, partly in honour of Colonel Cody and the Indian Scouts who were their film heroes at the time, but more to distinguish themselves from the others, the *Boy* Scouts in their fancy hats and neckerchiefs, toggles and belts. Among the local kids, the Scouts were an elite.

Ten of them, physically hard and agile, no fools and no weaklings allowed, mounted on bicycles that had been put together from scrap and a few new parts. They maintained control over something like half a square mile of the city's streets and playgrounds, exacting tribute where they wished, powerful because they worked as a gang. They even had a code of honour because Buffalo Bill and Robin Hood had ethical codes, so they stole eggs from the dairy to leave them on the doorsteps of old women whose cheerfulness they admired. They ensured peace at school for the teachers who offered them respect and hell on earth for the ones who didn't. In their black and white world, people were either for them or against them and, among those against, they counted pupils at Leeds Grammar School and Roundhay School. Their law was that boys attending either should step into the gutter when a Scout passed by. Naturally, the Grammar School boys objected, so there were fights; bitter fights they were, too, when a dozen large lads came looking for trouble. Sometimes the Scouts lost, but never for long because they were organized and the others never were.

So the boys who lived in or near Scout territory and had to cross it, often found themselves obliged to step into the gutter. One of them was Harry Philips.

Inevitably, the Scouts attracted camp-followers, among the local girls, and Verity and Sheeny Mannheim, as leaders, had their pick. At fourteen, both were widely admired and could afford to be discriminating. Sex was there and they took it, but they were far from obsessive. Sport and power were more important. Another Verity called Hedley was the cricketing hero of Yorkshire, and Tommy found himself having to live up to

57

his name and with natural gifts pushed forward by the spur of necessity, became a good cricketer. At fifteen he'd left his secondary school and been lucky enough to find a job in the garage at a local bakery, servicing the vans. At seventeen he passed a driving test, then left the bakery and became a driver's mate on long distance lorries. By this time he was playing, on Saturday afternoons, in the Leeds League, a big hard-hitting young batsman who had been to the county nets.

He hit eighty-six against Holbeck one hot afternoon and ran off the field lathered with sweat, and happy. He was taking his pads off in the dressing room when old Corey, the groundsman said, 'Eh, Tommy, tha's getten an admirer.'

'Oh aye?'

'Din'ta see? Couldn't keep 'er eyes off'n tha.'

'Ah.' He shook out the creases in his trousers and stamped his feet to make them hang better.

'Nay, lad. Have a look.'

'I'd rather have a cup of tea.'

Afterward, while they were fielding, he noticed the girl sitting on the grass behind cover, close to where he was positioned and heard her clap whenever he fielded the ball. Then he was moved round to long leg and she appeared there too, sitting to the side of the sight-screen. He grinned at her as he went back to his place and saw that she blushed. He also saw that she was very pretty and that she wore the blazer of the Girls' High School.

Two weeks later she was there again. He scored forty-eight, was beautifully caught on the boundary trying for fifty and ran cheerfully back to the pavilion. She was there, applauding hard.

He grinned at her and again she blushed furiously.

'Who is she?' he asked Corey.

'How the 'ell would I know? Posh, though.'

'Oh?'

' 'Er dad's got a big Rover.'

For the first time he was mildly interested: he'd never had anything to do with posh girls before. What it must be like to have a big Rover! So he lit a cigarette, went outside and strolled towards her; he was young but knowledgeable, familiar

58

with the phenomenon of the schoolgirl crush. As he passed her, she turned towards him, her scarlet face appealing; she was trembling. Would her God speak?

He said, 'Hello.'

She even stammered saying hello back.

'Didn't I see you a couple of weeks back?'

She nodded, looked away then back hurriedly in case he'd vanished. 'Yes.'

'Well keep coming then. You seem to bring me luck.'

Her face lit up. 'Really? Do you think so?'

'Well, I'd eighty-odd then.'

'It was a fine innings, too. Honestly!'

He grinned. 'Thanks.'

'No honestly. I'd rather watch you than Maurice Leyland!' Now again she blushed scarlet.

He didn't know why, but he was sorry for her: the agony was so visible, the self-torture so obvious. Where normally, if he'd liked the look of her, he would have taken her out and tried his luck, he didn't. Perhaps it was because he was taking a girl out that night, anyway; perhaps because it would be too easy. Instead he sat beside her, chewed grass and talked about cricket while she sat in adoration.

It went on all season and she became a kind of challenge to him, but a challenge entirely opposite in character to the one women usually offered. He was determined to see if he could get through the summer *without* touching her and if possible without hurting her. He didn't realize it at the time, but he was learning manners from her. He offered his hand to help her stand up, brought her cups of tea from the pavilion, spread his mac on the grass for her to sit on.

And one day when Corey said, 'I'll bet she likes it, Tommy lad!' he had to curb an impulse to thump him.

He didn't see her all winter and the next summer she wasn't at any of the matches, but he saw her by chance one day in The Headdrow looking into Lewis's window.

'Hello, Madge.' He tapped her shoulder and she turned, startled.

'Tommy!'

'How are you, then?'

59

She didn't blush this time; there was no trace of embarrassment. 'Very well.'

'Given up cricket, then?'

'I'm playing tennis instead. How's the batting?'

It was friendly but a little disjointed and over-polite and he was conscious of the cheapness of his suit beside her smartness.

'My luck's gone this season. I'm out to blinding catches every week.'

That was the end of it. They'd parted then, and a few weeks later he was in the army. It was in 1943, after Anzio, when he had the letter. There was a newspaper cutting all about his D.C.M. and the commission in the field he'd been awarded. And a sheet of Basildon Bond:

'Dear Tommy, I wonder if you remember me? I made a terrible nuisance of myself to you at cricket matches years ago. Do you remember? I saw you in the Yorkshire Post, cutting enclosed. I feel terribly proud to know you.

Also because I can say in a letter what it would be hard to say in person, I send you my thanks. You know why, I think. I also think you must be very kind.

I'm an S.R.N. now in the Brotherton Wing.
Yours sincerely,
Marjorie Young.'

He was home again and on leave in 1944, before the Normandy landings. The leave was long and tedious; he'd grown away from his family and they were only vaguely interested in him; his friends were all away or prisoners or missing or dead. On impulse one day he telephoned her at the Brotherton Wing. She wasn't off duty until nine, but she'd be delighted to meet him then, for a drink in Powding's.

They were both in uniform: she in the drab navy blue raincoat and gaberdine cap of nursing; he in battledress with the green Commando flashes.

He managed to get drinks and they wedged themselves into a corner of the bar. She sipped the beer and pulled a face.

'Don't like it?'

'Not much. Not beer.'

He said, 'It's funny. I spent years dreaming about beer in pubs and the first one was awful. I'd lost the taste.'

'Coming back now, is it?'

'It is.'

So she made him drink hers, too, and smiled at him.

He smiled back. 'I've a lot to thank you for. Yours was the only letter I got.'

She was deeply shocked. 'The only one?'

'Who'd write to me?'

'You mean, all the time you were abroad?'

'That's right.'

'Where were you?'

'North Africa, then Sicily, then Italy.'

'I know about Anzio. Were you at Salerno, too?'

He nodded.

'And you weren't hurt?'

He'd been nicked in the shoulder, otherwise, miraculously, he was unscathed. 'No.'

'I'd have written more if I'd known.'

'That one was marvellous. I've still got it.' He patted the battledress jacket.

'Really? She turned her head away and put her hand to her face. Then she pulled off her glove and put her hand into the mac pocket for a handkerchief and he saw the diamond.

He said, 'Who's the lucky lad?'

'Mm?'

'The lucky lad? Who bought that?'

'I don't know if you know him. Harry Philips. He's in the Navy.'

'From Moortown? Went to Roundhay?'

She nodded.

'I know him. Where is he?'

'At the Admiralty.'

'Lucky sod. Oh, I'm sorry.'

She smiled and he saw the tears still shining. 'I'm used to it. Hear worse than that.'

They walked out into the blackout and she took his arm. 'Tommy.'

'Yes?'

61

'I'm glad you telephoned.'

'I'm glad you could come.'

There was a pause. Then: 'I meant it. About being grateful.'

'I liked talking to you.'

She held his arm more tightly as they walked. He could feel her breast against his arm and he wanted her, suddenly and fiercely, but she was somebody else's girl and in any case—.

'I want a cigarette. Do you?'

He stepped into a doorway to light it and she followed him in, but didn't take the proffered Gold Flake.

She said, 'Tommy.'

He pulled deeply on his cigarette, her face showing serious in the red glow. 'Come on, love.'

'You can't see me blush and I can't see you. I just want you to know how much I admire you.'

'No,' he said.

'I don't know how it is, but you've always been a bit . . . well, god-like.'

'You're always on about blushing,' he said. He laughed to lighten the atmosphere, but the laugh was only half successful. She had linked arms again and her hand was clasping his own.

He said, 'You want to go canny. I've been abroad a long time.'

'I know. But I'm safe with you.'

God, but he wanted her! 'You're not, you know.'

In a moment her arms were round his neck, her mouth pressing his and her body tight against him. She could not fail to be aware of his arousal.

She whispered, 'I want you.'

'No.' He began to push her away.

'You want me, too. Oh, Tommy, Tommy.'

'You're another man's girl, Madge.'

'I'm not. Not really. He asked me and because he was going away I was sorry for him; I said yes. That's all.'

'He thinks you are. That's what matters.'

She tried to kiss him again, but he held her away. 'Listen Madge. There was a chap I knew got a letter from his girl.

She'd got another man. I watched him walk into machine-gun fire. Come on. I'll see you back.'

'I'm your girl, Tommy, not his. I always will be.'

'Come on, love.'

Verity had stayed out of her life after that night. She'd written to him twice, but he had not replied. In late 1945, she married Lieutenant Harry Philips, R.N.V.R. He'd neither seen nor spoken to her since, but neither had he forgotten. She remained in his mind and at times he was angry with himself for keeping her there, and angry with her both for being there and for being Madge Philips, and that was why he made the nasty cracks about her. That, and the possibility that someone might know.

Clare Fazackerly came over at about eleven, when he was sitting nursing brandy in a balloon glass in the common-room. 'You look like a fairly contented – what was it you said? – an old Tom from the backs?'

He grinned up at her. 'I knew you'd speak the language. Wasn't a bad dinner, eh?'

'Too many calories.'

'You're doing fine, love.'

She said, 'That brandy looks a good idea.'

'Over there. Hine, Cordon Bleu or Armagnac.'

'You mean it's self-service.'

'You're younger than I am.'

He watched as she went to fetch it, admiring her body as she moved across the room, the smooth curves delicately emphasized by the dress. She was neat and deft with bottles and glasses and she returned with a glass in each hand.

'Yours was nearly empty, so I took a chance and brought another.'

'Which?'

'Hine.'

'Wrong. It was Armagnac.'

'I'll have you know you're lucky to get anything.'

'Drinks usually brought to you, eh?'

'As a rule.'

'I take it you get one for your husband sometimes.'

She smiled. 'Julian has beautiful manners.'

'He'll be Mr. Fazackerly?'

'Mr. Porteous, actually.'

'You're one of the ones who keep their maiden names.'

'You don't approve?'

'No problem to me. I haven't a wife.'

'Really? Are you queer or pining for a lost love or what?'

'I told you. I'm an old Tom from the backs.'

'Mm. You were going to tell me things. A little history.'

'Was I?'

She ignored the evasion. 'Now where shall I sit?'

'There are three alternatives. My knee, the arm of the chair, or the carpet.'

She said reasonably, 'There's the chair.'

'Aye,' Verity grinned, 'but I'm using that.'

'You always treat 'em rough?'

'Not always. Depends whether I'm buying or selling.'

'I see. Oh, well . . .' She sat carefully on the arm of the chair. 'Now tell me.'

'What d'you want to know?'

'What sort of man he is.'

'Why?'

'I work for him. I'm interested. Natural curiosity. I'm feminine.'

'I've noticed. Well, he's a nice fellow.'

'I know that.'

'Behaves decently. The employees' share-purchase scheme was his idea; the unions have a lot of time for him. But you know that.'

She said, 'The boy is father to the man. What sort of boy was he?'

Verity could see him now, pictured clearly on some kind of screen in his mind. 'Always wore glasses, except when he was playing rugby.'

'He played rugby, did he?'

'Yes.'

'Well?'

'He was good. Wiry, as you'd imagine.'

'Guts?'

64

Verity looked up at her frowning. 'What do you want?'

'I'm just interested.'

'No. You're after something.'

She laughed. 'Hardly.'

'You want to know whether he's strong or weak, don't you?'

'Don't be—'

'But why?'

Clare said with a careful, light impatience, 'For heaven's sake, let's talk about something else.'

Malcolm Templeton

HE looked at the faces, most set in the familiar look of resentment, and laughed.

'You see it as some kind of assault on your virility, those of you who— No, let me put that another way.' The resentment vanished and they smiled or laughed.

'Personnel selection may not be a science, but we can take a scientific approach.'

Steele said, 'You're all the same, you boys.'

'I bet you can't find another like me between here and my twin brother,' Templeton said.

'Thank you. One is more than plenty. Perhaps,' Steele said savagely, 'you will allow me to make a point.'

Templeton kept on smiling. 'I'd be the last to stand in your way, Gerard.' He watched anger mount in Steele's face. 'Why are we all the same. Some of us, after all, are tall and others short. Some fat, others slim.'

'It's your small and uniform minds,' Steele said, 'and your arrogantly uniform attitudes, that I'm referring to.'

'At least that's clear. Care to explain?'

'I have no complaint,' Steele said, 'about true science or about those who practise it. I'm talking about the funny fringe, the phoney areas, the pseudo sciences.'

'You mean, psychology?'

'And sociology and all the other petty little ologies in which one man's opinion is as good as another's.'

'You think?'

'Some of the time, yes, I think.'

Templeton made a small, imaginary tick in the air. 'One up to you.'

Steele said, 'Let's not play bloody games. You try to count the uncountable, turn everything and everybody into figures. You set ludicrous norms and match people against them and if they don't match in every bloody particular, they're out.'

66

Templeton looked at him. 'Science consists of experiment and measurement, surely.'

'Yes, science does. You boys just try to use figures to back your own opinions. You're sabotaging the human race.'

Templeton said, 'Oh, come. By trying to put the right people in the right jobs?'

'By excluding everybody *except* the people who meet *your* standards. Christ, you'd never have let Churchill into the army. Answer me a question.'

'If I can?'

'Make me a matrix for an M.P.'

Templeton pulled a sheet of paper towards him and wrote, 'Steele. Wholly destructive in argument. Grudge against education, qualifications, scientific approach. Possibly paranoid.'

He looked up. 'I'm sorry? Oh yes, M.P.s. I'd say the best thing is six hundred and twenty-five individuals.'

'Ability to speak well and clearly?'

'It's important, after all.'

'Assuming you approve the party system, a strong sense of loyalty, specially when things are difficult?'

There was a trap being baited here, Templeton knew. Better the pre-emptive strike. 'You're going to tell me I'd have excluded Churchill or something.'

He was delighted to see Steele look furious. 'You would. Bevan, too.'

'Bad thing, do you think?' He got his laugh. 'Somebody else's turn, Gerard.'

Keyes said, 'I'm not sure I don't agree with Steele.'

'Look,' Templeton said, 'there's nothing sinister. I and people like me just try to put round pegs into round holes.'

Steele said loudly, 'A Freudian, by God. And obsessive about it.'

Keyes smiled briefly. 'It's the old army technique, used at the old War Office Selection Boards. I often used to think we kept out as many good men as we got in.'

Templeton suppressed a sigh. Whenever a group was introduced to selection techniques, there was always this wrangle.

67

'Look, this is ethics. We're talking about business: a man and a job.'

Keyes said, 'All right. But I prefer my business to have some ethical content.'

'Ouch.'

'Nothing personal.'

It never was. I hate your guts and every single thing you stand for, old boy, but it's nothing personal. He looked at Keyes and ached to slap him down.

'Guards, wasn't it?'

Keyes smiled that infuriating, impregnable smile they always had.

'Well, your standards were largely social and financial.'

'Agreed. I'm afraid money was necessary. The rest was simply tradition. You'd be surprised how tolerant everybody was.'

'Provided—' Templeton let the word hang.

'Oh, certainly. Bear in mind that I'm not necessarily defending it. Information only.'

'Do you defend it?' Templeton demanded.

'Selection by social standards? Difficult to avoid. We all do it, don't we, in picking our friends.'

Templeton grinned, holding his anger in check. It was this effortless superiority, this casual likeable arrogance, that kept Britain fundamentally Tory.

'That's all I'm saying really. Everybody who ever gives another bloke a job is applying standards. We just try to codify matters. It's not exact, as Mr. Steele said, but we score better than fifty per cent so. As far as business is concerned, we're saving money on wastage. I wouldn't pretend one test by itself tells anybody much. I.Q. tests don't really take any account of creativity' – he glanced at Steele to see if the olive branch was accepted, but Steele continued to glower – 'and Rorschach is only one indicator, not the final one. But if you give several tests to one person, in the end you get fairly close. Rorschach, by the way, is the old ink-blot caper. By the way, do you know the story about the bloke who went to a psychiatrist and the psychiatrist handed him a pair of socks. "What do they make you think of?" he says. "Sex," says the bloke. Next it's the table lamp. "Sex" this bloke says. The psychiatrist fishes in his pocket and pulls out a handful of change. "And this?" "Sex" the bloke says. "Okay," says the psychiatrist, handing him a blank sheet of paper, "What about this?" "Sex," says this feller. So the psychiatrist looks at him. "Funny," he says. "Four things: socks, a lamp, money and blank paper and they all make you think of sex. Why do you think that is?" And this feller looks back at him. "I never think of anything else," he says.'

The laugh came, Steele, Sinclair, Keyes and Jane Roper dissenting.

'Okay. Let's have some coffee,' Templeton said. 'Afterwards you can do a test.'

Steele said, 'No.'

'Okay. I just thought you'd be interested. The results will only be known to the individual concerned.'

Keyes said, 'And you.'

'Well yes. But you needn't worry about me. I'm secure as the Bank of – er, no. The Bank of Zurich, perhaps.'

While they drank their coffee and went to the toilets, Templeton went to the telephone in the mezzanine and dialled. A voice said, 'Yes?'

'Templeton.'

'Ah.'

'I believe I've struck your kind of gold.'

'Oh. A body?'

'Yes. Marketing man.'

'Good.'

'Spectacular results, I'm told.'

'And socially?'

'Ex-Guards.'

'School?'

'Harrow.'

'Age?'

'Thirty-nine.'

'All right. We were very pleased with Henderson.'

Templeton felt a spasm of pleasure. 'I'm glad.'

'Let me know about personality.'

'Of course. I'm doing the test this morning.'

He hung up, rubbing his hands. Another thousand if all went well.

At twelve-thirty he rang again. 'Yes?'

'High scores on both aggression and patience. Confidence, too, of course.'

'What kind of talker?'

'Urbane. Amusing.'

'Clever?'

'Certainly that.'

'Where is he?'

'The Princess. Princess Hotel, that is.'

'And the name?'

Templeton hesitated briefly. Once the name had been given he was helpless if they chose to renege.

'Come on, Templeton. The cash will be round by hand within an hour.'

'The name is Fullerton Ironside-Keyes. He's Marketing Director of European Communications Travel.

'Euromob?' The voice was doubtful.

'Don't let that worry you.'

Templeton was having lunch when the waiter approached. 'Mr. Templeton, sir?'

'Yes.'

'This just arrived for you, sir.' The waiter handed him a packet.

'Thank you very much.' He pushed the envelope into an inside pocket and turned to Jane Roper. 'I get forgetful sometimes. You will let me know if I start playing footsy under the table.'

She said, 'I doubt if you'd forget a second time.'

'That's what I like about this caper,' Templeton said happily, 'you get such a nice class of threat.'

Jane Roper

IT would be restful, she thought, to spend an hour away from all these prowling male libidos; to have a remark made to her that was not an oblique reference to sex and her own desirability, to be able to sit without wondering who was staring where, to be able to work without calculating an elaborate defence system that kept touchers and leerers out of range. Why did they bother anyway? It was obviously some kind of endless male optimism that kept them believing that the next pretty girl, or the one after that, would fall into bed moaning with delight. Jane was aware that this was the penalty for her spectacular looks but she did not underrate the concomitant advantages; it was just that there never seemed to be any respite.

She was leading a discussion, her eyes flicking to and from the sheet of paper on which she had set out the pattern she hoped the discussion would take. The leader's job was to control the conversation, but to do so gently and without strain, drawing in those people who were reluctant to offer their views, shutting up the over loquacious ones as discreetly as possible. She was sitting in a small, upright armchair, facing Steele, Giesing, Farmer and Sinclair, and the calf muscle of her right leg was pressing painfully against her left knee. She uncrossed her legs, placed her feet together on the floor and watched their eyes follow every movement. When Sinclair looked up, she was waiting for him.

'What do you think, George?'

He said, easily, 'There is an obvious need for a greatly simplified tax system, as there is a need for a simplified legal system. Happily for my profession and our legal friends, neither is very likely.'

'You believe not?'

'Too many vested interests involved. Look at the lobbies.'

She said, 'It's a viewpoint, but it's rather cynical. Don't you agree, Gerard.

71

'I think this whole thing is an exercise in futility.'

'All right, but what about reform of the Companies Act.'

Steele said, 'Saving your presence, I don't give a monkey's mandibles for the Companies Act. Or discussion groups.'

John Longbottom, sitting away to one side, cut in. 'The discussion group can be a very useful management tool. It can elicit valuable views from unexpected quarters. Bear with this one, Gerard, and you'll see.'

'There's an absolutely splendid view from this quarter, thank you very much.'

Jane said, 'Don't strain your eyesight.'

'You're supposed to blush a little and be flattered.'

'Look, we're talking about the Companies Act.'

'You may be.'

A little desperately she said, 'Mr. Farmer – er Mike.'

'Yes.' He was sitting in a curiously crouched position, bent over and staring at the carpet between his scuffed brown leather shoes.

'Any views?' Steele guffawed and she glared at him. 'What do you think?'

'Well something's going to have to be done about computer security very soon. Does that come under it?'

'Let's assume it does. What's the problem?'

'Magnets. And malice.' He grinned. 'They go together.'

'Go on.'

He looked round the little group. 'You don't see?'

Sinclair said, 'I see very well. I'm afraid I don't understand.'

Farmer frowned. 'You know, don't you, that computer information is usually stored on magnetic tape or on discs. Well, they're terribly vulnerable, you see. And something's got to be done.'

Jane smiled at him. 'You mentioned magnets.'

'Yes. Oh, you want me to explain? I'm sorry. Well, only the other day a trade union official in France got into a tape storage bank with a magnet and scrambled the lot.'

'Do you mean,' Steele asked slowly, 'that he destroyed the tapes.'

'Not the tapes themselves, you understand, but the magnet

affected the particles, in the coatings of course, and the recordings were ruined.'

Steele said, 'Bloody good.'

Farmer stared at him, shocked. 'The company now has no records. Don't you see? None at all.'

'Then they'll go out of business,' Sinclair said. 'And quickly.'

'That's right. In the States not long ago, according to a report on industrial sabotage, from Harvard I think, a man with a grievance built a powerful electro-magnet into a lorry and destroyed a bank of tapes from the street outside the building. The company went into liquidation in three months.'

'Three months?' Longbottom repeated.

'They lost all their orders, their records, their stock control documentation. Everything. They were helpless.'

Steele said, 'You've cheered me a good deal. I rejoice that man can still get back at your blasted machines. Did you say Harvard?'

'Yes. But for God's sake—' Farmer was obviously angry.

'I'd like to run an article. The report gives examples?'

'I'll lend you my copy. No need to get on to Harvard.'

'It's a good piece for *Viewpoint*. How to sabotage your computer. Or the Gas Board's, for that matter.'

Jane looked at Longbottom and shrugged. 'For chairing discussion groups, C minus.'

'It happens. Topics are self-propelling sometimes,' Longbottom was sympathetic. 'The ideal is a controlled four or five-way conversation. When you've been doing it for a while a kind of group dynamic develops.'

'Group rubbish,' said Steele.

Suddenly furious, Jane said, 'Where do you get this urge to hurt? And can't you give it a rest? It's infuriating. Don't you see?'

He grinned at her: a curious, lop-sided grin. 'No. But I see your knickers.'

She felt her eyes flicker downward, the blush on her cheeks, her hands move to the hem of her skirt, and brought herself under control quickly. 'From the way you've been staring, I imagine you've read the label.'

73

'That's right. Marks & Spencer.'

Suddenly she'd had enough. He was like a venomous little snake sliding round her and she had to stop him. She came out of the chair quickly and the slap of her palm on his cheek was surprisingly sharp and loud. She stood staring down at him then, her hand tingling from the blow, watching the skin of his face flare red.

He didn't touch it, didn't raise his hand to his cheek either to ease the pain or to ward off another blow. He simply stared back at her, smiling slightly.

Longbottom said in a shocked voice, 'That's enough, I think.'

Then Steele started to laugh. 'You have,' he said, 'a great gift for the incongruous, Mr. Longbottom. Longbottom.' He laughed again. 'Longbottom!'

'What's so funny about Longbottom?'

Steele said, between guffaws, 'Shorthouse.'

Jane looked at him, at the scarlet cheek and the face creased with laughter. Then, inexplicably, she, too, was giggling. She couldn't quite believe it and her mind asked coldly, why are you · laughing? But she continued to laugh.

She was lying in the bath, reading a rather damp *Evening Standard,* when the knock came at the door. 'Damn.' She climbed out, put on a towelling robe. The knock came again.

'Just a moment.'

When she opened the door there was a page with a large bouquet of flowers.

'For Miss Roper, ma'am.'

'Thank you. Over there.' She found her bag and give him ten pence and then, when the boy had gone, opened the little envelope. The message, in a large and untidy handwriting, read, 'Three cheers for pride, G.G.S.'

From Steele? She looked at the message again. How strange! Three cheers for pride!

The telephone rang and she picked it up. 'Hello.'

'It's Gerard Steele.'

'Yes.' What did one say to a man whose face one had slapped

74

not long before, 'Thanks for the flowers?' She said, 'I don't quite see . . .'

'You got them.'

'Yes. And they're lovely. 'But—'

'I'm not seeking forgiveness, don't misunderstand. But that was a splendid gesture. Most women would just have blushed or been embarrassed or said something stupid like, "I always go to Marks and Sparks." But you lash out. Marvellous!'

'Frankly, Mr. Steele, I find this incomprehensible. One minute you're brutally and disgracefully rude. The next you're—'

'Have a drink with me. Before dinner.'

'I'm sorry. There won't be time.'

He laughed. 'No subterfuge. You don't need them. You can always clout me again.'

A little helplessly, she found herself saying, 'All right. Where?'

'Not in that bloody common-room. There's a pub called the Guinea just off Berkeley Square. Round the corner. Know it?'

'Yes.'

'Fifteen minutes, then. The bar, not the restaurant.' He rang off.

What on earth, she asked herself in annoyance, made her do that? She was still dripping wet from the bath; there wouldn't be time to do her hair decently, and she didn't even want to meet him!

Dressed, she left the Princess and walked reluctantly along to the Guinea. Steele was standing in a corner, frowning to himself but he saw her and strode across, glass in hand.

'What do you drink?'

'Gin and tonic, thanks.'

He said, 'No, you don't. You sip that politely. What do you drink for pleasure?'

Anger flared again. 'Look, Mr. Steele—' she began.

'Bear with me. Now – what do you drink for pleasure? The nicest drink you've had, what was it?'

Suddenly she remembered a hot evening in North Africa and the faint, icy flavour of orange zest. 'Cointreau,' she said. 'On the rocks.'

75

Steele's hand clapped her shoulder. 'That's it!' He shouted to the barman, 'A large Cointreau. On the rocks. And more malt whisky. A pound tip if you serve me now.'

Jane felt herself blushing as angry office workers' eyes turned towards him; towards her, too. But the drinks came instantly and he handed over the pound. 'Do you often do that?'

'I invited you for a drink. I'm not going to keep you standing while I try to catch some barman's eye.'

She sipped.

'All right?'

'It's delicious.'

'You see.' Then he frowned. 'I'm not going to apologize.'

'All right. But why this?'

He looked up at her, still frowning. 'You're the only one with a mind among all those bloody zombies.'

Automatically she protested: 'No. They're—'

'They're conditioned,' he said. 'All of 'em. Good business behaviour. Disagree, but disagree politely. Don't lose the bloody order and think about the audit, and for Christ's sake don't touch the computer – that's true desecration.'

'And I'm not like that?'

'Oh yes you are. You're about two thirds conditioned. You behave decently and with decorum and people get away with bloody murder.'

She said, '*You* get away with murder.'

He nodded, vigorously. 'And you let me. Look how hard I had to shove before you did anything?'

She stared at him. 'You mean that was all deliberate?'

'Provocation? Of course.' He looked smug now, the frown gone. 'I was rescuing you from a world in which people are bloody rude to you and you have to smile and gloss it over because they're higher in the packing order than you.'

She sipped her drink and realized with surprise, when she looked at him again, that he was three or four inches shorter than she. 'You're fighting a losing battle. The human psyche's made that way.'

'I know. But there are degrees. I don't like to see gold being transmuted into base bloody metal.'

'Look,' she said, 'I can look after my own—'

76

'No you can't. You're like all women, you don't do things. You wait to be done.'

Jane put down her glass. 'There are better places to wait. Good night,' but his hand held her forearm.

'That's fine,' he said.

'Let go of my arm,' Jane was furious, 'or I'll wallop you again.'

'That's even better!' He released her arm.

Baffled, she stared at him. 'What the hell is the matter with you?'

'That's nice and direct. Straight talking suits you far better than all these bloody evasions. He mimicked her, skilfully and cruelly: ' "Don't strain your eyesight." Why didn't you say, "Stop looking up my skirt you dirty little bastard?" I'll tell you. It's because convention says you're supposed to ignore it.'

She spread her hands. 'All right. I'm a creature of convention.'

'You're not.'

'Oh?'

He took a mouthful of whisky. 'For a start, you're illegitimate.' Then he was fumbling in his pockets, producing cigarettes, and, when he offered them, smiling.

She said, 'What on earth! I mean, how do you—?'

'I found out.' He blew smoke about cheerfully.

'Somerset House. It's there.'

'I know. But why bother to look?'

He said, 'I wonder if Brother Farmer's got it in his computer yet?'

'I asked why you looked!'

'Frightening, isn't it, when people suddenly have information about you that they shouldn't have. Your bank balance, for instance.'

Suddenly she could barely see for fury. Her fingertips bent involuntarily, crooking the nails; she felt a sudden urgent desire to scratch his face again and again. She said, 'You bloody little swine!'

Steele laughed at her. 'I don't know your bank balance. How should I find out?'

'Then why? Tell me why?' she demanded. 'What the hell are you up to?'

'Have another drink.'

'I will *not* have another drink. But tell me why? Why?'

'I'll tell you,' he said, 'over the second drink.'

She should get up and walk out, but she couldn't. She had to know how much he knew, what he'd succeeded in finding out. His knowledge of her illegitimacy would only be awkward if he knew more. But it was significant that he'd found out even that.

She remembered how she'd heard it first, following all the best theories, when she was seven. 'We're not your real parents, Jane. That's why you call us Uncle and Auntie.'

'Then where are my mother and my father?'

'They died, dear, a long time ago.'

Oh yes, it had been a shock, but the real one had come later, when she was twelve and the realities of life and birth and sex had been explained to her. The story had always been that her father had been killed in the war and that her mother had died, of some unspecified illness, when Jane was very young. But Uncle Charles and Aunt Faith were her mother's uncle and aunt and they were getting older and less able to counter the adroit long-term questioning of a highly intelligent adolescent. Gradually she got nearer to the truth. One day, for some administrative reason, birth certificates had been required at school and she'd told them.

'I'll send it,' Uncle Charles said. But she noticed that the birth certificates of other children weren't *sent*: the other children *took* them to school. So Jane made careful inquiries and discovered the arrangements under which birth certificates were issued. She began to look for information; she went to the local library and looked in the files of the local paper for the announcement of her birth, but there was no announcement.

'Where was I born, Aunt Faith?'

'In Chester, dear.'

Chester? She wrote to the Chester Chronicle asking if they could tell her about the announcement and enclosing a stamped addressed envelope. 'Dear Miss Roper, I am afraid I can find no record of such an announcement. Yours sincerely. . . .'

Later she began to search the house, to go through the drawers of Uncle Charles's desk and Aunt Faith's dressing table in the hope of finding something. She found it the day of Uncle Charles's funeral. It was evening and her aunt had decided to walk and be alone. 'I'd like to be alone,' she said. 'You understand, dear?'

By herself in the house, Jane went upstairs, her own grief painful in her chest. The door of his study lay open and she went in, listening to the stillness, meeting the familiar smell of tobacco and books, looking round her at the room that had always been the same and now would never be the same again. His glasses lay on the desk, and his pipe, and the pouch she'd bought for his birthday. And his wallet! Her heart pounded. She stared at it for a long time, tears welling in her eyes. How could she go through it now? Now when he was no longer there to defend it. The room was full of his presence; he seemed to be watching from every corner, to know and to disapprove. But somehow she knew that the truth was there; that behind that worn, smooth cold leather lay the things she so needed to know. She said, 'I'm sorry, Uncle Charles,' and looked round the room. 'But I have to know. I have to!'

She found the cutting, carefully folded and tucked into one of the pockets. It was brief, old and terrible, and as she read it anger seemed to spread like hardening metal through her body, hot with hate at first, then becoming cold and solid and immovable. It said simply, 'At a resumed inquest on Tuesday, a verdict that she took her own life while the balance of her mind was disturbed, was recorded on Faith Doreen Roper of 227 Toll Avenue. The Coroner was told that a note Miss Roper left said she had recently given birth to an illegitimate child and that the father would have nothing more to do with her.'

That night she lay in bed, staring at the ceiling hour after hour, thinking about her mother and the man who had walked out, the man who would have nothing more to do with the girl who had borne his child. She tried to imagine the despair, the fear, the shame that preceded suicide. In the early hours, clear-eyed in the stillness, she promised that she would find her father. And somehow, she would ruin him.

79

Aunt Faith told her reluctantly when she was twenty-one. Jane, asked what gift she wanted, had said, 'To know about me. About my mother and my father.'

'But Jane, dear—'

'I have a right to know.'

Aunt Faith sighed. 'Can't you leave it, dear? If you can forget, it would be so much better.'

'Please. If you don't tell me, I'll never know. Never!'

So she heard how her mother, working in London, had met the man and become pregnant; how the man, faced with it, had denied all knowledge; how her mother had sworn that he was the only man she'd ever loved. She also learned his name.

It took her a year to find him, four more to equip herself for the job, another two to get it, to get near him, to work herself into a position near him, a position of trust. Now she was in that position. Sooner or later he would become vulnerable; sooner or later she would be able to contribute to his downfall. Sooner or later ... but not yet. She had no intention of doing slight damage, or wasting her effort inflicting unimportant wounds. When the chance came, though, it had to be taken. Meanwhile, she had a good job, and she had to hold it.

Jane watched Steele coming towards her, carrying the drink.

'So you believe,' she said, 'in being direct and truthful.'

'As much as possible.'

'So tell me now why you've been researching me.'

He grinned. 'Because I want to make love to you.'

Mentally, she groaned. After all the nonsense, this was what it was all about! Insults, flowers, meetings in pubs, mystery. All because he was feeling randy.

She said, 'Well, I'm sorry to disappoint you.'

'You mean directness won't work?'

'That's right.' She looked down at him. All her life she'd been brushing passes aside and this was easy. 'Did you think it would?'

Steele sipped his whisky. 'I think it will.'

Jane laughed shortly, deliberately contemptuous. 'Come on. We'd better go back.'

'You're scared.'

'This is getting more stupid every—'

'No,' he said. 'You're thinking about it.'

'I'm going.' She headed for the door and he followed her out into the mews.

He said, 'When you look like me, it's not enough just to smile and be charming. Beautiful girls don't respond.'

'I assure you, I shan't either.'

'I think you will. You see, I *have* made an impression, favourable or not. Small stout men can't bowl you over with their beauty. As the Good Book says, by taking thought one can add cubits to one's stature.'

'I wouldn't think this was a good context for biblical quotes.'

She heard him laugh beside her. 'None better. It's a very sexy bit of work, the Old Testament.'

'This is all rather disgusting, isn't it?'

'What do you mean, isn't it. Is it?'

She didn't reply, hurrying instead towards the hotel; but his hand was on her arm again, halting her. 'Oh, for God's sake!'

He said, 'I want to make love to you. I tell you so. Is that disgusting? If it is, what *should* I do?'

'Look, Gerard,' she said. She was impatient now and it showed in her voice. 'If you're feeling randy you'd better look elsewhere.'

'As a matter of fact, I'm not. It's not a matter of wanting to screw somebody, anybody. I want to make love to you. So think about it.'

A moment later, he escorted her into the lobby of the hotel.

Jane said, 'Thanks for the drink. And the flowers. Thank you, and good-bye.'

Steele looked at her in that curious way he had, half small boy, half cynic.

He spoke very softly. 'I'll be with you in spirit.'

George Sinclair

'NATURALLY he sees us as his own property. His baby.'

Keller smiled. 'For a man who's naturally distant, he can certainly loom.'

'I suppose it's all very human and excusable,' Sinclair said. 'After all, he ran the company for years. He's bound to have a sentimental interest, if nothing else.'

'I wouldn't say Hugh Salt was a sentimental man,' Keller said, then laughed. 'He's damned matter of fact. You know the old business about knowing the worth of everything and the value of nothing.'

'Oh, I don't know,' Sinclair began. 'He's—' but he was interrupted. John Longbottom was on his feet.

'I'm sorry, ladies and gentlemen, but Mr. Hodder has sent his apologies. He won't be able to get here tonight. And as you know, the other Euromob main board director who was supposed to be here, Sir Kenelm Scrivener, isn't well, so it looks as though the evening's blank.'

Sinclair let his eyes flicker round the table. Disappointment wasn't visible in noteworthy quantities.

Longbottom went on: 'So I suppose I'd better leave it to you. I could conduct a lesson on the properties in statistics of the bell-shaped curve, but I'm sure you don't want that.' There was a little mild laughter, polite rather than responsive. 'The table's here, and the chair and the booze. If anybody wants to stay and revitalize the lost art of conversation, fine. Otherwise, the evening is yours.

'Excellent,' Keller said. 'I can slip home for a couple of hours.'

'Where's home?'

'Hampstead Garden Suburb. You?'

'I'll walk a bit,' Sinclair said. 'That's what I miss in this place. It's all food and sitting on one's bottom.'

He went to his room and changed from dinner jacket into a

plain suit, slipped on a mac, made a telephone call and went out.

Sir Hugh Salt opened the door himself and looked mildly surprised to see his visitor. 'Oh, Sinclair, of course. Do come in. Come in boy. I was reading. One does become so immersed.'

Sinclair stepped into the panelled hall, began to slip off his mac.

'Give that to me,' Salt said. He tossed the mac on to a chair. 'Come this way. I'm in the study.'

Sinclair followed him into the book-lined room that looked out over the river, Salt talking over his shoulder. 'I expect you'd like a drink, wouldn't you.'

'Not especially,' Sinclair said. 'What are you reading?'

'Pliny's letters. Pliny the Younger, that is. Volume ten: the letters to Trajan. It's a terrible shame the rest was lost, you know. Tragic. Have you read him?'

Sinclair spread his hands. 'I'm neither more nor less well-read than most of my generation. But you make me feel illiterate.'

'I'm sorry. Shouldn't do that.'

'No. I'm envious. Deeply envious.'

Salt lowered his body on to the plain upright chair behind the big antique desk. 'Never envy the old, Sinclair. They haven't anything worth the envying.'

'Erudition isn't an attribute of youth. Can't be.'

Salt smiled at him. 'Don't butter me up.'

'I'm not. I envy your erudition, just as I envy you a house like this in Cheyne Walk.'

'The first, such as it is, is the product of Winchester and Balliol and some people who were prepared to be encouraging. The second, I'm afraid, is a matter of money. Most of it inherited.'

'I know.'

'Do sit down. What are you doing now?'

'I'm on a course.'

Salt frowned. 'Course? Oh, that management thing of Philips'. Is it interesting?'

'Occasionally.'

'Hm. Rewarding?'

'Possibly. I'd rather answer in six months. You're sure I haven't interrupted anything important?'

'That depends upon one's view of Pliny's letters to Trajan. I take it things are going well?'

'Very.'

'Go on.'

'Six per cent increase in turnover for the first quarter.'

'Over what?'

'Over the previous quarter. We're eighteen per cent up on last year at the same time.'

Salt chuckled. 'Good for you. Good for you. Where has it come from?'

'Fischer A.G.'

'In Frankfurt?'

'Frankfurt, Hamburg, Cologne, Essen. Et cetera.'

'That is capital,' Salt said. 'Supply problems?'

'Not for a few years as far as raw materials are concerned, but we'll need more land. More trees.'

Salt closed Pliny the Younger with a snap. 'It is really extraordinary. When I bought Ingrid Vik and Prince Patrick I thought I was being remarkably silly; that we'd never reach the end of it. You'll remember that? Buy as much as you can.'

'There'll be problems, surely, about the release of capital?'

'Don't worry. Not for that. It's vital.'

'You'll be opposed.' Sinclair said.

Salt stared. 'Opposed? Well, perhaps. All the same, I'll speak to Hodder about it. And Philips.'

There were, Sinclair thought, advantages to running the chairman's favourite subsidiary. He said, 'I thought you'd like to know about the figures.'

Salt got up and walked towards the door.

'Come this way, will you Sinclair?'

In the dining room, Salt opened the door of an exquisite corner cupboard which, if it was not Chippendale, was of almost the same period and quality. 'I have a brandy here,' he said. 'A Croizet. It's very old and fine. You might find it pleasing.'

After a moment he handed the glass to Sinclair. 'A very little, you see. Just enough to appreciate.'

84

Sinclair sniffed and sipped and sniffed again. 'I envy you this, too.'

Salt came with him to the door. 'Whenever you have news, Sinclair. Always glad to see you then.'

As he crossed the lobby at the Princess, the porter came forward. 'Mr. Sinclair, sir?'

'Yes.'

The porter gave him a piece of paper.

'Thank you.' He unfolded it and read the message: 'Mr. Carlo Hasso called. He is at Claridges.'

Sinclair glanced at his watch. It was after eleven o'clock. He crossed the lobby quickly, waited impatiently for the lift, went to his room and picked up the telephone.

'Claridges Hotel.'

'Signor Hasso, please.'

'Your name, sir?'

'Sinclair.'

There was a pause and a click. 'George! I call earlier but—' Sinclair could almost see the humorous regret, the spread hands.

'How are you, Carlo?'

'I am very well. Also very lonely.'

'Poor old Carlo. How is Gina?'

'Is very well. Also lonely – I hope!'

Sinclair laughed. 'What brings you to London?'

'I came to see you. On quick thought – what is you say?'

'Impulse?'

'Is right. Impulse. I need board. I say to myself, my friend George Sinclair. This time I buy from him.'

'I'll come round.'

'But not alone,' Hasso said.

Sinclair replaced the receiver. It was eleven fifteen now, which didn't make things particularly easy. He waited a moment for the line to clear, then picked up the receiver.

Twenty minutes later he was still on the telephone. Trade was evidently brisk in London tonight.

'Stevie? George Sinclair.' Stevie Wade was a tough blonde

85

in her forties who ran a company which produced advertising films, his own among them.

'At this time of night, Mr. Sinclair, I'm sure you don't want to talk advertising.'

'Hardly. I have a client in London.'

'I see-ee-ee-ee. He's important?'

'I'd like to keep him happy.'

'Then he must be. Look, it might help if you came round here. I have photographs and so on.'

'Right.' He left his room quickly and hurried out.

The taxi dropped him in Wardour Street a-bustle with the late crowds and he went down the stairs and knocked. Stevie, in sweater and slacks, opened the door. 'It's bloody difficult. I've made a couple of phone calls, but – well, you know. The ones I know aren't professionals.'

Sinclair passed on the pressure. Hasso would do business, but only *if*. He said, 'It would be bad news if you couldn't . . .' and let the words trail off.

'I'm not a magician, Mr. Sinclair. I'm thinking, believe me. I take it you don't want just the ordinary?'

He nodded. 'Not whores. Not at any price. Aren't there any aspiring actresses nowadays?'

She shrugged. 'It's so late, you see. Hey, wait a minute!'

He waited.

Stevie said, 'Why should it be only actresses? Just a sec.' She shuffled among the papers on a desk. 'That's it. She wants to direct films.'

'What's she like?'

'University of Sussex. About twenty-three. Comes to me about once a week begging for a job.'

'Pretty?'

'In an intellectual kind of way. High forehead and glasses.'

Sinclair lit a cigarette and listened. 'Juliet? Stevie Wade. You doing anything? . . . yes, now . . . just reading? . . . Listen, Juliet, could you get round here quickly . . . Yes, now . . . Don't worry, I'll pay for the cab. Fine.' Stevie Wade looked up at him. 'She'll be here soon.'

'From where?'

'Tatty part of Clerkenwell. It won't take long. Christ, why do I have to do this?'

'Survival,' Sinclair said, and smiled, remembering. 'That is the first duty.'

'I suppose so.' She opened a cupboard. 'Scotch?'

'Thanks.' She poured. 'I'd better be out of sight when you talk to her.'

'Hadn't you!' Stevie said. 'Just through there. You can leave the door ajar.'

He sat in the darkness, listening, conscious of guilt but turning away from it, and heard the girl's voice, eager and slightly breathless. 'I got here as quickly as I could, Miss Wade. What is it?'

Stevie said, 'I don't know, Julie. How badly do you want a job?'

The unseen girl's voice rose with delight. 'You mean you're giving me a job?'

'Answer the question. How badly?'

A tiny hesitation. 'More than anything. If I can just *get* in!'

'Words, Juliet. Do you mean it?'

'Oh, Miss Wade, you know I'd do anything.' She stopped and he heard the hiss of her breath. 'Is that it?' The voice was suddenly flat with dismay.

The silence lasted several seconds. Stevie must have nodded.

'Oh, God!' Then uncertainty again. 'Maybe I misunderstood . . .'

'No. You understood very well.'

'But that's – I mean, I'd be . . .'

'I asked you how badly.'

Another pause. The girl's voice, when she spoke, was very low. 'Just once? Just this time?'

Stevie said, 'This is important. It's to help keep us in the film business. I'm not intending it as a career for you.'

'No.' Then, 'Miss Wade, who is it?'

'A man. It's very simple. We have a client to keep happy. Our client has a client to keep happy. It's not your first time, Julie?'

Sinclair, trying to maintain his detachment, found it impos-

87

sible; his face burned and his hands were clasped tight.

'No,' the girl cleared her throat. 'No. I had a boy friend once . . .' Her voice broke.

'That's no use, Julie.' Stevie's tone was firm but sympathetic. 'I know it's not the nicest thing in the world, but you'll survive it.'

Again she cleared her throat. 'What would I have to do? I mean, would I—'

Stevie said, 'We're back where we started. How much do you want to work in films?'

A pause, then, 'All right.'

'Look dear,' Stevie said. 'This bloke may be a real pig. He may want it all ways. Don't go unless you're prepared to go through with it. Understand?'

'Yes. Oh, God!'

'And you get a job for three months. Just learning round the studio. On trial. Okay?'

'That's true? I mean, you wouldn't go back on it?'

'I won't,' Stevie said. 'But you won't either.'

The girl's voice was determined. 'I won't let you down,' she said. 'Now or ever.'

Sinclair rose, buttoned his mackintosh and went out. The girl was standing with her back to him. Stevie said, 'This is—'

'No names.'

'She's agreed. What about clothes? There are some odds and ends here. Turn round, Julie.'

Behind the big glasses, the girl's wide eyes stared at him nervously. She was wearing dark trousers, boots and a sloppy sweater. Her hair was long and dark, held by a wide scarlet band. She was tall and graceful.

Julie said, 'Are you . . .?'

'I wish I were, but no. Better get going.'

As her arms lifted to put on her coat, he saw the swell of her breasts and desire stirred in him.

They stood silent, waiting for a taxi, then got in sitting well apart. At the hotel the girl stood pale and silent beside him as they went up to Hasso's suite. It was only when they stood outside the door that she said quickly, anxiously, 'What's he like?' Sinclair tried to find an answer and couldn't. He said instead, 'If he's pleased you'll get fifty pounds,' and felt her stare as he knocked.

Carlo Hasso said, 'But she is mm-m-m—'

Julie was standing very straight, her arms loose at her sides, looking straight ahead.'

'May I introduce Julie? This is Carlo.' His voice sounded tinny.

Hasso took her hand and bent to kiss it.

Sinclair said, 'Julie wants to direct films.'

'She is very beautiful.'

Sinclair said, 'I'd better go.'

Hasso stopped him. 'No, I have brought your estimate with me.' He walked across to a table and picked up a file of typescript. 'I have made questions. If you could answer them now.'

Sinclair stared at him. 'Now? But—'

'I must leave London in nine hours.'

'Yes. But where?'

Hasso said, 'Stay here, in this room. Come, my little Giulia.'

Slowly she followed him.

Sinclair sat on the couch, working through the papers. Hasso's amended terms were hard, but the volume of business was big; one by one he disposed of the points. When he had finished he went over and poured himself a drink, then stood staring at the double door that led to the bedroom, trying not to think about the scene on the other side, forcing down in his own mind the guilt that was trying to surface. Who was it who'd said, 'We're all prostitutes if the price is high enough'? Well, it was a nasty cold world and this was the price. He drank the whisky quickly.

The door opened a little after two.

'You have looked at my questions?' Hasso said jovially.

'Yes. I have. I'm happy about things, if you are.'

Hasso laughed. 'Never happier. Never, never! So we have a deal, heh?'

Sinclair took the extended hand. 'We have a deal. The contracts will be with you in a day or two. Everything was, er, all right?'

'Was magnifico – magnificent, you say, hah! Giulia!' he called.

She appeared in the bedroom door. Apart from the black-framed glasses she was naked.

'Such a body!' Hasso gestured towards her proudly. 'I have to thank you. Such a girl!'

Sinclair glanced at his watch and Hasso laughed. 'Yes, I have finished,' then turned to her. 'Dress now,' he said. Julie reappeared, dressed, in a couple of minutes, and went directly towards the door.

Hasso nudged his arm, and when he turned, the Italian was winking. 'You try. Is wonderful.'

They climbed into a taxi outside the hotel and Julie gave her address, then sat back. He took out his wallet and counted off ten five-pound notes and handed them to her.

She said, 'I promised myself it was for work, but it's for money, too, isn't it?'

'I promised. He was pleased. Take it.'

She shook her head. 'He pleases easily.'

'Take it, all the same.'

She stared at him. 'Do you do this often?'

'Do what?'

'Pimp?'

He said, 'Julie, how long have you been trying to get a job in films?'

'Two years.'

'You've just got one in two hours. Take this money. Take your chance. Then, forget tonight. It's one incident.'

'All right.' She took the notes, rolled them up and put them in her pocket. 'What about you?'

'Me?'

'Aren't you— I mean, it doesn't worry you?'

'No.'

'I don't mean the ethics. I mean the urge.'

Sinclair looked. Her face was drawn, tight. 'Why?'

The driver flicked back the partition. 'Here we are, guv.'

He held open the door and she climbed out, then stopped and said, 'Come in.'

Sinclair shook his head.

'Please.'

'Why?'

'Because I don't want to be alone.'

He paid off the cab and followed her up the stairs. Her room was clean, almost Spartan: a bed, a tidy desk, a chair. A telephone. And books everywhere.

She went to the window and looked out. After a moment, she said, 'I'll spend the rest of my life wondering whether I'm a whore or not.'

Sinclair said nothing.

'He ... he didn't, you see.' Then, quickly, 'Would you like some coffee?'

'Thanks but no.'

'I expect you think I'm neurotic.'

'No. It must be a strange experience.'

Eagerly she said, 'Yes, it was. I was terrified at Miss Wade's. Then, with him, I wanted to laugh all the time, but I couldn't. I mean I daren't. But—'

'But what?'

'We used to talk about it. At university, I mean. What would it *feel* like to be a whore?'

'I told you. It's one incident. Forget it.'

She said, 'But I still don't know. Don't you see?'

'See what?'

'Well, you paid. You offered me money and I took it.'

'I must go.'

'No!' She walked again to the window and lifted the lower half. Cool night air flowed into the room. 'You'll stay.'

'No.'

'Then I'm going to scream. And scream.'

He looked at her, puzzled. 'Why?'

'Funny, isn't it? This way round, you don't even recognize blackmail.' She was smiling.

Richard Keller

As soon as he went into the house, he sensed something. Rachael had not heard the door, and Elgar didn't bark for him the way old Vaughan Williams had. Poor old Willie! Keller bent to pat Elgar, the beagle pup, listening to the sound of Rae's 'cello, the rich tones vibrant with excitement and importance.

'Listen!' he whispered sharply and watched the pup's head move into stillness. After a moment it rolled sad eyes at him and Keller laughed and scratched the silky ears. 'That's your 'cello concerto she's playing.'

He climbed the stairs quietly, two at a time, and came to the door of the bedroom which was now their music room. She was in jeans and sweater, hunched over the instrument, concentrating deeply. He began to move towards her, intent on surprising her. Was it cruel to enjoy the little oh! of surprise? Perhaps, but she wasn't frightened really and he loved to watch the look of pleasure suffuse her face. This time, however, Elgar intervened, slipping into the room ahead of him and interrupting her.

'Down,' she said, commandingly, then turned and saw him. 'Richard!'

'Evening off,' he said.

'Not for you, Sonny Jim,' she said. 'There's an urgent message. "Please ring Alex Hodder".'

She stood up and he took her into his arms. 'You're still vibrating to that A.'

She kissed him. 'I'll vibrate later. You must ring Hodder.'

'That urgent?'

'Very, very urgent.' She laughed. 'That's what he said. Melodramatic is the word to cover it, I think. You know.'

'I'll ring him now.'

Keller went into his study, picked up the extension phone

and dialled. A woman's voice answered. 'Mrs. Hodder? It's Richard Keller, the company secretary.'

'Oh, Mr. Keller, he's not here. I thought you'd know.'

'Know what?'

She giggled. 'Oh well, I'd better not tell you.'

Beside him Rachael said, 'He's at Euromob House.'

'All right, Mrs. Hodder,' Keller said. 'He'll be at the office I expect.'

'That's right, he is.'

'Thank you. Good night.' He put the phone down, mystified and glanced at the clock. Nine-thirty and Alex Hodder still in his office? There really must be something happening. He called Hodder on the private line.

'Hodder.' The voice was recognizable as Hodder's by its tone and timbre, but sharp and snappy.

'It's Keller. You asked me to—'

'Get in here, Richard. Quick.'

'Now?'

'Yes, now. And get a bloody wriggle on!'

The phone was put down at the other end and the connection broken. Keller looked at the handset, smiling ruefully. 'I think my star must be in the descendant,' he said.

'Did that man hang up on you?' Rae was laughing.

'He wants me in there.'

'Did you say *now*? I thought I heard—'

'So long,' he said.

'But why?'

'Who knows! But if Hodder's lost his easy charm, the millenium's here. Is there petrol in the car?'

'Darling, of course.' She purred at him. 'I put in two gallons only this morning.'

'Two!'

She kissed him. 'It will get you there and back. You *are* coming back?'

Keller grinned and kissed her.

He turned the Jaguar into the entrance to the basement car park and slid it into his space, then crossed to the lift and pushed the button. A moment later the doors slid back and he was walking down the carpeted corridor to his own office.

Surprisingly the light was on in his secretary's office. He pushed open the door.

'Jenny. What are you doing here?'

'Mr. Hodder's secretary asked me to come in.'

Keller said, 'What's going on?'

Jenny Walker was his senior secretary, able, unusually numerate, cool. 'A board meeting, Mr. Keller. An emergency one.'

Keller's stomach tightened. 'Since when?'

'Eight o'clock.'

'Two hours. Long, for this company.' He hurried down the corridor and opened the board room door. A wedge of smoke came at him and the buzz of conversation stopped instantly. Keller stepped into the room, conscious that all of them were watching him. For a moment he thought he saw relief on the face of Rylands Lankester, the director responsible for property, but Lankester turned quickly away.

Hodder stepped forward. 'I've been trying to get you, Keller. Where've you been?'

'I was at the hotel. Then I went home.'

'All right.' He raised his voice. 'May we begin please, gentlemen"

Keller watched them take their places. Harry Philips, po-faced on the left of the high-backed chairman's chair that stood in the middle of the long, oval table. Beside him Thornley sat, the finance man whose investments had taken a murderous caning during the recession. Lankester sat opposite, saturnine and confident as who wouldn't be in his position! Then Sir Ranald Duff of the Sapphire Assurance; Peter Cole of Universal Holdings; Lawrence Draper, director in charge of the Plastics Division; John Hyde-Compton of the Publishing Division and finally Scrivener.

Keller straightened his pad, eased a fraction more lead to the point of his gold pencil and waited for Salt to take his seat.

Hodder now walked to the seat on the chairman's left and said, 'In the absence of the chairman, somebody else must take the chair. Nominations.'

'Move Mr. Hodder take the chair.' It was very quick. Keller made the note, glancing at Hyde-Compton, who'd spoken.

'Second.' Peter Cole. Keller looked quickly at the faces. All were serious, set. It was as though everything had been decided and this was merely the formality. And Salt absent!

Hodder said, 'Thank you. There are no minutes. The minutes of the last normal meeting will be read at the next. No matters arising. Reports will not be heard this evening.'

Keller stared. What the hell was going on?

Hodder said, 'You have noted those present, Mr. Secretary?'

'Yes. I have.'

'Good.' Keller remembered suddenly that Scrivener should have been at the course dinner that night, but had cried off, pleading illness.

Hodder said, 'Standing order seventeen of this company says that any four directors acting together by agreement may call an extraordinary meeting of the Board. This meeting takes place at the request of Sir Ranald Duff, Mr. John Hyde-Compton, Sir Kenelm Scrivener and—' Hodder paused '—and Mr. Henry Philips.'

In the momentary silence, Keller said, 'Apologies for absence?'

Hodder said, 'No apologies. Mr. Secretary will you note that the four directors calling this meeting did so under the provisions of standing order nineteen excluding the chairman from the meeting.'

Amazed, he looked up. 'Please record it.'

'Of course, Mr. Chairman.' So that was it!

'This meeting has been called to hear a motion in the names of the four directors. Sir Ranald.'

Duff, a big, red-faced Scotsman dressed in immaculate City jacket, waistcoat and trousers, stood up. Irrelevantly, Keller thought about Duff's tailor; the man must be a magician.

Duff said, 'I have prepared copies of the motion.' He handed them round. Keller left his on the table, unread, noticing that the others did so, too.

Duff said, 'Mr. Chairman, I move that Sir Hugh Salt be removed from the chairmanship of the board of European Communications Corporation Limited with effect from noon tomorrow and further that he shall cease to be a director

95

of the corporation.' He blew his nose immediately and sat down.

Hodder said, 'You have heard the motion, gentlemen. Does it find a seconder?'

Scrivener said, 'Second.'

Brutus and Cassius, Keller thought. Brutal and callous. Neither had anything to lose or fear. Duff was chairman of an insurance giant; Scrivener senior parter in the most important firm of lawyers in London.

'Moved and seconded, gentlemen,' Hodder said. 'The motion is now open to debate.'

Keller noted Scrivener's seconding mechanically, but there was no need for an aide-memoire; he would remember this.

There was silence in the room except for the big antique clock ticking noisily in its niche above the fireplace. The whole wall had been designed round that clock, at Salt's request.

'No debate,' Hodder said. 'Please record, Mr. Secretary, that no comment was offered on the motion.'

Keller wrote: 'No debate'.

'Then I shall put the motion to the meeting. You know its terms. Those in favour?'

Keller looked round the table. Every hand except his own and Hodder's was raised.

'Thank you. I believe that was unanimous, but I will check. Those against?' Hodder looked round. 'The motion is carried unanimously.'

Duff rose. 'I have a further motion, Mr. Chairman.'

'You may put it.'

'I move that Mr. Alexander James Hodder be elected chairman of the Board of this company with effect from noon tomorrow.'

Hodder said, 'Is it proper for me to accept that motion, Mr. Secretary?'

'Yes, Mr. Chairman.'

'Second,' Scrivener said, his wide, florid face expressionless. He probably chopped chairmen like other men chop firewood, Keller thought.

'The motion is now open to the Board.'

Silence.

Hodder was sweating, Keller thought; afraid that even now, in his moment of triumph, some disaster would intervene.

'Those in favour? Thank you, gentlemen. That, too, was unanimous. I shall do my best to justify your confidence.' Now Hodder relaxed, visibly. 'Gentlemen, I believe we should place on record the Board's appreciation of Sir Hugh Salt's magnificent service to the company over a period of more than forty years.'

A chorus of voices murmured, 'Agreed,' and Keller noted it.

'Any other business?'

Silence. 'The meeting is closed.'

For a moment, nobody moved. Then Duff said, 'Well, it's been a long night,' pushed back his chair and went to the concealed bar. The others joined him quickly but Keller remained in his seat, still staggered by what had happened. Salt gone! My God, but there'd be headlines tomorrow. It was almost impossible to imagine Euromob without Salt. Or British industry for that matter. Salt had been its Cassandra, making enough noise about the state of industry for the ensuing silence to be deafening. Would he keep his seat on the Treasury Commission, even?

'Richard.' Hodder had materialized beside him, Philips and Scrivener with him.

'Yes, Chairman.' He looked at Hodder's eyes, seeing the tiny movement of the muscles made in response to that magic word.

'I'm afraid it is the penalty of your job that you have to deliver the resolution to Sir Hugh.'

'I realize that, sir.' Realize it, yes, but how would he be able to face him?

Hodder said, 'You know the exact wording of the resolution. However, we intend that Sir Hugh shall have the opportunity to make the implementation of resolution one unnecessary.'

'By resigning first?'

Hodder nodded. 'We must give him the opportunity.'

'And if he refuses to take it?'

Scrivener said, 'Tell him he'll be sacked. That's what the resolution says.'

97

Keller looked at Hodder. 'Do I say that, sir?'

'Yes, you do, Richard.'

'Yes, sir.'

'It's too late now. He goes to bed early.'

'You mean, in the morning?'

Hodder nodded. 'Very early, seven thirty or so. Now have a drink. It must have been a shock.'

Shock, Keller thought, is understating it. 'I was a bit surprised.'

'It's necessary, you know. We've got to do something.'

Keller took the whisky. 'Thank you. Good luck, Chairman,' he said formally, wondering whether he could not hear, already, the sound of knives being sharpened.

In his office, a few minutes later, he dictated to Jenny the minutes of the meeting. Salt was still a director. He was entitled to a copy. Hodder's girl was typing the formal letter from the Board.

Keller began to drive home thinking about Salt and then his mind switched to Scrivener. 'Tell him he'll be sacked.' Scrivener had said. A fat, red-faced solicitor who had lived all his life off other men's toil and problems, Scrivener was, he thought, about as loathsome a man as he'd met. Rich, powerful, he mattered in the City, mattered in the law, mattered in politics. And Salt. He was still up there on Olympus but about to be dragged down and torn to pieces. If the two of them represented success, then success was a thing to approach with delicate feet.

Rachael said, 'A drink?'

He shook his head. 'I'd better go to bed. I've got to be up early tomorrow.'

'For the course?'

'No,' he said. 'Not for the course.'

Tell me in bed, where we're comfortable.'

He left the house at seven. At that time half an hour ought to be enough time to cross London. The envelope lay on the passenger seat beside him, very white against the black leather, and he was reminded irresistibly of funeral announcement cards. He drove slowly, hating the errand, knowing that it was inescapable. Rachael had said, 'Try to be kind,' but it was the sort of thing that was beyond kindness. All that remained was fact and formality.

He parked the car on a double yellow line, almost as an act of penance. It was right that he, too, should pay something. He climbed the steps and pressed the bell. A maid opened the door, looking at him curiously.

He said, 'My name is Richard Keller. I wish to see Sir Hugh Salt, please.'

'I'm sorry, sir. He's not—'

'It's very important.'

'He never sees anybody bef—'

Keller gave her his card. 'Give that to Sir Hugh. Tell him the matter is urgent.'

She gave in, outgunned, 'Wait in here, please, sir,' and she opened the door to the drawing-room.

The envelope was in his hand and he became aware that his hands were sweating and wiped them down the sides of his suit. He stood, awkwardly, in the middle of the room, unwilling to sit or to take a dominant position by the fireplace.

Then Sir Hugh Salt came in, Keller's card still in his hand. He was wearing a dressing gown over his pyjamas and there were slippers on his feet. Keller noticed the old man's veins on his feet.

Salt said, 'I've no doubt it is important, Mr. Keller, but this is an extraordinary time to call on a man.'

Keller replied formally, 'I am here on the Board's instructions, sir.'

Salt looked at him closely. 'Are you, now? Are you really?'

'I am instructed to deliver this to you, sir.' He proffered the envelope.

'One need not be over-perspicacious to guess its contents, I suppose,' Salt's voice had always been dry, scholarly, older than it need be. Now it seemed cracked.

'I think you should read it, sir.'

'Of course. Please sit down, Keller.'

'I won't, if you don't mind, sir.'

He watched Salt fumble in his dressing gown pocket, pull out a leather spectacle case, put on the gold-framed half-lenses

99

that were among the most famous glasses in the country, and open the envelope.

Slowly, standing throughout, he read the two sheets of paper, then looked up. 'I see.' He took off his glasses and put them away. 'Is there anything to add?'

Keller said, 'Yes, sir. There is. The board has asked me to inform you that it is the directors' unanimous wish that you should resign and that, if you do, a compensation payment of one hundred and fifty thousand pounds will be made.'

'And if I don't?'

'Then I am instructed to say, sir, that the Board's resolution will take effect.'

'Resign or be sacked?' Salt's voice was not strong, but there were no hesitations.

Keller did not reply.

'That's it, isn't it, Keller?'

'I'm afraid so.'

Salt said, 'Who? Do you know? No – I'm sorry. It's improper to ask. You are waiting for my decision?'

'Yes.'

'Then tell 'em they'll have to sack me,' the old man said. 'Tell 'em that.'

Keller looked at him. Salt was very pale. He said, 'Sir, I think you should sit down for a moment. I have plenty of time.'

Salt said, 'There are only three reasons for resigning, ever. One is to get out. The second is honourable behaviour in dishonourable circumstances. The third is when you're caught out in dishonesty.'

'I'll remember that.'

Salt smiled. 'Do. It comes to us all. Though I must say, I never thought . . .'

Keller said, 'I realize this is your house, sir, but shall I get you a cup of tea, or something?'

'I'm not going to change my mind, Keller.'

'I didn't imagine you were, sir.'

'Ah, the shock. I see. Kind of you. But tell them they'll have to do their butchering in public. Where are they now?'

'The Board is due to meet at eight-thirty.'

Salt smiled. 'I've half a mind to go. Of course, I can do nothing. Not now.'

Keller, standing watching him, afraid Salt might collapse, found his thoughts intercepted.

'Don't worry, boy. I certainly shall not die for them. Now go, will you.'

'Yes. I'm sorry.'

'Are you? I wonder if I am . . .'

He rang Hodder from a call box on the Embankment.

'Well?'

'He declines to resign.'

'You told him about the money?'

'Yes.'

'All right, Richard. Come on back.'

'Sir!'

'What is it?'

'The statement. Jane Roper is on the course. She's staying at the Princess Hotel.'

'Thanks, Richard. Pick her up, will you. We'll need her here.'

'Right.'

'And Richard.'

'Yes.'

'Not a word to anybody.'

He had to find a passer-by to give him more change. Then rang the Princess.

'Jane Roper.'

'It's Richard Keller. You're needed at Euromob House.'

'What!'

'Yes. Quickly. Hodder needs you.'

'Do you know why?'

He said, 'I'll pick you up. I've got my car. Ten minutes?'

'Make it twelve. I'd like to clean my teeth.'

'I'll tell you then.'

They were all waiting in the boardroom when he entered.

Hodder asked quickly, 'What did he say?' He sounded anxious, Keller thought, and it was habit. Hodder had spent twenty years wondering what Salt would say.

'That he would not resign.'

'His words?'

'Tell them I will not resign.'

Hyde-Compton said, 'He would be a little more picturesque.'

'He said, "They will have to do their butchery in public".'

Hodder said, 'Pity.'

'Why?' Scrivener demanded. 'He's had his chance. So be it.'

'So be it,' Hodder said.

Lincoln Volans

SOURLY, Volans watched the concrete runway pattern tilting beneath the wing as the VC 10 eased in to its landing slot at Heathrow. In a few minutes he'd be down.

Volands did not, repeat not, like England. He did not, repeat not, like being sent back to school. He did not, repeat not, like big cities. Above all he did not, repeat not, like being dragged unnecessarily across the world, away from Mayjane and the kids. The sun was shining, but not brightly and in any case about eighty per cent of its light was blanked off by industrial haze.

Somewhere behind him a stewardess at a microphone in the galley was doing her routine farewell. 'British Overseas Airways Corporation hopes you have enjoyed your VC 10 Flight and that you will fly with us again. Thank you.'

It seemed like years, not days, since he'd last breathed the fresh clean air of the North-West but it was only four days since he'd left Seattle for New York and got snarled up in that ground control strike at J.F.K. He'd been tempted, damn it, to ask Mayjane to drive him to Vancouver and take the one-hop Air Canada flight, but with young Joe in New York it seemed a great opportunity to meet and talk for an hour or two while his kid brother was still his kid brother and not just another equal American adult. So he'd sat for three days at Kennedy. No point in going anywhere else, because they were all in the same state and the strike was expected to end any hour. Any hour now for three goddam days!

He felt the bump as the wheels hit and then the thunderous vibration of engines blasted into full reverse thrust. The VC 10 slowed and everybody stood up and began to fiddle with hand baggage. Taking his brief case, he walked across to the bus and then into the customs shed.

He was being paged. Would Mr. Lincoln Volans, passenger on BOAC Flight BA 501 from New York please go to the desk? Mr. Lincoln Volans, please.

'My name's Volans. You were paging me.'

The girl smiled. 'A cable, Mr. Volans. Here you are.'

'Cable? Thanks.' Volans ripped open the envelope. Who'd be sending cables, for God's Sake? Was something wrong? If it was they could take their London and their Princess Hotel and their VC 10 and they could jam them . . .

'Call me soonest. Startling news. Maintain silence. Love, Mayjane.'

Startling news? He read the cable twice. What the hell did she mean, maintain silence? What about, for God's Sake?

'Is there a phone?'

'Over there, sir.'

He started towards it, then stopped. It was 9.30 London time; Mayjane would be fast asleep. What would it be, two-thirty a.m. in their house overlooking the Sound? In his mind he could see her, sleeping gently with a window wide to let the cool air flow around, her hair dark on the pillow. No, he wouldn't waken her yet.

He took the airline coach into London and then a cab from the terminal to the Princess.

'My name's Volans. I believe you have a reservation.'

The clerk looked at him. 'Volans, sir. No.'

'Christ!' he said. 'Booked by European Communications—'

'Oh, I see, sir. One moment. Yes, it's one four one three, sir.'

The porter took his bags and the key and showed him to his lift. In the room, Volans gave him a ten-penny coin, told him he knew how bath taps turned on, and waited to be alone. He wasn't, though. On the bed lay a bundle of papers, folders, envelopes and a note on top signed by somebody called Long-bottom asking him to read the papers headed 'Course Documentation' before joining them in the Coward Room.

Volans hafted the papers. There was a good hour's reading, maybe two: he'd wait until after lunch and his call to Mayjane. Picking up the phone he asked the operator to book him a call at one-thirty. Seven hours pushed that back to six thirty Mountain time. Hell, she'd be up and about then. Meanwhile, the . . . what was it they called it here? Bumph, that was it. A good word. He slipped off his jacket, lay on the bed and began to read. At twelve he rose, put on his jacket and went out. A walk would do him good. Then he'd have a hamburger and some coffee in his room while he waited for the call to Mayjane.

In the lobby, a bunch of typical executives stood chattering. He thought they looked unusually animated and grinned. *They* couldn't be Euromob. But then he saw that George Sinclair was among them and knew it was. He slipped out into the street quickly and without being seen. After all those cooped-up days what he needed was space and air, not that there was much of either in this metropolitan gas-trap. The park would have to do. He walked in through the gates breathing deeply, lengthening his stride, straightening, and then for an hour he walked hard, revelling in the exertion, happy when the sweat broke on his brow and he could feel the cool breeze taking it in evaporation. Finally he had to hurry, really hurry, back to the hotel to be in time for the call.

It came through bang on the button with the line clear. Mayjane might have ben in the next room.

'Darling, you remember telling Cal he could spend the summer round your islands?'

Cal was her brother. 'Yes.'

'Well – hold your breath, darling – he's struck it rich!'

Had he heard her correctly? 'Did you say struck it rich? Mayjane, did you?' He could hear excitement throbbing in his own voice.

'That's what I said.'

'Gold? D'you mean gold?'

She said, 'Sorry, manganese. Good enough, though, isn't it?'

'Listen, is Cal right? I mean, is he sure?'

'For God's Sake, Lincoln, he's a qualified geologist. Just 'cause he spends his time fishing doesn't mean—'

'Sure,' he said, hastily. 'But does he have any idea how much there is? Quality. That kind of thing.'

'Listen, he's been up there since Spring. Right?'

'Right.'

'Only he came back and picked up a friend who assays professionally.'

'That Jim Forester he took fishing up towards Wrangell?'

Mayjane said, 'It's an island. A little one. Between Wrangell and Juneau. And they say it's just about made of manganese.'

'Jesus!'

'—'at's right! Lincoln, it's worth millions. Maybe tens of millions. Forester says it could be hundreds of millions.'

'Go on.' He could feel a pulse throbbing in his forehead, quite crisply like a drumbeat. Everything was ten times as clear as usual, every sound, every feeling.

'It's an ore called pyrolusite. And that's the main source. The island's stiff with it.'

'Did you say north of Wrangell?'

'Yes. Why?'

'That's spruce and hemlock land. Which island?'

'It's tiny apparently. About a mile and a half long and half a mile wide. The name is Whistler Island on the charts.'

Volans searched his mind. He couldn't even picture it! Whistler Island? The company might own it, but they didn't plant it, he was sure of that.

'Timber stands?'

Mayjane said, 'A fair amount of timber but it doesn't look like controlled forest. That's what Cal says.'

'Well, he ought to know.'

'Linc, what can we do? Could we buy it? Or buy the mineral rights?'

Volans groaned. 'Jesus, Mayjane, you know what it costs to buy an island?'

'Up there?'

'Oh, boy!'

She said, 'Sleep on it. Figure things out. You don't have to act. The stuff's been there a million years. Nobody's gonna find it tomorrow. But while you're over there . . .'

'Spy things out? Right.'

A few minutes later he put down the telephone and fell back on the bed. Tens of millions, maybe hundreds! He didn't doubt Mayjane or her brother, and the Forester guy who'd gone with him Volans remembered as both sensible and smart. Could he raise the money? Well, sure he could, by cutting somebody in!

The problem would be to get Euromob to sell. If they got one whiff of his reasons, if he so much as mentioned mineral rights, they'd descend on Whistler Island like a plague of wasps. Come to think of it, that was the trouble. He'd never met an Englishman yet who didn't think of Alaska in terms of gold-strikes and oil, Robert Service and Skagway. Even mention Alaska and bells would ring – more so in Britain than in Washington, Oregon or B.C.

That was the answer – B.C.! I'm a simple American and I want a part in your great Commonwealth. There's an island up there I'd like to own one day. My wife paints a little. You know? And the fishing for the kids! They'd look at it and say, 'That's the bloody Arctic, old boy,' and he'd grin and say, 'Listen, we like to live in the cold where I come from.' Volans laughed, thought of something, and picked up from the table beside his bed the list of course members. Sinclair! In the finish it would go through Sinclair, but Sinclair smelled rats quickly. Go to Sinclair and say please may I buy your island and Sinclair would say why. And the moment you said 'for fun' he'd laugh. So tell him it's for development, Summer lodges, a camp for kids. Tell him it's a small business enterprise of your own, long-term development, and he'll ask what percentage return you expect, look at you with contempt and take your money. Or will he?

Sniff around, Volans told himself. Understand a few attitudes, talk to the people. Don't move until you're sure. Meanwhile, who else is there? Keller, Richard Keller, company secretary. Well, he'd be likely as a source of information. Keller must be cultivated.

It was time to join the others. Volans tried to clamp a lid on the seething cauldron of his thoughts, put on a polite expression and went to the elevator.

PROGRESS REPORT 1. EUROMOB COURSE TWO

FROM: John LONGBOTTOM
       Malcolm TEMPLETON

TO: MULLER, URQUHART, NOSTELL MANAGE-
MENT GROUP.

DATE: WEDNESDAY P.M.

1. The course is so far having only moderate success.
Internal company tensions in Euromob are clearly such that a
great deal of time of every executive is taken up with politick-
ing, in-fighting and so on. This week's events, naturally, are
unlikely to be repeated and were bound to be the focus of
interest of course members, but we suspect the course members
give, in microcosm, a picture of the company, its strengths and
weaknesses.

2. Selection of course members has been both arbitrary and
unsatisfactory. There is one member (Steele) so resentful of the
return to a school-like environment that he is determined to be
disruptive. There is also a very beautiful girl who tends,
through no fault of her own, to be distracting, and a well-known
woman TV personality who often has similar effects. Another
course member is one of Britain's leading computing theo-
reticians who, though doubtless a major asset to Euromob,
lives in realms so abstruse that the course gets very little of his
attention.

3. Within these limitations it is now our view that the successful sessions so far have been Professor Small's on the Economic Environment and Dr. Lipton's on the Climate for
Management. The psychologist, Dr. James, who talked about
People at Work, would have fascinated an audience of novel-
ists, clinical psychologists or possibly criminals, but was no use
to managers. That case studies, as always, have triggered most
serious work.

John Michael Longbottom

'I'M sorry, Dr. Bennett,' Longbottom said. 'There just won't be a session this afternoon.'

Bennett frowned. 'You do realize I've come up from Bristol for this?'

'The fee, naturally, will stand, Dr. Bennett, Have you seen the papers?'

Bennett said irritably, 'I saw *The Times* this morning.'

'No, the evenings. Well, obviously you haven't.'

'I'm not in the habit of reading evening newspapers. What is this about?'

Longbottom said, 'The course consists entirely of Euromob executives.'

'Well?'

'Their chairman has been sacked.'

Bennett laughed scornfully. 'So they have all gone off to chase their tails, eh?'

'I know they'll be sorry to miss your lecture, Dr. Bennett. I suppose you couldn't stay over? We could rearrange tomorrow's sessions.'

'Hardly. No, I think I'll go straight back. I've a lot of work to do. Too much to waste a day . . .'

Longbottom watched him go, knowing it was an act, that Bennett would go to Timbuctoo to lecture if the fee was half-way decent and there was a free meal thrown in.

God! He was tired. Tired, tired, tired. And it would get worse; there was no end to it and no way out. He sat down and covered his aching eyes with his palms, found the sensation pleasant and rested his elbows on the baize-covered table. He sat that way for several enjoyable and restful minutes.

'I beg your pardon, sir.'

Damn! Why did somebody always have to break in! If John Michael Longbottom closed his bloody eyes for two seconds, there was always a reason why he should open them. He looked up, then stood up. A big man in a suit of unmistakeably American cut was looking down at him.

Longbottom said, 'I'm sorry. I was just—'

'Sure. I know. I'm Volans.'

'Nice to see you.' They shook hands.

'Have you eaten?'

'Thank you.'

'And your room's okay? Good. I'm afraid you've arrived at the wrong moment. It's all over for the day.'

'At two o'clock?'

Longbottom looked at him. 'You don't know, obviously Sir Hugh Salt has been sacked.'

'Sacked!' The same incredulity that had shown on all the others' faces showed on Volans'. 'You gotta be kidding.'

'No kidding. So you see. Everybody just vanished.' He thought, I wish you'd vanish too.

'Gee.' Volans shrugged. 'Well, I always did like missing school. Tomorrow?'

Longbottom said, 'I hope so. Nine-thirty.'

'I'll be there.' Volans sauntered out.

Two o'clock, Longbottom thought, and he didn't need to leave until eight. Six hours' sleep before he need go home and tackle it all again. He went up to the common room, certain it would not be in use for hours, pulled the curtains closed and stretched out on the couch. One thing about good hotels was that they had good curtains!

It was all so bloody unfair! He'd pulled himself up by his bootlaces and now the weight of it was dragging him down again. *He* hadn't a chance; the kids were suffering and *that* too would get worse. If only he'd never gone to that blasted dance. If the M.G. hadn't busted that gasket. An M.G. would have been too small and cramped.

He had not wanted to go, anyway; it would simply be too discourteous to refuse. The college ball was the major social event of the year, they'd taken the trouble to make up a party, even fitted him out with a friend's tails, and Mary Cullen had lent him her Chevrolet.

The date was blind and he arrived at 1149 Grant Avenue

anticipating an evening of slightly tedious formality in return for all the hospitality the Cullens had given him. Formality was the word, too. The father opened the door, invited him in, there were introductions to the family, then the cheerful paternal call to the girl waiting upstairs and she had floated down.

Then the dance in the Grant Hall, white and spacious, a mutation Acropolis in the Middle West, with its social rituals, its who-dances-with-whom-and-when. About eleven, he danced with Pat.

She was dark and very nearly beautiful, her rounded body on the plump side of perfection, but near to it, and she came close to him in the American way, her arm high on his shoulder, her body against his. 'This is a privilege, Englishman.'

'Why?'

'Oh, I know one or two of your students who wanted to get this close.'

He laughed. 'I was taught Greek by an old don who hadn't spoken a living language since nineteen. It's a good system. Keeps the mind on the translations.'

'Impossible!'

'He took all his meals in college and just pointed to the things he wanted. He made no conversation and when people talked to him, he just quoted tags back at them.'

'You're joshing me!'

'No. Honestly. There was a very special variety of intellectual snobbery involved, of course. A small group waiting for the jokes only they would understand.'

'Example?' She was laughing and her body moved against his. He concentrated on the anecdote.

'There was a man getting married – it's not really a joke, you know – somebody told the old boy "NOS ANIMORUM IMPULSU ET CAECA MAGNAQUE CUPSINE DUCT, CONJUGUM PETIMUS." It means, "Led by the impulse of our minds and by blind passion, we desire marriage." It's Juvenal.'

'Juvenile? I should say it is.'

He remembered his decision not to correct her. He'd decided earlier that university teaching was not for him. Instead he grinned down at her and said, 'If passion were blind, we'd be missing a hell of a lot,' and spun her into a turn that somehow contrived to bring their bodies still closer. He expected her, as they straightened, to disengage, move back a little into a more circumspect position; instead, astonishingly, she remained close and after a moment he felt heat rising in himself uncontrollably and still she didn't move. They dance three or four more steps, while his mind tried to accept it, and then he moved back and looked at her face. Her eyes were dark, the pupils wide and they looked back at him without reserve. The fences, the walls were down. His arm tightened round her and she leaned willingly against him.

It had happened in a few seconds, and surprise briefly seemed to paralyse his mind; they simply danced body to body, on a wave of anything but their own sudden, sharp desire, until the music ended and he had to return her to her table. He was half-way across the floor with her before he could speak, because his mouth felt thick. 'My date,' he said helplessly. 'I have to take her.'

'I know. But— 'she spoke softly. 'John.'

'Yes.'

'Take her straight home. Then come for me.'

'All right. Where?'

'Truman Hall. I'll wait.'

He could not bear to release her hand but it was necessary and he did and some sense-memory of her kept his fingers tingling where she had touched them. For the rest of the evening their eyes had remained locked across the ballroom until his date grew visibly angry. He was waltzing with her clumsily, his eyes following Pat's every move, when the girl said, 'I don't mind you preferring somebody else, but please don't show it so obviously.'

He mumbled his apologies and tried to concentrate on her, to talk, to be pleasant, but power of the attraction was too great and his mind kept emptying. To her credit, she ended by being amused, pretending to be doubtful of his fitness to drive her home but going with him cheerfully.

'I won't ask you in,' she said.

'No.' He made the effort. 'Thank you. It's been a wonderful evening.'

'Uh huh,' she said. Then, 'Hurry up. And drive carefully.'

He didn't of course. He drove like a maniac until he reached the drive into Truman Hall where a figure in white slid out of the trees, opened the door, and climbed quickly in beside him and when he moved to kiss her, said tightly, 'Drive the car. Quickly.' She took his hand and held it tightly, and as the car sped along the road he could feel her breast warm against it. He didn't know where to go, only that soon, somewhere, he must stop the car; there could be no more waiting. Then he saw the lane that led to the town's airfield and turned along it, grateful for the silent silhouettes of the flat Kansas country. A moment later he had braked to a halt and turned to her. In the light from the dashboard their eyes met and he could see the tension in her face and then they were too close to see and their mouths were searching, their arms tight about each other; they were plunging like divers into a swirling rapid of passion. Soon their clothes were gone and there was only the urgency of skin against warm skin and the strength of young muscles, and then, briefly, the sightless world of the uncapturable moment before release wild and demanding as their meeting.

Later he searched for his jacket, found cigarettes and they sat smoking in silence that grew longer and longer. What did one say to a girl one hardly knew when both of you were in naked post-coital peace in the front seat of a car? Eventually, driven by some distant impulse of ingrained manner, he murmured idiotically, 'I'm sorry.'

And she laughed, said, 'Yes, by Jove, old top,' and giggled and he watched in the dim red glow of their cigarettes, the movements of her body. Then he was giggling, too, and in a moment they were in another embrace, this time without passion but with liking at its centre and they began to talk in a surprised but happy way. Presently, and more slowly, they made love again, this time smiling at one another, their earlier urgency replaced by a gentler curiosity.

He could, of course, have vanished. It would have been easy enough. His year as visiting lecturer was almost over, the ticket for his flight back paid for. Perhaps she'd have followed him, dragged him into court for maintenance, but it was unlikely; she was as independent as her family, and they would have stuck together.

113

But Longbottom married her, barely hesitating. She had faced him, one day, trying to be light and confident but he had seen the wariness in her eyes. 'What is it they say in England, John – Preggers?'

'Oh, no!'

'Sorry, it's oh yes.' She smiled but there was a minute tremble at the corner of her mouth to betray her desperate uncertainty. He was deeply moved by the courage in her lightness – and by the fear it so ineffectually masked; nobody had been afraid of him before.

'Your father has a shotgun?'

She said stoutly, 'He sure has,' but moisture was welling in her eyes and he knew he was being unnecessarily cruel; that even a few seconds' delay was torment for her.

'Then I've no alternative. Will you make an honest man of me?'

Her face alight and her arms round his neck, 'Oh, John, John, John.'

'Well, will you?'

'Yes. Yes, please.'

There was a nasty drizzle falling as they landed and a mean, wet wind whipped at her. From that moment, Pat detested England. She had been brought up on the great plain of the Middle West where winter was cold and arduous, but where winter was also combated. England she found miserable. They got a flat near Hampstead while he looked for a job. It was on the second floor, without central heating, and a whistling collection of draughts attacked from every direction. Cold, she was unhappy, and the habit of unhappiness stuck. She was unhappy about shops, about prices, about traffic and parking, about doctors.

They moved from Hampstead, first to a semi-detached house near Bromley which stretched his resources to the limit and merely served to make her more miserable. The neighbours were mean and unfriendly, which was true enough; the shops were lousy, which wasn't. They had two children by now and Pat had turned from the warm and vital girl he had met into a lacklustre, complaining woman. She had also begun to drink. At first Longbottom had not realized it. She stuck carefully to vodka, which did not taint her breath, and there was little difference between her normal sullenness and a sullenness assisted by alcohol. She was already far over the borderline between social drinking and alcoholism before he realized she was even approaching it. Several times she was 'dried out', but each time she relapsed quickly afterward. The only chance there might have been lay in a return to Kansas, but he was not prepared to face a lifetime lecturing in remote American colleges, or, worse, going into American industry. Instead, he learned marketing and manufacturing in Britain, his capable mind absorbing quickly so that he was valued successively by both Unilever and Metal Box; he left both for the same reason: that a career could not be conducted with an alcoholic wife. It was not just that entertaining was impossible. As time went on it became more and more necessary to be free to be at home; modern industry demanded a quality of application he could not sustain. So he had moved to consultancy, the comfortable halfway house between teaching and business. It was, and he was aware that it was, an admission of defeat. He earned enough to employ a daily woman to see to the girls' needs; enough to keep a roof over their heads and a small river of vodka flowing into the house. But it was a bleak existence and without affection, for Pat accorded him none and to the girls he was remote, the man who came home every evening to a row they could only hide from.

A small sound awoke him and he lay still for a moment, briefly puzzled by the unfamiliar perspective of the room. The snap of the switch and the sudden light brought realization quickly and he watched Diana Hughes carry her portable typewriter across to the table. She still had not seen him.

He said 'Hello,' and watched her, and added quickly, 'It's me, John.'

'Oh, John!' Her hand lay flat on her chest as though to contain sudden fear. 'You gave me a fright.'

Longbottom rose, smiling. 'I'm sorry, love.'

'It's all right. What on earth are you doing here?'

'I was a bit tired. Thought I'd snatch forty winks. What time is it?'

'Four fifteen. I'll get you some tea.' She picked up the phone.

'I don't know why you don't go, too, Diana. It's not often we get a clear afternoon.'

'Tea for—' Diana looked at him questioningly and he nodded – 'for two. In the common room. Yes, that's right.' She replaced the phone. 'Be here in a minute. I could do with a cup myself. I've got these things Mr. Templeton wanted typing and I thought I'd get them done.'

When the tea came he watched her deal with it, neatly and smoothly, her hands precise. She was really extraordinarily nice and very capable: it was a pity she wasn't prettier.

'Here you are. The sugar's in.'

Longbottom took the cup and sipped gratefully. The tea was weakish, hot, thin-tasting and sweet; he liked tea that way and she always seemed to make sure that was how he got it. How different it was from home! 'Very nice,' he said, 'and very welcome.'

'How are the children?'

'Fine. Not that I see much of them.'

'No,' she said. 'I'm sorry.'

'For them or me?'

'Both.' He glanced up at her, ready to smile, but there was no humour in her face. 'It's a shame.'

'Yes.' He sipped his tea again. 'Still, it keeps me out of mischief.'

'They sent hot toast. Would you like some?'

Hot buttered toast! Longbottom could taste it as she spoke: hot buttered toast in his rooms at Oxford, fresh and marvellous and a million years ago. 'Yes,' he said, 'Yes, please.'

She busied herself. 'Strawberry jam?'

'By all means, strawberry jam.' When she had finished, the toast was already spread with butter and jam and cut into fingers. 'Soldiers,' he said.

She smiled. 'We called them that, too.'

'I think all kids do. Mine certainly do.'

She said, 'If I'd known you liked toast as much as that, I'd do some more often.'

116

'No, Diana, it's just – well, it's today. It touches chords and taste buds. Lovely!'

He realized with surprise that this was probably their first extended conversation. Diana had worked for him through three months and four courses, but the routine was not of a kind to encourage developing knowledge of one another. He sank back against the cushions of the couch. 'As a matter of interest, Diana, do you like your work?'

The rather plain face lightened. 'Oh yes. Yes, very much.'

'Funny, I don't think I've asked before.'

She said, 'If I didn't, I wouldn't be here.'

'Is there more tea in—'

'The pot is loaded. No, don't get up.'

She crossed the room to take his cup and brought it back a few moments later. 'There.'

'You spoil me.'

'Somebody has—' She stopped. 'I'm sorry. It's none of my . . .'

Longbottom said, 'It doesn't matter.'

'Yes, it does!' Her tone was almost fierce and he looked up at her in surprise. 'Well it *does*, John. No man should have to . . .'

'Yours won't, anyway.'

A brief smile. 'I haven't got one. And I don't . . . well, never mind.'

He looked at her. She was not ugly: a pleasant girl with a plain face and a slightly dumpy figure. The glasses and the dragged-back hair didn't help either.

'You'll make some lucky so-and-so a marvellous wife.'

He was staggered when she began to cry. At first he didn't realize she *was* crying, mistaking the little jerks of her shoulders for laughter, but then she put her hands to her face and said, 'Oh, dear' in a voice full of distress. Longbottom put down his cup and hurried across. 'Diana, what's the matter?'

'I'm sorry, it's nothing. Really, it's nothing.'

'If it's something I said . . .?'

She was still crying. He said helplessly, 'Diana, please. Did I say something?' and she shook her head mutely.

'Don't cry.' He put his arms on her shoulders, intending

117

reassurance, but her weeping intensified. 'Diana, please don't cry . . . At least, tell me what's wrong.'

She turned quickly almost grabbing at him, her arms round his waist, her face pressed against his jacket, and held on with a tightness near to desperation. Baffled, he gripped her shoulders, tightened an arm around her, and she said, 'Oh, John, John.'

Then he understood, and the realization hit him: the girl was in love with him! It was hardly unknown for secretaries to fall for bosses, but it was the last thing he'd expect of her. Poor kid! She must know, by now, precisely what her chances were in the market for husbands. Probably she had had her share of rebuffs and cruelties. And now she had fallen for *him* – a married man with difficult responsibilities and no prospects. He looked down at her, trying to soothe her, waiting until the tears stopped and she had control once more. She lifted her face and weeping had not improved it: the eyes were red, the mouth unhappy. 'John, I'm so sorry! I didn't intend . . .'

Longbottom smiled at her. 'Go ahead. It's good, occasionally, so they say.' She forced a smile in return, a small smile that was full of effort, and began to wipe tears away with the backs of her hands. He pulled the starched white handkerchief from his breast pocket. 'Here.'

'Thank you.' She dabbed her eyes, blew her nose and straightened, in control of herself again. 'John, I'm sorry.'

'What about that other cup of tea?'

'Oh yes.' She gave him a shy, grateful smile and poured.

'Better have one yourself.' It was a bloody nuisance! He needed a good secretary and it looked as though he'd just lost one; the result of unrequited love was either seduction or departure: that was one piece of established knowledge in the boss-secretary relationship. For a couple of months, devotion; after that, goodbye. Well, the hell with it! He wasn't going to tiptoe round the problem for months. Far better get it out in the open, now.

'Diana, is it me?' He tried to make his voice calm and paternal.

She blushed. 'I'm sorry, I . . .'

'If it is,' he said, 'I don't want to hurt you.'

She didn't look at him. Her hands held the cup and saucer, her eyes stared at them.

'Diana, I'm not worth the trouble. Don't—'

The cup rattled in her hands and she put it noisily on the table.

'All right, you know. I couldn't help it. I'm sorry.'

'I'm married, you know.'

'You're not!' She was looking at him defiantly.

He repeated, 'I'm married. I have two children,' and looked at her as he spoke, watched stillness come, and determination.

She said, 'It's too much. You can't carry it alone.'

'It's all right.'

'But it's not. I know about alcoholism, John. My father was ... well, I know. I know what it's like, every day, every night.'

'Really, Diana, it's not so bad. You're overstating ...' He was puzzled, uncomprehending. What was she getting at?

'No.' Her tone was firm, almost confident. 'I know.' Then suddenly she was nervous again, rising and walking to the other side of the room and pacing along it. She began, 'I'm not pretty,' then stopped suddenly.

He stared at her. There was no denying it. So he waited.

After a moment she said slowly, 'But it isn't necessary. What is it they say, all cats are grey in the dark?'

'Diana, I—'

'Please, John. Let me finish.'

'No, Diana. I'm married. I have children. I have to do my best for them.'

She was surprised. 'You think I want you to leave? Oh, John, No!'

'Then what?'

She faced him calmly now. 'I have a flat, near enough to your house – what is it, four miles?'

'I suppose so,' he was puzzled still. 'What are you saying?'

'Just that I'm alone. No boy friend, no husband. It's some where you could, well ...' She blushed quickly and her fingers were twined together.

John Longbottom said, 'How could I?'

'I'm a marvellous cook!'

That made it possible to laugh. 'I'll bet!'

Pat never cooked, now. The daily woman gave the kids their tea, he himself usually managed out of tins.

'And I can wash handkerchiefs better than this!' She held up his own.

It was impossible! Longbottom looked at Diana. 'How could I—?'

'Sleep with me? You don't have to!' She turned away abruptly and he hurried over, afraid of further tears, and stood behind her, his hands holding her shoulder.

'It's not that, you silly girl.'

'I'd enjoy feeding you, helping a bit.' She turned to face him. 'I like that kind of thing. But not just for myself.'

He became aware of the warmth of her shoulders beneath the blouse. 'You must see,' he said, 'that it's impossible.'

'I've thought about this. John, I know it couldn't be every evening, or all the time. But sometimes you could have a meal. Just sit and relax for a couple of hours. You need that.'

It was true. That was exactly what he needed: occasionally, somewhere soothing and warm and friendly.

She smiled up at him, 'Chicken Marengo and a bottle of claret. How about that?'

He smiled back. 'Steady with the temptation.'

They stopped at Sainsbury's on the way to her flat and bought the chicken and a few groceries. In the kitchen, when he tried to help, she put a glass of sherry in his hand and told him to sit and read the evening paper. Then she knelt in front of him and removed his shoes, took his glass when it was empty and refilled it.

The chicken was magnificent and they ate in near silence; but it was a warm and friendly silence, not the soggy, angry quiet of his home. Afterwards, as she cleared away, she said, gently, somewhere behind him, 'I still can't believe all this.'

'I'm a little surprised, myself. Here, let me help.'

She laughed. 'The kitchen is forbidden territory, except by invitation.'

'Then invite me.'

'No attempts to help then?'

'All right. He followed her in, watching her with pleasure. She wasn't pretty but there was a splendid womanly competence about her. Yes, that was the word – womanly. He stood behind her, bent and kissed her cheek. 'Thank you.'

She didn't turn; her hands were busy washing up. She said, 'Thank *you*.'

Now again he held her shoulders. 'Diana, I don't deserve this sort of kindness.' He looked down at her, watching her hands move in the bowl, aware suddenly of the swell of her breasts, her warmth. Involuntarily his own body stirred and he knew she felt it because her hands were briefly motionless. He realized then that he was holding his breath and released it; it came out in a long, shuddering sigh. 'I'm sorry.'

'No!' she said. 'Don't be! Please don't be sorry. Not *sorry!*'

'I didn't mean it like that.'

'I know.' She leaned back against him and again his body responded to her. 'There are no obligations, John. None.'

For a moment he did not move, could not move. His hands seemed paralysed and then, through them, he felt her warmth again and slid them round her waist, hugged her to him. Now at last, she turned. She took his hand and led him through to her bedroom and suddenly he wanted her blindly and desperately. He pushed her down on to the bed and began to pull at her clothes and at his own. She neither helped nor hindered, allowing him his way, and when she lay beneath him and the long, aching frustration of years was being exorcized in his violent urgency she held his plunging body.

'Oh John,' she breathed, 'oh John, John!'

PHILIPS' voice said very clearly, 'I understand both the paper's position and the company's, Mr. Steele.'

'Then you can't stop comment!'

'I can.'

Steele said, 'Over my dead body!'

'Yes, if necessary. Are you prepared to resign over it?'

'Over what?'

'The principle that an editor's right is absolute.'

'The hell with that,' Steele said. 'I just want to know the ruling.'

Philips spoke quietly yet crisply. 'No comment from the paper itself. No leader from you. But if one of the specialist contributors wants to comment, that's up to him. All right?'

Steele said, 'More or less.' He put the telephone down and bellowed, 'Sue!' There was a bell on the telephone. If he pressed it, she'd answer. There was also the intercom. He preferred the bellow, was known for it.

Sue came in. 'Yes, Mr. Steele.'

'What's the name of that bloody man who worships the ground old Salt walks on? Writes on African affairs sometimes.'

'I'm sorry . . .'

'You know. Little bloke. Fat. Black rimmed glasses. Was an M.P. till last time.'

'Mr. Jonas?'

'Is it Jonas?' Steele grinned. 'Came here about a month ago. Couldn't keep his eyes off you.'

He watched her remember, her short upper lip curling in disdain. 'Mr. Jonas *was* here a month ago.'

'Get him if you can.'

'On the phone?'

Steele nodded and watched her leave his office. The elegant

sway of her body reminded him of Jane Roper. He lit a cigarette and waited for the phone.

'Yes.'

'He's not in, Mr. Steele. They say if it's important they can get a message to him within half an hour.'

'Tell 'em to do it.'

'Very well.'

'And Sue!'

'Yes.'

'Tell the doorman I want to see Robert Hartney when he brings his stuff in.'

Two vehicles, by God! He rubbed his hands gleefully. Excrement would be set astir by this week's *Viewpoint*, in spite of Philips' warnings.

'Sue!' When she appeared he grinned at her. 'Coffee, my dear.'

She showed Jonas into the office about forty minutes later, her face thin with distaste. Jonas was a small, dark man, unmistakeably Celtic, his forehead creased, his eyes rather bulbous; he had eaten too much for too long and as a result his skin was muddy. If Jonas ever succeded in getting back to the Commons, he'd never get further than the back benches. But first he had to get back and he believed deeply in the power of the written word and the authority it conferred on the writer.

Steele beamed at him. 'Sit down now Idris, bach. Tea or coffee?'

'Tea, thanks.'

'Sue?' She gave his back a glance which said with eloquence that there was something wrong with a world in which *she* was serving something like Jonas.

'Very well.'

Steele watched her go. 'Nice, isn't she?'

'Very.' Jonas's eyes glowed.

'She's frightfully posh, you know. Daddy is a high-grade diplomat. Sir Frederick Lane Thurston.'

'Really. Yes, she's very lovely.'

Steele laughed. 'You're a dirty old Dai, bach. Look you!'

Jonas grinned uncertainly. 'Something I can do?'

'Not sure. I believe you mentioned that you knew Salt.'

'Sir Hugh Salt. Why, yes. Very well.'

'He's got the bullet.'

Jonas gaped. 'The what?'

'The bullet. Fired. Sacked. Call it what you like. Knife in the back and off you pop.'

'When?' The amazement was almost comic.

'This morning. Anyway, while the world must, of course, continue to rotate, a weekly like *Viewpoint* has a responsibility to examine a thing like this.'

'And you want me to . . .?'

'To do a piece on Salt's role in political affairs. Particularly in Africa. Can do?'

'Well, yes. I'm particularly well-informed about—'

Steele said, 'The silly old sod's gone now so you can whack away at him as hard as you like.'

Jonas's jaw sagged. 'But his role has always been—'

'He interfered where he wasn't wanted, right? He always knew best, right? He made friends with some of the most corrupt politicians on the whole damn continent, right?'

'Yes, but he also gave scholarships and—'

'Never mind. Now, you've got about two hours. I want a bloody good piece. Can do?'

Jonas blinked. 'You're sure you mean a knocking piece.'

'I didn't say a knocking piece. Just that he's not sacred any more.'

'And the . . .?' Jonas was hesitant.

'Hundred and fifty, if it's good. Fifty otherwise.'

Jonas said, 'Thank you. My name will appear?'

'Of course it will.'

Sue came in with the tea and Steele got up, smiling. 'Good old Jonas. Never lets us down!'

Sue handed Jonas the cup.

'You'll have to take that with you, old boy.' Steele laughed, and as Jonas took the cup, slapped him on the back. Tea filled the saucer. 'Sorry, old boy,' he said.

The man who came in a couple of minutes later was a very different character. For him Sue brought an occasional table; the cup and saucer were china. He barely looked at her. Robert

Hartney had been in the Cabinet until a few months earlier and would be in it again when his party returned to power. In the meantime he was working on Volume Four of his Political History of England.

Steele said, 'You know about Salt?'

Hartney's nod was barely perceptible.

'Then what do you think?'

Hartney shrugged. 'These things happen. He did well to stay there so long.'

'You're not surprised?'

'Surprised?' Hartney considered the word. 'No. No, I'm not. I was, a little, last night, when I first heard.'

'Last night?'

Hartney smiled faintly. 'Just a whisper.'

'And you know it's Alex Hodder now?'

'As long as the institutions will have him.'

'Any views on the pair of them?'

'Don't be naïve, Steele. It's not appropriate.'

Steele felt himself flush. 'Naïve?'

'You know perfectly well what I think.'

'Not about Salt.'

'Ah.' Hartney's glasses flashed.

'Or about the company.'

'I see. It is, of course, their paper.'

'Yes, it is. But this one, this paper, also belongs to everybody. Specious, perhaps, but it has had a long and honourable role.'

'You want me, I take it,' Hartney said, 'to write about Salt, Hodder and Euromob.'

Steele nodded. 'If you will.'

'Hmm. All right. I can say what I like?'

'Those are the terms of your contract.'

'How long have I?'

Steele glanced at the clock. 'Two hours or so. Do you want a room?'

'I'd prefer to dictate.'

Steele pressed the intercom button. 'Bring your book, Sue.' When she came in, Hartney rose and Steele said, 'My secretary, Miss Lane-Thurston.'

'How do you do. Freddie's daughter?'

'Yes.' She smiled and sat down.

Steele said, 'You can manage, can you, if I stay here and get on.'

'Oh yes,' Hartney said. 'Now, Miss Lane-Thurston, let me see . . . we'll start, er yes: "For if the Salt have lost his savour, wherewith shall it be salted?" '

Sue asked, 'Wherewith?'

'It's a Biblical quotation, my dear.'

Steele looked up. He had never seen quite so much of her thigh before but reluctantly he looked away.

Hartney's voice went on. 'This Salt, the titanic Hugh of the ilk, had certainly lost his, whether through age or obsession. He threw too many stones, while living under glass himself. Too much power, for too long, perhaps.'

Mentally, Steele rubbed his hands. He pretended to read, but his eyes stared sightlessly at the papers in front of him.

' ". . . On the other hand the European Communications Corporation – Euromob – needs powerful flavour. Salt in his prime was right, for Sir Hugh was one of the men who can flavour a great business. A pinch of the best Salt was enough.

' "But Euromob, having thrown Salt in the fire, have now nothing with which to add flavour to the frying pan. Alex Hodder is able, no doubt, but he has spent his life in Salt's shadow, venturing out to try his strength in the sunlight only infrequently. It is as though the Euromob dish, having been flavoured so long with Salt, will now only taste of—" ' Hartney paused elegantly. 'Do you think, Miss Lane-Thurston, that strawberry or vanilla is the more . . .?'

She said, 'Prâline sounds more . . .'

'It does, doesn't it. So ". . . will now taste only of . . ." Let's make it caramel, burnt sugar! ". . . taste only of caramel." '

Within twenty minutes Hartney had finished a corrosive piece of prose that virtually demanded an end to the current management and its replacement by authoritative financial men. He accepted a drink while he waited for Sue to type the article and sipped the whisky while he read the evening paper. When the copy was ready, he handed it to Steele. 'There.'

Steele read it, gloating. 'Nobody can say,' he said in the end, 'that we don't have freedom of expression.'

Hartney smiled. 'I do hope that's true.' He folded the carbon copy and put it in his pocket.

Jonas's article was entirely different. Where his own ingrained respect for Salt had clashed with Steele's instructions, there had simply been no contest. Jonas praised Salt for everything he was and had been, did and had done. He was writing about a Titan, he said, but in Salt the faults had not been Titanic – only the virtues. Steele grinned as he read it. Then he called Euromob House.

'Miss Roper's office.'

'Gerard Garvin Steele of Viewpoint.'

'I'm afraid she's busy, Mr. Steele. You can imagine.'

He said, 'I can. However, she'll want to know about this.'

'All right, I'll see.' The girl's tone was doubtful, but Jane Roper came on a moment later.

'Yes, Gerard.'

'I knew you'd say it one day.'

She said, 'For God's sake! What is it I'll be so anxious to know?'

'Robert Hartney.'

'What about him?'

'I've got his copy for this week. He absolutely tears into Salt.'

'Pity,' she said, 'but I think we can stand it.'

'Ah,' Steel smiled to himself, 'but he also puts Hodder in the machine.'

'What does he say?'

'Minces him. Little pieces. Does everything but say he's queer and he hints pretty broadly at that. And Philips.'

'Says he's queer too?'

'Incompetent is nearer. Doesn't actually say it because he's too clever to say anything actionable unless the four safe walls at Westminster are strongly about him, but he's not wildly impressed.'

She sighed. 'Well, thanks very much, for your contribution to my happy day. Spike it, will you?'

'I can't, love. Sorry.'

'Why not? You're the editor.'

'Can't touch a word. This stuff comes engraved in kerbstones

127

and direct from the mountain. Hartney's got a good contract and a lawyer to match.'

'Okay. Thanks for telling me. You'd better await instructions.'

'I've had mine,' Steele said. 'Outside contributors can say what they like.'

'Who says?'

'Philips.'

'Oh, Harryboy,' she said.

'And that's not all.'

'It must be.'

'No.'

Jane said, 'You're a toad, Steele. Somebody got a conjuring set and turned you into the semblance of a man, but you're a toad underneath.'

Steele laughed. 'You haven't seen underneath, yet.'

'What's the rest?'

He said, 'Idris Jonas, ex-M.P. You know?'

'He pinched my bottom once. Dirty little . . . !'

'He's a worshipper at the Salty shrine. Shedding Salty tears.'

'The little creep! Salt used to subsidize his African trips, you know.'

'I guessed. He says Salt was Africa's best friend in Britain. He doesn't quite suggest that sacking him is an offence under the Race Relations Act, but he comes close.'

'Well, you can put him on the pin!'

'Agreed. But he balances Hartney. You see?'

'I see you in my mind, squatting on your lily pad, croaking. You dreamed this lot up yourself.'

Steele said, 'Prove it.'

Hodder's Rolls picked him up outside *Viewpoint*'s old and rambling office and took him to Euromob House. The Directors' lift whisked him upstairs. Jane Roper was with Hodder when he went into the office.

Hodder said, 'Hello, Gerard. Jane told me.'

'Awkward.' Steele paused for puncuation and added, 'May I offer my congratulations.'

'Shake my hand, there's a viper up my sleeve?' Hodder said.

'He's under contract. The contract says no touching. Anyway, he'd howl blue bloody murder.'

'He'll howl blue bloody murder every chance he gets as long as I'm Chairman,' Hodder said. 'May I see the article?'

'Of course.' Steele handed it to him, winking at Jane as he read it.

Half way through, Hodder whistled. 'Listen, Jane. "In every great corporation there are always the jealous men, smaller, full of spite and envy. When a great industrial figure goes one thinks inevitably of Julius Caesar, bloody knives and et tu, Brute?".'

She said, 'He doesn't want anybody to misunderstand.'

'Nobody will. The trouble is, it's not true.'

Steele, enjoying himself said, 'Once Hartney says it, it *becomes* true!'

Judy Kernon

'I'D like to speak to Mister Philips, please. It's Judy Kernon.'

Philips' wife said, 'I'll get him.' Click. 'Yes, Judy?' Philips' voice was flat and unemotional.

She said, 'In view of events, does that selection question still arise?'

'Selection? Oh yes. Yes it does. And Judy?'

'Yes.'

'No change in the requirements, except that there is some urgency now.'

She hung up, wondering why. What swirling side-current from the directorial whirlpool up there made the appointment of a deputy more urgent? She wondered who had played what part in the assassination. Hodder was a Brutus of sorts, Philips was possibly a Cassius. She supposed the board must be crawling with envy and dislike, with wounds and wounded pride. There would be Cascas aplenty. But had Philips really played the Cassius?

Judy gulped down her coffee and went back into the room. Templeton was standing at the front beside a huge scrap pad.

'Righto,' he said, 'We're going to do a case study this morning. As you know, these things are always based upon a real company situation, but the names are changed to avoid actions for libel, slander and possibly rape. This one is the Krunch Khrome Ko. All Ks. They make bicycles and have done for a thousand years. They were founded by Granddad Krunch who's been dead this many a year. The Chairman and managing director is Father Krunch. His sons Crispin Krunch and Ken Krunch are directors. So is Tom Dough. He's sixty-eight now and financial director. He's not qualified, but he's good. There are two other directors. One is Axel Frame the designer (he's Swedish) and the other is Freeman Wheel, a solicitor who represents the large holding the Croesus Bank has in Krunch Khrome.

'Now, here's the problem. Father Krunch has thirty-two per cent of the shares, Chris fifteen, Ken fourteen, Dough twelve, Frame six and the bank twenty-one. Pa wants to retire to the South of France and sleep in the sun with his friend Milly Fayne. He doesn't think either Chris or Ken is up to snuff. Dough will retire when Father goes. Frame doesn't want to manage, just to market his new bike which Father has, so far, sat on and refused to pedal. That leaves our pal Wheel who can't take over, anyway, because as I said, he's a solicitor and he's very busy conveyancing. But, at Wheel's suggestion, Father has decided to call in a consultant to make recommendations. You've got it. Here's the last balance sheet, character assessments of the various bods, produced by somebody like me.

'So now,' Templeton beamed, 'you'd better go away and think what you'd recommend. Use one another's rooms. I want you to do this in threes and I've made a little list. We'll all hear the answers first thing. The reason for doing this exercise after dinner, as you'll appreciate, is that the modern business executive is blotto three-quarters of the time and we like to make you practise thinking while squiffy. Or, to put it another way, it may sometimes be necessary to work at night.'

Judy opened the bedroom window, letting the cool night air flood in from the park. 'I have not the slightest objection, gents, if you remove your jackets.'

'I'm okay, thanks.' Richard Keller was slim, cool and immaculate. Giesing, however, was sweating, his forehead beaded with droplets.

'Nein,' he said.

'Come on, you're among friends.'

'No. Thank you, but no.'

What was the matter? She looked at him anxiously, almost sure he was trembling. 'You okay Reinhard?'

'Yes.' He swallowed. 'I am all right.'

'Okay.' Judy let herself relax.

'What do we do about old Pa Krunch?'

Keller's slender, neat fingers were turning the balance sheet, his eyes picking with precision among the figures. 'They're making money,' he said. 'Twenty-six per cent gross. Wouldn't want to interfere too much with that.'

'But if we don't,' Judy said, surprised to find herself fascinated, 'it looks as though the ship will go down with all hands. Look, it says here that Chris Krunch is stubborn, old-fashioned and a soak. Ken, on the other hand, is a forty-year-old hippy who may or may not be taking trips on something other than a bicycle.'

There was silence. Both looked at Giesing, who sat silently staring at his hands which lay, white-knuckled, in his lap.

'Reinhard?' Keller said.

Giesing looked up. 'Sorry.' Judy watched how his eyes flicked from one to the other, and thought, disbelieving it, that he looked frightened. But how could he? What was there to be frightened of? She said lightly. 'You got any ideas?'

Giesing lit a cigarette and inhaled deeply. His forehead was slippery with sweat and he took out a handkerchief and mopped it. He said, 'This company cannot survive without management from aus – from outside. They either appoint new directors from outside or join with other company whose management is strong.'

Watching him and listening as he spoke, Judy became more puzzled. Giesing was obviously utterly sure of his decision, yet he seemed to be speaking with only half his mind, and having to concentrate fiercely to achieve even that. She glanced at Keller, who shrugged, then yawned. 'I haven't the slightest doubt that he's right. I'll go along.'

Judy said, 'But what about the family?'

'No mention of Momma,' Keller said, 'so no family, I suspect. One hairy beery, and one happy hippy and dad anxious to be off with his lady love. No, there's nothing to save except their income.'

'It seems a pity just to say, sell it,' Judy said.

'They can bring in outside directors. Get Templeton to pick a couple. Or you, Judy.'

'Gee, thanks.' She looked again at Giesing, feeling worried. He looked ill, she thought. Maybe this was a thrombosis or something equally serious. 'Okay. I'll go along. I reckon you should go to bed, Reinhard.'

'No!'

'You don't look well.' Keller supported her. 'I would if I were you.'

He looked from one to the other, eyes still hunted. Then, 'Ja,' he said. 'Ja, I go to bed.'

Judy went with them to the door, watched them walk away down the corridor, Keller entering his room and Giesing heading for the far end of the corridor, stopping outside his door. He glanced round quickly and seemed about to go on again, but saw her and went, instead, into the room.

What on earth was it? She stood for a moment, looking along the length of the now empty corridor, then went back to her room. Something was wrong, clearly wrong. She sat on her bed, thinking. Should she call a doctor? Surely, one couldn't do that without his permission. On the other hand, what if it was an embolism of some kind? She thought of her own father, who had died alone in his car and remained there, unnoticed, for hours. Giesing's life might be at stake! Still, he'd said he was all right and it was a monstrous impertinence to . . . She began to get ready for bed.

Twenty minutes later she was still worrying. The man might be seriously ill, lying there in an hotel room in a country which, if not strange, was not his own. She ought at least to check once more. She slipped on a robe, walked to his room and knocked. There was no reply and she knocked again.

'You will have to come in and capture me,' a voice said clearly on the other side of the door.

'It's me,' she said, 'Judy Kernon. Are you all right?'

'I will not surrender myself.' She stared at the smooth woodwork. Was he mad? Capture him?'

She said, 'Reinhard, it's just me. Please open the door.'

'There are others.'

'No,' she said. 'I'm alone. Are you all right?'

'Go away. Leave me.'

Obediently she turned. He had a right to privacy, but . . . She knocked again. 'Please, Mr. Giesing, open the door. Please.'

133

There was a pause, and then he did, and stood slack-shouldered. 'Very well. Take me.'

'I'm sorry? I don't—'

Giesing was suddenly almost shouting, his voice throbbing with something close to anger, or hysteria. 'Take me. Shoot me. But do not torment me. I know who you are. Take me!'

Judy said, 'Sit down. Over there, on the bed,' and was surprised when he obeyed. The big German slumped down, his eyes resigned, the outburst over.

Then he said quietly, 'How did you find me?'

'Find you?'

'You find me. How?'

Judy managed to grin. 'I just came along the corridor and knocked.'

'No,' he said angrily, his mood changing yet again. 'You find me. How did you know?'

It had to be some kind of persecution complex. The man was afraid of her; afraid but curiously resigned. 'Whom do you think I am?'

Giesing looked at her. 'I tell you. I surrender, but do not play games like this!'

'Who?' She tried to make her voice gentle.

'I no longer care,' Giesing said. 'No more. I have lived with this thing. If you send me to prison, I . . .'

'Prison?' She was trying desperately to understand what she was supposed to be. 'I can't send you—'

'Then kill me,' he said. 'If you have to kill me, do it!'

There was some crime, real or imagined, and she was the instrument of retribution. She said, 'You are guilty?'

'Of course!' He seemed almost eager to confess. 'I did it. I admit it. It has not been easy.'

He assumed she knew, that was the odd thing! How could she get him to tell her? 'You want to make a statement?'

'Ja. I make a statement. You have paper?'

'I'll listen first, then we'll talk about it.'

He began to talk and Judy listened at first with incredulity, then with horror. He described the journey in the truck, the look in the woman's eyes, but he did not look at Judy and the recital was flat-toned, low. As it ended he spread his palms. 'That is it. That is what I did.'

134

Now she knew who Giesing imagined her to be; he saw her as a member of one of the Israeli squads who hunted down war criminals. The guilt-ridden words had painted scenes in her mind and she could picture the despair of the woman, her awful sense of the inevitability of events. And the nervous boy with his bicycle, frightened of a sergeant, who betrayed her.

'Do you know what happened?'

'She died. She must have died. She was Jewish and Polish. She must have died. Auschwitz, perhaps.'

Judy shuddered, as she looked at the hunched figure in front of her, the expensive suit, the neat, polished shoes, the strong hands. It seemed inconceivable that she should be listening to this, here, in this shiny modern room in a shiny modern hotel in London. It seemed impossible that he could have done the thing he had described. Yet he had; it was no fantasy and his guilt was real.

'You see,' Giesing said, 'I deserve to be punished.' Now at last he raised his head and met her eyes. 'She died,' he added dully. 'She died. In a concentration camp. They would have starved her first. Forced labour, starvation. Because I betrayed. Do you see?'

She looked back at him, her mind heavy with despair, with the knowledge that this story, this moment, would always live with her. She saw with astonishment that his eyes were wet, that he was weeping. 'Punish me,' Giesing said.

'I can't. I'm not here for that. I had no idea until you told me.'

She watched the tears with a detached fascination, the droplets like lenses magnifying the skin and fine stubble of his cheek.

'But I must be punished. There can be no forgiving. There is no way to atone. I must be punished!' His head swayed from side to side, the neck muscles tense, the jaw clenched. 'Do you not see. I *deserve* to be punished.'

There was nothing she could do, or say. She had lived her life, her whole life, with stories of the brutalities to which her people had been subjected and there was an all-consuming horror in her at the enormity. If you were Jewish, the people who died were not numbers, but names. They were your mother's brother, your cousin, the father of your school friend, your teacher's entire family. Judy knew and had known dozens, even hundreds of people in whose lives the 'final solution' had left a scar. But now, she realized, she was looking for the first time not at a victim, but at a victor. The man sitting now on the edge of the bed, beside himself with grief and remorse, was one of the *herrenvolk*, one of the people who had done it.

So why didn't she hate him? She felt, with a curious clarity, the contraction of her brow in a frown. Perhaps because the mind is equipped to bear grief, to suffer it and recover from it; whereas remorse and guilt linger. Perhaps it is easier to bear communal resentment or hatred, however severe, than it is to sit alone for ever with a knowledge that cannot be revealed.

'Who else knows?' He did not reply and she repeated the question.

'I know.'

'No one else?'

'Who?' Giesing's fists clenched. 'Who could I tell?'

'You told me.'

'Only because—' he stopped. 'Because I thought that it had happened. That you were here to bring an end.'

'You want that?'

'Yes, I want that!' He was on his feet suddenly. 'You understand why I want that! Because I am weary. I have lived for thirty years with it. There is no way of lifting the burden. I have to carry it, but there is no rest. Do you see that?'

Judy felt pity welling up in her and was amazed by it. Pity where there should be nothing but hatred; pity where there should be contempt.

She heard herself say, 'You have no need to look for punishment.'

'That is stupid. I wish sometimes they would kill me. Sometimes I think to kill myself, but I have no right. When they come for me I must be here!'

'Punishing yourself.'

'But you are Jewish!'

She looked up at him. 'Yes, I'm Jewish. So somebody else knows now. One Jew knows.'

'And you will tell them?'

136

Judy shook her head. 'If I did that, if they came and took you, would I not be an informer, too?'

Giesing frowned. 'I am sorry.'

'I think you'll have to tell them yourself. And I doubt if they'll do anything.'

'What? Why?'

'It is one crime in millions. Thirty years ago.' She shook her head. 'I can't forgive you. I ought to hate you, but I don't.'

'Then—?'

Judy said, 'I can say it is time to stop torturing yourself. No one can pay for another's life, so you should stop trying.'

'A Jew can say that?'

'I don't know. I'm a Jewess. I can say it. You've been telling yourself you're not fit to live. All these years you've been telling yourself. It proves something. The fact that you feel guilty means your values aren't wrong. You transgressed, that's all. Once and very badly. But only once.'

'You believe that. Truly?'

She met his eyes. 'I believe that. I don't know if there's a God. Maybe if there is he'll be angry some time. But now it's time to put it aside. Or to try.'

She went back to her room, climbed into bed, lit a cigarette and lay staring at the ceiling, smoking thoughtfully, unable to get him out of her mind. All her life she had shuddered at Nazi crimes against the Jewish people, but the Nazis had sinned against Giesing, too, had taught a boy new attitudes, encouraged brutality, encouraged the strut of victory. Giesing was a victim, with his thirty years of guilt; he was a fundamentally decent man with one heinous crime on his conscience; Hitler, Goebbels, Streicher were gone but a boy they corrupted lived on to bear their guilt. After a while she reached for the telephone and asked to be connected with his room.

'Are you in bed?'

'No.'

'Get dressed. I'll meet you in the lobby in a few minutes.'

He didn't ask why and when they met he followed as she led the way out into the street. They walked in silence along Knightsbridge then turned into the park. They walked for an hour, then returned to the Princess and up to the fourteenth floor. She opened the door of the common room, found a bottle of brandy and poured two drinks.

'Listen to me,' she said. 'I know, now. And I have walked with you. Talked with you. I am now going to drink with you. In spite of what you did. Now drink.'

They drained their glasses. Judy said, 'Somewhere in hell, Hitler and Goebbels are talking . . .' He was watching her, intensely serious. '. . . and they wonder what life is like on earth. So Hitler sends Goebbels to find out. When Goebbels comes back, he says, "It's amazing. The Jews are doing all the fighting and the Germans are doing all the business." ' As he looked at her, she held his eyes, willing him to laugh, and after a moment, he managed it. 'We can laugh together too. Jew and German. We can laugh together.'

He put down his glass and held out his hand. Judy hesitated, then laid her own hand on it. Giesing bent low and kissed it. 'I am honoured,' he said.

Alex Hodder

ONE might look, Hodder thought wryly, like a lion stalking the corridors of power; but the lion was caged. He wondered often where true freedom lay. Certainly not at the bottom, where he'd started, and where you could feel the weight of everybody sitting on everybody else up above. Equally, it wasn't available at the top where clever men made bonds and fences in case other clever men tried to be clever in the wrong direction. Perhaps there was freedom in the learned professions. A lawyer could, if he felt that way, tell a client to do something unpleasant to himself and the only person who suffered was the lawyer. But imagine being a judge, listening for three months to the intricacies of a financial fraud! Parsons? Nearer . . . They could have freedom if they chose to be unscrupulous.

He looked around him at the smiling faces, the outstretched hands, listened to the murmurs of congratulation, recognizing the tinny sounds and level eyes of sharp envy. As soon as they got out of earshot the knocking would begin: 'Of course, he's only a jumped-up reporter! The City won't wear him for long.' And, above all, following him endlessly for the rest of his life, 'What a bastard. Old Salt made him, then he turns round and sticks the knife in. The treacherous bastard!'

What would they say if he told them? They wouldn't believe him, that was certain. Perhaps they'd think it was an elaborate piece of self-justification, dreamed up by some PR man, or *woman* – That's what they'd think! Jane Roper's a shrewd little number dreaming up one like that; they probably scheme together in bed at night!

But if he said it? If he stood up now and said, 'I didn't want the job. I have never wanted power'? No – disbelief. Only people who strain after power, fight for it, have other men's blood beneath their fingernails and on their consciences, only those men actually *reach* power. He'd noticed Keller watching

139

him at that critical board meeting and read his mind. Keller was thinking, 'Look at him sweat. Even now he's scared the prize will slip away!' And Keller was a civilized man, likeliest of all to believe the truth, but conditioned by profession and environment to the inevitable and unvarying cycnicism. Now Keller was standing over there, waiting for the little speech, thinking like the others about the complex move and counter-move that must have preceded Salt's dismissal. And now he, Alex Hodder, would have to get up and offer bromides. No change that will affect your jobs. Onward progress. Growth of the corporation. Nobody regrets what happened more than I do. No! He wouldn't say that. Well, then, partings, however sad, are necessary and inevitable. That had the right hypocriti-cal ring.

He'd said goodbye to Salt a few hours earlier and there was a pain in his chest now that felt as if it would never go. In a way, he hoped it never would.

He had been sitting in his office when his secretary buzzed, her voice cracking with strain.

'Oh, Mr. Hodder.'

'What's the matter?' he'd asked, meaning her.

'Sir Hugh, Mr. Hodder. He asked if you can spare him a moment.'

'Of course.' Instinct had Hodder half out of his chair, then he sat down again heavily. He'd been answering that summons for thirty years. Could Mr. Hodder spare him a moment? It had always been a courtesy, a characteristic courtesy, of Salt's, to phrase it that way. Now, when he had to ask, ironically he phrased it the same way.

Hodder pressed the key. 'Where is Sir Hugh?'

'In his office. At least—'

'We'll all have to get used to it. Don't worry. I'll go and see *him.*'

He walked along the corridor to the big office beside the boardroom, hesitated, knocked. The knock was his first. Always before he had walked in.

'Come in.'

Salt was sitting behind his huge antique desk, its surface littered now with papers.

Hodder said, formally, 'Good morning.' Another change from the friendly 'Morning' they usually exchanged. Nor would it be Alex and Hugh; it had taken twenty years for Salt to stop saying Hodder and start saying Alex. Now it would be Hodder all over again.

'Oh, Mr. Hodder. I wanted to speak to you.'

Mister! 'So my secretary said.'

'I have come in to sort and remove my possessions,' Salt said.

'There's no need to hurry.'

'I had hoped,' Salt said, 'to complete the task this morning. Unfortunately, I underestimated the volume of material.'

'Plenty of time,' Hodder said. 'Please don't hurry.'

'I have the one car,' Salt went on. 'And I intended to return that this morning However, I have to ask you whether you will allow me to use it for the rest of the day to continue clearing all this . . .'

'Of course,' Hodder said, somewhere near to tears, yet near to smiling, too. How typical of Salt to use the vast chairman's Rolls as a removal van! It wasn't even a gesture, just part of the way he lived. 'If I can help in any way.'

'Thank you. But I think not, Mr. Hodder.' The meticulous *mister* again! No question that the old boy believed he was the ringleader, the treacherous servant. He wished desperately that he could tell Salt, knowing that if he did, Salt would not believe him. The rules were strict. Within them it was possible to depose the ruler for the good of the kingdom; but it was not possible to do that and retain friendship.

And this was a very old, very valued friend, whom he could call friend no more . . .

He had gone to see Salt for the first time early in 1939 when, at the age of twenty-two, he had just completed his first year on the City page of the old *Evening Post*, now long dead. Salt was in his late thirties, then, a young tiger. Already he had built up the family wrapping paper business into a strong public company, and if there was no war, then Salt seemed to promise rapid expansion. But a whisper had reached the City Editor of a slightly reduced dividend and Hodder had been sent to find out why.

He found Salt sitting at ease, reading. Reading Juvenal, of all things, at eleven o'clock in the morning and far keener to talk classics than finance. Finally, however, Hodder had asked the question.

'Dividend?' Salt said. 'They're extraordinarily lucky to get one at all.'

Hodder smiled. 'Shareholders do tend to expect dividends, sir.'

'They expect a great deal too much. In my view, Mr., er—'

'Hodder.'

'They ought to be glad to see money going into investment. And that's where ours is going.'

'Into timber?'

'That and land. Land suitable for timber.'

'I see.'

'Every penny we have to spare will increase our holdings of resources,' Salt said.

'The shareholders don't matter?'

'The shareholders can wait.'

'So if it's a choice between them and new acquisitions, the new acquisitions win every time.'

Salt smiled. 'Not *every* time. But a good deal of it. The companies which invest now will become great companies. That is my view.'

Hodder wondered if Salt knew about Atna and sat for a moment, barely listening. The City office of the *Evening Post* took a selection of newspapers from round the world and Hodder, reading a two-week-old copy of the Vancouver Sun, had seen an article about Atna Holdings.

He said, 'There's two hundred and thirty square miles of British Columbia up for sale.'

Salt looked at him. 'Aforested land?'

'A company called Atna Holdings owns it. They haven't declared a dividend at all for four years. They're in trouble.'

'It would seem so. When, Mr. Hodder, did you learn this?'

'Yesterday.'

'One moment.' There was a big bookshelf in Salt's office and he took down the Times Atlas of the World. 'Ah. Atna. Mount Atna, I suppose. That is the coniferous belt. How interesting.'

Then Salt rose. 'Thank you, Mr Hodder.' And Alex Hodder was out of the office almost without realizing it.

Three weeks later he received a cheque for a thousand guineas. Salt had bought Atna and his shareholders received no dividend, either, in 1939. Hodder wrote a note of thanks.

'Dear Mr. Hodder,' came the reply. 'Valuable information is valuable. Yours sincerely, Hugh Salt.'

Their next meeting arose from a story in the English language newspaper in Buenos Aires. There was a lot of trouble between a big British ranching company and its American canners. There was also, in another part of the paper, the story of the death of the owner of a local canning plant. He telephoned Salt. 'To the best of my knowledge you're not in canning, but ...' he explained. Salt went into canning and paid him a further thousand guineas. That was in June, 1939. Salt took him to lunch and they agreed war was near.

'Will you go?' Salt asked.

'I think so. Sooner or later they'll take me. I might as well get there first.'

'Stay in touch with me.'

He was fond of sailing, so he joined the Navy and found himself as a sub-lieutenant on a corvette during the battle of the Atlantic. He was torpedoed three times and rescued from the water each time. Eventually he had his own corvette and with it twice sank German submarines. He was awarded the D.S.O. It was a hard, brutal and often short life and he was lucky to survive. Several times, on leave in London, he telephoned Salt and visited him in Cheyne Walk to drink sherry and talk, or at least listen as Salt talked, about business and about the classics. By common consent, the war was avoided.

In 1945, Hodder took back to the United States a lease-lend destroyer and spent four months there, waiting for his passage home. It was a time of parties and happiness, of admiration for young heroes and especially young British heroes. He was invited everywhere and decided to use his time learning something about American industry, rather than play tennis all day and fornicate all night. He had heard of nylon, though not of other developments in plastics, and visits to Dupont and other major companies enabled him to learn a good deal. Finally, he

143

wrote a long report and sent it to Salt. Summarized, it said, 'Get into plastics.' And Salt did.

Newly demobilized, he went to see Salt.

'What will you do?'

'Journalism, I suppose.'

'I should like you to join this company.'

He did. His job was information, and his motto was Salt's dictum, valuable information is valuable. He had two multilingual girls and half the world's newspapers and he was required to report only when he discovered something worth reporting.

After three months, he said, 'I'm going. I'm bored sick.'

Salt nodded. 'I'm not surprised. I am contemplating the purchase of a gravure printing house. I should like you to find one that is for sale.'

'How?'

Salt said, 'I hope you won't ask again. There are never any set rules.'

Hodder toured the country. After a month he was little wiser. After six, he'd heard of a company in Leicester, checked his road and rail maps to see how good the city's communications were, and checked in at the Bell. A week later he recommended purchase and named the price. Salt bought.

And so it had gone on. He began as Salt's little finger. The years made him Salt's right hand, made him a director, made him the successor. Then they made him the executioner.

He looked at their faces. Here were Euromob's real resources: not all of the corporation's able people, but enough to make a cross-section. And if he were to succeed as chairman he needed to kindle enthusiasm in people like these; the first pronouncement, therefore, was important. On the other hand there must be no promises he could not fulfil. It was, Hodder thought, rather like being a party leader at election time: one had to promise enough jam to get the votes, but not be committed to jam forever. He said, 'I've been in this job, ladies and gentlemen, for almost no time. Many things need to be done and, though naturally I have thoughts, I do not yet wish to embark on any statements about the future.' He paused. Their

144

faces were blank. He was giving them bromides and they were taking them. His words mattered to neither speaker nor listener. That must change. He noticed that Steele, the exception, was smirking, and a thought came to him.

'Except this,' he said. 'All of you are senior enough in this corporation to have a very great deal of freedom. By that I don't mean authority – one can have authority and still be oppressed oneself. Freedom is what Mr. Steele has. I will give you an illustration.' Hodder felt pleased at the direction of his sudden inspiration. 'Mr. Steele's paper this week will carry a ferocious attack upon me by Robert Hartney. I don't like that. Who would? But I will allow it to run.'

Hodder glanced at Steele, saw the smile, the pleasure in power.

'Now, two of you, Miss Roper and Mr. Steele, know that Hartney is under contract to *Viewpoint*; that the magazine is *obliged* to publish his material without alteration. So it may perhaps seem that I had no alternative.' Steele was nodding and Hodder knew now, with certainty, that the article had been written at Steele's behest. 'But there is another course which I could easily have taken. I could have closed *Viewpoint*. Immediately. Any observations? Mr. Keller, what would be the consequence, do you suppose?'

Keller said, 'Well, it wouldn't make you popular along the liberal fringes or with the literary establishment. On the other hand, the big investment houses would approve.'

'That was my own view. This corporation cannot really afford *Viewpoint*. Capital is tied up there without earning. On the other hand, if I am to practice the freedom in which I believe, it is necessary that freedom be visible. I see my role, in part, as the protector of that freedom of action. If it is misused – and I don't mean in *Viewpoint* any more than elsewhere – then I shall act. But I want to extend its limits. And I want you to do so, too. I will make one promise and it is this: I will never discourage a man or woman who has a positive suggestion or recommendation to make. I have one to make myself. It's time we ate.'

There was a scatter of handclaps and they drifted through to where the table waited.

145

The question, really, was a simple one. Would they give him any time? Euromob might be pulled round. *Might*. He might be able to do it. *Might*. But only *if* they'd give him time. Scrivener had unseated Salt without mercy and Hodder knew that the honeymoon period of his own chairmanship would be short.

A waiter approached. 'Mr. Hodder, sir? Telephone.'

'Thanks.' It was Harry Philips, and the news was bad.

'I've just talked to Con Summers of the drivers.'

Hodder said, 'Is it at General Secretary level already?'

'They're steamed up. Nobody seems to know quite why, but they want a showdown.'

'The men?'

'Yes.'

'And what's Summers say?'

'He doesn't see how he can hold them.'

'Unless we surrender?'

'Yes.'

'What did you tell him, Harry?'

'That we wouldn't. That total surrender to the drivers now would lead to a round of claims we simply couldn't stand.'

'I see. And he said?'

'On your own head be it.'

'I don't know him. What's he like?'

'Uneducated. Shrewd. Good mind of its kind.'

Hodder hung up. A bunch of strikes would finish him before he started, a fact which must be clear to anybody with half an eye. So why was Philips being implacable when diplomacy was the item required? Harry was deep. Always deep. Hodder remained puzzled about Philips' part in the unseating of Salt. Ostensibly he'd had no part in it, simply voting with the others. But! There was always a but with Harry.

'Tell Mr. Verity I'd like a word with him, please.'

Hodder watched the waiter approach Verity, who was busy charming Clare Fazackerly. He smiled. A man's reach should exceed his grasp or what's a heaven for? Verity looked at the waiter, frowned briefly, and asked her to excuse him, then walked over.

'Have a drink, Tom.'

146

'Thanks. Scotch.' He could feel the scrutiny of Verity's hard, dark eyes. 'Something wrong, sir?'

'I've just spoken to Mr. Philips. He, in turn, has been talking to Con Summers.' He watched Verity react.

'I wish he wouldn't.'

'Summers rang him.'

'It's possible to be out.'

Hodder smiled. 'Yes, it is. Tom, Summers says this is a nasty one. They want to strike. Why?'

'Because this is a rich company.'

'Not really. That's all?'

'More or less.'

'And Summers?'

'He likes to run with the hares and hunt with the hounds. A moderate to the bosses and a bloody revolutionary to the lads.'

'Nasty.'

Verity said, 'We'll solve it.'

'How?'

'The way we always do. Talking.'

'Sure?'

'Not *sure*. But it's what I think. If they'll let us get on with it.'

'Who's they?'

Verity grinned. 'For the time being, I think all negotiations should still be conducted from the transport office. If it has to get to the boardroom, I'll let you know.'

Hodder looked at him, wondering. Verity exuded massive confidence; was it justified or was he over-confident? He thought that, for the moment, he must go along. 'I'll pass the word.'

'Thanks.' Verity rose and walked away; back, Hodder noticed, to Clare Fazackerly. And *she* gave him a big smile. Verity must be a considerable operator, he thought, and the thought gave him confidence. Hodder glanced at his watch. There was one other thing he intended to do that night.

Fullerton Ironside-Keyes

'WHERE do you live, Mr. Volans?' Keyes was talking to Volans because nobody else was and this was a practice of his. People who weren't being talked to were often grateful to the man who broke the silence.

'Seattle. Y'know it?'

'I have been. Briefly, I'm afraid. But I know what Puget Sound looks like.'

'You do? My home overlooks the Sound.'

'How wonderful,' Keyes said. 'You're very lucky, you Americans, with all your scenic grandeur. We have to manage with a couple of trees and the Thames Estuary.'

'Yeah. It's a shame. That's a great country we got. Mind you, I'm not sure the Canadians aren't even luckier. You been to B.C.?'

'Again, briefly. Into Vancouver and out again.'

'Ain't that a great place? That B.C. coast, y'know, clear up to Alaska. Boy, oh boy!'

Keyes listened politely. He had an ear for nuances, an eye for details of behaviour, and it struck him that it was highly unusual for Americans to concede superiority to anybody, in particular Canadians.

'I seem to remember,' he said, 'that this was a subject of great debate between you people and the Canadians. Whose scenery is the more beautiful. Whose skiing? Whose boating? And so on.'

Volans' eyes narrowed. How *very* interesting. Keyes watched him take a grip on himself and project again. 'Gee, Mr. Keyes, I'm an Anglophile. Canuckophile too, if you like. It's not treason.' Volans grinned almost convincingly.

Keyes smiled. 'It's uncommon. But pleasant, I must say.'

'Well, y'know. We got this thing about land.'

'But you call it real estate,' Keyes said smoothly, watching Volans' eyes react again. How very fascinating.

148

Volans said. 'No. We tend, I think, to say real estate when we mean building land and property. Land is farms and forests.'

'I see. And you like farms and forests?'

'That's right.' This time the grin was genuine, Keyes thought. Volans *did* like farms and forests.

He asked the simple question. 'Have you any?' Again he was rewarded.

'My house, that's all. But I'd love to. Gee, I'd love to.'

'Where?'

'Oh, up the B.C. coast.'

Keyes left it there. 'I hope you'll manage it, one day,' he said. 'Though I must say that if I spent my days in the wide open spaces, I should prefer a – er, contrast in the evenings.'

Volans laughed. Was there the tiniest suspicion of relief in the laugh? *'Chacun a son goût.'*

'My *goût*, at the moment, is another brandy,' Keyes said. 'Can I get you one?'

'Thanks.'

'And I think you should meet some of the others. Do you know Richard Keller?'

'Only, well, I know who he is.'

'Nice chap. Come on.'

He parked Volans smoothly on Keller. who saw what was happening and was both too pleasant and too wrong-footed to prevent it, and crossed to Sinclair, sitting alone with the *Evening Standard* City page.

'Treacle mines up?'

Sinclair looked up at him. 'Couple of points.'

'Mind if I join you?'

'Not a bit.'

'It's odd, isn't it,' Keyes said, 'that Salt's departure didn't move the price one ha'penny. Up or down.'

Sinclair said, 'You think it should?' His eyes were very blue, Keyes thought, and very cold.

'I'd expect something. Mind you,' Keyes stretched, looking with pleasure at the polish on his shoes, 'the City baffles me anyway. I was at school with any number of idiots who "carry weight" as they say. Just money, of course.'

149

'Just money,' Sinclair agreed.

Keyes sipped hs brandy and watched Volans talking to Keller, noticing a tension that should be absent from this kind of social event. It wasn't, in any case, a social tension; not at all the sort of excruciating accent background clash; it was rather a kind of excitement. Yes, that was it. Volans was all a-quiver. He really must see if he could discover why. For no reason at all it seemed important and Keyes had learned to trust his instincts, though it intervened in his life only occasionally and for no clear reason. Sometimes a still small voice said do or don't and experience had taught him to listen.

A little later, he moved across to Keller. 'Nice chap,' he said, smiling.

'Very,' Keller agreed gently. 'Very American.'

'Oh? He seemed very pro-Canadian to me. Dreams about land.'

'I envy him that,' Keller said. 'Imagine owning an island. Peace and silence. After all this, eh?'

'Not for me,' Keyes said. 'I would prefer to own an hotel, preferably the Crillon.'

'He's got more chance of seeing his wish come true.'

'I suppose so. But islands come costly, I believe.'

'Oh, I don't know,' Keller said. 'It's a little one and very remote.'

Keyes programmed himself into a shudder of distaste. 'He's actually planning to do it?'

Keller laughed. Oh, yes. We own it, as a matter of fact. Tiny little place, apparently, but very beautiful.'

'Where?'

'Off the coast of British Columbia. It's called Whistler Island.'

'Are we selling?'

'I wouldn't be surprised. It's unused.'

'Ah? Well, good night!'

'Night.'

Keyes went to his room, picked up the telephone and dialled. 'Ministry of Defence, Navy,' the operator said. Not Admiralty any more, Keyes remembered with a pang.

'Is Commander Young on duty tonight?'

'Commander Young, sir? One moment.'

A moment later, he was speaking to Young: 'Jimmy? Fuller Keyes. Listen. Can you tell me anything about a place called Whistler Island?'

'Where, Fuller?'

'Off the Canadian coast, West coast.'

'I'll find it. When do you want to know?'

'Now,' Keyes laughed. 'You've nothing else to do.'

'Okay, I'll call you back. What is this, a bet?'

'In a way,' Keyes said.

He waited. A few minutes later Young rang back. 'It's not Canada, it's Alaska.'

'Really?'

'It's about two miles long, a little less, perhaps, and half a mile wide And covered in grizzly bears and mosquitoes, I shouldn't wonder.'

'Thanks, Jimmy.'

'Nothing of it, old boy. My pleasure.'

'Where, exactly?'

'You wouldn't know if I told you. You'll need an Admiralty chart.'

Keyes said, 'Don't you call them Ministry of Defence charts now?'

'Not me, old boy. Night, night.'

So. So maybe it was all genuine. A nice little island. Very small, probably not much value. But why the hell did Volans say it was in British Columbia when he knew damn well it wasn't?

Quickly Keyes went downstairs. When the chance came, he invited Volans to stay in his flat for the weekend.

'Well, gee, that's real kind of you, Mr. Keyes. But I guess I wanna be a tourist. If you don't mind, I'll stay right here.'

'Of course.'

Keyes lay thinking. The evidence was sparse, but its weight didn't matter; what mattered was that instinct said he was on to something important. But what? Alaska meant oil, but that was miles away on the Arctic shore. What else? Defence? There was the giant radar operation at Nome. Alaska also meant

Robert Service, gold and the Trail of '98 It meant timber, which was Volans' business. Snow and ice plus natural resources then: these were Alaska. And what natural resource could exist on Whistler Island? He thought again of Volans' suppressed excitement. There *was* something, something important. It was a pity that it was all so far away . . . Keyes sat up very straight. How far? Eight or nine hours? He could be there and back in a weekend. Thoughtfully, he reached for the telephone. There were advantages to being in the travel business.

Tommy Verity

'AND what,' Clare asked, 'did God say?'

Verity looked cautiously both ways and dropped his voice to a whisper. 'That he's going to show us.'

'Oh?' She pursed her lips. 'What?'

'He's going to make another world to give us some competition. Only this time he'll do it in six days.'

She smiled. 'Every line a laugh, as we old troupers say.'

'You could do a lot of those, couldn't you?'

'A lot of what?'

'Well, "Every tort a tangle", as we lawyers say!'

Clare said, 'Or – let me see – "Every audit an ordeal, as we accountants say!" You ought to play panel games.'

'He's like me. Worried about a strike.'

'Who's on strike?'

'Nobody – yet. But the lorry drivers may come out.'

'You'll notice we have no trouble with women.'

'I don't have much trouble with them myself.'

She said, 'Tell me, did you go to the comedians' school, or are you self-taught?'

'I went to a funny school, love, and I'm a self-taught bastard.'

'You have a way,' she said, 'of short-circuiting my humour.'

'It's too subtle. All you clever people are the same. Take too long getting there.'

'And you don't?'

'I'm nearly there now.' He watched the flush rise in her cheeks.

'What does that mean?'

'Did I tell you that's a smashing dress?'

'Yes, you did, but I don't mind your telling me again.'

'I'd better say summat different—'

'Why do you say "summat"?'

He laughed. 'You're learning.'

'I know.'

They grinned at one another. He knew the thought that was going through her mind: she was surprised it should be such fun to spar with this product of the northern working classes.

He said, 'You'd be surprised,' and watched her eyes widen with the knowledge that he'd read her thought.

'At what?'

'Too late, love. And the answer to the other question is, just like this.'

'Other question?'

' "Is he like this in bed?" '

'You're becoming coarse.'

He laughed. 'I know two things about a horse and one of them is rather coarse.'

'Whch one is that?'

'Dunno. I only know the couplet. But I can guess and so can you.'

He watched her look at him, met her eyes and held them, saw them widen for a moment. Then the pupils contracted and she glanced away in slight confusion.

'Why can I guess?'

'Because women have dirty minds.'

'You seriously believe that?'

'Yes. They love jokes about lavatories, nappies, that kind of thing. Watch your next audience.'

She said, 'We don't make jokes like that on my show.'

'Ratings might be better if you did.'

'I'm there to be ladylike. Not to make lavatory jokes.'

'Are you a lady?'

'What *is* a lady?'

'Well, according to the seaside postcard definitions, a lady only swears when it slips out.'

'I see. Well—' she stopped, staring at him.

Verity laughed. 'That was a beautiful double take. A gentleman, definition from the same source, is a man who takes his weight on his elbows.'

'Oh.'

'And I'm not a gentleman.'

154

'That,' Clare said coolly, 'is true beyond doubt.'

'You don't know. Yet.'

'I am a married lady. I have two children. I'm sure there must be easier places for you to look.'

'I never said easy.'

'You'd better not!'

He said, 'But it would be, come to think. Just along the corridor.'

'Good night, Mr. Verity.'

'Night, love.'

He went to fetch another brandy and Judy Kernon said, 'How far is it from Barnstaple to Doncaster?'

Verity turned, smiling. 'Two-seven-three miles.'

'I heard you could do that.'

'No magic. I just learned the distances. If transport's your job you might as well know. A brandy?'

'Thanks. Must be nice,' she said reflectively, 'to do a job you understand.'

'If you don't understand it, you *can't* do it.' He handed her the drink.

'But you can control?'

'If you can trust your subordinates. Otherwise there's chaos. Why?'

'Dunno. We just drifted into that. I spend my whole damn life talking about jobs, so it was habit, I guess.'

'Yes? What's a good American lady doing working for something called Euromob?'

'Running away, what else?'

'From what? A man?'

She shook her head: 'Plenty of men over here. Though it's getting harder to separate them.'

'From other men, do you mean?'

Judy Kernon laughed. 'No, I meant visually.'

'The girls are the ones with the nice behinds and the . . .' his hands gestured.

She frowned. 'You sure? My memory's not what it was.'

Verity looked at her, smiling. 'Let's test it. How d'you make gefillte fish?'

'Bream for breference.' She switched to a heavy New York

155

Yiddish accent. 'And don't forget the ground almonds.'

'And charoseth?'

'You're pretty knowledgeable, mister.'

'I come from Leeds.'

'So?'

'Rag trade. They used to call it the land of the waving palms, when I were a lad. How do you make charoseth?'

'With apples and sultanas and almonds and cinnamon, Thomas Verity. And care. So why this thick northern talk?'

'It's Yorkshire.'

'Yorkshire, schmorkshire. Who cares as long as they make the puddings! Say – what's the secret of those puddings?'

'You want to know?'

'I asked.'

'Right then. What you need is an old kitchen range with an oven heated by coal. The kind you black-lead? You know?'

'I know. We're out of date in New York, too.'

'Then you make the batter the night before and let it stand. That's important – to let it stand.'

'Right.' He noticed that her face was serious. Somewhere behind the eyes, all this was being noted.

'Then, when it's cooking, you need beef in the oven, too, with a little of the juice dripping down on to the pudding.'

'Okay. So leaving aside the schmaltz, I can do it.'

'I say.'

'Yes.'

'Don't go serving it with the beef.'

'No? Roast beef and Yorkshire?'

' 'Appen it's why we're so uncouth. But you don't serve it. You bring it on the plate, tip the gravy over it, and eat it. If you leave it half a minute too long, it turns to leather. You eat the beef next.'

'Such authority!'

'It's like the mileage. Worth knowing.'

'Don't you bother with things that aren't?'

'I bother. But it *is* bother.'

'What do you mean?'

'Simple. If you like something, if you're interested, learning's easy. Otherwise you have to work.'

Judy laughed. 'You have some refreshingly simple attitudes, Thomas.'

'All the girls say that.'

'Just before they boot you out?'

'Perhaps.' He was intrigued, suddenly. She was chatting him up and the conversation wasn't as random as it might seem. 'I'm not booted out a lot.'

'Your charm, naturally.'

'Naturally. You ever been married?'

She looked at him squarely. 'No.'

'Why not? Good cook like you.'

'My business.'

This was fascinating. Talk about yourself Mr. Verity. Talk freely, but be careful with the questions. He said, 'Where I come from we mind everybody's business.'

'Okay.' She shrugged. 'Korea.'

'Korea was a bloody long time ago. You'd only be a kid.'

'Eighteen.'

'Nay, damn it.'

'You've not married, either.'

'No.'

'And I don't *think* you're a fairy.'

Verity laughed. 'I don't think I am.'

'So?'

It was funny, really He was mocking her, but his war was years earlier than hers. 'I'm like you. Faithful to a memory.'

'In your fashion.'

'I may look it, but I'm not made of stone.'

'Well, gee Mr. Verity!'

Strange to be having a conversation like this with a woman and no sex content in it. He didn't fancy her; she wasn't flirting with him. Odd ... He decided to offer her a helping hand. 'How do you like working for this lot?'

'Euromob?' She frowned. 'They're good to work for, I think. Bit amorphous.'

'The word,' he said, 'is soft.'

'Define your terms, mister.'

'I forgot you don't speak the language. Soft means lacking strength.'

'Where you come from?'

'Aye. Too polite to be bloody nasty, even when you need to be nasty.'

'What kind of nasty?'

He looked at her, sensing the interest in his answer. 'Some things have to be done. They're not nice. Cleaning out, that kind of thing.'

'And Euromob needs a clean-out?'

'I reckon. Don't you?'

She grinned. 'We've just had one, damn it.'

'Salt?'

'Yes.'

'That wasn't a clean-out. It was enforced retirement.'

'So where would you start?'

Verity felt the laugh coming, suppressed it, then decided to let it happen. 'The question is, where would you stop?'

A little later, he lay in the bath, brooding. She was a nice lass, Judy Kernon, and shrewd. What had he told her? That he learned easily and liked work; that he wasn't either queer or a compulsive satyr; that he'd sack and go on sacking; that he thought he knew what was wrong. All fair enough. The question was, at whose bidding were the questions being asked? Because one thing was certain: Harry Philips didn't need to be told about Tommy Verity. Funny . . . what time was it? He glanced at his watch on the table beside the bath. Twelve-twenty. Well, if people were asleep at this time it was just too bad! Verity climbed out of the bath, dried himself quickly, went to the phone and dialled. It rang four or five times. A voice said, 'Hello!' Angrily, Verity thought. Not tired, angry.

'Wilf?'

'Eh? Oh, yes, Tommy.'

'Asleep, were you?'

'Asleep? No, no, no! No, I was just—'

'You're a dirty old man, Wilf.'

'Y'what?'

'*You* know. And at your age. You ought to be ashamed.'

He heard Wilf Stokes laugh, and went on, 'D'you want to ring me back?'

'It's all right,' Stokes said. 'It'll keep.'

'Not too long, at your age. Look, you know that Brighton business?'

'Yes.' Stokes's tone was suddenly neutral, and he could imagine Mary Stokes looking at him.

'Tomorrow. Let Summers know, eh?'

'Tell him, you mean?'

'Not tell him, Wilf. Let him know enough to be worried. Just an odd word. A name.'

'Okay, Tommy.'

'But delicately. And just Summers.'

'Righto.'

Verity said, 'Ride 'em, cowboy,' and put down the phone. Summers was looking for trouble and he'd find it.

The whole thing had been Wilf's idea. Immediately after the last strike, eighteen months ago, he'd come into Verity's office and beaten about no bushes. 'Summers has got it in for you.'

'How do you know?'

'I know. He told somebody I know that he was going to smash you. And he might, at that.'

'Why, Wilf?'

'Because you were a driver and you became a boss.'

'I'm not the only one.'

'No. Just the one he's out to do.'

Verity leaned back. 'Not much I can do.'

Wilf Stokes said, 'There is.'

'Oh?'

'Fix him.'

Verity laughed. 'Strong arm, you mean? Get him duffed up? Christ, I can't do that kind of thing.'

Stokes shook his head. 'Not that. But he's a bugger for the women.'

'What do you mean?'

'Look, Mr. Verity, he's got a wife like a bloody hatchet.'

'Go on.'

'He's frightened of her. If she found out some of the tricks he gets up to!'

'That's blackmail.'

159

'What do you think he's doing?'

Verity laughed. It would be sweet indeed to have a hold on Summers, a rest from the threat of strikes held forever over his head.

'How?'

'Do you want to know?'

'Just tell me.'

'We meet him in Brighton. For a long informal talk about the future, that kind of thing. You, me, him and the chairman of the Euromob branch.

'You're planning to fix Tuckett, too?'

'He's another randy little sod. Also a crook. He sells a load at least twice a year.'

Verity said, 'I know. Go on.'

'Well, we don't stay in an hotel. We stay in a flat we've rented for a week. Okay? And then we leave. And for a few quid I organize a couple of girls to pick 'em up. They'll never resist it.'

'So they enjoy themselves?'

'No,' Wilf said. 'Film.' He said the word briefly, harshly, and it created silence for a long moment.

Then Verity said, 'Christ, Wilf!'

And Stokes just grinned. 'Don't worry. It's easy as falling off a log.'

It was, too. The meeting began on a Friday and then the pre-arranged telegram came in from Verity's office. Family illness, he'd have to go, but why didn't Summers and Tuckett stay for the weekend, as planned. No point in letting a perfectly good flat go begging.

Well . . . they hesitated, anxious to accept, but wondering, and Wilf said, 'If you decide not to, there's always a train later. Just leave the keys on the table.'

The two girls, already installed in the upstairs flat, came down to borrow matches for the gas stove a few minutes later and after that there was no question. Summers and Tucket stayed. The camera was mounted in the loft. The operation had cost three hundred pounds and knowing it was up his sleeve had given Verity a lot of confidence in his dealings with the union.

He grinned, now, remembering the film. Summers would get a nasty shock. But then Summers should think before the act.

Like him.

He picked up the telephone again and asked to be put through.

She said, 'Hello,' her voice quiet but puzzled.

'Hello.' He let the silence hang. Long seconds ticked by and Clare said, 'That is you?'

'Nobody else.'

Again silence. 'Then what—? No, don't answer. You'll only say, "What do you think!" '

'That's right.'

'I doubt if this will be much of a conversation.'

'We'll manage.'

'Not if you're monosyllabic.'

'I'll say something.'

'Good, Go ahead.'

'I fancy you.'

He could almost feel the silence. Then she said, 'Good night,' and he listened, waiting for her to hang up. In a moment, she would.

'What are you doing?'

'Sorry?'

Pleased at his timing, he said, 'What are you doing?'

'Reading.'

'Anything interesting?'

'That depends on your interests. "The Trial of Robert Emmet." '

'Feller who draws the comic trains?'

'No. Before that.'

'I know. Irish. There was a girl called Curran. They hanged him.'

'Let that be a lesson to you.' He could hear her amusement.

Verity laughed. 'You sound pleased with yourself. Reading in bed?'

'Yes.'

'Nice and warm and snug.'

'That's right.'

'I thought you were going to hang up.'

'I was. And am. Good night.'

'I say.'

'Yes.'

'It's a nice name, Clare.'

'Thank you.'

'It fits, too.'

'Good.'

'In fact you're a right cracker all round.'

'Thank you again.'

'Which is why I fancy you. I say.'

'What now?'

'Do you wear pyjamas or a nightie?'

She laughed. 'Why?'

'Some research I'm doing.'

'You'll have to list me as a don't know.'

'I don't think so. If you were a don't know you'd have put the phone down before.'

'I very nearly did.'

'Why didn't you?'

'I will now.'

'No,' he said. 'We're both enjoying this. I am, anyway.'

She didn't reply, and he smiled to himself. 'Aren't you?'

'What?'

'Enjoying this?'

'This conversation?'

'Yes, it's fun, isn't it?'

'In a way.'

'It's fun because it's naughty,' he said.

'I see.'

'I wish I did. Which is it, pyjamas or nightie?'

She sighed. 'A nightdress.'

'Colour?'

'As a matter of fact, it's white . . . a sort of white lace.'

'I approve.'

'That's nice. I'm so glad.'

He said, 'It's a good job I'm not there. I'd be after you and I'm a big, strong, rough feller.'

'I expect you are. Big, anyway.'

'You have no idea.'

He heard her breath hiss. Then, 'I really think I should go to sleep now. Goodnight!'

He could her the throb in her voice.

'Good night.' he said.

He gave her five minutes, then telephoned again. 'I still fancy you.'

'Oh, please. I thought we'd—'

'We did.'

'Then—?'

'It's the thought of *you*. All nice and warm and snug in a white lace nightie. Were you asleep, or reading?'

'I'll put the light out.'

'I wish you'd lend me that book. I can't sleep.'

There was silence again.

He said, 'I'm sorry. I shouldn't have – Good night.'

'No, you can borrow it.' She spoke quickly.

'Thanks.'

'I'll leave it outside the door.'

He said, 'That's taking a chance. Somebody might steal it.'

'Who?'

'Anybody.'

A pause. 'Do you really want it?'

'I want it.' He enunciated the words clearly. 'I want it very much.'

Her voice was low, hesitant. 'Then if you just . . . you know where?'

Verity felt his jaw aching from tension. He said slowly, 'I haven't any slippers.'

'Oh?' He could hear her breathing. 'Oh, God! I can't come to your—'

'Just bring the book. It'll only take a second.'

'Oh, God! Don't make me come to you!'

'Only a second, and then . . .'

She said, 'All right,' and the phone clattered down. Verity clipped off the lights, leaving just one, and went to the door, opening it, waiting.

'I've brought your book.' Her voice was unnaturally loud and she was holding it out.

Verity took it, and her hand. He pulled and closed the door.

'No, please. Please, Tommy.'

He wrapped his arms round her and kissed her. For a moment, a brief moment, she tried to resist, a tiny noise of protest beginning, then ending. He squeezed her body against him, almost crushing her and after a while she relaxed against him, then responded and urgency tensed her body . . .

He said, 'I'll look at you on the telly and I'll say — do you know what I'll say?'

She smiled up at him. 'Yes I do. You'll say, Ee, by Gum, I've 'ad 'er.'

'No.' His hand shaped her hip. 'I'll think that. But I'll say, there is a hell of a hunk of woman!'

'La, sir. Your elegance and style!'

He grinned. 'Tha's got a grand bottom.'

She tried to wriggle away, but the smack caught her. 'You're a brute.'

'Nay, lass.'

'Oh, yes you are.' He watched her expression change as she looked at him. 'Why wouldn't you? Why did you make *me*?'

'It doesn't do to spoil women. They get uppity.'

'Me? Would I get uppity?'

'More than most.'

'Don't let me, will you?'

Verity grinned. 'Don't try it.'

'Or?'

'No more sweets.'

He looked down to where she lay in the crook of his arm, smiling quietly. 'Now,' he said 'it's time to get out of a nice warm bed and go home.'

George Sinclair

HE was crossing the lobby after lunch when the man spoke. 'Mr. Sinclair?'

'Yes?'

'My name is Simon Fenlis Smith. I work for *Action This Night*.'

Sinclair was instantly irritated. The young man wore King's Road clothing and hair round his shoulders. 'Again please.'

'*Action This Night*. On T.V.'

'I've heard of it. Do you want me on it?'

'No.'

'Then good day.'

'Mr. Sinclair, we're trying to get Sir Hugh Salt on to the programme. You know him I believe.'

Sinclair stopped. 'I know him.'

'Will you help?'

'Why should I?'

'Well I suppose we can manage a fee . . .'

'Stuff your fee,' Sinclair said. 'Have you asked him?'

'Yes. He won't.'

'I'm not surprised.'

'Why?'

'Some smart little sod like you sitting there with a long list of carefully researched awkward questions and trying to make him look stupid.'

'It isn't always like that.'

'Often enough to make people leary of you.'

Simon Fenlis Smith said, 'There are a lot of shareholders in Euromob.'

'Of whom he is one.'

'They're entitled to know.'

'Obviously, he doesn't want to say anything.'

'You won't help?'

'I'm not sure if I could. And I'm quite sure he's had enough without some smartarse chopping him up.'

Smith handed him a card. 'If you change your mind, call me.'

The afternoon's lecture was on Discounted Cash Flow, an accounting technique for calculating in advance the required flow of money. Sinclair, familiar with it, listened for a while. but his mind kept going back to the T.V. man.

The money Salt had promised for development would not now be forthcoming; that much was certain. And he wanted that money, the road upward depended on it. Without the money he'd remain a successful, middle-level businessman. With it he could go a very long way, but not in Euromob now, and certainly not with Salt gone. What did that leave? Either quitting Euromob himself or – and his mind raced at the thought – the break-up of Euromob!

At four o'clock when the course broke up for the weekend, he went to the telephone.

'I wonder if I might come to see you, sir.'

Salt said, 'Not much point, now.'

'All the same.'

'Oh, very well. At eight this evening?'

'Fine. Thank you.'

When he arrived, Salt led him through into the study. A reading lamp glowed on the desk.

'Juvenal?'

'Eh? Er, no. As a matter of fact, I was reading the Companies Act. Do sit down, Sinclair.'

'Thanks. How are you, sir?'

Salt smiled. 'A little surprised, still.'

'Bound to be.'

'Oh, no. One has no business being surprised. All's fair, you know.'

'I should feel pretty rancorous.'

'Yes. One does. Helpless, too, unfortunately.'

'Hardly that.'

'My dear young man, what do you suppose I can do with my little shareholding against the board? I can make small noises of protest at the annual meeting. It really won't matter.'

'That's months away. May?'

'A long time, I grant. But one must wait.'

'Unless.'

'Unless what?'

'Were you ever worried about a take-over?'

'Take-over?'

Sinclair said, 'I think Euromob is hanging there like a plum for Slater or somebody.'

Salt was looking at him with the scholarly blankness with which he usually masked the speed of his mental processes. Sinclair smiled. 'Of course, it would depend on asset values to a large extent.'

'Yes. Yes it would.'

'And the shares are low enough.'

Salt said, 'One cannot act against the interests of the shareholders, naturally. However, the shares are extremely depressed, and so—' his smile was gentle – 'is the mood of the stockholder. But if they were to get a fair price . . .'

'They'd be bound to, sir. The current price barely reaches asset values.'

'Which are in any case undervalued,' Salt said. Then stopped. 'This is revenge, pure and simple. Tempting, but childish. I would not have put Euromob together had I not thought its future must be enormously successful.'

'Do you still think that, sir?' Sinclair found he was nervous even asking the question. Two days was not long enough to lose the habit of inferiority.

Salt looked at him. 'As a matter of fact,' he said, 'I don't. I believe it was a mistake. I have, in fact, thought so for some time, but one could hardly admit it. Even . . . even to oneself.'

'That is a very interesting situation,' Sinclair said.

'Yes. I suppose it is.' Salt chuckled. 'It is not without charm, is it. That which thou sowest, that shalt thou also reap.'

'A T.V. programme called *Action This Night* asked me to persuade you to appear.'

'I know it. As these affairs go it is moderately respectable. When is it?'

'Monday.'

167

'Your interest in this, of course, is the continued strength of our company?'

'And myself.'

'Very well. Now let me see, you're an accountant by training?'

'Yes, I am.'

'We'd better start going through the papers. I have a lot of documents, of course. There's a property valuation in Manchester and Glasgow that was completed last week. And another for Frankfurt.'

'That's interesting.'

'Very. I promise you.' Salt's eyes, for the first time since Sinclair had known him, were twinkling. 'Do you have many, ah – engagements during the weekend?'

'None, sir.'

'Good.'

'Except that I could perhaps play golf with Ray Toller. On Sunday morning.'

'Of Toller Securities?'

Sinclair grinned. 'Yes. He's a member of a club I play at.'

'Oh, by all means. To miss that would be most unwise. Tell me, does he play better than you?'

'No,' Sinclair said.

'Then he'll lose?'

'Not this week. We'll both have to struggle, but I think he might have a chance.'

'What do tigers play for?' Toller asked.

Sinclair laughed. 'I usually say "What you like," but not now.'

'Since you're bound to win, I don't see why not.'

'Bound to? What are you?'

'Ten.'

'I had the worst thrashing of my life from a ten-handicap man. What about five pounds on the first nine, five on the second nine and five on the match?'

'Fine by me.'

'Right, I'm giving you seven shots. Off you go.'

He watched Toller drive. Not smooth, not lissom and weakish hands, but efficient enough. 'Good shot.'

'You mean "good shot – now watch this",' Toller said.

He took two practice swings, stepped up to the ball and smacked it two-eighty yards in a long, low straight line.

Toller said, 'I'm impressed.'

'Some people can hit golf balls. Some can make money. Which would you rather?'

'*You* might make a lot of money. I'll never hit a ball like that.'

'You wish you could?'

'Not desperately. But yes, I do.'

Sinclair said, 'That's how I feel about money,' then paused and watched Toller's second wood shot finish in front of the green. His own shot needed a nice seven iron. He took a five and hammered it.

'You're a mile through the back. Hard luck!'

Sinclair had a ten foot putt for the half. He missed it without difficulty.

As they came off the ninth green, he handed over five pounds. On the seventeenth a further five. The third followed on the way to the clubhouse. 'To him that hath.'

'Unfair, isn't it. Two and one *and* one up on the last nine. I enjoyed that.'

'So did I.'

Toller said, 'A tip, by way of thanks. Buy Sprangue. They'll go up this week. Twelve and six to about eighteen.'

Sinclair said, 'Thanks. I will. Can I give you one in return?'

Toller turned to look at him and changed, on the instant, from amiable opponent to stony financier. 'Well?'

'Buy Euromob.'

Toller said, 'I wondered what this game was about.'

'Now you know.'

Toller said, 'Everybody's had a sniff. It has its attractions. But why now?'

'Hugh Salt's on the telly tomorrow.'

'Saying what?'

'He doesn't believe it will work. I don't know if he'll say it. And there's a new property valuation.'

Toller relaxed. 'Come on, I'm thirsty.'

Salt said, 'Let us be quite clear about this. I have agreed to answer these questions and these alone.'

'That's right,' Don Grange said. 'There's film first, then we'll go through the questions in the agreed order. All right?'

'Yes.'

Watching, Sinclair was surprised by the old man's calm. He'd been on T.V. before, of course, but plenty of pros would sweat before the appearance. 'Not nervous, sir?'

Salt turned to him, puzzled. 'Why on earth should I be?'

'People often are.'

Grange said, 'Excuse me, but who are you?'

'I'm the moral support.'

'Fine. Only it has to stop short of the studio floor. Would you mind sitting in the producer's box?'

'Not a bit.'

There was a snatch of the curiously old-fashioned swing melody that Grange had adopted as his signature tune – then they were running up. Sinclair watched the producer cueing telecine and cameras, saw Salt waiting, coolly.

Grange said, 'Well, it's been quite a week for you.'

'Surprising, yes.'

'After how many years?'

'I don't know. I'm sure you will have it written down, somewhere.'

'Yes I have. Almost forty. Sir Hugh, what happened?'

'You know what happened. I was sacked.'

'How did it feel?'

'I was surprised.'

'Shocked?'

'Doesn't that word imply disapproval? I was startled.'

'You don't disapprove?'

'The board had every right. Its members acted perfectly properly. I may think they are wrong, but that's unimportant.'

'Do you think they were wrong, Sir Hugh?'

'Naturally.'

'You are succeeded,' Grange said, 'by Alex Hodder. He's a very old friend, isn't he?'

'He was, certainly.'

'Was? Isn't he a friend any more?'

Salt said softly, 'One can afford to lose such friends.'

'Who needs enemies, eh?' Grange laughed. 'Sir Hugh, the reason for the sacking isn't far to seek. Lack of growth, poor profit performance, dissatisfied shareholders.'

'True.'

'There's some justice in it.'

'They think they can do better. Mind you, they haven't so far.'

'The directors, you mean?'

'Only the chairman has changed. They couldn't produce profit before. I see no reason why that should suddenly change.'

'Are they able?'

'You must judge them by their record.'

'So they're not?'

'That's your judgment. Since I appointed many of them some of the responsibility is mine.'

Beside Sinclair in the box, a watching executive of the T.V. company murmured, 'He must have talked the shares down a bob already.'

Sinclair thought, but did not say, 'Wait until he's finished.'

Grange said, 'It's a lifetime, Sir Hugh. You built Euromob from a family business into a giant international corporation.'

'Not entirely single-handed.'

'You guided it all.'

'Oh, yes.'

'What's it feel like now, Sir Hugh. You must feel as though you're in limbo, cut off from everything you knew.'

Salt said, 'I am a little rusty on my Catholic theology, but limbo is the waiting place for hell, is it not? In that case, I am most certainly not in limbo.' He smiled. 'Quite the reverse.'

'Heaven to be free?'

'Something like that. The responsibilities of being chairman of a company like Euromob are enormous.'

'And the salary. Forty thousand a year.'

'Eighty-five per cent to the Chancellor.'

'The Rolls and the rest.'

Salt said, 'I shall not be without a Rolls.'

'Or a pension?'

'You can take it that, whatever I may die of, it will not be malnutrition.'

'Do you feel a sense of loss?'

'Of course.'

'Will you describe it.'

'I have been thinking about it,' Salt said. 'There is a popular expression about the loss of an arm.'

'That's how you feel?' Grange said eagerly. 'As though you'd lost an arm?'

'A diseased arm,' Salt said. 'As though the pain had suddenly gone.'

Sinclair sat up. The agreed questions were past. This was adlib time.

'Diseased, Sir Hugh? That's a curious expression.'

'It's a curious situation. I put the corporation together in the belief that it would become one of the dominant companies of Europe. I'm afraid I was wrong.'

Sinclair's lips tightened. He wondered if Toller were watching.

'Wrong? That's quite an admission, Sir Hugh. How were you wrong?'

Salt said mildly, 'I took over several perfectly sound companies, all of which were functioning satisfactorily, and I made this impossible Colossus.'

Grange was pleased, and looked it. This interview was financial dynamite. 'Impossible?' he asked softly.

'Oh yes. It can never work. The whole thing is impossible to administer, that's the trouble.'

'So you don't think your successors – your former colleagues – will succeed where you failed?'

'Where we all failed. No I don't.'

'Then will it fail? Surely a company like Euromob can't fail, just like that?'

'No. It withers. It crumbles. It is not a bicycle shop on a street corner which can be closed by one piece of ill fortune. But it can never, I'm afraid, do what I hoped.'

'How long, Sir Hugh, does a company like this take to wither?'

'It's withering now. But of course, there are vast assets. In land, machinery, raw materials . . .'

'Take-over bid, Sir Hugh?'

Salt looked at Grange as though the thought had not occurred to him before. 'Take over?' he repeated. 'Well, it's a very big bite. But it would be a bargain.'

'Why a bargain?'

'Principally property. There are new property valuations of which the share price takes no account.'

'So there might be an even bigger Euromob, soon?'

'No. It ought to be broken up. There are highly successful companies in the group; there is a great deal of very valuable property. The rest should be scrapped or unloaded.'

'But is that possible?'

Salt said, 'To one or two very expert gentlemen in the City, it is as easy as falling off a log.'

'Sir Hugh, time's almost up. Do you have any word for the people who sacked you? For your former colleagues?'

Salt said, 'Yes. I wish them luck.'

'Thank you, Sir Hugh Salt.'

Sinclair said, 'May I use a telephone, please?'

'Of course.' He was shown to an office.

'Toller speaking.'

'George Sinclair. Did you see it?'

'Yes.'

'And?'

'I thought it unnecessarily vindictive.'

'That's all?'

Toller said, 'I take it you have a bulging briefcase?'

'I have three.'

'Then if you'd bring them round. Oh, and by the way. Does the name Keyes mean anything to you? Ironside-Keyes?'

'Yes it does.' Sinclair was puzzled. 'Why?'

'I wondered.'

173

Mike Farmer

HE was awake. He'd been so for some time, watching the hands of his watch tick towards seven fifteen. Only the sheet and blanket covered him as he pushed his toes towards the corners of the bed so that the bedclothes would lie without creases, revealingly, on his body. He was enormously excited and his heart thumped heavily; it seemed its pounding must be audible, must make the room move, but it didn't seem to because none of the girls took the slightest notice. They simply came in each morning carrying the tray of tea and the paper and laid them on the table beside his bed. He always watched, squinting through lowered lids, waiting and hoping for some reaction, but there was none. Would it be the Spanish girl, or the dark Irish one? He hadn't seen the Scandinavian blonde since the first morning and had almost given up hope, but one never knew! He lay tensely, ready to feign sleep.

His nerves jumped as he heard the key in the lock. He opened his eyes a tiny fraction to watch as she came in: it was the Spaniard, the swarthy, rounded little Spaniard, closing the door behind her with a shove of her bottom and walking round the bed to the table. He could have wept: she was taking no notice at all, damn it! As she came near to the bed, he had to close his eyes in case she guessed what he was doing. He pretended to awaken as she put down the tray.

'Oh, good morning.'

'Morning, sair.' She was brisk. The tray was down, the papers beside it and she was on her way out again.

Farmer said, 'Er, would you mind pulling the curtains?'

The girl nodded but did not speak, walked to the window to pull curtains back and Farmer watched every breathtaking movement of legs, of body, of arms.

'Thank you. It's easier to read the papers in daylight.'

She nodded and went out. Damn! Damn! Damn! She couldn't have missed seeing! Why the hell did they always ignore? He reached out for the papers, the *Sun* and the *Mirror*, searched for the day's pin-ups and eyed them appreciatively. I bet, he said to himself, that the people who take those pictures don't go short. 'No, dear,' he muttered, 'lean back a bit and undo another button. That's right. And a little bit more thigh. Now come here!'

Farmer climbed out of bed and began to pour the tea. Why? Why would no woman have anything to do with him? Even the worst scrubbers seemed to walk past him with their noses in the air, yet everybody else seemed to manage. He'd have to pay again; wait until midnight and then go to Shepherd Market or Soho and take the same ghastly bloody risk. All the same, it had to be done. Pressure was building up. He drank the tea eagerly, scalding hot, glad to direct the attention of his senses to some other area of his body. Now the shower. He went into the bathroom, turned it on and climbed in, turning up the hot water until he could hardly stand it, then gradually turning it off and letting the cold spray hit his body. That was better. He was under control again now, refreshed and ready for work if only there was something to work at instead of this stupid management course. If only, he thought, people would let him get on with his work! If only sex didn't bother him! If only other people's stupidities didn't intrude! He'd have liked to go to work on that idea of Steele's, but he was imprisoned in this bloody hotel.

Shaving, he stared at his face in the mirror. He didn't look so awful. A bit bony perhaps. Jill had said he was bony. But it was an intelligent face. And he could afford to be generous, so what was wrong? If only he could get this interminable, aching, sex problem out of his mind, he'd be able to work so much better. With Jill, for a while at least, everything had been fine. He'd been able to get on. But then the bitch had—. Well, she could whistle for money. She'd never see another penny from him, court order or no. How could any woman be such a cow? The way she'd carried on on the phone last night, too; she'd found out where he was and was demanding money again. Or else! Or else what? It would be a pleasure to go to prison for her, by God!

But meanwhile the weekend stretched interminably before

175

him, a prison in itself: a prison of boredom and inaction and therefore, inevitably, a prison of growing frustration. How he hated weekends!

He breakfasted alone and then went out, wondering how to pass the day. Pick up a girl, his mind said, but it was no use: he was no good at picking up girls. He almost missed the little sign off Oxford Street, because he was watching long smooth legs swinging by, but the word caught his eye and he looked at it. 'COMPUTAMATCH,' it said, 'Computer Introduction Bureau for friendship and marriage. The perfect mate by computer.'

Farmer went hesitantly up the stairs, anxious not to be made a fool of. Two floors up there was a door, freshly painted, on which it said, 'Please come in'.

The girl looked up and smiled brightly. They always smiled when they were paid to smile; never otherwise.

'Tell me about this,' Farmer said.

'It's very easy,' the girl said. 'You just fill in a form and we code the information for the computer and it sorts out the most suitable person.'

'How many names in the bank?'

'About fifteen thousand, sir. You just pay five guineas, you see. And if a marriage results from one of our introductions, there's a further fee of twenty-five pounds.'

'I see. Okay.' Presumably of fifteen thousand, at least half must be women. Surely one among them . . . He pulled out his wallet. 'How long does all this take?'

'A few days, that's all. Thank you.'

'Days?' Farmer said. 'Computers work in millionths of a second. Real time.'

'Oh, yes sir. I know.' The girl produced the form. 'If you will just complete this.'

'Right.'

'But we have to forward your details to the lady concerned and she'll have to get in touch with you.'

'Do me a favour?' The skin was tight at his temples. Thousands of women, one of whom might even be free today!

'What, sir?'

176

'I take it that's the terminal.'

'Yes, sir. It's a keyboard terminal.'

'So you can feed in straight away?'

'Yes.'

'And a print-back answer?'

'Yes.'

Farmer said, 'I'm all alone in London, you see. If I gave you ten pounds, could you speed things up?'

She looked at him doubtfully. She was pretty and secure and had the instinctive distrust of her kind for those who weren't. She said, 'Perhaps when I've seen the form, but you'll get me shot.'

The questions were routine, age, height, colouring, glasses or not. Some indication of education. Job? He wrote statistician. The girl might work near a computer but she would no more understand autonomics than she would Mandarin. Salary?

'This is, of course, confidential?'

'Oh yes. We keep the document here. In the computer, you're just a number.'

He nodded. Salary, £10,000 p.a. Interests? What did one put: sex? Well, he could play chess. Chess, then. And carpentry – he could do that. And he knew about engines. Was that enough? No, women liked food and fashions and theatres. The theatre, then.

Had he a car? No, damn it, he hadn't. Still, he could hire one.

He handed the form over the counter and watched as she read it. At one point she glanced up at him in surprise, probably, he thought, because she didn't expect him to earn a salary like that.

He said, 'Please.'

'Oh, all right, then.' He watched her walk across to the keyboard terminal and sit down. The ring on her finger, with its tiny diamond, said she was bespoken. If she hadn't been, would he have had the nerve to ask her out?

'Excuse me, is that one thousand or ten?'

'Ten.'

She stared at him. 'Oh. That *is* a lot.' After a moment she continued typing. 'Now we wait. Just for a second.'

177

The print-out was slow. The machine must be second generation.

Farmer's legs trembled. There were names on that list, names of girls who wanted to meet men as badly as he wanted to meet girls. 'May I see it?'

'Oh, no.' She was shocked. 'I can't do that.'

'Then what?'

'Well, I could ring one of them up, perhaps. I'll just get the forms out.'

He watched her, aching. If she knew what he was thinking, Farmer thought sourly, she'd have called the police. He forced a smile. 'Any luck?'

'Well there is one.'

'May I see?'

'No. I'm sorry. But she's thirty. And dark. She's a mathematician.' The girl almost shuddered.

'Where?'

'The Chant bank, it says here.'

'Can I ring her?'

The girl said, 'You did say ten pounds.'

'I'm sorry.' He pushed the money across the counter. 'There's five more, if— Can I ring her?'

'No. I daren't. That's against the rules. I'll have to.'

Farmer said, 'Ask her if she can make it tonight.'

'You'll have to make the arrangements, if she agrees.'

She picked up the phone and dialled, then stood listening. Across the office Farmer, too, could hear the ringing tone and counted the rings. It sounded as though there'd no reply. Oh no! Please not that!

The girl shrugged meaningly, ready to hang up, but then there was a click.

'Oh, Miss Richards?' She winked at him. 'This is Computamatch. Yes I'll hold—'

The girl covered the receiver with her hand. 'Closing the door. They usually do. Oh, hello? Yes, Computamatch. There's a gentleman on our list now who might. . . . Yes, well the computer put your name at the top of the list.'

She listened. 'All right. I'll give you the name now, on the phone if you like. Right. No, it doesn't say he's interested in maths. Just statistics.' Farmer nodded vigorously and the girl said, 'I expect it's the same thing, really. He's staying at the Princess Hotel.'

He raced back to the hotel, up to his room, and sat waiting. Would she ring? The girl had refused to give him the number. Farmer paced up and down his room, torn with anxiety. It was suddenly desperately important that he should not be turned down, sight unseen.

She telephoned at a quarter to one.

'Mr. Farmer?'

'My name is Wendy Richards. I expect Computamatch told you I—' she stopped, her embarrassment evident even on the telephone.

Farmer said quickly, 'Oh, yes.'

'Well, I, er – I rang.'

'Yes.' Farmer felt suddenly tongue-tied. Oh, God! What did one say?

'Thanks.'

There was a moment's dead silence, then she said, 'I don't know what happens now. I haven't. . . .'

'Neither have I. We meet, or – well, we meet.'

'Yes.'

'Well, then?'

'Tonight?'

She was uncertain, 'It's awfully short not—'

Farmer found words, 'Please. We can do – well, anything you like. Theatre, or something. If seats are available.'

'Gosh. This is . . . well, I mean.'

'I'll pick you up. Can I pick you up?'

A long pause. Then, 'All right. But I'll meet you.'

'Where? Here?'

'No!'

'I'm sorry. I didn't mean – how about, oh, God, where? Do you know the Law Courts in the Strand? There's a big clock.'

'I know.' She sounded breathless. 'What time?'

'Seven.'

'All right. Seven o'clock.'

179

He had expected Temple Bar to be quiet on Saturday evening, but people were milling about. Farmer cursed, realizing that they hadn't made any arrangement about recognizing each other. No evening papers tucked under the arm, or yellow carnations. He glanced up a hundred times to align himself precisely beneath the clock. That, at least, made him identifiable.

He waited. Soon it was a quarter to seven, but then time began to drag as he became more and more certain that she would not come. When it was seven o'clock and she was still not there, he knew. Somehow, with that instinct they all seemed to have, she had detected in him what they all seemed to find abhorrent. And she wasn't going to turn up. Well, he wasn't going to wait, either. He'd just give her a few minutes, then go. If she hadn't the courtesy to be on time, there wasn't much point. . . . He watched the legs twinkling towards him and away again, the pert and pretty girls who climbed off buses and hurried off. Surely *one* of them. . . .

At quarter past, he became conscious of a woman on the other side of the road. He knew she'd been there for some time because the ochre coat had been part of the scene around him. But that was the wrong side of the road; they'd agreed to meet under the clock. Farmer looked at her again. She'd be thirtyish. Certainly she was dark. And wore glasses. She'd nice legs, certainly; strong legs. She looked worried, too, anxious even. He noticed she was carrying something in a leather case, something he recognized, a spherical slide rule!

He almost went under a car in his haste to get across, but then hesitated. She turned and saw him and their eyes met. She smiled tentatively.

'Miss Richards?'

'Mr. Farmer?'

They both laughed nervously. 'It was the slide rule,' he said, pointing. 'I recognized it.'

'I thought it must be you, standing over there, but I wasn't sure and it would have been awkward, you know, if—'

'Yes.'

She had prominent teeth, but it didn't matter. At least she was not looking disapproving, nor looking away.

He said, 'I'd better tell you, I'm married. But we're separated. Have been for two years.'

'Oh.' She didn't seem concerned.

Within half an hour they knew they both worked on computers and Wendy Richards said, 'Gosh, you're *that* Mike Farmer!'

Farmer grinned. 'Well—'

'Gosh! You know, I heard you lecture, once, at Imperial College.'

'I bet I was a bore,' he said happily.

'No. You were talking autonomic theory. It was marvellous!'

'I'm flattered you enjoyed it. Where are you?'

'Phineas & Falkenstein. They're merchant bankers.'

'I know.'

'I think of you in the computer context. Development.'

'Euromob just provide the hardware,' he said. 'Listen, it's marvellous to meet a woman who understands all this!'

'Or a man!' She smiled. 'Listen, how far do you think you can take this parallel with the human nervous system?'

Farmer said, 'As far as you like. How many nerve ends are there in a finger tip? It's just a real time problem.'

'No,' she said. 'It's primarily conceptual. Persuading other people. You do a superb missionary job. . . .'

They were still talking when Sir Hugh Salt was interviewed, but they didn't see it and wouldn't have cared if they had, for by that time they were utterly absorbed. They parted at twelve-thirty, having arranged to meet again at ten-thirty next day. When Farmer went to bed he couldn't sleep, thinking about her. He realized suddenly that he hadn't thought about sex the whole time he was with her.

'Gosh!' he said. And grinned.

Richard Keller

THEY saw Jane and Francis and Clifford Crane to the door, watched them put their instrument cases in the car and drive off, waving. As Richard closed the door, Rachael leaned against him.

'That was lovely, darling.'

He put his arm round her shoulder and they walked slowly along the hall. 'I don't know. It's a big thing to say, about Mozart particularly, but I think the quintet for clarinet and strings is m . . .'

She nudged him hard. 'Don't dare say favourite. Don't dare, Richard.'

'You mean the E flat major?'

'And the G minor and the C major and the quartets and the sonatas and the concertos. Not to mention the Masses.'

'All right. But it's supremely lovely.' He looked at her. 'Like you.' Her eyes went dark as he watched and he bent and kissed her.

After a moment, she pushed him away. 'You'd like coffee?'

'No. Not after that. Mozart isn't coffee.'

She mimicked him. 'Mozart isn't coffee. Coffee is Berlioz!'

'Mozart is sparkling Moselle!'

'In Salzburg?'

'In Hampstead.'

She smiled and he thought how beautiful she was: calm and beautiful, smooth and beautiful. Beautiful and beautiful.

'But it's so late, darling.'

'We're celebrating.'

'Celebrating?'

'Finding that clarinet for tonight.'

'All right. Sit down. I'll go.' She went out and came back a few moments later with the bottle in an ice bucket. 'A few minutes,' she said. 'Now, sir, name your record.'

He stretched. 'Vivaldi, I think. Spring.'

Rae shook her head. 'Too planky.'

'Planky?' he said. 'Plonky!'

'Well, plinky, then.'

He tutted. 'Something smooth, then. The intermezzo from Cavaleria Rusticana?'

'Saccharine.'

He said, 'I shall put on Ravel.'

'I see. La Valse?'

'Bolero.'

She crossed to the turntable. 'Listen.' It was Albinoni, the haunting sweetness of the tiny work for violin and organ. 'Is that right?'

'I love you.'

She sank down beside him and kissed him sweetly and lightly. After a while, she whispered, 'Really, Richard. The *Bolero*!' Her laughter bubbled.

'I haven't seen you for days.'

'And nights.'

'No.' He pulled her to him. 'Darling?'

'Mm?'

'Let's forget the Moselle.'

'Yes.'

They were on the stairs when the telephone rang. Rae said, 'I wonder who . . .?'

'I'll get it, darling.'

'Yes. But – be quick.'

He smiled and hurried to the phone.

'Hello.' It was Philips.

'I'm sorry, Richard, but you're going to have to come in.'

'Tonight?'

'I take it you didn't see *Action This Night*?'

'No. I was—'

Philips said, 'Sir Hugh was making music too. He more or less invited a take-over bid. So we'd better marshal our strengths.'

Keller said, 'Right, sir. But what about Mr. Thornley?' Thornley was finance director.

'He was in Chichester, but he's on his way.'

'I'll be along soon.'

He hung up and went upstairs. The bedroom door was not closed and inside Rae sat at the dressing-table brushing her long dark hair with grave concentration. Keller watched for a moment, then smiled. There was a small table with a semi-circular top against the wall and he began to drum on it, softly, pom, pa-pa-pa pom: the low insistent drum beat of the *Bolero*. After a moment, he heard her laugh quietly but he continued drumming, increasing the tempo, increasing the weight of the drumbeats with a musician's care. Then at last, he stopped.

He left his clothes where he had been standing and slipped quietly into the now-darkened room and into bed.

Rae said, 'You were like an advancing army.'

'I feel like an advancing army.' He reached for her and brought her warmth against him.

'All those drums.'

'Very insistent, drums.'

'Who was on the phone?'

'Philips.'

Under his hands her body tensed. 'Not tonight, not again!'

'Afraid so. Sorry.'

She held him tightly. 'I won't let you go.'

'You'll have to. But not yet.'

'No.' Rae sighed happily. 'Not yet.'

Later she drove him to Euromob House and they sat quietly, fingers touching occasionally, turning their faces from time to time to smile at one another. When he got out, he felt as though a part of himself had remained in the car.

Philips said, 'Sorry, but we must look at this.'

'I understand.'

'We're in luck, as a matter of fact, because my girl happened to be watching and she took a note. She's typing it now.'

'Good for her.'

Philips told him briefly the content of Salt's broadcast. 'Now Richard, what we need is figures. Figures that are as accurate as possible about this year's prospects. We also need those up-dated valuations.'

Keller said, 'I don't understand that one. I know of no new valuations.'

'Nor do I. But he wouldn't have said it if—' He broke off as Hodder came in.

'Alex, do you know anything about these valuations?'

Hodder shook his head. 'You know what Hugh's like.'

Philips said, 'But he can't have taken the only copy surely. Not even he . . .'

Keller said, 'It's a company document,' and felt himself flush at his own naïveté.

'Be your age, Richard. And get going!'

He worked steadily through the board's papers, compiling a rough profit picture and attempting a forecast. About two-thirty, James Thornley came in to join him and they worked on, frequently handicapped by lack of information, but assembling, gradually, an impression. Coffee was on tap throughout the night and breakfast was ready at seven; red-eyed and weary, they attacked the bacon and eggs. Afterwards Hodder said, 'Richard.'

'Yes?'

'There's a rather delicate little task I'd like you to do.'

Keller waited, watching Hodder hesitate. Whatever the task was, Hodder didn't like asking.

Finally, embarrassed, he said, 'I want to know exactly what every director has been paid by the Corporation over the last three years.'

'All right.'

'Salary, directors' fees, expenses, perquisites. Everything.'

'I understand.' Who was Hodder gunning for? Everybody?

'Everybody, Richard. And one other thing. I don't want anybody else to know what you're doing. This is a report to the chairman only.'

'All right. Except yourself.'

'Including myself. How's the rest of it going?'

Keller said, 'It's a working brief *now* if you need to use it.'

'Good. Thanks. Somebody may be on to me today. City Editors or somebody.'

'I'd be surprised if they weren't.'

He slept for a couple of hours in one of the bedrooms of the directors' suite, then went back to work. All payments to directors were made through his office rather than through the Salaries Department and he had copies of all the returns made to the Inland Revenue. He began to work through the figures, smiling occasionally at the little fiddles. Hyde-Compton found frequent visits to both Menton and Big Sur necessary to discuss books with writers. It was almost certain that the trips cost more than the books made. Thornley apparently had enough wine in his office to supply El Vino's; Keller wondered whether the Chambertin and the Haute Sauternes went home in his briefcase.

Heavens above, he hadn't telephoned Rae! He glanced at his watch; it was almost eleven. Keller sat at his desk smiling, waiting for the warm softness of her voice, listening to the ringing tone. He realized suddenly that there would be no reply: that the tone of the ring had that indefinable quality which meant the house was quiet. Perhaps he'd mis-dialled and picked up a wrong number! Carefully he dialled again. Still no reply. Probably she had slipped out to a shop or taken Elgar for a walk on the heath.

He worked on, going through all the files one by one, unearthing the minutiae of the directors' lives. Everything seemed pretty straightforward. If the Inland Revenue chose to examine any director's remuneration too closely, they'd be able to drive a procession of buses through the gaps, but they were only the gaps every businessman left. There was just Salt's file now; should he bother? The old boy wasn't his concern any more. Still . . . he opened the file and started to go through the documents. Then he sat up: what on earth was *that* doing there?

That was an authorization for work to be done on a house. It sometimes happened that the Corporation stood the cost if some sound reason could be found. In this case the house had been painted and decorated, and carpeted throughout, a new kitchen and new bathrooms had been fitted, a curved staircase had replaced the old one. 'Purpose,' he read, 'use in advertising brochure for Europaint Division'! Well, that was a nice little fiddle at seven thousand pounds; they'd practically rebuilt the house! He recalled his visit to Salt and the comfortable, lived-in look of the house in Cheyne Walk. Strange that the house hadn't been done up and Salt didn't have another. He turned the paper and immediately knew two things: first that it was not Salt's home which had been done; secondly that the paper had not been signed by Salt – only by the house's owner. And that was almost a year earlier!

Obviously it must all be a mistake. Philips had forgotten to put the paper in front of the Chairman and, intending to, had tucked it into the Chairman's personal file. Well, he'd have to try to straighten that one out quietly. But hang on a minute, he couldn't! Hodder had demanded to know. He'd ring Rae again before he decided.

The phone rang endlessly and he listened with growing concern, wondering where she could be. Had she been going out for more than half an hour or so, she would have telephoned him, surely. He was a little surprised she hadn't telephoned him anyway. Well, damn it, it *was* Sunday. He'd slip home for an hour. He closed the file, put on his coat and went to look for a taxi.

The garage door was open and the gleaming bonnet of the Jaguar suggested she must be back. He pushed his key into the lock, opened the door and stepped back grinning as Elgar rushed out, barking joyously. He watched the dog rush off to attend to a tree, then stepped into the house.

'Rae!'

Curious. There was no answer. The house *felt* empty, too.

'Rae, darling. I'm home!'

Still no answer.

He went into the kitchen, the sitting-room, the dining-room. Ashes were cold and fires unlit. Suddenly he felt afraid. She wasn't in the bedroom, either, or the music room. Cold, now, Keller came downstairs. What on earth could have happened? He stood, indecisively, in the hall, listening to Elgar barking in the stillness. Barking! He hurried out of the door, looking for the dog, realizing the barking came from the garage. And there he found her. Rae lay dead in the front seat of the car, dressed as she had been dressed when he had left her the night before. Her body, when he touched her, was cold, stiffening, bent unnaturally by death into a gracelessness that would have been impossible to her in life.

Keller sat in the car beside her for a long time, holding her dead hand and remembering. There were police to be called, things to be done, he knew. But they could wait until this last communion was over. He saw the radio and switched it on to seek music for them, but the radio was dead and that fact began to tell him what had happened because lights and ignition were on, too. Finally he went into the house and began to telephone.

Alex Hodder arrived about three, Jane Roper with him. Keller stared at them angrily and resentfully, as he had stared at everyone: at the police and the doctors they had brought; the mechanics who had examined the car, the reporter from the local paper who had arrived like a rat up a rope. They'd taken Rae away now, for ever. He knew it was for ever but could not believe it, could not believe that they would play no more, that he wouldn't hear her voice or her music or her laughter; that this ghastly cold numbness he felt had replaced the warmth in which she had loved him.

Hodder said, 'Richard, you mustn't be alone. Come home with me, for tonight at least.'

'No. Thank you, but no. I'd rather be here—' They'd surely understand that.

'All right. It's no use saying anything, I know. But if there's anything at all I can do, I want to do it.'

'Thank you,' Keller said dully. He didn't want Hodder there, or anybody else. He turned and went back into the house as the car started up and drove away. Could it really have happened? Could it be only last night they'd played the Mozart quintet? He searched for the record and put it on, then sank blindly into an armchair as the music swept over him and his grief began to vent itself. Hours later, it seemed, there was a click and a door opened and a woman came in carrying a tray. Keller's heart thudded. 'Rae! Rae?'

But it wasn't. Jane Roper had stayed when Hodder left and had made him some tea. Keller shook his head in wild despair and she put the tray down and went out. It was evening when Elgar began to scratch on the door and Keller's mind came out of the black tunnel into a sad, cold world. He got up, opened the door, comforted the dog and set off to find him some food.

Jane Roper was still in the kitchen. She said very quietly, 'I won't intrude, Richard. But somebody should be here.'

'There's no need.'

'I'll go if you insist. But I'd prefer to stay.'

It no longer seemed to matter. The citadel that had been breached would never be a citadel again. 'Thank you Jane. You're very kind. It's Elgar, here.' He smiled wanly. 'He's hungry, poor old chap.' By the time the police telephoned to tell him how it appeared to have happened, he had regained control.

It had been the car. She'd backed it into the garage and somehow got the gear into first instead of neutral. When she took her foot off the clutch, the forward jerk had broken her neck. 'What we call a whiplash injury, sir,' the policeman said.

'Thank you. I understand.' But he didn't: it was a crazy way to die, in a car, in your own garage, barely moving. 'But for them,' he said savagely, 'she'd still be alive.'

'Who?'

'Hodder, Philips. That pig Scrivener. They killed her, damn them!'

Jane Roper said nothing and it seemed to him like a denial. 'I tell you they did. Grabbing for power, hostile to everybody. That's why I had to go in. That's why she's dead.'

'I see,' Jane said quietly.

'They're bastards. The whole lot of them. They don't give a damn for anything, Jane, except themselves and what they can grab.' He told her about Hyde-Compton's trips, Thornley's wine. Finally he told her about Philips' house.

And she agreed with him. 'You're right, Richard. Bastards is what they are.'

John Gaunt

HE stared at the brown, mahogany door of Steele's flat and listened to the unmistakable guest noises on the other side. Well, it was too bad. Steele must be spoken to and something done quickly.

A woman opened the door; thirtyish, fairly smart, a little loud.

'Mrs. Steele?'

She said, 'That, succinctly, is a blueprint for hell.'

Steele appeared behind her. 'What is?'

'To be your wife, my sweet.'

Steele stared in surprise at Gaunt. 'What on earth?'

'Did you see Salt on *Action This Night*?'

Steele's face narrowed. 'No I didn't, damn it. Tonight?'

Gaunt nodded.

'Come in and tell me about it.' Steele flung the door wide. 'Toss your coat over there.'

Over there was a couch with twenty or so coats on it. Gaunt put his on top. 'What would you like to drink?'

'It doesn't matter. Tonic, something like that.'

'Gin, old boy?'

'No. No thanks.'

Steele said, 'Drink what you like. I'm the last to interfere. Look, old boy, can you stay for a bit? I'd rather not abandon all these people.'

'Certainly.' Gaunt was looking round, recognizing one or two faces.

'It's my Sunday night,' Steele said, leading him forward. 'I always do this. If you can wait, I'll introduce you to one or two people. Here, meet Julian Ferranti, he's not related to all those pound notes but he wishes he were, eh Julian?' Steele laughed loudly. 'And this is Sarah McLennan. She's an artist. Sculptor, actually. Julian's a critic. Also of sculpture.'

'How do you do?' Gaunt said, mentally groaning. She would

want to do a head of him. 'I've seen Miss McLennan's work.' He could remember some large, sexually symbolic lumps of stone at one of the East End galleries.

'Me, too,' Ferranti said. 'Like it?'

Gaunt thought, there's nothing like being put instantly on the spot. He glanced at Sarah McLennan, a dark girl with large eyes behind even larger glasses; the hand which held a cigarette to her lips hadn't moved since he was introduced. She was looking at him impassively. He said, 'I think everybody's tired of external symbolism. Miss McLennan seems to do for her figures rather what Ghil Ray did for sitar composition.' And pick the bones, he thought, out of that!

'You may be right,' Ferranti said. 'I hadn't seen her as quite like the sitar.' He nodded and detached himself. 'You must excuse me.'

'Do you think,' Gaunt said, 'that I offended him?'

'Julian? No.' Sarah McLennan was suddenly staring at him. 'I say! You really have a most remarkable head.'

Gaunt looked at her. Should he let her do the head? He laughed deprecatingly. 'Me? Don't be silly.'

'My dear boy, it's magnificent. The eyes especially.'

He said, 'What's so special about my eyes?'

'God, they're fantastic! Will you sit for me, Mr. – er—?'

'My name is Gaunt.'

'Will you?'

He stared at her, watching the eyes have their old magnetic effect. It was, he thought, like capillary action: he didn't know why it happened, but it always did.

'Such eyes,' she breathed. 'God, if I could catch that!'

'Really?' He decided to make her work. 'I'm not sure I like being spoken of in the third person.'

'Mmm?' She was staring, not listening.

Gaunt said, 'The eyes, the head. As though they're detached.'

'It's a way of speaking—'

He interrupted. 'It's as though I were to meet you, a total stranger, and say, 'What a body. I'd like to sleep with that. You'd slap my face.'

'Possibly. Sit for me?'

'Just you and me in a studio, Miss McLennan, and there won't be much sitting.'

'Has it been done before?'

Gaunt laughed. 'I've lost my virginity, yes. Have you?'

'Not lately,' she said. 'Look, please will you?'

Steele's voice said, 'And this is Irina Pedersen, she's a ballerina.'

Gaunt turned.

'And Eric Ericson. So is he. They're from Denmark. They came with Alan.'

They shook hands, Gaunt with relief, glad to be out of Sarah McLennan's clutches. He switched his attention to Irina Pedersen, watched her glance at him, then meet his eyes in a swift double-take. Her own pupils widened, almost in fear.

He said, 'Miss Pedersen is exquisite,' and she smiled at him. 'So fair and such grace.' He turned to Sarah McLennan. 'You should sculpt her and not me.'

'You are a sculptor?' Irina Pedersen said, 'How wonderful!' But she was looking at Gaunt. A few minutes later when he wandered away, she followed.

'Mr. Gaunt.'

'Hello.' He met her eyes, watched them widen and felt himself wanting her.

She said, 'You are the most beautiful man I have seen.'

'Thank you. But men are not beautiful.'

'You are,' she said simply. 'You are beautiful.'

'I should like to see you dance.'

She nodded. 'I dance for you. Now I dance!'

'Where?'

'You come. I show you how I dance.'

Gaunt said, 'I wish I could, but I must stay.'

'Then take me somewhere.'

He looked around, round the crowded room, the jumbled flat.

'There is a roof,' she said. 'Come to the roof.' He stared at her. Her eyes did not move from his.

When they left the flat, entered the lift and pressed the top floor button, she took his hand and he could feel hers, trembling. At the eighteenth floor they got out. A door was marked 'Roof'.

Gaunt opened the catch and together they climbed the grubby stairs, out through a door at the top, out on to a concreted roof.

She looked at him, her eyes deep in the moonlight. 'See,' she said, 'your skin is so dark and mine so fair.'

He reached for her and she floated to him, then away. 'Irina!'

She placed her finger on her lips. 'Shhh. It is necessary to dance.'

She kicked her shoes off and began to sing softly; something from Giselle, he thought. Then softly, unbelievably lightly, she began to dance and he watched her, thinking that it was like a scene from a film. The silhouetted roofs, the moonlight and the beautiful ballerina dancing to her own music.

'Irina!' Still she floated, pirouetting with cool, precise elegance. 'Irina!' Suddenly she obeyed his tone, turning into his arms, her eyes and her lips seeking his. She whispered, 'Please now.' His arms tightened round her, her thighs, her belly, her breasts were hard against him. He said, consciously filmic, 'This is the world of the sweep. Soot. Ugh!' He shuddered theatrically.

'I am very small and very light. You are strong.' She laughed in her throat. 'I am good at being held.'

Blindly now he reached for her, his hands first working at her clothes, then lifting her. He felt like a giant standing there in the night, holding aloft a world of sensation and pleasure and beauty.

'I help you,' she whispered.

And then there was no way of knowing time or finite things, for he was in a world of movement and raging coloured sweetness with her lips pressing down on his as he stamped his way into paradise.

Steele said, leering, 'What happened to you?'

'Miss Pedersen had lost an earring on the way here,' Gaunt said. 'I helped her find it.'

'Ye-e-es.' Steele's attention had already gone. 'They'll all be gone in a moment.'

When they were, Gaunt described Salt's television appearance and Steele listened with glee. At the end, he said, 'They squabble like rats, don't they!'

'And like rats,' Gaunt said, deliberately, picking up the hyperbole, 'they destroy.'

'What do you mean?'

'That if Toller, or somebody like him gets hold of Euromob, you and I can start looking for jobs.'

'I suppose so,' Steele said. 'He's not a charitable organization.'

'No. Nor is philosophy in management his territory. His only philosophy is more money. That's why I came to you.'

'What the hell can I do, old boy?'

Gaunt said, 'You have a paper.'

'Yes?'

'There must be discreditable things about Toller.'

Steele said, 'What makes you so sure it's Toller.'

'Philips is afraid of him.'

'My God, but this is a dangerous trick to play.'

'You must know people.'

Steele looked at him. 'I do.'

'Then why not find out? You don't need to publish anything.'

Steele's glance showed admiration. It might be and was reluctantly conceded, but it was there. Steele said, 'You think strategically.'

Gaunt grinned. 'Just to some purpose, I hope.'

He left then, walked to the lift and went down. In the lobby a girl rose from a seat as he walked towards the door.

'Irina, it's very late.'

She nodded gravely.

'And I might have been hours.'

She smiled; a small, glittery smile. 'One *pas de seul* and one *pas de deux* do not make a ballet.'

From: John LONGBOTTOM

To M.U.N.P. MANAGEMENT GROUP

Date: SUNDAY

This report is in two sections for reasons which require no explanation.

Longbottom: The unseating of the chairman of Euromob naturally smashed any hope of conducting a calm and effective course. Members have been arriving and departing like trains at a junction and have been giving only part of their attention at the best of times.

Templeton: It has been interesting to observe the behaviour under stress of the various personnel. One can have no inkling of what they are doing, but it has been interesting to observe how they have been doing it. As is well known, excitement emphasizes most behavioural characteristics. *Sinclair* is a notably quiet man, self-contained to an unusual degree. He has clearly been busy at *something* (one cannot know what) and has done whatever it is with clarity and dispatch. A most able man.

Verity: A very fast mind and an opportunist. Began by regarding the course as desperately serious; now is extremely selective about the things to which he gives his attention.

Giesing: Is deeply worried. It may be, though this is purely speculation, that he is concerned the palace revolution may affect him detrimentally. Hardly mixes socially except with Miss Kernon. They seem to be friends. Nothing else implied. Friends.

Steele: Antagonistic; disruptive. Likes to hear about other people's disasters. May be expert journalist, but never a manager in this millenium or the next.

Keyes: Secretive and opportunistic. A good mind but clearly does not care to apply it to management theory. Apparently decisive.

Roper: Suffers the disadvantage that she has her hands full trying to prevent others getting hands full. Balanced and clever. First class potential.

Gaunt: Difficult to fathom. No comment yet.

Keller: A classical type: highly numerate, highly intelligent. Balanced personality with firmly-based convictions.

Farmer: Should not be on the course. So much a leading specialist in one field and so uninterested in others that his presence is disadvantageous.

Fazackerly: The course queen bee. Has worn an arch and superior air for some days.

Kernon: In a sense what applies to Farmer applies to Kernon. Gifted, no doubt, but management selection is her field, not management.

Volans: Out of doors type who is clearly a good manager in his own field – or forest. Feels out of depth here, perhaps partly because he has not been made welcome.

Clare Fazackerly

IT wasn't that the dinner jacket was badly cut; far from it. Nor was it because Verity was uneasy wearing it; in fact he wore it almost too easily, like a bandleader. No, she thought, looking at him as he talked with Scrivener, it was because he was tough and dinner jackets did not suit really tough men. Once at a T.V. party, she had met Burt Lancaster, smooth and charming as a man could be, but wrong in a dinner jacket because there was too much muscle on too much shoulder. Of course, Scrivener was tough, too, but it was a different *kind* of toughness. Scrivener would now be weak as a kitten, physically; it was his mind that was granite, unyielding as Verity's body. At the thought, she felt a shiver across her back; her contact with Verity's body had been too recent, and too moving, for thought of it to be neutral.

She wondered what he would say when he saw Philips. And *Mrs.* Philips! He'd skated round Mrs. Philips, but Clare's instinct told her a bone was buried somewhere beneath that tree. For that matter, it might be amusing to watch the Philipses when they saw Verity. And Scrivener. Mentally she hugged herself: it would be an utterly unnerving evening with a bit of luck. Getting Verity there at all was a brainwave, but when he discovered who else would be there he would be angry.

They had walked together, on Friday afternoon, from the last session, in which two members of Parliament, Labour and Tory, had been discussing the two parties' attitudes to business. They had been as predictable as they were dreary, and as tedious as they were obvious.

Verity had grinned. 'Away, mm?'

'Yes.' Clear and bright.

'Have a happy time.' The big dark face was an unlikely source for schoolboy words. His unlikelihood was, she thought, one of his principal attractions.

'I doubt it.'

197

'Why?'

'Somebody has backworded on my dinner party.'

'Shame.' He drew the word out mockingly.

When they walked along the corridor towards their rooms, he stopped outside his own door and opened it. 'Coming in?'

Clare laughed. 'At this time? Four fifteen!' Then she felt her stomach contract at something in his face.

He said, 'One time's as good as another.'

'Really?' She knew her smile was over tense.

Verity glanced calmly down the deserted corridor then took her wrist. A second later she was in the room. 'Are you going to change before you leave?'

Puzzled, she looked at him. 'Well, yes.'

'Then you'll want a bath.' She watched him stride into the bathroom, heard the water flowing into the tub; knowing what he intended made it impossible. She opened the door and slid out into the corridor. Fortunately nobody was there and she went quickly to her own room, trembling now.

She sat on the bed, hands clasped tightly. How did he know? How did any of them know? What was it in her face that gave her away? She stared at the door, knowing what would happen, hoping she'd find strength. She opened her handbag and found a cigarette, fingers stiff and awkward, then inhaled the smoke gratefully, leaning on its weird strength. Once is enough, she told herself. You must not become his creature. Must not, must not, *must not*! There was a soft knock on the door and Clare's fingers tightened.

'Page, ma'am,' a voice called. His, of course, and she could imagine his face twisted like an actor's as he sought for the right, deceptive timbre.

'Ma'am.' Still she held the silence, her whole body crying out for him, her mind holding it with difficulty.

'I will *not*,' she muttered, 'I will not. I will not give in. Not now. Not at this hour. No . . .'

It was not – and she knew that it was not – a straightforward case of nymphomania. That was an itch that always needed scratching; its sufferers insatiable. She was far from insatiable. No, this was a more complex thing, a curious mixture of capacities and complexes and shifting balances. She knew a great deal about it, but knowing it didn't control it; recognizing the causes didn't help when she felt the need building inside her. If she went to an analyst? But no. She knew too many who had taken up the endless examination of themselves. Besides, how could one go to a man in a white coat and tell him, admit to a brutal and ugly compulsion? The trouble was, she was afraid that it was getting worse. A year or two ago the incident with Verity would never have happened . . .

The trouble really was that it had always been too easy to excel. She had excelled as a child, comfortably ahead of all her school contemporaries. Older, with examinations to pass, she faced them with the easy confidence that a first-class mind and physical beauty can give. Examiners, impressed by written papers, were charmed in oral examinations. She ran, swam and played golf with a perfect co-ordination that allowed her to compete with men, and win. In her accountancy examinations she was the national silver medallist; when she was admitted as a solicitor she received personal letters of commendation from the Solicitor-General and the President of the Law Society.

Everything easy: her husband rich, her children attractive. And then, suddenly, the unbelievable business of being whisked into television. 'We think you'd be good at this panel game.' And then fame . . . recognition everywhere; shop assistants running to serve; a world of glitter that complemented, but didn't destroy, the world she knew. She moved through life behind an armour plate of self-confidence. Then the chink had been made.

She'd been at home, that day. It was before the children left play school to go to school properly and she became free and joined Euromob. She had been irritable because the housekeeper was away and things went wrong. The new dish washer failed to work and she telephoned the shop angrily then realized the wall plug was still switched off.

She answered the doorbell and saw a man standing on the step. There was a van in the drive.

'I'm from James's Electrical.'

'Oh. Well it's all right. I found out what was wrong.'

'Better have a look, all the same.'

199

'No. It's all right.' An edge to her voice. 'It's working.'

Stubbornly he said, 'Better to be sure.'

'It was just the switch.'

'Look, ma'am,' he said. 'I sold you the machine. I want it to work right.'

Something about him made her angry and she flared. 'Go away, you stupid man!'

She began to close the door quickly, but he put his foot in the angle.

'Take that foot away!'

He said, 'Do you always carry on like this?' He looked like a great, patient horse.

'Take your great foot out of my door,' she said furiously, 'and your fat head away from my house.'

He just stood there. 'I'm waiting.'

'Can't you see, you great fool, that there's no need for you?' She slammed the door and the sill must have hurt his ankle. He looked at her angrily. 'In two seconds you've said I was stupid, a fool, and dim.'

'Well, aren't you!'

He said, 'Apologize.'

She stared at him. How dare he? How dare this lout say that to her!

'To a *thing* like you?' She injected all the contempt she could muster into the question.

'You want your bottom tanning, missis.'

She laughed at him.

He said, 'You drag me here, then you try to shut the door in my face. And you're shocking rude. Apologize!'

'Is it likely?' Who did this ox think he was?

'I don't have to take it. Not from you or anyone else. I'm my own master. Apologize.'

Her temper had evaporated by now, leaving her a little ashamed, but amused. 'Master?'

'Somebody should,' he said. 'Somebody really should.'

She looked at him, smiling. 'Should what, little man?'

'Tan your arse for you.' He turned away.

'That,' she said, intending it as a final word, 'would require a very remarkable man.'

He turned slowly. 'You reckon I couldn't?'

Unbelievably Clare felt her heart thump, a lurch in her stomach, the old response to challenge. 'No,' she said, 'I don't think you could.'

'Well, I'm damned!'

'You're like all men. You're a blusterer. You simply would not have the nerve.'

He laughed. 'You think?'

'I'm sure.'

His mouth had opened in a playful grin. Suddenly he lunged for her with his arm and she saw what was happening and closed the door on it, imprisoning him. Then his body hit the door and she was hurled back into the hall, staggering, grabbing at the wall for support. He loomed in the doorway. 'Right,' he said. He took a step forward. 'You're like all women. First thing you'll do is scream for help.'

She looked at him, at the cheap, scruffy suit and the dirty cuffs, the heavy, oily working shoes. He was slow in mind and slow in body. One swift, strategically placed kick would do, and she knew enough judo anyway to take him on.

'Don't worry,' she said. 'I can cope by myself.'

'Oh, yes?'

'Easily.'

'Aren't we cocky, then?' He came forward standing upright, hands by his sides. He extended one arm, and edged forward. Clare chose her moment, waiting until his foot moved, then grabbed at the wrist and swung him into a hammer lock.

She laughed. 'You see.'

'Bloody clever,' he said. He began to straighten his arm and as she grasped his wrist she could feel the power of his muscles. Suddenly her hands moved. She looked at them in disbelief; he was moving them against the lever hold by sheer strength. She looked down at his bent back, aware suddenly of its breadth. Then her hands gave again. She couldn't hold him. Well, she wasn't going to lose; it would have to be his thigh, the sciatic nerve. She lifted her knee ready to strike and as she did so his arm jerked irresistably and his hips pivoted and she was on the floor. She slithered away from him, quickly, then realized she was in the corner.

'That's right,' he said. 'You're cornered.' He was laughing at her, contemptuously in control. She should never have started it, but having done so, she must finish it. Her right foot flashed at his groin, but he moved in an easy reflex and she missed, hurling herself off balance. In a second her wrist had been grasped and she was dragged to the foot of the stairs, where he sat down and pulled her across his knees. There was a sharp sting as his hand smacked at her and she yelped. He said, 'I told you I'd tan it and I will.'

She struggled, beating with her fists at his leg, but his left hand held her down while his right administered the spanking. It was painful, now, but she was damned if she'd beg him to stop; instead she changed her tactics, searching the muscular calf for the pressure points. When she found one and dug in her fingers he yelped with pain. 'Right, you minx,' he said. 'More you fight the more you'll get.' The next blow was harder, the sting sharper; her skirt must have ridden up. He smacked again; his hand was like a bat and her skin smarted. 'You swine,' she gasped furiously as he laughed, then smacked her again.

'I'm enjoying this,' he said.

She stared at the carpet as her head hung down and she realized that she could still reach, still damage. But he saw her stretching hand.

'Right,' he said. 'You asked for it, love.'

She felt the elastic moving across her hips and buttocks and then a tremendous smack on her skin.

He said, 'I can see my fingerprints.'

'All right. You've had your fun. That was a sexual assault.'

'If I did that, you'd know, too!'

'I'm a lawyer,' she said. 'And I'm telling you—' Smack!

'That's a smack on the behind,' he said. 'Lawyer or no lawyer.' His hand remained on her, still for a moment. Then it moved and Clare gasped. 'That's what you were talking about.' She lay across his knee, picturing herself lying there, bottom in the air while this oaf— He did it again and she felt her stomach contract.

'You see the difference?' Smack! 'Answer!'

'Yes, I see.' Could that be *her* voice?

'Right, apologize.'

'I'm sorry.' She seemed unable to move, her voice appeared to be coming from somebody else.

He released her. 'You can get up.' And when she didn't, another smack that was lighter. 'Come on. You can get up.'

Then a pause when she didn't and at the end of the pause his hands came to her again and his voice, infinitely knowing, said, 'I see . . .'

Since then there had been others; how many she preferred not to think, but they had had in common that they were big men, men with an air of strength and ruthlessness to match their physical power. Verity was merely the latest.

She walked across and he said, 'Nah then, Clare.' She smiled. 'Another drink?' Scrivener shook his head but Verity nodded. She was on her way to get it when the bell rang and she put the glass down instead.

'Good evening, Mr. Philips. You must be Mrs. Philips. How d'you do. I'm so glad. . . .' Clare was in the room, a couple of minutes later, when they came in. She kept her eyes on Marjorie Philips, waiting for recognition to strike. Meanwhile, she talked: 'I'm so sorry about Julian. He was in late from a meeting in the City, poor man, and he's still dressing. He sends his apologies.'

Philips murmured something and his wife smiled. Clare said, 'Now I think you'll know everybody. Sir Kenelm Scrivener, of course.'

Scrivener turned, 'Evening Philips, Mrs. Philips.'

Clare said, 'And Mr. Verity. Old friends, I believe, as well as colleagues.'

Marjorie Philips paled noticeably and Clare smiled to herself. One way and another, it could be quite an evening.

Sir Kenelm Scrivener

HE had eaten sparingly and still felt uncomfortably bloated thanks to that blasted beef in pastry thing he'd had at lunch. He'd eaten too much of it, forgetting he was out to dinner. Why, for God's sake, did people have to invite guests on Sundays, these days! Damn nuisance! He glowered round the room, his gaze stopping at Philips.

'Things any better now Salt's gone?'

'Bit soon to feel the difference.'

Scrivener stared at him. Something about Philips' damn provincial smugness irritated him. 'Need to be quick. Look at last night.'

'Do you think anybody'd take him up?'

Clare's husband, Julian Porteous said, 'It will depend on the property, eh Scrivener?'

He nodded. 'Toller may bid.'

Philips said, 'You represent a large holding. Would you sell?'

'For a profit, always. To avoid a loss, always. To cut a loss, always.'

'And Euromob?'

'We've already lost on our investment. I can't see the price gaining at the moment.'

'So you'd sell?'

Scrivener looked down at his cigar, lifted it, drew. He said, 'Salt's a damn fool.'

'Why is that?'

Scrivener looked up. Verity had asked the question. He said, 'Because that kind of thing won't do.'

'In the City?'

He nodded.

Verity said, 'Still, I'll bet he enjoyed it.'

'Hardly the point,' Porteous said. 'The criterion is not enjoyment.'

'All right, what is it?'

Scrivener drew on the cigar. 'What's right.'

'For whom?'

'Don't be naïve, Mr. Verity.'

Verity was persistent. 'You tell me, Mr. Porteous.'

Julian said, 'Stability.'

'The status quo?'

Nobody bothered to answer.

After a moment, Verity said, 'I understand money-is-power. I understand money-is-holy. What I don't understand is money-is-right.'

Porteous said, 'Is Hodder going to reply?'

'I believe he'll be on *Evening Hour* tomorrow,' Philips said. 'He's been invited, anyway.'

'Then he'd better go on. Look an even bigger damn fool if he doesn't.'

'Damn fool?' Verity said.

Scrivener sipped his brandy. What a tedious man this was, this boor from the back streets. What did he matter, anyway? 'Damn fool,' he said.

'Why?'

'Oh, for God's sake! Because that's how he was made.'

'He was also made chairman.'

'You'll learn that nothing's final.'

'I see.'

'Even you.'

He glowered at Verity, seeing the sudden access of anger rigorously controlled. He looked at the others: Philips quiet; his wife looking as though she might cry; Clare's eyes agleam, Porteous impassive.

Verity sat back in his seat, clearly raging inside, anxious to fight but waiting another chance.

Porteous said, 'The question, Philips, is whether you can make it.'

'Me as me, or me as Euromob?' Philips looked calm but his wife's eyes were frightened.

'Either. Or both.'

Philips said, 'The problem is to make Euromob work. Right?'

'The problem,' Porteous said, 'is whether good money goes after bad.'

'If you mean, will there be a profit tomorrow, the answer's no.'

'Better if Toller did break it,' Scrivener said. 'Shake some money loose.'

Philips said, 'We also employ a lot of people.'

'Not my concern.'

'As a director?'

'Nominally, then.'

'But only that?'

'What do you expect, Mr. Philips?' Porteous asked. 'We're businessmen, not benevolent institutions.'

Verity said, 'Funny how insurance companies never say so. They're always United and Friendly and Provident.'

'Emotive words,' Clare said, 'in the nineteenth century. Nothing dragged out the widow's mite like virtues with a capital letter.'

'It is necessary, of course,' Porteous said, 'to genuflect occasionally. Managing directors of large companies must at least appear to be avuncular.'

Scrivener grunted. 'In a very limited way.' Even a glance showed Philips' tension. He was the cold type, with everything bottled up; a prime coronary candidate. The other one was harder, whatever his name . . . Verity. He was hard. How good was he? Scrivener had an impression that the naïveté lay thin. He let his glance come up slowly and saw Verity looking across the room, his expression soft. Scrivener followed the look to Marjorie Philips. There was more in this than a meeting of childhood friends, he thought. Then he realized suddenly that Clare was watching them too.

'What would you do, Mr. Verity?' Scrivener watched the face turn towards him, black eyes hard.

'About Euromob?' And when Scrivener nodded. 'It would be wrong of me to say.'

'Why?'

'Because Mr. Philips is my boss.'

Philips said, 'I'd be interested anyway. Let's hear.'

'Right,' Verity said. 'I'd do it very simply. I'd start by deciding what made profit and what made loss. Then I'd look at assets and try to decide potential. Then I'd scrap the present loss-makers and the assets we can't develop.'

'Woman's Press?' Clare said.

'Tell me its situation.'

'Makes a small profit,' Philips said.

'Rising or falling?'

'Slight fall.'

'Future?'

'Debatable.'

Verity said, 'It sounds the kind of thing that bleeds you white while you wait to make a bit of money.'

'So?'

'I'd need to be a bit clearer. But I think I'd get shot of it.'

'And lose money?' Scrivener said. 'It cost us seven millions.'

Verity looked back at him. 'That's lost already.'

All right my beauty, Scrivener thought, but would you *do* it? Really do it? Or is this talk?

Verity said, 'I told you. Now you tell me something. What would you do about our transport strike?'

Scrivener said, 'That's a day-to-day management problem.'

'Mr. Porteous?'

'I agree.'

'Come on,' Verity said. 'We're talking in the air. What would you do?'

He was alight inside; Scrivener could see that.

'You've beaten them?'

'I believe so. Not certain, yet.'

'Then I should do what you did.'

Verity said, 'Aye. Maybe you would.'

Scrivener wondered what Verity *had* done; how the strike *had* been pushed aside. He said, 'You just talked.'

A hard smile flowered on Verity's jaw. 'Aye.'

'And they listened?'

'Aye.'

'Why?'

'I had some persuasive arguments.'

207

Porteous said, 'I suspect you might be a hard liner, Mr. Verity.'

Verity nodded. 'And I'm not the only one in this room.'

'I seem to be in a minority of one,' Philips said softly.

Scrivener smiled. 'Not if you're sensible.'

He looked across the back of the Rolls to where Philips sat, and said, 'It will happen.'

'All right.' Philips sat pale and impassive against the soft upholstery.

Philips could not, Scrivener knew, bring himself to believe it. Scrivener said, 'Your problem isn't the job. You'll get the chair before long. But what do you do *then*?'

Philips said, 'Work.'

'Not enough. There's too much fat. You need to be a butcher.'

'Like Verity?'

'He's crude, but he's right.'

Philips said, 'I'm thinking of him as my deputy.'

'That's sense. You'll let him swing the hatchet.'

'For a while.'

Scrivener felt a cough of amusement building in his chest. He let it out. 'Then reap the harvest. He's a bull. Careful where he works. Keep control.'

'If you'll drop me here,' Philips said.

As the car drew away, Scrivener looked back at Philips standing on the kerb, waiting until his car pulled up with Verity and Philips' wife in it. He wondered idly whether Verity was having an affair with her. Unlikely, he decided. Far more likely that they'd had one in the long ago. He'd been a bit wrong about Verity earlier in the evening. Under the boorishness there was a lot of shrewdness; he had built a fence round Philips quickly enough. Wrong class, of course, not even lower middle; Verity came from the back streets, which never made for acceptance. Well, that was his bad luck.

He was almost back at Belgrave Gate when he remembered the books. Damn! He'd have to go and get them or Dorothy would play hell. He'd missed her birthday morning before and it wasn't worth it. Scrivener leaned forward and tapped the glass screen.

'Yes, sir?'

'Euromob House.'

'Yes, sir.' The partition slid into place again and the Rolls glided smoothly back into the one-way system.

Scrivener used his key and rode up in the directors' lift, then trod heavily across the central reception area towards his own office. The parcel was on the sideboard and he picked it up, put the light out and stepped out again and went to the bathroom at the end of the corridor. He was coming back when he heard the noise. Scrivener stopped and listened. Everything was quiet. Buildings like this were full of noises; perhaps it was something inconsequential. But then it came again: a filing cabinet drawer closing in Keller's office. Was Keller here? Surely not. Not after that business of his wife's death. Then who? Not a burglar; the directors' suite was elaborately secure. He stepped forward and opened the door. A girl stood behind Keller's desk, a file open in front of her. It was that public relations woman, Miss Roper. As she became aware of him, her head jerked up in fear and surprise. She looked guilty as hell, Scrivener thought, guilty as hell.

'What are you doing here?'

'I – I was looking for something,' she said.

'This is not your office. It is eleven p.m. You have no business in this suite or this office.'

She said defiantly, 'I have a key issued by the chairman.'

'That file?'

She picked it up and thrust it into a drawer, then closed it quickly.

Scrivener wondered whose file it was. He said, 'You are on enclosed premises at night without permission. That is a felony. I shall report this to the police.'

'Mr. Keller asked me to fetch something,' she said. 'I stayed with him today, Sir Kenelm. You know about—'

'I know,' Scrivener said. 'I shall telephone Keller. Unless you are here with his express permission on a particular errand, I shall call the police.' He walked to the grey outside phone on Keller's desk, picked it up.

'No.'

Scrivener looked at her inquiringly. She was very pale, breathing quickly. 'Well?'

'It was something, well – personal, Sir Kenelm.'

'You were searching the office of the company secretary. I shall call the police. This is very serious.'

'No.'

'You do not appear to realize—'

She said, 'Please don't call the police, Sir Kenelm.'

Phone in hand, he looked at her, then began to dial.

'Please!'

Something in her voice made Scrivener look up. He could see the fear in her face.

'Please?' It was softer, a rising inflection. Scrivener's eyes flicked over her.

'Don't, Sir Kenelm, please. I'll—'

'Well?' But Scrivener knew now. He felt the pressure at his temples.

'I'll—'

'What?'

Her eyes were very wide. Suddenly they dropped and when she spoke, the word was a whisper. 'Anything.'

It was a long time – by God it was a long time! – since he'd had a girl like this! Scrivener looked at her, letting his eyes move from her face to her breasts, to her waist, to her hips, to her legs and back again. She blushed furiously, but remained still.

Deliberately, Scrivener dialled the second digit, then the third. 'Don't. Please!' She came quickly round the desk and stood in front of him and Scrivener hesitated, feeling need building inside his head. He put his finger to the dial again and she clutched at his hand, holding on to it with taut fingers.

He let it remain there and looked at her. 'Tell me why I should not call them?'

'Because—' She stopped, biting her lip. 'Because I—' She looked down at his hand. Then, slowly, she raised it and placed it on her breast and, as Scrivener's fingers moved over her, she said, 'I will do anything.'

He tried to smile, but his cheeks seemed set. His voice hushed as he said, 'I shall be difficult to please.'

Her hands squeezed his hand against her. 'I shall try, I promise.'

Sweating, Scrivener replaced the telephone. 'In my office,' he said. 'We can lock the door.' He looked at her with satisfaction. 'And take our time.'

Fullerton Ironside-Keyes

VINER, the man from Cloudair, said, 'Anything to help, Mr. Keyes. It's a pleasure.'

'Unfortunately I had to come unexpectedly. There wasn't time for bank clearance and it's the weekend, anyway.'

'Don't worry. Here's five hundred bucks. You can use the yellow Pontiac convertible over there.'

'It's very kind of you.'

'What the hell, it's only money! You'll be on the noon flight Sunday, right?'

Keyes laughed. 'Always assuming there's a seat.'

They shook hands and he slung his grip into the Pontiac, climbed in and switched on. A moment later he was bowling out of Vancouver International Airport at Sea Island, heading south for Bellingham, Mount Vernon and Everett to Seattle.

The time was a little after midnight – strange to think he'd landed in Vancouver at the same time he'd taken off from London eight hours earlier. Strange, too, to think what had happened in London! He tried to keep his swarming mind steady as the night highway unfolded in front of him, to concentrate on driving, on staying awake. There would be time to think when he got to bed. At the immigration post at the frontier, the guard asked only whether he intended staying.

'I want to see an old friend in Seattle,' Keyes said.

'How long will you be staying, sir?'

'I'm flying back to London on Sunday.'

'Have a good visit.'

He was away. He held the Pontiac down with difficulty to a steady sixty, his foot anxious to apply more pressure. The glittering lights passed in clusters, then the night was dark again until the next cluster. At two-fifteen he stopped at a motel outside Seattle, checked in, showered and went to bed. He ached for sleep; his eyes felt as though they were full of gravel, his limbs heavy, his stomach disembodied. But his mind couldn't wait. *What the hell was it all about?*

'Mr. Keyes?' The man had been quietly dressed, unostentatiously waiting in the foyer of the Princess Hotel.

'Yes.'

The card had come out then: *G. W. Zander.*

'Yes, Mr. Zander?' He had been puzzled by the expression on the other's face, a look somewhere between bland and confident. 'Have we met?'

'Not until now. I should like five minutes' conversation with you, Mr. Keyes.'

'I'm sorry. I'm flying in a few hours. I'm in rather a hurry.'

Zander said, 'I haven't a lot of time either. It is important.'

'I have no need for further insurance, Mr. Zander.'

Now Zander smiled. 'Nor I. I'm selling nothing, Mr. Keyes. I just might be buying.'

'Buying what?'

'You. Sit down, Mr. Keyes. For five minutes. No pressure. After that I go. Right?'

'All right.' Keyes sat obediently on one of the couches.

Zander said, 'My organization seeks and employs executives of the highest class.'

'You're a body-snatcher?'

'Not in the sense you mean. We don't serve others. Just ourselves.'

'I see.'

'No. You don't Mr. Keyes. But I shall explain. The organization for which I work has expanded very quickly and is continuing to do so. It needs able men.'

'So?'

'Your name has been given to us.'

'By whom?'

Zander shook his head. 'Our secret.'

Keyes waited and the silence lengthened. For a moment he was puzzled, then he understood: it was a stress trick. How would he behave? He stared at the wallpaper and slowly began to count the repeats of the pattern. Finally Zander said, 'What is your salary?'

'My secret.'

'If you are recruited, it will be doubled.'

Keyes frowned. 'Whatever it is?'

Zander's silence somehow said yes.

Zander said, 'How long have you run your company?'

'Four years.'

'And turnover has . . .?'

'Increased fourteen times.'

Zander said, 'That's good, but too long.'

'I know.'

'Will travel expand?'

Keyes smiled. 'What would prevent it?'

'And profit?'

'Inevitably.'

'What, Mr. Keyes, would be the next three areas to open up? In your judgment?'

Keyes laughed. 'Hell, Hull and Halifax.'

'Okay. You *do* know?'

'I know four with certainty. After that less surely. Other factors arise.'

'We're going into travel.'

'Who is we?'

'I wouldn't be surprised,' Zander said, 'if it's you and me. Or you and us. Will you meet my boss?'

'Certainly. When?'

'Next week, early.' Zander rose and held out his hand. 'Five minutes I said, five minutes it was. Safe trip! I'll be in touch.'

And then he was gone.

Keyes stared at the ceiling of his Seattle motel room, running over and over the words that had been drumming in his mind since they were spoken: 'If you are recruited, it will be doubled'! Who on earth could make promises like that? There was something American about Zander, but he wasn't American; rather he was international and that could mean anything or anybody from oil companies to shipping to petrochemicals – anything. The only other clue was Zander's phrase 'Going into travel', which meant they weren't in it already.

He told himself over and over that there was no point in thinking about it, but it was difficult to haul his mind back to the purpose of the trip; finally, however, he believed himself and dropped into sleep.

He came awake, slowly, at seven, got out of bed quickly, showered, dressed and had a quick cup of breakfast coffee, then he left. By seven thirty he was knocking on the door.

'Mrs. Volans?'

She was a dark, handsome woman, housecoated, suspicious, a chain taut across the gap of the partly-open door. 'Yes?'

'I'm Fuller Keyes. From London.'

'Oh yes?' Her hand held the neck of the housecoat.

'I have met Lincoln in London, Mrs. Volans. I thought I'd call. I realize it's very early, but—'

She looked at him doubtfully. Almost, he thought, fearfully.

She said, 'Linc's away.'

'Ah. I'm Euromob, too.'

'I suppose you'd better come in.' A trace of hospitality asserted itself. She was quite an attractive woman, Keyes thought. But not for him. 'You had breakfast?'

'Coffee. You know.'

'Yeah, I know. Better feed you, I guess.'

'You're very kind.'

Keyes was conscious of picking his way through a verbal minefield. Information had to be elicited without her clamming-up. 'It's lovely here,' he said.

'We like it.'

'It's curious how attitudes differ,' Keyes said carefully. 'To me *this* is marvellous, but Linc says it's too big and too busy.'

'He would. How 'bout cornflakes, ham, eggs shirred?'

'Wonderful.'

Mayjane Volans said, 'He's okay?'

'Fine.'

'When did you see him?'

'Yesterday. Yesterday morning,' Keyes amended carefully.

'Gee, it's incredible.'

'Yes.' She came back into the room and began laying a table. Upstairs there were the thumps of a family rising. He'd have to be quick.

Keyes said, 'He's making a bid for an island.' She had a cup and saucer in her hand and it rattled; she used the other hand to steady it.

'Yeah. Well, it's nice.' There was strain in her voice and she followed up quickly, 'What do you do, Mr. Keyes?'

Keyes watched her carefully as he said: 'Land.' Her hands were very still.

'Like ours?' she said with tinny brightness.

She was frightened. Not of him, but of what he knew. 'Like *ours*,' he said. 'Like Whistler Island. Important assets.'

She said, 'Oh,' too casually, the lie clear on her face.

Keyes probed further. 'These are tricky games to play, Mrs. Volans.'

'I don't know what you mean, Mr. Keyes.'

'No?' He was on the right lines. 'It's potentially dangerous. Do you see?'

'Dangerous?'

'People don't buy islands for fun, Mrs. Volans. Certainly not islands like Whistler. I have already given orders for a survey.'

She sat down heavily, her face in her hands. Then she looked up. 'Don't bother.'

'Oh?'

'It's manganese.'

Something happened inside Keyes' chest. Manganese! He lit a cigarette, inhaled, then spoke as calmly as he could. 'Confirmed?'

'Gee, yeah. Mountain of it.'

'By whom?'

'Minerologist. Friend of my brother's,' she looked dully at him. 'What happens now? You fire Linc?'

'Well it was rather foolish,' Keyes said. 'But I don't know. After all, he . . .' he let the words hang. 'I'll do my best. There'll be documents, of course.'

'Yeah. Geological report. Assay samples. The lot.'

Keyes said, 'Thank you. I'll give you a receipt naturally. Perhaps you'll be happier if I don't stay for breakfast. Oh, and one other thing.

'Yes.'

'Please do not inform Lincoln of our conversation until I speak to him myself.'

'Why not?'

'Not, at all events, if I am to be able to help,' Keyes said.

He was in Vancouver by noon, had a sea food lunch, then drove out to Sea Island. Viner said, 'That was quick.'

Keyes smiled at him. 'We English,' he said, 'do not allow grass to grow.'

'See your buddy?'

'He was away,' Keyes said.

'Shame.'

'One of those things. Is there a flight before tomorrow's?'

Viner frowned. 'Not one of ours. There's Air Canada, of course, but that's dough.'

'That reminds me. Here's most of yours back.'

'Gee, thanks. Look, there's Two Ocean Air Stream. They have a flight tonight to Manchester.'

'That would be useful.'

'Know them?'

'By name. We don't charter from them.'

Viner grinned ruefully. 'Now's a bad time to start. C'mon. I'll take you over . . .'

At ten p.m. Martin of Two Ocean walked across the tarmac with Keyes. 'I'm not trying to steal you away from Cloudair, Mr. Keyes. We oughta build our own, not steal other people's.'

Keyes grinned. 'But?'

'But I'll make you a suggestion. I'm told Britain has two million fishermen.'

'Yes.'

'Canada has the finest fishing in the world: salmon, trout, steelhead. The finest bar none.'

'It's a good suggestion, Mr. Martin.'

217

'Fly 'em here on Two Ocean airplanes.' Martin grinned. 'The jets with the friendly hostesses.'

'That's how to fill an aeroplane,' Keyes said.

Martin frowned. 'It's not full enough tonight. At least you'll have a comfortable ride.'

They shook hands. 'Thanks.'

'Bread upon the waters, Mr. Keyes. Think kindly of us. And let me know if the staff get drunk and throw things.'

'I'll do that.'

As the Seat Belts light went off, the girl said, 'Mr. Keyes?'

'Yes?' He looked up at her. She was fair, a well-brushed girl, smiling pleasantly.

'I'm Marilyn Westcott and I'm executive hostess aboard this flight. May I get you a drink?'

'Thank you. Scotch.'

'On the rocks?'

He nodded. She returned in a moment with the glass on a little tray. He said, 'No uniform?'

Marilyn Westcott smiled. 'I'm only half stewardess. The other half is public relations. If you'd care for a fresh steak of grilled Cohoe salmon, Mr. Keyes, we've got some aboard that was only caught today.'

'I'd care for that very much.' She smiled and he watched her walk off down the gangway, the slim, youthful flanks swaying inside the dark dress. 'I care for that very much indeed,' he repeated softly to himself, sipping his Scotch.

The jet landed briefly at Edmonton, for no purpose that he could see. They took on fuel, but a take-off and landing would make that necessary anyway, and after that they took off again, heading at first across the lonely immensity of the Canadian plains, then north towards the Pole. Keyes always enjoyed this moment of a long flight: the gradual dimming of the lights as people settled to sleep after dinner, the silence except for the muted whistle of the great engines out there in the icy, lethal cold that began a foot away from his seat. He reached up and clipped out his own light; now there were only two others, both up front, and as he looked, one went out. Keyes lit a cigarette and stared out at the moonlit cloudscape below. Beneath it were mountains and rivers and glaciers and lakes; bears and wolves;

great forests and plains of wheat. He could never quite detach himself from the magic of flight.

'Pretty, isn't it?'

Keyes turned. Marilyn Westcott was standing in the aisle, looking past him. He nodded. 'It seems a pity to cross it all without any of it making . . . oh, memories.'

'I know just what you mean,' she said. 'There's so much. And it goes by. Would you like a blanket, sir?'

'No thanks.' Keyes smiled. 'I'll have a brandy, though.'

'Very good.' '

'Will you join me?'

'I'd like that.'

She was back a few moments later with the drinks. Keyes sniffed. 'That's good brandy.'

'It's from the special locker. Croizet.'

'Thank you.' He raised his glass a fraction in acknowledgment, then sipped. 'Marvellous. Tell me, what does an executive hostess do?'

'Well-l-ll,' she said. 'In flight, we take over if there's a problem with a stewardess, or an awkward passenger. We also try to look after people who are particularly important to Two Ocean.'

'I see.'

'Like you,' she said.

Keyes said, 'But I'm not.'

'You could be, so Mr. Martin says. You charter planes, don't you, Mr. Keyes.'

'Endlessly,' he grinned.

She grinned back. 'You see. Maybe you'll charter us.'

Keyes pulled out his case. 'Cigarette?'

'Thank you.'

He struck his lighter and held it for her and she steadied his hand with cool fingers. 'It's nice.'

'What?'

She sighed. 'A drink and a cigarette like this. In the quiet.'

'Yes it is.' He finished the brandy, savouring its warm smoothness on the lining of his mouth. Up front, a hand lifted and the last pool of light vanished. 'Now everybody's asleep.'

219

'Mmmm.' She sounded deeply content and he turned to look at her.

'I doubt if you're allowed to sleep.'

'No.' She smiled. 'But I can snuggle.'

Keyes raised his arm and lowered it round her shoulders. 'Then snuggle up to me.'

'I do believe I will, sir.' She leaned across to rest her head on his shoulder and giggled.

'What the matter?'

'These charter seats.'

'I'll raise the arm.' It pivoted easily upward on the hinge. 'That's better.' His hand was on her shoulder and under its pressure she came easily towards him, her body soft and softly-perfumed.

'Chanel?'

'*Joi*,' she said.

He moved closer, inhaling the fragrance more deeply. 'It suits you.' His arm tightened round her and somehow she moved with it, her body turning towards him, her face near and up-tilted. He kissed her gently, and afterwards took her cigarette and stubbed it out with his own then kissed her again, more passionately this time and when it was over her eyes were wider but she was smiling. He reached for her as she pulled away, but she put her finger to her lips and rose to reach up into the rack over their heads. Keyes saw her body arch taut above him for a moment, then she straightened and laughed softly.

'I'd better tuck you in, sir.' She sat beside him and reached across to cover him with the blanket and Keyes, her breast against him, felt his body responding. He took the other corner of the blanket from her, draped it across her, then kissed her hard. She murmured softly against him as his hands moved over her and Keyes, aware of the people sleeping nearby, was almost unbearably excited.

'Why,' he said savagely, 'do we have to be in this damned aeroplane?'

She laughed quietly. 'And on these seats!'

'You're mean with tourists.'

'You're not a tourist.'

'I'm a V.I.P.,' Keyes muttered. 'I for Impossible. I for Impatient.' She was looking at him, her eyes dark, and her body was warm and smooth to his eager, seeking touch.

Keyes' laugh was sudden and harsh, half way between frustration and amusement.

'What's the matter?'

'I've got a complaint about the service on this damned airline.'

'I'm sorry to hear that, sir. Anything I can do? I'm the executive hostess. Is it the food?'

'No.'

'The liquor, sir?'

'Not the liquor.'

'You're warm enough!'

'Too warm, if anything.'

'But you aren't satisfied.'

'No,' he said. 'I'm bloody well not.'

'That's a pity,' she said, 'and you a V.I.P. I shall have to do *something.*'

'It's the seats. They're too small.'

'Please use as many as you like, sir.' Her eyes sparkled.

Keyes grinned. They moved awkwardly and she kept the blanket over them. 'It's still a little cramped.'

'Well you see, sir, we don't get a lot of call for this kind of thing.' Her lips lifted to kiss him. 'I can't imagine why.'

'It would fill a lot of seats.'

She giggled beneath him. 'We could stack people in layers.'

Keyes laughed. 'It's a pleasure to fly with you Miss Westcott.'

Her arms tightened round him. 'I hope you'll fly again, sir. Many times. Many, many, many, many times.'

From Manchester he flew to London, bolt upright, B.E.A., thinking hard. The knowledge and the facts he had were of the greatest possible commercial value. The mere existence of a vast discovery of manganese on Euromob territory was the most critical new factor in Euromob history. If the preliminary survey was correct, and it seemed the man who made it was good, then the strike was very big and very valuable. The

221

question was, what should he do with the information? He thought of Zander with his mysterious approach and promises of doubled salary, of Hodder and Philips, either or both of whom would give their teeth for the information. So would every stock market speculator in London! Christ, it would be easy enough: just buy in Euromob shares, which were, in any case, as depressed as hell, then let the manganese announcement come out. That was the sure way, certainly. But with shares at sixteen shillings, covering a vast range of assets, you'd have to have a hell of a holding to make a big killing. It was a problem. A large and difficult problem. And in the meantime it was complicated by the fact that another man knew. He'd have to talk to Volans.

It was seventy-thirty p.m. when Keyes arrived back at the Princess Hotel. He felt weary, purged, untriumphant. The flatness was something to do with fifteen thousand miles of travel, but it was also to do with his dislike of uncertainty, his dislike of situations in which the next move was fraught.

Keyes turned the shower on, mixed the water until it was as hot as he could bear it, and stood in the spray until he felt as though he had been boiled. Then he turned it to cold and waited until he shivered. Drying himself, he picked up the telephone and asked for Volans. He heard the operator ringing.

'I'm sorry, sir. There's no reply from his room.'

'Page him, then.'

'Yes, Mr. Keyes. Should he telephone you?'

'Please.'

He dried himself, lit a cigarette and began to dress. Then the phone rang. Keyes said, 'Mr. Volans. We must talk.'

'Why, sure,' Volans said.

'I'll see you in the bar – the American bar – in five minutes.

Judy Kernon

'WE ought to turn Catholic, you and I,' she said.

'Why?'

'Well, we know the value of confession.'

Giesing said, 'It worries me. Since I tell you – now I can bear, you know.'

She nodded, smiling a little. 'I know. What's more, I'm glad.'

'No, Judy. It is wrong. I feel easy. I should not feel easy.'

'I don't think you feel easy, Reinhard. I think you feel a little less bad.'

'I do not have that right.'

She shook her head. 'I think time will reconcile you a bit.'

Giesing said, 'Have you ever killed, Judy?'

'Yes.' She smiled at his look of surprise, then the smile vanished as she remembered. 'A chicken.'

'A chicken!'

She said soberly, 'It's just the same. You put out the light that can't be lit again.'

'I have killed seven times. Six men. And the woman.'

'The men were soldiers?'

'Ja. Soldiers.'

'And you feel less badly about them?'

Giesing said, 'I was a soldier; they were soldiers, too. But when you see a man die, something happens to you.'

'I believe you.'

'No. Unless you have done this thing, you cannot understand.'

'I didn't say I understood. I said I believed you.'

They were sitting in the common-room just after midnight, having spent the evening watching television.

Giesing said, 'I am sorry. It is a bore. Bore is right?'

'You're not a bore,' she said. 'All the same, I'm going to bed.'

They turned as the door opened and Verity strode in. 'Aha!' he said briskly. 'The guilty lovers sprang apart.'

Judy grinned at him. 'If I were going to spring this far I'd have to do it in two parts with a rest in between.'

'Go on, he's blushing!'

Giesing was on his feet, indignant. 'I assure you . . .'

Verity held up a placating hand. 'Crude English humour, mein herr. A drink to make up?'

'No. I—'

'Brandy, then,' Verity said. 'And for you, madam?'

Judy groaned. 'If you're gonna be bright and pressing like this, Tommy, just a teeny drop.'

'Of brandy, naturally?'

'Of brandy, naturally.'

'When I came in here,' Verity said, 'it was a bit like going into the Egyptian room at the British Museum. Lively and gay. Everybody dancing.'

Judy glanced at Giesing and said on impulse, 'We were talking about death.'

'Judy!' Giesing looked at her warningly.

'Did you kill anybody, Tommy?'

'What the hell's that—!' he said in sudden anger. Then he controlled himself. 'In the war, you mean? Yes. Yes I did.'

'I take it you feel it still.'

'It's not a thing you forget, love!' He seemed to remember the drink in his hand and took a swallow.

'That's what Reinhard says.'

She saw Verity glance at the German. She said, 'Here we are. Jew, Kraut and – what are you, Tommy?'

He grinned, the machinery of anger hidden now. 'I was a Pom to the Australians, a Limey to the Yanks and a Tyke to everybody else.'

'And now we're all together in this great and glorious enterprise called Euromob,' Judy said. 'Marching onward and upward together to the bright plains beyond. I wonder if you two fought.'

'No,' Giesing said. 'I was on the Russian front.'

'Poor sod!'

'Hein?'

224

'Never mind.'

'You, Tommy. Where were you?'

'Middle East, Italy, Normandy. The usual.'

She looked at him, wondering if she dared ask. What the hell! she thought. He can't kill me. 'Did you ever do anything *really* foul. Did you?'

She felt the black eyes on her like a pair of cannon while the lips smiled sociably beneath. Then Verity said, 'Women always mean sex when they say a thing like that. And I'll tell you – there's been nowt like me in the Middle East since the Thousand and One Nights.'

Judy said, 'I didn't mean sex.'

Again the eyes, staring into her. 'What the hell,' Verity said, 'makes you ask?'

'Bear with me.'

'*Ho* did, eh?' He gestured towards Giesing.

'Yes,' she said. She heard Giesing groan and kept her eyes on Verity.

'Why should I tell you? Even if I had?'

'You did?'

'I'm not saying that.'

'But you did?'

She watched Verity fumble for cigarettes. At length he said, 'You're a shrewd bugger, Judy.'

She waited.

Verity sat down. His voice, when he spoke, was curiously quiet. 'It's funny,' he said. 'Nobody knows but me. You always want to tell, but it's too big and too nasty to own up. You know?'

'I'm learning.'

'What did *he* do? What was it, Reinhard?'

Judy said, 'You first.'

'Me?' Verity drew on the cigarette, throughtfully exhaled and looked hard at her through the smoke. 'All right,' he said. 'It was very simple. There were about twenty of 'em in a dugout. I'd just got a mortar in position when they started climbing out to surrender.' He held up his hand. 'I had the bomb in this hand and the tail was actually in the tube. I actually saw 'em with their hands in the air.' He shrugged.

Judy looked at him. Like Giesing a few nights earlier, he was staring at the carpet, shoulders hunched. 'Why?' She said it as gently as she could but there was no way of being gentle.

His head jerked up. 'How the hell do I know why? I just let the bloody thing go, that's all.'

'Tell me.'

Verity said, 'They were just standing, most of 'em, with their hands in the air. It killed the lot.'

'They were soldiers,' Giesing said.

'They were boys! It was 1945, just this side of the Rhine.'

Judy said, 'Reinhard here betrayed a Jewish woman. He thinks she'd have been killed.'

The two men were looking at one another. Judy rose silently, took their glasses and filled them.

'If I said it was a long time ago?'

Giesing spread his hands. 'It's in the head. In the mind.'

'How much do you think about it?'

'As little as I can,' Verity said. 'But it bobs up sometimes and you can't help it.'

'Which was worse?' She felt them both looking at her with a kind of dull resentment that she should insist on raking and re-raking over these old coals. 'No, tell me. Which was worse?'

'Me. Mine,' Giesing said. 'It was betrayal. Nothing is worse than that.'

'Tom?'

'Mine was murder.'

Judy said softly. 'At least you're not the only one now. Neither of you. You both know somebody else did something foul.'

'I don't understand you,' Verity said. 'I don't understand you at all.'

'I'm a believer in peace and goodwill, that's all,' Judy said evenly. 'The Jewish mother syndrome. Now I'm going to bed.'

Giesing rose. 'Good night, Judy.'

'You started this. You can stay,' Verity said. 'I won't sleep tonight and I don't suppose he will. You're not walking off to bed.'

She looked at their faces and sat down again.

'You want to talk, we'll talk,' she said. 'But first let's order some coffee.'

It was three-thirty when Giesing told them. The conversation had ranged from the siege of Leningrad to the bogdown at Cassino, from the rebuilding of Germany and the expansion of the U.S. to Britain's continuing problems.

Judy said, 'Sure you're smart. You think of everything, you British, but you always handle it badly. Penicillin, jets, hovercraft.'

'Only because governments give it away to those bloody pirates over the water,' Verity said. 'Given a similar discovery by a private company, we'd cope very nicely.'

Giesing smiled. 'Are you sure?'

'No. But we would.'

'Look at this company now,' Giesing said. 'It's big, diffuse. It does not know where it goes. It has fighting at the top. Could this company do it?'

Verity smiled. 'There are some very efficient areas in Euromob. Sinclair's lot, for one.'

'Agree,' Giesing said. 'You see . . .' Judy felt him appraising them. He ended lamely, 'I don't know.'

She got up and filled his cup. 'Come on, Reinhard.'

Almost lightly, he said, 'We have such a thing.'

'Y'what?'

'Yes, Tommy. We have.'

'Go on.'

'I am not sure.' He hesitated, then seemed to decide suddenly. 'The copying machine. We have a new principle.'

Verity said, 'Xerox, Addressograph,' he was counting on his fingers, 'Copycat. Now even I.B.M. have moved in.'

'We have a new principle.'

'Go on.'

'It is cheaper. It is better.'

'Photographic? Electrostatic?'

Giesing shook his head. 'Magnetic. It also has means of shaping, composing.'

Judy said, 'Cost?'

'About half.'

227

'And just what,' Verity asked quietly, 'are you going to do with that little lot?'

'It belongs to Euromob. It was discovered in the laboratory of the wallpaper printing plant in Germany.'

'Do they know? The management?'

'Not yet.'

'Why not?'

Giesing said, 'It can save Euromob. Turn it from an expensive problem to a major world company. I am not sure the right people are in control.'

'And you'll keep it till they are?' Judy stared at him.

'I will.'

She asked, 'Who are the right people?'

Giesing said, 'Until tonight I did not know. But why not us?'

Judy watched the two men frowning at one another, each trying to peer into the other's mind.

'How far on are you?'

'The prototype works.'

'Patents?'

'Prepared. Ready to file world-wide.'

Verity said, 'They'd never let us. Never.'

Judy felt herself smiling and got up. 'You never know, boys. Good night.'

She telephoned Philips at seven-fifteen, feeling baggy-eyed after three hours' sleep. Philips sounded brisk as ever. She thought resentfully that he was always bright-eyed and bushy-tailed, however early in the morning.

'Yes, Judy.'

'Verity. Thomas Verity.'

'Yes?' She heard a cup rattle.

Judy said, 'I think he's a genuine tiger. At first I thought he was a straightforward old standard-type leopard but he's bigger than that.'

'I'm interested to hear you say so, Judy. You think he has positive virtues?'

'Oh, he's positive all right. He's tough and he's decisive. We had a long session last night, he and Giesing and I.'

'I was talking to him last night, too,' Philips said.

228

'Oh, you were? You agree?'

Philips said, 'Any faults?' Oh you crafty old bastard, Judy thought. All questions, no answers.

'Plenty.'

'Go on.'

'Well, he's guilt-ridden.'

'What about?'

'Who knows,' Judy said. 'But he is. And, pursuing the cat image, I suspect him of being a bit on the tomcat side.'

'He's not alone.'

'You don't have to tell me,' Judy said.

'In particular, or in general?'

'Suspicion only.'

'And the suspect?'

Judy laughed. 'That's slander. Are you taping this conversation?'

'Naturally, Judy. I'm having my usual breakfast of bacon and two scrambled tapes. Who? Is it somebody on the course?'

'Well,' Judy hesitated. 'Yes. Yes, it is.'

'It has to be Clare Faz,' Philips said. 'That's interesting.' I wonder why?'

'Maybe he's big, strong and masterful.'

'What other faults?'

'Precious few scruples.'

'All right. But tough?'

'Very,' Judy said. 'By the way . . .' She waited for him to ask. He didn't. She picked it up again: '. . . Giesing is a good dark horse.'

'Oh? He's German.'

'We're called Euromob,' she said. 'Will you appoint Verity?'

Philips said, 'First things first. In this case, cold scrambled eggs. Thank you, Judy.'

She was listening with half an ear as John Longbottom said, 'The business that welcomes change employs people who make a profession of change.' And a busy-bodying, know-it-all collection of schmucks they are, she thought. Then the door opened and Templeton tiptoed melodramatically in, robbing poor Longbottom of what attention his audience was granting.

'It seems,' Longbottom said, 'That one or two amongst us are summoned to the presence of the most high.'

Templeton grinned. 'Sorry to disturb. Mr. Philips wants Mr. Verity, Mr. Giesing and Miss Roper. Apparently it's urgent.'

The three rose, shrugging, and tiptoed out. Longbottom said, resignedly, 'We'll go on for a bit, but we'll stop if it's grinding to a halt. The theme was to be managerial planning of change. If you just let change hit you it'll scupper you. It's necessary to plan.'

A thought struck Judy and she glanced at Clare Faz. The familiar profile was calm and composed. Have I, Judy thought, been deceived by my own beady observation, or by her carefully projected image? Clare Faz was well-pressed, well-groomed, serenely intelligent and, if the impression she gave on the telly was anything to go by, irreproachably decent. Odd that they'd exchanged hardly a word throughout the course, but on further thought, not so odd: Faz usually went to and from lectures with Verity.

Today there was no Verity. Judy carefully strolled out beside her.

'Clare, how would you like to forget all these standing up cupsa tea and have a nice formal afternoon tea in the lounge?'

Clare Fazackerly smiled. 'But how extraordinary! Yes, I would like that very much. China.'

'With nice crisp linen and hot water jugs!'

Clare poured and waited. 'To your taste?'

Judy sipped. 'Perfect. Funny that we haven't talked very much. All the men, I suppose. One must circulate.'

Clare said, 'Did you find out?'

'What?'

'Which is the sexiest.'

Judy grinned. 'There are ten men and we're only at the eighth day. Gaunt strikes me as pretty giddap'n'go. I think poor Mike Farmer's a bit obsessive.'

'He undresses one with every glance,' Clare shuddered.

'Creepy as that?'

'Awful!'

'I think he's a touch frustrated,' Judy said. 'Doesn't know where to start.'

'Or to stop.' Clare sipped at her tea, beautifully at ease.

Nothing was to be given away, that was clear. There would be no girlish gossip; Clare was playing the tea table game with a crisp sweetness that was totally impenetrable. At last they got up and went up together in the lift. Why is it, Judy asked herself, that you want to know so badly? Pure, feminine curiosity? Or this instinct of yours?

They strolled together along the fourteenth floor corridor and with a sudden, brutal inspiration Judy stopped outside Verity's door. 'Well, thanks for the tea.'

She was rewarded. A dull, red flush spread across Clare's face and she stared at Judy with hate. 'No,' she said. 'My room's along here.'

'Of course,' Judy said. 'Stupid of me.'

Evening Hour began at nine: a rough-house of news and features that had suddenly emerged from the flat plain of the television scene. The principle was attack: tough interviewing of a personal kind. Why, Mrs. Mother-of-four, don't you take the Pill? Why, Mr. Singer, do you wear a wig? The usual game, Judy thought, of hitting where people are weak. She chose to watch in her own room, preferring to avoid the inevitably crowded, speculative common room. Hodder was showing a lot of guts appearing on this show to answer Salt. For the moment he counted as one of the weak, and if he handled himself badly, they'd tear him apart.

The show's signature tune came on, a few bars of *In a Monastery Garden*, sneeringly played on violin and muted brass, and the wait began. There was a footballer unlucky enough to have been filmed committing a spectacularly nasty foul; a Woman's Liberation protester who'd stripped and burned her bra at the Conservative Women's annual conference. Then came the break when a brand-new pop group played its first and only record – *Evening Hour* found five new pop groups each week – and then it was Hodder, faced by the trendy-old face of Kevin Milk.

Milk introduced Hodder waspishly: 'The long-time Crown Prince who succeeded, the Sparrow who killed Cock Robin, the man who put Salt on Salt's tail.'

Hodder sat through it politely, then said, 'I would like to make it clear that I have nothing but respect and regard for Hugh Salt.'

Milk raised an eyebrow. 'But *he* feels differently, Mr. Hodder. He said,' – Milk looked at the clipboard on his knee – 'he said you were the sort of friend he could afford to lose.'

'Nonetheless, I regret the loss.'

'But not the sacking, eh? You're still glad you sacked him.'

'Sir Hugh was voted out of office by the board of the company. No one man did it.'

Milk said, 'He didn't seem to think so.'

'No? Then I am sorry. The problem is that Euromob is a very big company, a very large and complex organization—'

'Making small and unsatisfactory profits?'

'Yes,' Hodder said. 'We have to change that.'

'Sir Hugh Salt says it won't work. That Euromob is nothing but a big mistake, a monster he should never have put together.'

'Naturally, I don't agree.'

'He says the best thing would be a take-over, then for the whole thing to be split up into workable pieces.'

'I know what he says,' Hodder said. 'I believe Euromob can work and work well. If—'

Milk interrupted spitefully. 'If?' The word was drawn-out, up-accented, disbelieving.

'If some really intelligent decisions are taken quickly. Euromob has vast resources, both of fixed assets and goodwill. If you think of the vast packaging organization, the paper-making. We own vast tracks of the finest timberland in the world, both in Scandinavia and Canada. The value of these properties alone will rise inevitably.'

'But somebody might sack you, Mr. Hodder.'

'Not *somebody*. The board can. At any time.'

Milk said, 'What area do you think has the greatest growth potential? Paper, packaging, travel, publishing. Which of all these things . . .?'

'Publishing has least. For the rest, there is no discernible limit to the potential for expansion.'

'So anybody who made a bid would get a bargain?'

'I would have to leave that to his judgment.'

Milk smiled. 'I'm surprised you haven't mentioned the latest mechanical wonder.'

'Which is?' Hodder asked.

'Really, you don't know?'

'Not from that description.'

Milk muttered something. The words were inaudible.

'I beg your pardon.'

'Your new copying machine,' Milk said with sarcastic clarity. The producer punched Hodder's face up quickly and the chairman's puzzled frown was clearly visible in millions of homes.

'You bastard!' Judy said softly to herself. She could feel the tears stinging in her eyes.

Milk said softly. 'You have *heard* of this revolutionary new principle, Mr. Hodder?'

'Well . . . naturally.'

'Developed in the Euromob paper laboratory in Germany?'

'Of course. But it's early days . . .'

'Early days, Mr. Hodder? I'd say it's too late. Especially when it was developed in *Germany*. Do you know the principle, Mr. Hodder?'

Judy couldn't bear to look. Hodder had clearly never heard of the machine and had lied. Now he was to be ripped to pieces. What a bastard Verity was! And why had he done it? For Philips' sake?

She heard Hodder say, 'Do you know the name of your floor manager, Mr. Milk?'

'We're talking about Euromob,' Milk said.

'Answer my question.'

'All right.' Milk grinned. 'Floor manager stand up.'

'I didn't ask if you'd recognize him if you saw him. I asked his name.'

'Who's interviewing whom, Mr. Hodder?'

Hodder said, 'You're as bad as I am, but with less excuse. We have eighty thousand employees in twenty-six countries.

Naturally I don't know everything. But Euromob *is* sound and will succeed. That's a promise!'

Milk said, 'Alex Hodder, new chairman of the giant Euromob corporation, fighting for his business life. And now we turn . . .'

There was a knock on Judy's door and when she opened it, Giesing stood there, ashen-faced. He said, 'It was you or Verity. Which?'

'For God's sake,' she said. 'Do you think *I'd* betray *you*?'

Gerard Garvin Steele

EVERY editor, every journalist worth his salt, has a contacts book. It is likely to contain the home telephone numbers of convicted felons, fashion writers, film stars, illicit bookmakers, crooked motor dealers, doctors who will say anything for a guinea, girls who will do anything for ten, libel lawyers, insurance salesmen, public relations operators, male and female, by the dozen. Steele looked under C for City. The established City Editors were no use to him, but he needed a man with their kind of knowledge, their contacts. The name of Alasdair McFarquhar loomed up at him. McFarquhar was in P.R. now. Would he talk?

Steele reached for the phone. 'Alasdair? I wondered how the fleshpots were treating you.'

'Buy Euromob, Gerard.'

'There'll be a bid then?'

'Somebody's got to do something. If there isn't a bid Hodder will have to hand out money in self-defence. But be quick. The market will move upward.'

Steele said, 'Your words are wondrous silky. I haven't heard you talk for far too long.'

'Which is why you're ringing?'

'Right. I want to feed you on oysters and things.'

'For lunch? I'm a bit—'

Steele said, 'So am I. Dinner? Dinner tonight.'

'Urgent?'

'I need a fix. A few wise words.'

'All right.'

Steele cut the evening's course dinner and met McFarquhar in an overpriced Italian basement in Soho. Over the second large whisky, he said, 'Let us now, as the lesson-readers say, praise famous men.'

'In particular?'

'Their beginnings.'

235

'Ah. You're after dirt.'

'Interesting · to hear you say that,' Steele said. 'There's always dirt at the beginning?'

'There's always dirt. Where were you looking?'

'The financial operators.'

McFarquhar laughed. 'Are you numerate, Gerard?'

'I can count to a hundred in guineas.

'Delighted to hear it. But you need to be a high-grade accountant even to distinguish what is dirt.'

'How very disappointing.'

'We're talking about highly technical operations like bond-washing and dividend stripping.'

'It's the first hundred thousand that's so fascinating.'

'Yes, indeed,' McFarquhar said. 'Where *do* they get it?'

'Let's order and you can tell me.'

'You promised oysters, Gerard.'

Steele grinned. 'Settle for spaghetti and a hundred and twenty.'

Later with the Frascati and the Valpolicella gone and the Stock '84 going, McFarquhar said, 'Toller!'

'Toller.'

'He's a dangerous chap, Gerard.'

'In what way?'

'Every way.'

'How did he begin?'

'Well, you know the story. He undercut everybody for that first two miles of experimental motorway, the by-pass to Leeds.'

Steele said, 'It's in the cuttings. I need better than that.'

'Not from me, old boy. I like money, but.'

'Okay, Alasdair.'

'I'll give you one piece of assistance and a few words of warning. The warning is first – Toller is always prepared to be rough. Really rough.'

'Violence?'

'Can take many forms. Now the help. You know Leicester Deptford?'

Steele laughed and nodded.

'He knows more about Toller than ... well, let's leave it there.'

Deptford's daughter answered the telephone. She always did, always ready to say she was sorry but Daddy wasn't there while in the background Daddy took steps to make the statement true.

'Pru, it's Gerard Garvin Steele.'

'Oh, hello.'

'Is your father there?'

She sounded worried. Steele knew she was trying to work out whether he was, for the moment, a friend – or a threat to the Deptfords' precariously balanced lives.

'Hello?'

'Leicester, I want information.'

'All right.'

'Can you come to the flat?'

'Now?'

'Now.'

Leicester Deptford said nothing for a moment. Then he said, 'All right. Good-bye.' He arrived three hours later, in the early morning, by which time Steele was in bed and had to get out, angrily.

'You took your time.'

'Did I?' Deptford held his left hand clasped in his right like a nervous and rather smarmy parson. He offered no explanation.

Steele glared at him. Deptford was waiting patiently, an expression of polite inquiry on his moon face.

'Have a drink?'

'Thanks. Yes. Er, thanks.' Steele handed him a large glass of whisky which Deptford held without sipping.'

'I'm trying to get at some City background.'

'Mmm.'

'You know, Leicester,' Steele said carefully. 'Everybody's always portraying the City as a mass of tradition, propriety and confidence when you and I know—'

'Terrible people,' Deptford said. 'Awful. They'll do anything, you know. Anything.'

'Things you wouldn't?' Steele couldn't resist it – Deptford's

237

total amorality was as well-known as his ingenuity and his charm.

'Oh, come now Gerard. I wouldn't – I mean. Honestly, some of it's really terrible. Every perversion known to man, honestly.'

Steele nodded. If he'd been asking about architects or the compilers of dictionaries, they would have been guilty. Deptford loved to ascribe disgraceful traits, preferably to people of extreme propriety. In a moment Steele could begin to ask for detail.

'Your drink, Leicester.'

'Oh yes.' Deptford looked at it as though he'd forgotten all about it, then swallowed a good two ounces of whisky at once.

'It's the beginnings I'm interested in.'

'That's when they're worst you know. I mean, some of them actually have murdered their grannies for the first few thousand.'

'Ah. Have they?'

'Terrible men. There was a Lord Mayor . . .' Deptford went into a brief and slanderous anecdote that was certainly fictional.

Steele tutted. 'I heard about Toller the other day. He's a bit of a . . .'

'Ray Toller? Oh, what a man!' Deptford beamed. 'Honestly, he's *so* evil. I mean, really evil.'

'Go on. You know him?'

'He was my sergeant, Gerard. During the war. Ran a chain of brothels all over Southern Italy till the Mafia stopped him.' Steele listened, lips pursed. The problem with Deptford was to separate truth from fiction.

'Brothels?'

'Honestly. He had about ten at one time. Made a fortune. Gave it all to a Lebanese woman.'

'So he was broke?'

'Hadn't a cent.'

'What about the motorway?'

Deptford looked surprised. 'You know about that, surely!'

'Only that he undercut everybody.'

'But you know how?'

'No.'

'It was stolen Government machinery. No, honestly. Stolen. Every nut and bolt.'

'But how?'

'Well it was all spare. At an airfield. He just went and took it away, painted it yellow and went to work. By the time the Ministry had decided to auction it as surplus, the road was built.'

'But they traced it to him, surely?'

'How?'

Steele said, 'The machinery for one thing.'

Deptford shook his head in wonder at this naïveté. 'He hadn't got the machinery.'

'Then? But how did he . . . I mean, where was it?'

'Buried. In the road. It's all there, about a million pounds' worth, buried under the motorway. In a couple of pits, under about ten feet of concrete.'

Steele whistled. 'What happened?'

'Nothing happened, naturally. The Ministry hushed up the fact of the missing equipment for obvious reasons. Our hero was in business. The road cost a million a mile. He put six hundred thousand in his pocket.'

'How do you know?'

'Me?' Deptford looked astonished. 'Because he told me.'

'Why would he do that?'

'Because he's vain, you see. He likes to boast. And after all, there's a limit to the people he can tell.'

Steele said, 'I'd limit it even further, Leicester. What made him tell you?'

Deptford smiled. 'You don't understand, do you Gerard?'

'Well, he knows you talk.'

'Ah. But he also knows nobody believes me. At least, not all the time.'

'So?'

'It's a way of building the image. People like to pass on stories, true or untrue. He's doing his boasting by proxy, you see.'

'I see.'

'Yes. And he's a terrible pervert. Little boys, you know. And black girls from the Sudan. He has them flown in.'

'Has he?' Deptford was inventing again. The information had stopped flowing.

'Oh, yes. The airlines do it for him, you know. Some terrible people in the airlines.'

Steele grinned. 'I understand. They're worse in America.'

'Yes, but nobody here is half as bad as the Russians. Do you know what they do in Kazakhstan?'

Steele said, 'When you appear before your Maker on the final day of judgment, Leicester, and he says, "is this true about the machines?" what will you say?'

'On my honour.'

'If the alternative is a thousand years in hell?'

'Oh, I'd choose hell, old boy. I couldn't bear not to see you for a thousand years.'

Feeling foolish, Steele persisted. 'But it's true?'

Deptford's moon face turned to him innocently.

'Printing true?'

'Yes?'

'Be careful of Roy Toller,' Deptford said. 'Night Gerard.'

'Why?'

Deptford was already half out of the door.

'Because he means it.'

Hartney said, 'I'm not going to raise that in the House.'

'But it's true!'

'So what? It was a long time ago. He's probably protected by the Statute of Limitations. Think of the public racket if we dug up two miles of motorway. Half the country would sieze solid.'

'You don't care?'

'Of course I don't. He's a useful chap, Toller. Busy. One of the people who makes change.'

'And he gives money,' Steele asked, 'to party funds?'

Hartney said, 'To all three parties, I should think, if he's any sense. And he has.'

'So society is helpless where the Tollers of this world are concerned?'

240

'Society is never helpless. Society evolves, it creates and destroys.' He smiled. 'Ask not who is the Toller of the Bell!'

'Very neat.' Steele said.

'But *you* are helpless, Gerard. Against Toller, anyway. Paper against property? Ideas against money?'

'Ideas have been known to win in the end.'

'Perhaps. But the end is a long way away, and all the means are his.'

Lincoln Volans

KEYES said, 'The problem is the bid. Surely you see that?'

'Yeah, okay.' Volans looked at the elegant man in the armchair. To think he'd always regarded the English as effete. 'But the problem is also to hang on to what we got.'

'It's always difficult.'

'That's okay for you, Keyes. But I've lost half of it already.'

'To me?'

'Yeah. I'm not figuring on losing all the rest.'

'No, my dear chap,' Keyes said. 'But under the existing conventions, once the bid is put in, nothing major can be done.'

'It's not major. One little island.'

'One little island of manganese?' Keyes smiled. 'It's very major indeed. But English attitudes are curious and the bid regulations reflect them.'

'But surely business goes on?'

'Naturally. But property is a word with mystical significance. Salt intoned it on television. They wouldn't dare dispose of one square yard.'

'So we do what?'

'We need money. We need power.'

Volans said, 'Great. We got neither.'

'So we must acquire an ally. Or allies, but preferably just one.'

Volans could see Whistler Island whistling goodbye. He said, 'Does it occur to you, Keyes, that we don't have to do anything, not one goddam thing, right this minute? We can sit on this information until the time is right – until it's better than it is now, anyway.'

Keyes shook his head. 'It is high time both of us were rich.'

'I'm prepared to be patient.'

'Perhaps,' Keyes said. 'I, however, am not. I have been poor long enough. I wish to be rich.' He smiled. 'Forthwith.'

Volans was conscious of dull, red anger mounting inside him against this smooth pirate who had not merely stepped in to demand half, which was bad enough, but had now taken control of the whole thing. 'We'll lose the lot.'

'Don't be so doom-laden. If we're quick and skilful, we can do this.'

Volans said, 'That stuff's been there for a couple of thousand million years. Nobody's gonna find it next week. Wait a bit.'

He watched Keyes shake his beautifully-barbered head. 'I have decided that among the directors of Euromob there is one who can command enough private money and enough sheer pressure within the corporation to pull this off. We'll go to him.'

'Who?'

'Scrivener.'

'He's the lawyer, right?'

'That's him, Volans. He represents money– very big money indeed. That's why he's there.'

'Represents?'

'Lord Mingulay, the petrol man. He's got six per cent, whatever it is, of Euromob. Scrivener's on the board to watch it.'

'How much is Mingulay worth?'

Keyes shrugged. 'God knows. Rumour suggests three hundred million or more. Now do you see.'

Volans stared at him miserably. 'I see this guy taking our pants. High-priced lawyers exist to screw people like me.'

'Nonetheless,' Keyes said, 'We will see him.'

Scrivener had not risen. He sat behind his desk, fat hands clasped on top, and looked truculent. Volans thought the man's complexion looked like raw liver and that he had never seen a man he liked or trusted less.

'Your father,' Scrivener said, 'was a damn fool.'

'I know,' Keyes said, 'and I agree.'

Volans stared. Nobody, but nobody, would say that to me about my old man.

'The question,' Scrivener said, 'is whether you are a damn

243

fool chip off the damn fool block. I hear not, but I don't know.'

Keyes said, 'We have information. There is literally a very large fortune in it.'

'So make it.'

'It's difficult.'

Scrivener nodded. 'You have no idea, Keyes, how many times I have had this conversation. All you need is money.'

'No.'

'Then what?'

'Money and influence.'

Volans watched Scrivener's elaborate sigh. 'They are the same thing.'

'Perhaps,' Keyes said. 'But they will perform separate functions in this.'

'All right, tell me.'

Keyes glanced at Volans. 'There are difficulties.'

'I'm not stupid. This man's presence tells me it's in Canada or the U.S. He's a timber expert, therefore it's timber. What's so difficult?' Scrivener's eyes swung at Volans. 'This is your idea?'

'Yes.'

'So why is Keyes here?'

Volans said evenly, 'Because he muscled in on me.'

'Good for him. His father'd never have done that.'

Keyes said, 'Leave this to me. We're talking about minerals, Sir Kenelm.'

'What minerals?'

'I'm sorry.'

Scrivener said, more softly, 'I have to know. You see that?'

'Of course. It is a valuable mineral.'

'Quantity?'

'Large.'

'How large?'

'Perhaps hundreds of millions.'

'Whose land?'

'There,' Keyes said, 'is the rub.'

244

Scrivener laid his hands flat on the table, looked at them for a moment, then said, 'What makes you think Euromob would sell to me?'

'I didn't say it *was* Euromob.'

'You didn't have to. You realize, do you, that what you suggest is highly unethical, even criminal?'

'I'm aware that nobody *gives* fortunes away. They have to be taken.'

Scrivener said, 'How much money?'

'Less than a million pounds.'

'How much less?'

'That,' Keyes said, 'is where the question of influence comes in.'

'Let me ask you something, Keyes; and you, Volans: let me ask you how you imagine you'll keep control of me?'

Keyes said, 'We'll have to trust you.'

'Not very good.' There was something approaching a smile on Scrivener's face. No, not a smile, a sneer, Volans thought. First he was robbed by Keyes and now this fat cat was going to take over. He said, 'Look, Scrivener, I don't trust you.'

'Ah. Don't you? So what do you propose?'

Volans said, 'Just don't double-cross us, that's all.'

Scrivener laughed. 'And how will you stop me? I mean, look what you have told me already. That there's a valuable mineral deposit on the corporation's territory in North America. That's the whole story, details apart. No doubt a search would find it.'

Volans nodded. 'Eventually, maybe.' He looked at Scrivener, fat and secure behind the desk, powerful and contemptuous. What would worry Scrivener? And then he knew.

Volans said, 'How's your health?'

'What?'

'Your health. You look to me like a hypertension case. How's your heart?'

'My health is no concern of yours.'

'Didn't say it was,' Volans said. 'I just reckon you're a man who'd die easy.'

'If you're threatening me—'

Volans interrupted. 'I'll just make you a promise. If you can push this through you're in for a one third share. If you double-cross me, you'll die. You hear?'

Keyes said angrily, 'Don't be stupid, Volans.' Volans turned and saw Keyes' face, saw that the threat had scared him. Keyes was unscrupulous, but his kind never actually involved themselves in the rough physical stuff.

'Listen to me, Keyes,' Volans said, 'there's enough for all of us and I want mine. If you double-cross me, I'll kill you, too.'

'The wild man from the West!' Scrivener's tone was jovial. 'Well, I suppose it's a basis for trust. Where is it?'

Volans hated each word as he said it, hated the necessity to pass on part of this glittering prize to a man who had done nothing to earn it. He told Scrivener about Whistler Island, its latitude and longitude, about the survey and the assay. Scrivener sat still, nodding occasionally.

In the end he said, 'And the metal?'

'Manganese. It's an ore called pyrolusite.'

Scrivener smiled. 'I shall attend the course dinner tonight. Perhaps I shall have news.'

Jane Roper

SHE listened, sympathizing, as Hodder spoke. The chairman was puzzled, and clearly felt badly let down and was entitled to. But more than that was in the air; there was a knife out; Hodder was the knife's intended target and Hodder knew it. He said, 'You are the people who knew. Mr. Giesing told Miss Kernon. Together they told Mr. Verity, who conveyed the information immediately to Mr. Philips. Mr. Philips told Miss Roper because as head of public relations she would have to deal with the press. The question is who told Milk and *Evening Hour*?

They stood there, she thought, like naughty children confronting an angry but baffled headmaster. Hodder went on, 'I'm not suggesting for a moment that it was done deliberately. A word slipped or was overheard and I would like you all to be absolutely sure that nothing like it happens again. I did not enjoy last night's interview. Nor am I enjoying these—' Hodder gestured towards the daily papers.

Philips looked bland and assured. He was frowning but it was a token frown, displayed because concern was expected rather than because it was felt. Philips must be everybody's prime candidate, including Hodder's. The fact that he was unworried meant that he felt very strong.

'All right,' Hodder continued. 'I know, now, how far along we are. Mr. Giesing deserves the strongest praise for the development of the copier. I intend that it shall do this corporation nothing but good, after this nasty start. Now, if you'll stay, Jane and Mr. Giesing, we'll work on a statement. See if we can undo some of the damage.' The pointed exclusion of Philips was lost on neither Philips nor anybody else. Hodder, at least, Jane thought, had no doubts about the culprit. When they had gone, he smiled at her, but it was a strained smile. 'All right, Jane, how do we go about it?'

What, she wondered, would he say if he knew she had

telephoned Milk's secretary, anonymously, half an hour before the programme? Goodbye, that's what he'd say. Whatever her reasons.

'I think,' Jane said, 'that what we must try to do is emphasize the autonomy of the separate divisions. If we say that the results of the German research and development were to be presented to the next board meeting and that they had, until now, been kept within the German operation for security reasons, we have a case.'

'*Do* you, Jane?'

She said, 'We'll work on it. We could say that the information had been passed to Milk by a dissatisfied employee.'

'Probably true at that,' Hodder said. 'But don't.'

Giesing said, 'I believe that I know who—'

'Proof?'

'Not proof, no.'

'Then forget it. Innuendo and half-truth are terrible hazards in this kind of situation.'

Jane said, 'I had a little idea. I can possibly sell it to somebody on one of the newspapers.'

'Go on.'

'Well, it's a round-up story,' Jane said. 'They telephone the chairmen of half a dozen companies: ask a shipowner if he knows where a particular ship is; they ask a tyre manufacturer how many car tyres he made yesterday; they ask an insurance chief if he knows the cost of £1,000 with-profits life policy for a fit man of forty.'

Hodder said, 'On the grounds that none of them will know?'

'Yes.'

'You'll destroy confidence in British industry,' Hodder said. 'No, let it die its own death apart from that first bit about security. Okay?'

Jane nodded. Hodder seemed determined to play it straight – or as straight as possible.

'Right,' Hodder said. 'And thanks again, Mr. Giesing. I promise that you will be well rewarded. And all the members of the development team.'

'Thank you,' Giesing said.

'Now go back to your course.'

They spent the afternoon examining the fortunes of a sewing machine company in a Harvard Business School case study. The company – thinly disguised by the name Wizard, but unmistakeably Singer – had had a rough time for many years as market after market in Russia, China, Eastern Europe, closed down. Jane was sure it was fascinating, but working up interest was not easy. She felt sorry for Longbottom and Templeton who were trying to struggle through the course on the periphery of the interest of its members. So she listened, her attention wandering constantly, but forcing it back from time to time to the lecture.

In front and to her left, Steele sat. He was noticeably less bouncy today and she wondered why. Hodder's neat slap-down the other day? Possibly. Whatever it was, Steele sat brooding, not even pretending interest. Sinclair, too, was mentally elsewhere, calculating on a scrap pad. Keyes and Volans, an unlikely pairing, sat beside one another and she noticed the odd way each turned, from time to time, to stare at the other. Strange how things had moved in a few short days.

At five o'clock she went into the underground car park, picked up her TR5 and headed across town through Holborn for Hampstead. Richard Keller was faced with the ordeal of the funeral tomorrow. If somebody (meaning me, she thought) didn't make him eat, he wouldn't eat, and he was near enough already to the point of collapse. She flicked the Triumph through the traffic with neat precision, driving with half her mind; the other half free to think.

She was surprised she felt so unscathed by Scrivener. To allow her mind to dwell on that ghastly hour in his office was to shudder, but otherwise her memory seemed able to suppress it. It had been necessary, she told herself firmly: necessary to enable her to keep her job, necessary to know about Philips. The information about his house was not enough in itself to damage him seriously, but if it could be thrown into the balance at the right moment, when the scale was tipped against him, then it might prove critical. For that pleasure she'd face a dozen Scriveners.

Keller came to the door. There were dark circles round his

eyes and his skin was pale. He had shaved either cursorily or not at all, but he was wearing a business suit.

'Are you all right?' she asked softly, affected by the depth of his grief. He nodded, blinking, and tried to smile. 'Thanks, Jane. Yes, I am.'

'Where's Elgar?'

At the mention of his name, the Beagle ran busily towards them, tail high-pointed and wagging briskly.

Jane said, 'Take him on to the Heath for twenty minutes. I'll get you something to eat.'

'I'm not hungry,' he protested. 'And I have to go to the office.'

'Why on earth—?'

'You would think, wouldn't you,' Keller's hands made a helpless motion, 'that for a couple of days . . .'

'But is it *so* urgent, Richard?'

He shrugged. 'A transfer of some property. Apparently it's vastly urgent.'

'Surely not tonight! Mr. Hodder wouldn't—'

'It's not Hodder.'

'Then who?'

'Scrivener.'

Inside her chest her heart gave a thud. She said, 'You're going nowhere until you have eaten. Take Elgar. Just twenty minutes.'

She watched him walk down the path, like a man in a trance, the dog bounding at his heels, then she busied herself: hot soup, a steak, a glass of wine, black coffee. By the time Keller returned it was ready. Keller ate slowly and in silence and when he had done, got up.

'Do you really have to go?'

Keller said, 'Lord Mingulay must have his island. When Mingulay wants something, he means now. I'm quoting Scrivener.'

'Island?' Jane was puzzled.

Keller smiled wearily. 'Apparently it's some mosquito infested speck off Alaska. Mingulay wants to build a private yacht harbour.'

'And for that, Scrivener's making you—' Jane paused. 'What island?'

'It's called Whistler Island. Old Salt bought it years ago

when he was busy buying up half British Columbia and Alaska. Suddenly everybody's wanting islands up there.'

The door closed with a clunk on the empty house. Keller said, 'That's what's so awful. The emptiness.'

'Richard!'

He turned to look at her.

Jane said, 'She was lucky, too, to be so much loved. Try to think of it that way.'

There was just time to shower and change and race downstairs to the ante-room where they were all having drinks before dinner. As she entered, she felt the eyes swivelling towards her, the men admiring, the women assessing. She stood quite close to the door, making small talk with Templeton and Longbottom, until dinner was announced, then went in, to find herself sitting beside an empty chair. She glanced at the card: it was Scrivener's place. Unfortunately it was impossible for her to move.

Scrivener came in a few minutes later, sat heavily in the chair beside her.

'Ah, Miss Roper. I have the pleasure again.'

She looked at him, smiling formally, then returned her attention to her plate.

Scrivener said to Templeton, on his right, 'I'm a lucky chap. Miss Roper and I are old friends these days.'

Jane smiled tightly, thinking: why don't you say it, you bastard? Why don't you make them jealous; tell them about an hour on your office floor? She had thought, two hours ago, that she was unaffected; now her flesh crawled as she glanced sideways at his hands and remembered. She forced herself into the light conversation that flowed round the table; effortlessly in some places, more laboured in others. Scrivener himself was positively jovial, but across the table Steele sat glumly, and at the far end Keyes and Volans, still together, looked tense.

'All well, Sir Kenelm? The voice came from behind her chair and Jane looked up, half-turning. She was in time to catch the warning shake of Scrivener's head. Keyes now stood behind her chair.

'I have no reason,' Scrivener said, 'to think otherwise.'

251

'Good. Thank you.' Keyes went away quickly. Keyes and Scrivener? She watched Keyes take his seat and whisper to Volans. That made three of them. And the urgent transfer, at Scrivener's insistence, of land owned by Euromob!

She said, 'That was an intriguing little conversation,' and watched Scrivener's face turn to her, his eyes glittering.

'It was nothing.'

'Really?'

'Well nothing much.' Scrivener had a large piece of duck on his fork. He put it into his mouth and chewed with satisfaction. He would tell her nothing. Scrivener had kept too many secrets over too many years to spill one casually. But perhaps she could get a hint. She had a feeling that it mattered.

Jane said, 'I've been thinking. You're a pretty remarkable man.'

'Oh?' Pleasure glowed in him. 'Why?'

'You are obviously trusted by so many people. And you're powerful.'

'Trusted? Well, I'm a lawyer. Powerful? I don't know about that?' He grinned at her.

Jane said, 'Oh yes, you're powerful.' She allowed her eyes to meet his for a moment and saw the lust harden in them. As she looked away, his knee pressed against hers. Should she move it? No, she decided. Not yet. Five minutes later, she did and watched amusedly as Scrivener tried covertly to reestablish contact.

Halfway through the dinner, a bulky letter was delivered to Scrivener by a waiter. He put his fork down and slit the envelope. Jane, glancing boldly at it, could see Keller's signature on the covering letter. Scrivener grunted with satisfaction and put it in his inside pocket.

Jane said, 'Intriguing.'

He laughed. 'Curious?'

'Naturally.'

'Women always are.'

'Intriguing or curious?'

'Both.'

She allowed his knee to touch hers again. 'And men aren't?'

'Not compulsively.'

Jane said carefully, 'The other, er – day. Didn't you . . . well, wonder?'

Scrivener's look was suddenly shrewd and assessing. 'Why you were there?'

'That and – other things. Other whys.'

'Yes,' he said. 'I wondered.'

'You see? And you still wonder?'

He'd relaxed again. 'I can control it.'

Jane moved her own knee minutely and felt his jerk in nervous response. She said, 'That wasn't my impression.'

He was peeling a pear and his hands stopped moving. He said, 'Your impression is wrong, Miss Roper.'

'No.' She looked at him. 'It's there now. In your eyes.'

'And in yours.'

Jane said 'I did.'

'What?'

'Find something. What I was looking for.'

'In what sense?'

She made herself laugh. 'Fascinating, you see? Very revealing. One learns a lot.'

'What about?'

'Oneself.' She looked at him. 'And other people.'

'And what did you learn?'

She said, 'When something is important to you, you react very – er, positively.'

'You think so?' He was almost purring, but watchful still.

'I'm quite sure.' She was silent then, determined to let him reopen things. Volans and Keyes kept looking at Scrivener almost, it seemed, pleadingly. He, on the other hand, seemed to avoid their eyes, or at least to look consistently in another direction.

After a moment, Scrivener laughed. 'I can almost feel your curiosity.'

'Can you? Whatever it is, it's important. I know that.'

He laughed again. 'How do you know?'

'You're excited and tense.'

'Ah, but that's—'

'It isn't,' Jane said. 'Not all of it.'

253

Scrivener looked at her, eyes level. He said, 'You're clever.'

'As well.' She met his eyes coolly. 'I can tell something else. It's not just important, it's very important. Very important indeed.'

'How do you know that?'

'Your eyes. And you're sweating. But not with fear, or because it's warm.'

'You forget.'

'No. I understand now. You *are* clever.'

'Observant. I have noticed several things. Keyes and Volans, for instance.' Surprised, Scrivener blinked rapidly once or twice. She went on, 'And it's about land. An island.'

Scrivener said, 'How the hell do you know?'

She put a cigarette between her lips and waited in vain for him to light it. Eventually she rolled her lighter and inhaled comfortably.

'It's that bloody man Keller.'

'Richard?' Jane said. 'Is Richard involved, too? No, I heard a little conversation the other night.'

He was glowering and she laughed because his discomfiture was infinitely sweet. And then she began to realize that her careful inventions had been close to the truth. He *was* worried that she knew. She said, 'In North America, somewhere, and when his eyes flicked at her she added on impulse, praying that she was right,'The West Coast.'

Scrivener's eyes widened, but his tone was unconcerned. 'You're guessing.'

She said, 'I was wrong a moment ago.'

He looked relieved. 'I told you.'

'Not about that. I said you weren't afraid, but I think you are.'

He said, 'Afraid?' in a dismissive kind of way. 'Of you?' But he was startled.

'Of what I know.'

Scrivener stared at her hard. 'I think that after dinner we must talk seriously.'

She'd won! Won, won, won! Careful, now, she told herself.

'Certainly, Sir Kenelm,' she said. 'I should like that.'

Mike Farmer

THE dinner seemed interminable and he picked at each successive course until the waiter took it away. Around him the conversation ebbed and flowed but he knew none of it would interest him and detached himself from it and from the others. Why did he have to be here at all, damn it, when there were so many better ways of spending one's time. Work, for example. And Wendy! He'd telephoned Wendy just before he'd come down to dinner and it had been magical, as every moment spent with her had been magical; yet here he was, sitting at this blasted dinner, waiting until he could decently depart and phone her again.

For the fiftieth time he glanced at his watch. The port and the brandy circulated to him and he passed them on. Nine o'clock. Who was going to speak? Longbottom was rising, which must mean somebody was!

Longbottom said, 'Ladies and gentlemen, one or two of you may have met Fergus Carnegie, the City commentator, during the pre-dinner session. He's going to talk for a few minutes about the City, then answer questions. It's not often we ordinary people have the mysterious curtains pulled back for us and I'm sure this will be interesting.'

Carnegie rose and began a fervent defence of the market place as the criterion of all things and when, after twenty minutes, the question and answer session began, Farmer rose and excused himself, pleading a migraine. He hurried up the stairs and across the lobby towards the lifts and then he stopped suddenly as a flash of ochre caught his eye. Could it be? Surely not. He moved hesitantly, unsure, expecting his hopes to be dashed. They weren't.

'My God, Wendy!'

She shushed him delightedly. 'You're shouting, Mike.'

He said, 'I feel like shouting. Gosh, what are you doing here?'

'I wanted to see you.' She spoke shyly, afraid she was going too far, that he'd be offended. 'Do you mind?'

'Mind? It's marvellous!' He gripped her shoulders, convinced that if he didn't she'd disappear as magically as she had arrived. 'You wanted to see *me*?' He repeated the words disbelievingly.

'Well, yes.'

He said, 'They're still at it. Talk, talk, talk. I was on my way to telephone you.'

'Honestly?' She sounded as though she didn't believe him.

'My God, yes. I couldn't wait. I wanted to hear—'

'Me too.'

'This is fantastic!'

She laughed with pleasure. 'Yes. It's wonderful.'

Suddenly daring, he reached and took her hand. 'Let's go somewhere. Out of here, I mean.'

'Yes. Away from people.'

'There are millions out there.'

'I know.' She squeezed his hand as they walked towards the door and then stopped. 'Oh, dear!'

It was raining.

Farmer said, 'I have a coat you can—'

'But what about you?'

He stopped, defeated. 'Well, we'll just have to stay here. There's a restaurant and a bar . . .' he thought of the dinner downstairs and all the people who would come out, the inevitable introductions. 'Oh damn!'

Wendy said, 'It would rain, wouldn't it? I was hoping . . .'

'Privacy,' Farmer said savagely, 'is a luxury.' He thought of his room upstairs and was slightly shocked at his own presumption.

'I don't mind if . . .' her voice was low. 'After all, it's not . . . I mean.' She glanced towards the lift.

Farmer's scalp felt electric. 'I couldn't ask. You . . .'

She blushed. 'You didn't. It was me. I'm forward!'

'You'd be all right, honestly,' he assured her. 'Honestly.'

They looked at each other uncertainly, aching to be alone. 'All right,' he said in sudden, almost schoolboy excitement. 'Come on!'

256

He felt strangely guilty as the lift rose and as they hurried along the corridor. Were they breaking some law? Retribution *must* be around the corner. Then the door was closed and both sighed their relief, smiling at one another with a sudden happiness that turned, in a second, to embarrassment. The walls seemed to be closing in, the room to consist of nothing but a bed; he had to apologize.

She said, 'Sorry? Why?'

'Well, you shouldn't be here, really. I mean, in my bedroom!'

'I know,' Wendy said. 'Mike!'

'What?'

'Oh, nothing. I mean, I don't know. I wanted you to speak.'

'Did you?' He looked at her. Her eyes seemed huge and very deep. If he kissed her would she be angry? He wanted to kiss her and her face seemed to be coming nearer to his. Then he was kissing her, awkwardly, and their teeth clashed but the kiss went on and his arms went round her. He drew back and looked at her in astonishment. 'You don't mind?'

'Mind?'

'Gosh.' They kissed again.

He remembered the early days of his marriage, when there had still been affection, took her hand and led her to a chair that faced away from the bed, sat down and pulled her down on to his knee. There was worry in her eyes.

'Don't be afraid.'

'It's just – someone might come.'

'No. Not without knocking. You're not afraid of me?'

'Of you?' She looked at him with serious eyes. 'No, Mike. I'm not afraid of you.'

He said, 'People seem to be, you see. Girls . . .'

She kissed him. 'I can't think why. I'm not. I think you're wonderful. Honestly.'

'And you. You're beautiful.'

'I'm not!'

'Yes, you are, Wendy. Beautiful.' He wanted to give her something, anything, a gift to show that . . . 'Will you wait?'

'Why?'

He smiled nervously. 'Just for a minute.'

'All right. What do I do if somebody comes?'

'Read *The Times*.' He handed it to her. 'But they won't.'

He went to the lobby, remembering the glass cases with lighters and jewellery. He looked quickly and one of them had a necklace. They took his cheque doubtfully, 'A hundred and twenty guineas is a lot of money, Mr. Farmer,' while he chafed and fretted and then saw a big box of chocolates and bought that too. Then he went back upstairs and knocked.

'Who is it?'

'It's all right! He felt happily conspiratorial as she let him in. 'Now. Do you like chocolates?'

She looked at the box. 'Yes. But – it's an enormous box.'

'Close your eyes.' He thought she looked like a little girl, standing with her eyes tightly-closed. 'Now turn round.' She trembled a little as his hands fastened the necklace, but she stood still. 'Right.'

'Oh, you shouldn't!' She was squinting down at it, 'Mike, you shouldn't. Oh, thank you. Thank you.' She kissed him quickly and hurried to the mirror. 'Oh, it's lovely!' Then her expression changed. 'It's gold.'

He stammered. 'I – I think so. Hope so!'

'It must have cost the earth!'

'No, honestly!'

'But it must. Oh, Mike, you shouldn't!'

He didn't know what to say. The only word that would come out was, 'Please.'

'I couldn't. Oh, Mike!' She was in his arms.

'Mike that's an awfully extravagant – I mean . . .'

'You're here,' he murmured. 'That's what I don't believe. You're here.'

'Oh, yes. With you. I don't want to go away.'

Farmer shook his head with a kind of puzzled wonder; he'd been avoided for so long that acceptance, let alone eagerness, was incomprehensible. 'I don't want you to. I'd hate it if you did.' Then he realized what he'd said and blushed. 'I'm sorry, Wendy. I didn't mean . . .'

She laughed shyly. 'You're sweet, Mike. Really, so sweet!'

258

'That's a funny word.' He hadn't been described as sweet for thirty-five years.

'It's not. It's the perfect word!'

'For you, perhaps.' Suddenly they were kissing one another hard.

'Oh, Mike!'

A thought struck him. 'Champagne! Do you like champagne?'

'Well . . .'

'If you do . . .?' he asked anxiously.

She nodded then, eagerly, her eyes shining. 'You're awfully extravagant, Mike.'

'Extravagant! Me? No, honestly I'm not.'

'Chocolates, champagne – and this wonderful necklace. I'd call that extravagant!'

'But that's for you.'

'Oh, Mike, Mike.' She held him tightly. 'And I brought you nothing.'

'You brought yourself,' he said. 'That's the best thing of all. Honestly, the best thing of all.'

'Is it? Do you really . . .?' Delight was clear in her face, in the bright eyes and the smooth brow.

'Really. Really, really, really!'

'Me too,' she said. 'Oh, me too!'

'I can't hold you tightly enough.'

'Let me try.' She squeezed and they strained together. 'Oh, that's wonderful.'

His body responded quite suddenly and with a power that astonished him; he'd been deliberately avoiding thinking of her in sexual terms because to do so would be to contaminate something beautiful. But now his body was betraying him. He stepped back and away from her, in confusion, turning his back so that she should not see.

There was dead silence. He thought: God, what will she think of me? She's nice, decent, and I have to rear up like that. He held his breath, waiting for the inevitable slam of the door.

'Mike.' Her voice was little more than a whisper. She sounded almost frightened and he cursed himself.

259

'Wendy, I'm sorry. I couldn't help— Just ... oh, I'm so sorry!'

There was a silence behind him. He could imagine that she was reaching for her coat, disgusted. After all she was a highly intelligent woman, not some tart.

'I'm not.' Her voice trembled as she spoke and for a moment he did not understand. 'I'm not, Mike.'

'What?' She couldn't mean what he thought she meant. Not a girl like this! He said, 'I didn't mean – well, you know.' He couldn't turn, but he looked back at her, over his shoulder and was astonished to see tears in her eyes.

'Oh, Mike, it's all right.' He watched a tremulous smile appear. 'Honestly. I thought you mustn't ... any more.'

'Oh, God!'

'Mike, please!' She gave a little cry and came towards him and he tried awkwardly to embrace her without making a contact that would frighten her.

'I'm sorry,' he muttered. 'It's just ...'

'I'm not offended, Mike.'

'No?'

'No, honestly.' She was very nervous, blinking quickly, afraid of every nuance of her own words. 'I think I'm proud, really. Of myself.'

He looked at her blankly, 'Proud?'

'To be able to ... I mean that you should want ... should want ... me.' Her eyes dropped.

Farmer put his hand under her chin and raised her face. 'But Wendy.'

She said. 'So I don't mind, you see. Is that awful of me?'

He wasn't sure. Perhaps it *was* awful. Perhaps she *was* forward. But proud. Proud! Didn't she realize? 'No,' he said. 'I don't think so.'

'I was frightened,' she said suddenly.

'Why?'

'I thought you'd decided you didn't ... like me.'

'No!'

'Honestly?'

'My God, no! It was me. I was all—'

'I know. You were embarrassed.'

260

'Yes, I'm sorry.'

'Please,' she said. 'Oh, *please* don't be sorry. Smile for me. It's minutes since you smiled and I like you when you smile.'

He began to smile and felt it turning into a grin; then, when she smiled and said 'That's better!' he began to laugh and she laughed too and their embrace was awkward no longer, but confident.

'Champagne,' he said.

Wendy nodded and he picked up the phone and ordered it and added, 'Two glasses.'

'What *will* they think?'

'That we're celebrating. There's a marvellous view from here. The park. Come, look.'

They stood staring out of the window, arms round one another's waists, content simply to be close, until the wine arrived; Wendy stayed by the window, then came towards him when the waiter had gone. He handed her the glass. 'To you.'

'No, to you.'

He looked at her. Dare he say it? Her expression was soft, somehow defenceless, her eyes warm. He decided he dared. 'To us?'

'Oh yes. To us.'

They drank and smiled and drank and smiled again and then she said, 'That was awful.'

'The champagne?'

'No.' She laughed and then was abruptly serious. 'No. Me frightened and you embarrassed. Was it terrible for you?'

Farmer nodded. 'I didn't know what to do. You shouldn't be frightened. Not of me.'

'And you shouldn't be embarrassed. Let's make a promise!'

'What?'

'You promise never to be embarrassed and I promise never to be frightened.'

'I don't think I could,' Farmer said.

'Promise to try.'

'All right.'

She raised her face and he kissed her gently, embracing one-armed because they still held the wine glasses. Farmer said, 'Cheers.'

261

'Cheers.' They kissed again and after a moment his body responded to her again and again he began to turn away. 'You promised,' she said.

He couldn't look at her. 'I know. But—'

'Don't move.'

'It's getting worse,' he said.

'Kiss me, Mike.'

'Wendy . . .'

'Please.'

He kissed her lightly, then again, his mind focused on his arousal, his body feeling as though it were paralysed. Nor dared he have moved, even if his body would have allowed it. The sheer presence was enough without . . . but the pressure was growing. 'Wendy, my God!'

The softness of her stomach was against him, she must know, be able to feel . . .! Then he could stop himself no longer. He pulled her hard against him, surprised that she moved easily, willingly, astonished when her lips parted with his and their tongues were touching, moving, building. He felt enormous, now and she couldn't possibly . . . he must not do this! He pulled away, almost roughly and went to the window. After a moment he heard her move, come nearer.

He said, 'I'm sorry, Wendy.'

'I broke the promise too.'

'You?'

'I was frightened. Just a bit.'

'I'm sorry!'

'It's just . . . I didn't know, you see.'

'Didn't know?'

'How, well – strong. But it's not *you*, you see.'

'I'm a rotten—'

'No, Mike. I don't think I'd be frightened again.'

'You would,' he said miserably.

'I don't think so.' She came and stood beside him, looking out. 'After all, thousands of people out there . . .'

He turned and held her again and she pressed herself against him with nervous deliberation. 'There. Are you embarrassed now?'

'A bit.'

'I'm a bit afraid, too. But not as much.'

'No.' He stood for a moment, knowing it was true, that embarrassment *was* fading; that with Wendy it wasn't necessary. 'You're wonderful,' he said, looking down at her and seeing the tension in the planes of her face. 'Don't worry. I wouldn't hurt you for the world.'

'I know,' she said. 'It's just that . . . well, you see, I don't know very much.'

'You mean you're . . .' He couldn't say the word.

She blinked, nodding. 'At thirty. Silly, isn't it?'

'There'll be plenty of time, Wendy.' He pulled her to him in sudden, deep compassion. 'I told you, I'm married. We're not divorced, you see, just separated.' Then he realized what it must sound like: an assumption that she'd marry him. 'I mean, if you will . . . if you'll wait until—'

'Oh, Mike. I don't want to.'

He felt as though he'd been hit. 'I should have asked you properly. I want you to marry me. When I can. Please, Wendy!'

She laughed, near to tears. 'Oh yes, Mike. Yes.'

'You said you didn't want to?'

'To wait.'

He stared at her. 'But you're . . . you're a . . .'

She said in a small voice, 'I've waited already. For you, you see.'

'Christ!' He reached and pulled her closer, wrapping her tighter with his arms. He'd burst, soon. Her arms were round his neck and her body was against his, tightly against his, her thighs against his, her belly and her breasts against him, her lips on his lips. And when the kiss was over and they strained against each other so hard they seemed to be trying to become one body, he heard her whisper, 'I love you, Mike.'

He raised his head to look at her and she leaned back in his arms.

'I do, Mike. Do you mind?'

'Mind!'

She smiled and moved against him and in wonder he took his hand from her back and guided it towards her breast, but he had to stop before he touched it.

'Go on,' she said, and her head bent. 'I want to see you do that.'

Farmer hesitated and she said 'Mike,' very softly. Then lightly he cupped her breast and his tight-held breath came out in a great sigh and so did hers and they laughed together, her breast alive in his hand.

'You're beautiful.'

'So are you.' And when he protested, 'Mike, it's time!'

He looked down at his hand. 'I can't quite believe, you know, this.'

'That's just my dress. A brown, woollen mound.' She smiled, impishly. 'It's not really made of wool.'

'No?' It feels like wool.' He tried to take up the game. 'I must find—' but banter was not his world and the words died.

'Yes, yes, you should.'

He looked at her helplessly, at the tight bodice of her dress, and she laughed and blushed and touched her side. 'Here. But it's awkward. I didn't know you'd—' She stopped, and a flicker of fear crossed her face.

Farmer knew her thought. She was wondering if she'd gone too far, if he'd think she was a tart, leading him on. He said, 'I'd never have dreamed.' He put his hand to her side and found the zip and moved it down but when he'd done so it was no help, so he kissed her and said, 'It's all right.'

'It's not. Not tonight. Oh, Mike, I wish . . .'

'I wish, too. But I can wait.'

'I don't want you to have to wait, Mike. I love you. I want—' She blushed and lowered her eyes, then leaned forward and pressed herself against him. 'Mike, I want you,' she whispered, and his body jerked against her. 'I want you just so much.'

'You can't,' he said. 'Not as much.'

'It's just – it doesn't show.'

'No.' He felt himself going scarlet. He couldn't be having this conversation with her! It was impossible. 'I'm afraid it does with me.'

'Mike.'

'Yes.'

'I don't want to go. To leave you. Not tonight.'

264

'But you must. You mean here?' He could see her eyes were misty with tears.

She said, 'Anywhere. But with you.'

Farmer said, 'There's only here.'

She squeezed his hand against her. 'Mike, go into there.' Her hand pointed to the bathroom.

'Why?'

'Please.'

'All right. ' Obediently he went, half-knowing what she intended but still dazedly unable to believe it. He stared at himself in the morror, the flushed face, the tousled hair, as a minute or so dragged by. Could she find him attractive?

'Mike.'

He went back into the room. Her clothes lay on a chair and she was in the bed, the covers up under her chin.

'My God, Wendy. Oh, Wendy!'

'Please, Mike. Hurry.'

He turned and went into the bathroom and began to rip off his clothes, tossing them on the floor. The light went off in the bedroom and he went through into the darkness, making his way towards the bed, turning the covers back, climbing in.

When he touched her it was like an electric shock. Somehow he had not expected nakedness; his wife had never been naked. He found her breast and held it in a gentle hand.

'Oh, Mike!'

And after he'd kissed her, she said, 'I told you it wasn't wool.'

'Silk,' he said. And despite the urgency, he was smiling. 'Finest silk.' And kissed her again.

'I'm shy, Mike.'

'No. Not now. I love you.'

'Too shy, darling. Isn't it silly. I can't—'

Farmer took her hand. 'Here.'

In a moment she said, 'And steel.'

'What?'

'Silk and steel. Oh, Mike, Mike, please!'

'You might have a baby. What then?'

'Your baby? Oh, Darling, I'd pray for that.'

She cried out briefly as the thirty years of waiting ended, and he was motionless for a moment, guilt-stricken, but then her arms were softly round him and he moved again and the guilt ebbed away as he plunged on.

It was late when they slept, bodies fitted together like spoons, warm and happy; late, too when they awakened as the girl came in with Farmer's morning tea and *Times*. It was the Spanish girl; the one he'd wanted so badly, and now he could wonder why when she was so clearly so ordinary.

Beside him Wendy tensed. 'Oh, God!'

He said softly, 'It doesn't matter,' and then to the Spanish girl, 'Would you bring another cup, please.'

She did not react; merely said, 'Si' and went out, returning in a moment with the cup.

'She saw us!'

'It doesn't matter.'

'But—!'

Farmer said, 'All that has changed.'

She laughed; it was almost a giggle. 'Yes, it has, hasn't it? Do you take sugar?'

'I'll pour. It's my side.'

'No, it's a woman's—' she had begun to get out of bed and she stopped.

'What's wrong?'

'I have no clothes on.'

'It's all right. I'll pour.'

'No, darling.' She climbed out and he turned to look at her. She said, 'Last night I didn't dare let you see me. Now I'm . . . well, proud to.'

'You should be.' He reached for her and she skipped out of his way.

'*Do* you take sugar?'

'Three lumps.'

She poured the tea and sat on the bed beside him while they drank it.

He put the cup down half-full.

'You don't want it?'

'Yes, I want it,' he said, reaching again.

'You'll spill the tea!'

266

'I will indeed. So put it down.'

She replaced the cup on the side table as his hands took her, pulling her down to him and his mouth found hers.

At ten-thirty he was called out of the lecture to the telephone.

'Hello?'

'Mike?'

'Wendy! This is marvellous. They called me out.'

'I told them it was urgent.'

'Good for you.'

'I love you, Mike.'

'And me.'

'I had to tell you, but I feel terrible about it.'

Something bounced in his chest. 'About what? Are you all right?'

'Oh, yes. I'm fine.' She laughed softly. 'Never better. I had a marvellous night.'

'Then what?'

Wendy said, 'Toller Securities *is* making a bid for Euromob. We're just going to run the figures through. It'll probably be announced tomorrow.'

'How do you know?'

'We're Tollers' bank. It's quite true.'

'How much?'

'Twenty-one shillings, I think. Looks that way. Now I must go. They'd sack me!'

He said. 'They would, too. You shouldn't really have told me.'

'I couldn't have you *not* knowing.'

'No. Thanks. Wendy, thank you.'

'What will you do?'

'I don't know. I'll have to think.'

'I had to tell you. 'Bye, darling.'

She was gone and he stood for a moment, thinking, before he realized the telephone was still in his hand and replaced it. What *did* one do with that kind of knowledge?

He thought of the new installation that was being completed now at Tunnel House. In six months the hardware would be in

267

and he would be able to start working on making his dream into actuality: turning Euromob, the whole gigantic enterprise, into an autonomic creature capable of reacting on lightning reflexes to the minutest change registered in the most distant part of it. Would Toller allow that? He didn't know much about Toller, but the little he knew made it doubtful. Philips would, though. It was Philips who had backed him, forcing the scheme through an unenthusiastic board, finding three and a half millions for hardware. Without Philips he'd have quit Euromob long ago. So Philips had the right to know.

Tommy Verity

MARJORIE PHILIPS smiled. She was still a very attractive woman at fifty, Verity thought. Her hair had its natural colouring and if it had been assisted then the assistance had been carried out with subtlety. 'Do you remember the last pub we were in?'

'Polly's?' He wouldn't forget.

She nodded.

'I remember very well.'

'When the world was simple. Or maybe it wasn't.'

'Simple's all right,' Verity said. 'But don't confuse it with good. There was a war, remember?'

'I remember.' She was smiling from the eyes and they were good eyes, lined but with lines of kindliness. 'A quarter of a century. It's hardly believable.'

'It's a long time.' He watched her, covertly. It was a *very* long time. He wondered what she would say if she knew.

'A long silence.'

'Yes.' He offered her a cigarette and when she refused, 'You won't mind?'

'Of course not. It's funny. I remember Polly's, too. We weren't allowed in pubs in uniform, you know. You'd have got me sacked.'

'It was dark, as I remember.'

Her eyes warned him. A warning? Or a plea?

She said, 'How've you been all these years?'

'Getting older.'

'Still got your hair. More than Harry's got.'

'Man liveth not by heads of hair alone, Marjorie. Harry's done all right.'

Again the glance. 'I suppose so. Have I changed, Tom?'

'Not a lot. I'd know you.'

'And Harry?'

Verity said carefully, 'It's a long way from Leeds Grammar

School to the job he's got. He was bound to change.'

'Yes.'

'*You* think he has, then?'

'Oh, yes.'

'You could have knocked me down with a wet haddock.'

She laughed. 'A long time since I heard that.'

'I believe you. Circles you move in, it'd be a Dover sole or nothing. Why did you?'

'The note?'

'What else?'

'I've been thinking, since the other night. I thought I'd like to talk.'

'I'm glad you did.'

They were in a pub just off Knightsbridge to which a note, left at the porter's desk at the Princess Hotel, had summoned him. He'd debated ignoring it, then decided to go.

'Tommy!'

'Yes.'

'It's funny you should be working for Harry.'

'Funny?'

She laughed. 'I'd forgotten that trick of yours. Pulling people up. You know what I mean.'

'I know.'

'He admires you.'

'Hardly that.'

'Tough and resourceful. I quote.'

'Maybe. I'm his backstop.'

'That's how you see it?'

'That's how it is, Marjorie. He thinks he can depend on me.'

'And can he?'

He ignored the question. 'You know why?'

'Roots go deep, Tommy.'

'No,' Verity said, 'not that. I'd deferred once I'll defer again.'

'Defer?'

'I agree: it's the wrong word. Honourable once, always honourable. Only it's not true.'

'Oh?'

270

'I'll tell you something, young Marjorie. I've been a right swine with women.'

'I don't believe you.'

'It's true.'

She met his eye. 'Not with me.'

'I wonder.'

'Oh, Tom. You're too sharp for me.'

He looked at her, and found himself smiling with pure pleasure. 'Tha knaws summat?'

'Go on, lad.'

'Ah feel about ten year owd.'

'You know summat?'

Verity laughed, 'Go on, lass.'

'Tha deean't look it.'

'I don't think I ever did.'

'Are you very tough, Tommy?' she asked suddenly.

'I don't know. Probably a bit hard.'

'I'm soft, you see.'

'I believe you.'

'Not that,' she said. 'I'm serious.'

'Tell me, then.'

'I don't know whether you'd approve.'

'Approve?' He was surprised. Intrigued but surprised. 'Is that important, Marjorie?'

'Yes, Tommy. As a matter of fact, it is.'

'Go on, then.'

She hesitated. Whatever it was that she wanted him to know, must be important.

'I don't think,' he said, 'that you could do much I'd disapprove of.'

Amusement crinkled the corners of her eyes. 'I did once.'

'You did an' all.'

'I can see your face yet, Thomas Verity. All severe and disapproving.'

'I could have gobbled you up. Why I didn't, I don't know.'

She said, 'Toller's bidding for Euromob.'

'Is he? I hadn't heard.'

'You wouldn't, till tomorrow.'

271

Why had she told him? So that he could buy shares and make a profit. For old times' sake?' To pay a debt, an imagined debt? Or what? He asked, 'Where does that leave Harry?'

'I don't know. High and dry, perhaps. He'll want to fight it. Refuse the offer.

'I expect his contract's all right.'

'I expect so. But it would be the end of his career.'

'You'd be sorry?'

'He would. He's ambitious. What about you?'

'I expect I'll be all right. Why did you tell me?'

'So you could protect yourself. If you need to.'

'Protect myself?' He looked at her in puzzled amusement. 'What could I do?'

'Tommy, you're not a man to be pushed. You do your own pushing. I just wanted to give you the chance.'

'But why?'

'I don't know,' she said. 'I'm fond of some of my memories and that includes you. I don't want people like Toller muckin' about wi' 'em.'

'Sither'!'

'So think on,' she said, 'and do summat.'

'I still want to, lass. And if you're not out of here in thirty seconds, I very likely will.'

Her eyes flickered, then she leaned across, and kissed him quickly on the cheek and hurried out.

He was back at the Princess in time for coffee. All the way there, thoughts had flashed in his mind like the lights of a pinball machine, and each had been extinguished as quickly. *Was* the information useable? Marjorie believed he was a man to make things happen, but that was based largely on thirty-year-old memories of a cricketer and one wartime night when what he'd done was precisely nothing.

He could tell everybody, or nobody. He looked round the dining-room, wondering what would happen if he simply stood and said loudly, 'Toller's bidding a guinea a share. Tomorrow, after the market closes, the offer will be announced.' What would they do? It occurred to him that they'd want to know

272

whether it was true, whether the knowledge came from a reliable source, how he came to have it? Funny, Verity thought, that he hadn't doubted it for a moment.

What *would* they do? Longbottom? Longbottom would slip out to buy shares, as many as he could afford, and probably a lot more. So would Keyes, but with more discretion. Templeton would observe the scurryings with an amused eye; Gaunt, too. Mike Farmer? Verity smiled to himself. Farmer would probably see it as an essay in calculation. Volans would buy; so would Judy Kernon, but not greedily. She'd be good-humoured and hopeful and use the money on some cheerful extravagance.

Clare? It would bother Clare. Just knowing would bother her. She'd be wondering, as he was, what she could do with the knowledge. No doubt her husband and his insurance company would benefit. But who else? Verity put his cup down, rose and crossed the room.

'Now, Clare.'

She looked up at him, smiling. 'Hello, Tommy. Where were you?'

'I had a date.'

'Ah.'

Very cool and a little aloof, he thought, and grinned, remembering other circumstances. 'It was interesting.'

'Really? How nice.'

'Important, too.'

Clare said, 'Whoever she was, I hope she enjoyed it.'

'Whoever she is, she usually does.' He watched her jaw tighten. 'But it was information, not indulgence, Clare.'

'Useful, I hope.'

'Profitable. Very profitable, I might tell you.'

'Oh?' She put a cigarette in her mouth. 'Tell me?'

He said, 'You light it.'

'Nice of you.'

'I'm not nice. But I'm very well-informed. And they say knowledge is power.'

'You're interested in power?'

'Not like you.'

She was pale now. 'That's brutal.'

273

'Remember what they said the other night? Money is all that matters. Money's right.'

'Who said?'

'Your husband. Scrivener.'

'And you don't agree?'

'Who said I don't?'

He turned away and she said, 'Where are you going?'

'Upstairs. My room. I fancy a bath.' Verity walked quickly to the lift.

In his room, Verity undressed quickly and turned on the bath, watching with satisfaction as the generous flow of hot water flooded into the big, blue tub. He almost failed to hear the knock, but he turned the tap back and went to the door opening it only a little, putting his head round it.

Clare began to move foward, into the room, but the door stopped her. He said, 'Yes?'

'Are you going to tell me?' She looked from one side to the other, concerned not to be seen.

'I'm running a bath.'

'Are you going to tell me, Tommy?' She looked round again. 'Look, please don't keep me standing here.'

'The water's running.' He grinned at her.

'Please let me in.'

'All right.' He stood back and opened the door and she entered quickly. 'Now I see you, I reckon you could stand a scrub.'

She stopped, startled. 'You're naked!'

'I don't take baths with my clothes on.' He walked into the bathroom and climbed into the tub, leaning back comfortably. 'Clare!'

She was still in the bedroom. 'Not so loud!'

'Come and wash my back.'

She appeared in the doorway. 'You were going to tell me something.'

He looked at her, at the face that smiled with well-bred charm from the TV sets, the woman who was quoted on every subject under the sun. 'I don't talk business in the bath.' The sponge was floating beside him and he picked it up and threw it

274

at her. She caught it dexterously enough, but water splashed her from head to foot.

Clare said, 'You're a bastard, Tommy.'

'A dirty one. That's what the sponge is for.'

'And you'll tell me?'

'What time is it?'

She looked at her watch. 'Ten past two.'

'I'll tell you,' Verity said, 'Some time between three and three-thirty.'

'Why then?'

'I'm thinking of the Stock Exchange.'

Clare moved towards him, the sponge in her hand. 'All right. Lean forward.'

He said, 'And then I'll give you a scrub, eh, love?'

Clare didn't reply.

'I said, eh love?'

'Yes, Tommy.' She began to scrub his back.

He told her at three-fifteen and she said, 'I see,' and reached for the phone beside the bed.

'Who are you telling?'

'Julian.'

'What do you think he'll do?'

'Buy shares in Euromob, I should think.'

He took the phone from her and replaced it on its cradle.

'I think so, too. What else?'

'Accept the offer, when it's made.'

'I believe that, too. So Euromob goes?'

Clare said, 'It's no great loss, surely?'

'It will be to a lot of people. Philips for one. He'll want to fight.'

'Philips is a fool.'

'And Hodder?'

'Another fool.'

He laughed. 'Here you are, stark naked on my blankets, talking about fools.'

She flushed. 'It wasn't my choice.'

'Philips was, though. At least I thought he was. Your husband and Scrivener seemed to fancy Philips. What's it about?'

'Please hand me the telephone.'

'I told you. You tell me.'

She said, 'Convention demanded that Hodder replace Salt. It also demands that Philips replace Hodder. But after Philips there was no heir apparent. It doesn't matter now.'

'So the institutions would get their man in.'

'Simple, wasn't it. Phone please.'

'One other question. You and your husband. It's a funny set-up?'

'We suit each other.' She dialled the number.

'Julian? Clare. I'm told Ray Toller is bidding for Euromob tomorrow. The offer is a guinea—'

Verity tickled her and she wriggled, glaring at him.

Julian's voice said, 'What's the matter?'

'It's all right,' Clare said, 'just a touch of hiccups.'

'A guinea, you said?'

Verity slapped her bottom noisily.

Clare said, 'Yes. Look, I'd better get off the line.'

'What is it?' Julian asked.

Verity slapped her again and she hung up quickly. He said, 'Poverty of invention, that's what it is. Will you tell anybody else?'

'Of course not.' After a moment she turned her head quickly, questioningly. 'Will you?'

'I'm not sure.'

But he was. He felt amused, tolerant, almost light-headed. Angry, too, with the Tollers and the Scriveners and the Porteouses. The hard poverty of the thirties had left scar tissue in his mind. Toller would smash up Euromob, not caring who got hurt in the process. It seemed wrong that it should happen without some sort of battle. Also it was necessary to defend oneself.

Who else knew? Philips, presumably. But who had told Philips? And why had Marjorie told him herself? Only, surely, because she knew he wouldn't learn it from Philips. Was it possible, then, that Philips was the only person who *did* know? Verity dressed carefully, went downstairs and took a taxi, but half-way to Euromob House he stopped it and got out. If Philips *were* keeping to himself all knowledge of the bid, then

Philips would be suspicious of any move out of the ordinary, and the sight of his deputy-to-be pussyfooting into the chairman's office would, at the very least, surprise him. Verity went to the telephone, but Hodder's office said he was out. Then Verity remembered.

'Is he at Mrs. Keller's funeral?'

'Yes, Mr. Verity.'

'Thanks.' Verity looked in the E–K directory, then found himself another taxi.

'Hampstead.'

'Right, guv.'

'When we get there, I want you to drive past the house, not stop. Okay?'

'You the bleeding secret service?'

He grinned. 'No.'

'Rozzers, then?'

'No.'

'Bleedin' nuisance, they are.' The driver pulled away.

They climbed up the hill and the driver said, 'Along 'ere somewhere, guv.' Verity began to look, checking the numbers on the gates, counting down. It should be here, now, the next but one . . . There was a white Triumph in the drive.

'Stop further along.'

'Right, guv.'

He sat in the car, waiting. About twenty minutes later three cars appeared, the last of them Hodder's Rolls; it stopped outside the house and Hodder got out, bowed rather formally and shook hands with somebody, presumably Keller, in the leading car, and then climbed back into his own.

'Follow that Rolls.'

'You bloody are,' the driver said. 'You're a bloody rozzer.'

'No.' Verity said, feeling slightly ridiculous.

'Cos' if you are,' the driver went on, 'I don't want any nonsense in me cab; it's a new cab, this, and I don't want no scratches nor nothing.'

'Look, pull up alongside him when you get the chance. What's on the clock?' He handed over fare-plus-tip and sat back, waiting. At the Marylebone Road traffic lights he slipped out of the taxi and rapped on the door of the Rolls.

277

Hodder looked up, frowning, saw who it was and nodded. The chauffeur turned and opened the door and Verity climbed in. 'Mr. Hodder, there's something you ought to know.'

'As urgently as this?'

Verity said, 'Maybe you know already. Ray Toller will make an offer for Euromob shares tomorrow. It's expected to be a guinea.'

Hodder's eye was leary. 'First, how do you know? Second, why the cloak and dagger act?'

'I know because I was told.'

'By whom?'

'Sorry, I can't tell you,' Verity said. 'But it is a good source.'

'Reliable?'

Verity thought: is she? 'Absolutely reliable. And the secrecy is because I didn't want to talk on the ordinary phone – I don't have your private line number – and I didn't want to come to your office.'

'Why not?'

Verity was silent.

Hodder said thoughtfully, 'I take it you didn't want to be seen. By whom?'

'I'm sorry.'

'It has to be Mr. Philips, doesn't it!'

'Would you mind dropping me, Mr. Hodder?'

'All right. Roberts, will you stop at the Shaftesbury Theatre, please.'

They rode in silence until the Rolls slid to a stop and Hodder said, 'Thanks.'

'You should know, after all.'

Verity's feet were on the pavement and he was turning to close the door when Hodder leaned across. 'Verity.'

'Yes?'

'Mr. Philips. Does he know already?'

'I haven't told him.'

'But he knows?'

Verity said, 'I have every reason to believe so.'

He watched the Rolls move off. Either way, now, he was safe.

PROGRESS REPORT 3 EUROMOB COURSE TWO

FROM: John LONGBOTTOM: Malcolm TEMPLETON

To: M.U.N.P. MANAGEMENT GROUP

DATE: SECOND WEDNESDAY:

As seemed likely, the course has been so disrupted by the changes at the top with Euromob that it has served almost no purpose. The best that can be hoped is that a few eyes may have been opened to the opportunities in management education. It has been apparent that course members have been involved in various skirmishes and there is an air of tension among many of them as they await results.

M.U.N.P. Potential: 1. It is clear that Euromob has no real idea of the capacities of its staff and no attempt has been made to analyse and record, in spite of their massive computer installation. Suggest approach to Mr. Harry Philips seeking instruction in this task.

2. There appears to be no coherent management philosophy within the corporation. M.D.'s 'Think-tank' has not produced one and the Board, largely composed of individualistic people, unlikely to. We should do it for them.

3. So far as is possible to tell from conversations, there is a great deal of potential within Euromob for development of assets. Philips aware (Lists of holiday subscribers passed to books dept. etc.) but much more to be done. M.U.N.P. should be retained to consult.

4. Suspect from conversations with Farmer and with relevant director (Hyde-Compton) that publishing division's accounts badly handled. M.U.N.P. should be retained to consult.

5. Entire management structure is unsatisfactory. M.U.N.P. should approach Euromob to restructure, but there is obvious danger of 'structuring = McKinsey' (i.e. we suggest it; McKinsey get the job).

Gerard Garvin Steele

'So in conclusion I will return to the point at which I began: my own definition of public relations. I hope I have shown you why I describe it as that part of faith which actually moves the mountain.' The speaker smiled and sat down, smoothing his elegant silver hair, straightening the creases in his trousers, looking benevolent.

Longbottom said, 'Thank you very much. That was fascinating, Sir George. And I've no doubt you have said enough to start a barrage of questions.'

Sir George Franklin nodded, lips pursed in satisfaction. He had been PRO to two Prime Ministers, one broadcasting authority and a giant industrial company.

Longbottom went on, 'You have given us a very neat run-down on precisely why PR is an essential complement to the complex communications of our industrial society. Questions?' Steele stared back at him, aware of Longbottom's mute plea not to be savage now. Around him there was silence; he was aware that they all expected him to jump in first. Well, he'd jump in second or third.

Finally, Jane Roper, one public relations operator to another, said, 'I must say I find it is a great advantage to know the mind of the management.'

'Absolutely,' Sir George agreed smoothly. 'Unless one does it is difficult to keep control of the picture.'

It will have to be second, Steele thought grimly. He said, 'What makes you think you're entitled to control?'

Longbottom said quickly, 'Mr. Steele edits *Viewpoint*.'

'Does he? Oh, that Mr. Steele. The journalist?' Sir George dripped the word out. 'I didn't say anybody was *entitled* to control, Mr. Steele. Just that you should—'

Steele said, 'Leave me out of it, please.'

'. . . that *one* should seek to acquire it and, having acquired, seek to maintain it.'

281

'And anybody's free to try?'

'Naturally.'

Steele felt angry. Angry generally, but angry particularly at his own fear of Toller: he'd been put off Toller not by any threat from the man himself, but because other people said Toller was dangerous. 'And are we equally free to define public relations?'

Sir George said, 'To try. Many have tried.'

'And all have failed? Your own definition excepted?' Steele watched the flush of anger blossoming on Sir George's pale, smooth skin.

Longbottom said, 'Please, Mr. Steele.'

Sir George raised a manicured hand. 'Don't worry, Mr. Longbottom. I enjoy healthy debate.'

Steele said, 'You seemed to be saying that public relations is a kind of graphite, or oil, to the machinery of industry.'

Sir George nodded. 'That is my view.'

'Not mine,' Steele said carefully. 'Try this: Public Relations is the vaseline applied to the public anus to facilitate penetration.'

'There are ladies present,' Sir George reddened. 'I hardly think—'

Steele grinned and turned to Clare Fazackerly. 'You offended?'

'Only by a certain lack of elegance.'

'And you Jane?'

Jane Roper said, 'It's not as good as Humbert Wolfe on journalists.'

'Admitted,' Steele said. 'And Miss Kernon?'

Judy Kernon grinned. 'Listen, kid, I've read Portnoy's Complaint.'

He turned with pleasure to Sir George. 'Now we've disposed of that, would you like to argue that you and other PROs are not paid panderers.'

Longbottom had risen with an embarrassed grin. 'Okay, okay, let's try to cool it. Sir George is willing to answer questions, *not*—'

Steele said, 'Face the truth.'

Sir George was dark with anger. 'I'm damned if I see why I should be attacked like this.'

282

'You're being paid,' Steele said. 'The whore is worthy of his hire.' He watched Franklin struggling to control his temper, searching for words, finally achieving a simulated blandness.

'Mr. Steele,' Sir George said, 'must have had an unpleasant experience at the hands of a PRO. But when I was at Downing Street, I had excellent relations with the political correspondents. Including the man from *Viewpoint*.'

'You were the pap they sucked on,' Steele said. 'It was necessary to be nice to you.'

'Now look,' Longbottom raised his voice, 'there's no need for a brawl Mr. Steele. Can't we—?'

Steele said, 'Can't we all be nice and obedient and consent to being manipulated!'

'Sir George was talking about public relations as a tool of management.'

'It is dangerous, specious claptrap,' Steele said. He looked round the room, a little surprised that nobody else seemed much concerned. Well, they were business automatons, zombies with obedience programmed in. 'I have never accepted it elsewhere I'm damned if I'll accept it here.'

Longbottom said, 'All right. We know your views. Give somebody else a chance.'

Steel shrugged and sat down.

At the end, Franklin came to him, hand outstretched. 'Well, Mr. Steele, we put some life into it.'

Steele looked at him, took the hand, held on to it. He said, 'Sir George, have you heard a story about a financial gentleman who stole a million pounds' worth of Government equipment to build a road, then buried it in a hole and made half a million?' He watched Franklin's eyes narrow, then widen as the answer was prepared.

'Can't say I have. Sounds a good story.'

Steele said, 'He's a very important gentleman. Should the story be told? If not, why not? What is the public relations view?'

Sir George pretended to consider. 'I think the PR view is: look forward, not back. Who gets hurt and how badly?'

Steele said, 'It's like the old bit in the romantic novel. Many get hurt, but none get hurt like Raymond.'

Franklin's eyes flicked at him.

Steele smiled. 'Or was it Algy?'

'Whoever it was, if somebody's going to get hurt, isn't it best forgotten? For Heaven's sake, I'm as idealistic as the next man but this is the real world we live in and the trick is to stop people being hurt.'

'All people?'

'Certainly. People don't like fuss and trouble. Life's hard enough, surely. They like quiet rest and relaxation when they can get it.'

Steele said, 'There is more joy in Wigan over one millionaire who is convicted than over a thousand and one petty fiddlers.'

'And that's your job? The job of the Press?'

'Yes. The press has two main jobs – investigate and inform.'

Sir George shook his head. 'Old fashioned, Mr. Steele. You haven't been watching.'

'Oh?'

'The job has changed. Now it's another form of entertainment. It's not the daily bulletin any more, it's the eight o'clock show.'

'You make it sound like *1984*.'

Sir George said, 'That's only a few years away, now.'

'And coming?'

'Certainly it's coming. The thing is to decide. When it happens, do you want to be a prole?'

As Steele watched Franklin leave, John Gaunt appeared beside him. 'He doesn't mind. He just pretends he does. And does that rather well.'

Steele said, 'I thought at one point he was genuinely angry.'

'No. He's a judging kind of man. Living proof that the upper classes have still the upper hand.'

'Warning in every word, anyway,' Steele said.

'Was there?'

'You've read *1984*?' And when Gaunt nodded, 'Didn't you notice? His last words were, do you want to be a prole?'

Longbottom said wearily, 'I'd rather like to get through a session without unpleasantness,' and Steele, noting the accusation in his eyes, glared back at both Longbottom and the young man beside him.

'This,' Longbottom said, 'is Ken Ware. He's one of the Müller, Urquhart Nostell partners, an accountant. Before he joined us he was in management accounting at Shell. He's an expert on the Discounted Cash Flow technique.'

'Arising from that,' Steele said, 'and from your earlier observations about peace and concord, I think you'd be better off without me for this little session.'

'It's useful,' Longbottom began.

'Not to me. I have to take my shoes off to count past ten. Good afternoon.'

Steele took a taxi to his office feeling rebellious. Between pompous PROs and management accountants it had not been much of a day.

Sue, his secretary, looked up in surprise. 'Hello! How's it going?'

'It is uniformly ghastly.' Steele opened the door of his own office and went in. 'Come on in, Sue. Tell me all.'

She followed, head down, looking at her notebook. 'Not much, really. Oh yes, a writ.'

Steele's heart thudded. 'From whom?'

'Malcolm Sandwich, says our review was defamatory.'

'His book was disgusting,' Steele said. 'He hasn't a chance. That all?'

'Expenses. Admin. There's a great big basketful.'

'There would be. Sue! Sue, 'tis a vile and filthy world.'

She smiled, smoothy blonde, secure and confident. 'Weltschmerz.'

'Angst in my pants,' Steel said. 'Very uncomfortable.'

She laughed and Steele looked at her admiringly. 'One of the nice things about educated upper-class girls is that they understand one's jokes. Some, anyway.'

'I don't think I want to understand them all.'

'That's another thing they do very well – fail to understand.'

'We have courses, you know, at Cheltenham.'

'In what?'

'The technique of the snub. Some hints on reproof. Mastery of the icy stare.'

'Okay, let's have the paperwork and we'll shift it with the maximum economy.'

While she sat making notes, taking letters as directed, Steele went rapidly through the accumulated routine work. After about ten minutes he picked from the basket what looked like a blank sheet of paper. 'What's this?'

Sue said, 'Oh, from some crank. It just says "don't".'

Steele looked again. The single typewritten word had been almost lost in the folding of the sheet.

'How did it arrive?'

'Plain envelope,' Sue said. 'Addressed to you.'

'Posted?'

'No. Just your name on it,' Sue said. 'I expect he pushed it through the door to save a stamp.'

He nodded and worked on.

The telephone call came about an hour later, on his private line. 'Mr. Steele?'

'Yes.'

'I'm sure,' the voice said gently, 'that you will take this in the best possible way—'

'Who is that?'

'You have been pursuing a line of inquiry, Mr. Steele, that is misguided.'

'What line? Who's speaking?'

'You know the matter concerned, Mr. Steele. I am giving you good advice, worth taking.'

Steele said angrily, 'This is mad! What the hell are you talking about?'

'You do know, Mr. Steele. Or so it is to be hoped.'

At the other end of the line the receiver was replaced and Steele listened to the sudden purr of the dialling tone.

Sue said, 'What on earth was it?'

'The usual nut.' But Steele knew it wasn't. There had been a flat certainty about the voice; that could not have come from the usual nut.

'If he wouldn't say who he was, it may be the same one who

286

phoned twice before and asked for you, then rang off when I said you weren't here.'

'Today?'

'Just after lunch.'

Steele scowled. It could only be Toller; either McFarquhar or Leicester Deptford had reported back on Steele's interest. He picked up the telephone.

'Hello.' Deptford's guardian daughter again.

'Daddy there?' Steele identified himself.

'Hello.' Deptford was on the line.

Steele said, 'Leicester, word has reached our friend Toller.'

'Wasn't me.'

'I didn't say it was. But only two of you knew I was inquiring.'

'Then it's the other chap, whoever he is. What's the warning?'

'How did you know it was a warning?'

Deptford laughed softly. Steele could picture him at the other end of the line, the moon face bent into puffs of humour. 'It had to be, Gerard. Threats are his weapons.'

'All right. An unspecified threat.'

'Then do be careful. I told you. Toller means it.'

'So?'

'Listen and I will tell you a story.'

Steele listened and finally hung up. He was a little puzzled, very angry and considerably frightened.

Sue said, 'Is it a *real* threat?' She was frowning, concerned, giving him her interest as well as her attention.

'It does seem so.' He could feel the tension in his facial muscles; his skin seemed stiff and stretched.

'Will you give in?' In his mind the end of her sentence composed itself. She had not said 'Will you give in, *little man*?' but in some blend of tone and inflection, the words had been implicit.

'You think I will?' He stared back at her resentfully but her eyes were clear of meaning.

She shrugged. 'I don't know. How can I?' And again Steele seemed to detect the implicit belief in his weakness.

'Go on.'

Sue said, 'One shouldn't run away, of course, if one can win. You only run if you're bound to lose. That's what courage is, surely.'

'Cynical!'

She frowned. He could see her wondering how her realism could be seen as cynicism. 'Could you win? I mean, could you put him into a position where he couldn't strike back because he'd be doing so in public.'

'Ingenious.'

'Well, it's pretty obvious!'

Steele smiled. So much depended on one's point of view; it had been far from obvious to him. He asked how and watched her shake her head.

'I doubt it,' he said.

'Then you'll have to forget it!' She was quite sure; dismissive now. It was almost obscene, Steele thought, that she should be so at home in these byways of power.

'Have to!' Steele said. 'Have to?'

'Well it's chancy, otherwise.'

'I don't care, damn it!' Steele heard himself say the words out loud and once it was done felt obscurely compelled to underline them. 'I'll damn' well expose him.'

'You're exposing yourself,' she said, then blushed quickly and violently, and his pleasure in her discomfiture, delight at the sudden puncturing of her armoured shell, forced everything else from Steele's mind.

He laughed and looked down, deliberately vulgar. 'I don't think so. I'm all zipped up.'

Sue's lips were pursed tight, her cheeks crimson; Steel had not before seen her embarrassed. He said, 'But pursuing the allusion, I'll kick him right there. In the balls, where it hurts.'

'I don't understand why you do this?' Sue said.

'Do what?'

'This innuendo all the time. The minor obscenities. The anatomical asides.'

'For God's sake!' Steele felt himself flushing too. 'Now you object to small pleasantries?'

Sue's blush was disappearing now. She looked determined,

even angry. She said, 'It's like your threat to Toller. You deal in talk.' She got up and walked out of the office. Raging, Steele watched her go: the little madam – flouting her bottom at me! As the door of her office closed he hurried over and opened it: 'Just what do you mean?'

'Do you want me to say it?' she asked quietly. 'Do you?'

'Yes I bloody well do.' He was hot and angry.

'You haven't got the nerve.'

'Oh, I haven't?' Steele somehow couldn't avoid sounding schoolboyish.

'You think I daren't go for Toller?'

She lowered her eyes. 'I'm sorry. I should not have said—'

'Never mind that,' Steele shouted. 'You think I daren't, don't you? Well, I'll bloody well show you! Come in here, sit down and I'll dictate the story to you.' He could feel his jaw thrust forward. 'Straight away!'

She followed him back into the room and Steele said, 'No, sit over there.'

She stared at him blankly. 'All right. But why?'

'So I can see your legs,' he snapped. 'Is that direct enough for you?'

She did not reply and he said, 'Right. The story begins, quote:'

Steele dictated four paragraphs. 'And is that poisonous enough for you?'

'If you print it.'

'I'll print it.' His anger was mixed now with satisfaction. 'I'll bloody well print it. Right? And if I want to say balls, I'll say it.'

She got up and left the office. After a moment he heard the faint clicking of her typewriter and opened the door. 'If you don't like it, you can always leave.'

She looked up at him coolly. 'I shall quite enjoy it I think. I'm not one of those who can't stand the sight of blood.'

Fullerton Ironside-Keyes

'YOU will remember our conversation on Friday, Mr. Keyes.'

Keyes was in shirt and socks in his room, changing after the afternoon session. He wondered how Zander had managed to time his call so perfectly.

'I remember.'

'It would be convenient if you could spare a little time now.'

Keyes hesitated. He'd been hoping the call, and the interview, would be delayed until it was clear whether Scrivener had succeeded in prising Whistler Island out of Euromob's grip. As one third owner of a small mountain of manganese, neither Mr. X nor Euromob would have anything to offer him. If not, well he remembered very clearly Zander's casual remark about a doubled salary. In either circumstance, he didn't need to grovel. He said, 'All right. In an hour I have an engagement. Will that be long enough?'

Zander laughed gently. 'Nobody gets an hour. I'm in the lobby.'

'I'm half-naked. Two minutes.'

'Right.' He dressed, knotting the Brigade tie above the striped shirt. Bowler? Yes, he thought, a bowler. A bowler not for its business connotation but for its social ones. He wore it very straight and well forward.

Zander rose as Keyes crossed the lobby. 'I have a car.'

'Good,' Keyes said. 'Do you always work like this?'

'You mean this sub-James Bond business? No.' He held the door. 'It's just for you.'

'It's appreciated.' Keyes was half-smiling. 'Perhaps you'll tell me, now, whom I shall see.'

Zander stopped beside a silver-grey Mercedes. 'No.'

'Why not?'

'He may change his mind between now and then.'

290

Keyes laughed.

'Don't laugh, Mr. Keyes. About people he's almost never wrong.'

'Very well.' Keyes sat quietly as Zander threaded the Mercedes through the late afternoon traffic and stopped off Jermyn Street.

'Into the lift. Second floor.'

Keyes stepped out of the car and went into the building, holding the door open for Zander, but Zander wasn't there; the Mercedes was already moving off.

A little puzzled but unsurprised, Keyes went inside and pressed the lift button, stepped in when the doors opened, and pressed the button for the second floor. The lift was silent, opulent, smooth. He stepped out into a corridor, quite short and panelled in some matt, black substance. There didn't seem to be a door, but Keyes looked carefully round to make sure and then waited. It was, he thought, a little like being called in to see the adjutant at Birdcage Walk, and remembering, he placed his feet apart and his hands behind his back and stared at the wall opposite. Whoever was waiting for him was doubtless observing from somewhere or other; it made sense to be immobile.

A couple of minutes went by, then the panel at the end of the corridor swung back revealing itself as a door, and a man appeared in it.

'Come in, Mr. Keyes.' The figure was in silhouette against the light behind.

Keyes walked forward, through the door as the man stepped back. In the light he recognized Ray Toller. 'I wondered.'

'About me? Sit down.'

Keyes sat. 'No name was mentioned.'

'But you wondered?' Toller sat with deliberation in an easy chair.

'One is bound to wonder. It is a situation made for speculation.' He looked at Toller: smallish, neat, undistinguished; nothing to make one suspect the hundred million Toller had made.

'And now?'

Keyes' mind went back to his school, to a master who had

said, 'All your life people will try to ask you awkward questions. They are disconcerted if you answer very simply.' He had found the advice good. 'Now I know.'

'All right, Mr. Keyes. Is your curiosity satisfied?'

'I think so.'

'No questions you wish to ask me?'

Keyes reflected. 'I think not.'

'As you stood in the corridor outside, I was able to see you, Mr. Keyes. Clearly you knew that. So do most other people who stand there. It is, in its way, a small stress test. You exhibited less curiosity than anyone I can remember.

Keyes looked at him, decided not to be drawn, and raised his eyebrows a little politely.

Toller said, 'I value curiosity.'

'Not, I imagine, pointless curiosity.'

'It is difficult to know when it *is* pointless.'

'Often,' Keyes agreed. 'But not this time.'

'Properly at ease.' Toller changed tack swiftly.

Keyes smiled. 'Easy, in fact. It is a relaxing way to stand still.'

'You have strengths, Mr. Keyes. Have you also weaknesses?'

'Inevitably.'

'And they are?'

'Private.'

Toller said quietly, 'Once a man works for me, they cease to be private. I require to know.'

Keyes looked at him. Toller sat very still, hands resting lightly in his lap, knowing he held all the cards. Except one, Keyes thought. Until the game actually began they were equal; after that Toller could walk all over him in hob-nailed boots. It was important, until that moment, to win. He rose. 'A pleasure to meet you.'

'You misunderstand, Mr. Keyes.'

'Do I?'

'I shall explain. I make a living, if you will accept the expression, out of knowing the strengths and weaknesses of companies. This balance, as I call it, is my criterion. So with my staff. I demand ability, judgment, literacy, numeracy, the ability to concentrate and absorb, good social ability and a deal of ruthlessness. Sentimentality has no place in this organization. Fair?'

'It seems so.'

'I employ people for their abilities. Their weaknesses concern me only if they are likely to bring weakness into my organization. I have no moral objection to homosexuality, but my people do not pick up Guardsmen in the Park. You see?'

'Yes I do.'

'Then what are you?'

Keyes said, 'Sorry.' He felt slightly ridiculous, standing.

'There are seven sins, are there not? Pride is one. Which others?'

'No.'

'Mr. Keyes, let us be clear. If I am satisfied, you will be offered a job here worth fifteen thousand pounds a year.'

'It is necessary,' Keyes said, 'for me to share that satisfaction.'

Toller looked up at him and Keyes had to make an effort to remain still. He was wrong-footed and it would be difficult to regain balance.

'Why did you go to America?'

'I beg your pardon?' Keyes felt a tingle of nervousness in his spine.

'America?'

'On business.'

'Euromob business?'

'What else?'

Toller said, 'I don't know. I have a report which makes me curious.'

'On my trip to America?'

'And on yourself. You did nothing save visit a family called Volans in Seattle and meet various airline representatives, namely a Mr. Viner of Cloudair, a Mr. Martin of Two Ocean Airstream.'

Keyes stared. 'You had me followed?'

'Why not, Mr. Keyes? Then there was a Miss Marilyn Westcott, also of Two Ocean Airstream.'

293

He felt his cheeks redden and cursed himself.

Toller said, 'Your relationship with Miss Westcott was on your side a matter of impulse; on hers an attempt to win business. I think you were unwise but no more. Mr. Viner and Mr. Martin were contacts; your meetings with them were not the reason for your trip. You went to see the Volans family. Why?'

'That, too, is private.'

'When Mr. Volans is here in London?'

For God's sake, how much did Toller know? What on earth had made Toller set detectives on him in the States? That, certainly, was what had happened, but it was difficult to imagine its being done, or the reasoning behind it!

Toller said, 'I see you disapprove.'

'I am—,' Keyes smiled, recovering a little of the initiative, 'I am curious.'

'Ah!' Toller nodded. 'My reasons are simply as I explained them. I need to know.'

'It was a social visit.'

'I think not, Mr. Keyes. Had it been, you would, by now, have been angry. As it is, you are concerned. I shall, I promise you, discover the reason.'

'Why, when it doesn't matter?'

'To be sure that it doesn't. Even today, people do not fly fifteen thousand miles without reason.'

Keyes managed a shrug. He must get to Volans quickly; hold a council of war; let Scrivener know. Or should he?

Toller said, 'I see uncertainty.'

'This is my first stress interview.'

'Interesting that you should see it as stress.'

'Stress is easy to detect in oneself.'

Toller rose slowly, neatly. He walked to an antique escritoire at the other end of the room, opened a drawer, and took out a paper, glanced at it and then looked at Keyes. 'The offer is fifteen thousand pounds a year; an Aston-Martin car and such expenses as you need.'

Keyes blinked but recovered himself quickly, straightening his knees, his hips, his back until his body was upright. The offer was there: fifteen thousand! *Fifteen thousand!* It was unbelievable. He said, coolly, 'I should like to think about it,' but he was conscious of fear in his chest.

'Why?'

'Perhaps because your stricture on impulsive action found a mark.'

Toller smiled. 'Until nine in the morning, Mr. Keyes. At that time the offer becomes invalid. Telephone me here.' He crossed the room, handed Keyes a small card, and shook hands.

'I shall let you know by nine.'

Toller said, 'When you accept, I shall require the information.'

He took a taxi back, a lift to the fourteenth floor and hurried to Volans's room. There was no response to his knock. Damn! Keyes hurried to the common room, but only Longbottom and Templeton were there. Where, then? He went down again and into the Prince's Bar; no Volans. Keyes cursed, remembering Zander's Mercedes, sure now in his own mind that Zander had gone back to the hotel to talk to Volans.

'What bars are there, here?' he asked the head porter.

'The Prince's Bar, sir. The Duke of Plaza-Toro Bar, the Maids-in-Waiting Bar. And, of course, the Tiara Bar on the roof.'

Keyes thanked him. Would Volans be up there? He had a brief vision of Zander leading Volans to a high place and showing him all the kingdoms of the earth, but he rejected it; Zander wasn't that kind of devil. They'd be talking quietly in some suitably discreet place, probably outside the premises. He went to the telephone.

Scrivener said, 'No it isn't signed. Hodder was at a funeral this afternoon.'

'But it will be?'

'I see no reason why not,' Scrivener sounded annoyed, but Keyes was familiar with his temper.

'When?'

'How do I know! As soon as possible. Good-bye, Keyes.'

'Sir Kenelm!'

'Well?'

295

'Time matters.'

'Of course it does. Don't be a fool, boy.'

Keyes said, 'Then let's get a move on.'

'Don't be impertinent.'

'The word, Sir Kenelm, is impatient. And I am.'

'And I am late for dinner,' Scrivener said. He hung up.

Keyes bought the *Evening Standard* from the bookstall and took a seat in the lobby.

Volans returned alone and thoughtful and Keyes watched him as he slowly crossed the lobby towards the lifts. Certainly something was up. He rose and hurried across.

'Been talking to a man called Zander?'

Volans spun round, his face blank with astonishment.

Keyes said, 'I'm a mind-reader.'

'How the hell—'

'You have, though?'

Volans shrugged and nodded. 'Zander talked to me. You know him?'

'I met him.'

'So who the hell *is* he?'

Keyes ignored the question. 'He wanted to know why I went to Seattle. Right?'

Volans said, 'Right.'

'And he knew I'd talked to your wife?'

'Yeah.'

He also inferred that I was some kind of international seducer, but you know better than that?'

'Do I?' Volans' eyes were hard.

Keyes said, 'For God's sake, it was the papers I wanted. I wasn't in the house half an hour.'

'What about the stewardess!' Volans snarled.

'What did you tell Zander?'

'Never mind.'

Volans began to turn away angrily and Keyes grabbed his shoulder. 'This is what Zander wanted. That we should quarrel.'

'Quarrel? We supposed to be friends or something?'

'We're harnessed together for the moment.'

'Are we? So what's Scrivener doing? Has he got that signature?'

'Not yet.'

'Uh huh! I'll tell you something, smartpants. I am being sideswiped and I know it. I don't trust you and I don't trust Scrivener. Why should I when you're robbing me?'

'But you'd trust Zander? You must be mad!'

Volans said, 'Yes, I'm mad. So long, Keyes.'

'One question. Did he ask about your brother? About the trip north?'

Volans grinned. 'It's no fun losing. But it's sure one hell of a kick pulling the others down with you.' He turned shaking Keyes' hand away from his powerful shoulder, and Keyes watched him go, mind racing. It was impossible now to learn what Volans had told Zander, so he must assume the worst: that Zander now had got some hint that mineral deposits were involved. It was unlikely, though, that Volans had told him the whole story. He'd still be hoping Scrivener would get the signature that would make them all rich. Unless Toller had promised him the earth – and Toller hadn't seen him yet – that remained Volans' and his own best hope. There were, however, two others. He could let Toller know about the manganese: or he could let Hodder know. Either *should* reward him spectacularly, but it was an ungrateful world.

He went again to the telephone. 'Sir Kenelm Scrivener, please.'

'I'm afraid Sir Kenelm is dining, sir.'

'Interrupt him, then. My name is Keyes. Ironside-Keyes.'

'Very well, sir.'

Keyes waited. The servant's voice, when it came back on the line, was a shade less deferential. 'Sir Kenelm does not wish to be interrupted, sir. He asks if the matter is very urgent.'

'Say one word,' Keyes said savagely. 'No, make it two. Toller, that's tee-oh-double-ell-ee-ar, and Whistler, double-you-aitch—'

'Very well, sir.'

A moment later, Scrivener's voice said, 'What the hell's all this about?'

'Ray Toller. He either knows – or he's got a damn good idea – about Whistler Island.'

'Don't be bloody silly, boy! How can he?'

'His staff work is good. I was followed to Seattle and he's got somebody working round the Volans family.'

'Very well, I'll see Hodder first thing. It's dangerous. He might suspect something. But I'll see him.'

Keyes said, 'Tonight.'

Scrivener's voice was gravelly with rage. 'I said tomorrow.'

'Tonight.'

'Don't dictate to me, boy.'

'If you don't move tonight, all the dictating will be done by Toller.'

'Then let it.' The phone crashed down.

Back in his room, Keyes lay on the bed cigarette in hand, thinking. Perhaps he had been foolish to try to push Scrivener; there wasn't much even Scrivener could do at this time of night. If Scrivener were to rush round to Hodder demanding signature forthwith, Hodder would rightly smell fish and refuse. But if he didn't get the signature soon, then the pressure of events and the widening knowledge of the existence of the manganese would bring the whole thing out into the open. And at that point he, Fullerton Keyes, could bid it a fond good-bye.

A couple of cigarettes later he had reached certain conclusions: regretfully he had decided to cut his losses and acquire such benefit from his knowledge as might remain to be acquired. There was no guarantee of the generosity either of Toller or Hodder and the choice between them was difficult if not impossible.

Those were his conclusions. The decision remained. Fullerton Ironside-Keyes frowned and reached for another cigarette.

Harry Philips

'WHEN you have a moment, Harry.' Philips glanced at the intercom speaker and depressed the button labelled *Chairman*. Hodder in at 8.30 in the morning?

'In just a couple of minutes, if that's all right.'

'Fine.' With a click, Hodder went off the line.

No use wondering what it was about: it could be about any of a million matters. Unlikely, however, that it would be about Toller's bid because Hodder didn't know about it. Philips sat for a moment, reflecting, examining his own position. He had in no way dirtied his ticket, whereas Hodder had; he had the support of Scrivener and the institutional directors, where Hodder had not. The more modern-minded senior staff supported him because they saw him as the key to the future: Farmer's tip-off about the Toller bid indicated that clearly enough.

He rose, straightened his jacket, took off his spectacles and replaced them more comfortably, then walked out of his office, had not yet summoned either the nerve or energy necessary to move into Salt's. Philips knocked lightly, once, and went in.

'Good morning, Harry.' Hodder looked up briefly, wrote something, then laid down his pen.

'Morning, Alex.' Philips waited, watching Hodder get up stiffly and walk to the window. They had never been friends; true they had worked in harness with Salt's hands on the rein, but that was more a matter of not being enemies, nor even rivals. They were rivals now, though, Philips reflected, whether Hodder recognized it or not.

Over his shoulder, Hodder said, 'You have a loyal staff, Harry. I envy you that.'

An alarm bell pinged in Philips' mind, tensing his mental reflexes. 'Oh?'

'Mmm,' Hodder said. He continued staring out of the window towards St. Paul's and the silence lengthened. Philips looked at him, trying to decide what Hodder was after. The tactical silence was hardly an indication of happiness, so what was it? He decided to wait, to let Hodder speak, but it became increasingly obvious that Hodder would not; the chairman stood by the floor to ceiling window silhouetted against the sky, immobile. Philips, standing by the door, felt increasingly marooned. He could not withdraw, nor could he stroll forward; his voice, now, would sound odd and unwelcome in the silence. All the same, pressure to speak was building inside him. So was a wish to move. A man could stand, like Hodder, staring out over a great city, for hours; it had the same fascination as watching an anthill or a beehive, but standing as he stood now was uncomfortable and increasingly so. Philips realized suddenly why: Hodder had put him in the wrong, subtly and ingeniously. His silence was a hostile one and both of them knew it. All right, then, he'd break it.

'Something I can do?' His dry throat betrayed him and his voice came out hoarse and nervous. Damn!

'You want it very much, Harry?' Hodder turned slowly to face him.

Philips cleared his throat, feeling the colour rising in his cheeks. Get hold of yourself he told himself furiously. 'It?'

Hodder smiled. 'This.'

If you're going to be simple, direct and patrician, Philips thought, good luck to you. He said, 'Should I understand?'

'I'd be surprised if you didn't.'

'You'll have to explain.'

'I'd have thought it was a simple question. Do you want this?' Hodder's hand indicated the office, the surroundings.

Philips said, 'This is the office intended for the Deputy Chairman.'

'And you would like to be Chairman?' Philips found himself surprised at Hodder's urbanity, strangely because Hodder was naturally urbane and urbanity was to be expected.

'I am normally ambitious, Alex, if that is what you mean.'

'So I had thought.'

'I see.' Philips spoke carefully. 'You are unhappy about something I have done?' Let Hodder be specific.

'Harry, as a director of a publicly-quoted company, you are

300

required to declare the extent of your holding in the company.'

Philips felt his cheeks tighten. So that was it! Hodder had learned about yesterday's purchase of Euromob shares! 'I declare it every year.'

'Increases in the holding should be notified to the company secretary immediately.'

Philips manufactured indignation. 'For heaven's sake, Alex. Give me the chance.'

'I am asking the extent of your holding now.'

Philips said, 'Roughly sixty thousand.'

'Shares?'

'Pounds.'

Hodder went to his desk, picked up a copy of the previous year's annual report. 'It was fifteen thousand shares last year. You have bought heavily and very recently.'

'That is true.' Philips felt, and hated the feeling, like a guilty but defiant schoolboy.

'Why?'

Philips said, 'You are entitled to know about the purchase but not the reasons for it. However, you know the situation as well as I do.'

'You mean Toller's bid?'

Philips looked back at him, his mind turning the question over fast. Presumably Hodder must know, but how? Or was he guessing?'

'A bid of some kind. Hugh invited it.'

'It's a big gamble on a possibility. Fifty thousand pounds, Harry?'

Philips nodded, saying nothing.

Hodder said, 'I wasn't aware you were a gambling man, Harry. Particularly with money you don't have.'

Philips concentrated on remaining bland. The new stock market account had begun on Monday; he had almost three weeks in which Euromob shares could rise on Toller's bid, before he'd have to pay his broker. By that time he'd have sold again and even allowing for capital gains tax, he'd do quite nicely.

'All right.' Hodder shrugged. 'It's your business. I do think, however, that as a director of this corporation, simple decency would demand that you inform your colleagues of important news concerning it.'

'Like what?' Philips said.

'Like the bid Toller is making. At twenty-one shillings a share.'

'Is he?'

'Don't be naïve, Harry.'

Philips felt anger bubbling and suppressed it. The word decency had stung, more so because he recognized the correctness of its use. 'I heard rumours. I would have reported them to you this morning.'

Hodder said wearily, 'As you would have reported, on Tuesday morning, the development of the copier.'

'That's the real grumble, isn't it Alex,' Philips said. 'You think I was behind that.' It was time to counter-attack.

'You knew.'

'I had heard, the same day. I was seeking more information, that's all, before I reported.'

'And you did not tell me.'

'Tell you what?' Philips said. 'Some half-baked story about a great invention. Do you imagine I would want it shouted about if there was nothing to it?'

'From where I stand, Harry, it makes an unattractive picture.'

Philips said, 'If you want my word that I had nothing to do with telling the TV people about Giesing's copier, I will give it happily.'

'Then who told them?'

'I have no idea.'

'Perhaps,' Hodder said, 'it was the same person who told me you knew about Toller's bid. That's all I know just now, Harry: that the bid is coming tonight, after the market closes, and that it's for a guinea. I had no idea you'd have bought, but I guessed you would.'

Philips sat at his own desk, sipping hot, black coffee, aware of his crisis and the speed at which it could develop. He felt curiously dead, inert, unexcited. He should have felt vividly

alive and was disappointed that he didn't. The accusation about
the shares didn't worry him: he had intended to tell Hodder
that morning and the use of a few hours' grace to make a little
money was a practice hallowed by time and repeated use.
Scrivener or Duff or Salt wouldn't have hesitated. The fact
that Hodder *would* didn't make it criminal.

But the accusation that he told the obnoxious interviewer
Milk abut the copier stung a little. Philips would not do it and
resented the general belief that he might. So who had? No, he
told himself, don't chase that hare. You have other things to
do.

He finished his coffee and picked up the telephone.

The car dropped him at Peter Jones's and he walked from
there, against the one way traffic, to Scrivener's house. Scrivener took him into his study for a whisky.

'What makes you think it's time to go? Seems a bit soon to
me. Destroy the market price.' He didn't know. Philips said, 'I
think that broadcast and the subsequent newspaper comment
has done a terrific amount of damage. There's more this morning. Have you seen the *Mail*?'

Scrivener nodded. 'Price crept back two coppers last night,
though.'

'Somebody in the market. Toller possibly. You've heard the
rumour?'

'It's the reason I'm listening.' Scrivener's liver-face swung
towards him. 'If the price drops again, the corporation will be
gobbled up.'

'You have no objection surely?'

Scrivener said, 'This copier makes a difference. If it's as
good as it seems it's a world-wide profit maker. Look at Xerox.
What it did for Ranks!'

Philips sipped his whisky. 'I agree it's very soon after Salt.
But If all the trouble is out of the way . . .?'

'Yes.' Scrivener seemed deep in thought. 'Help yourself to
the whisky, Philips. I agree Hodder's acting a bit oddly. Odd to
me, too.'

'Oh?'

'Mingulay wants an island. Got his eye on a bit of rock we
own off the Canadian coast. Made a fair offer, too.'

303

'But?'

'Hodder said no. Wrong time to dispose of property. I ask you!'

'Mingulay annoyed?'

'Wouldn't you be?' Damn place is nothing but rock anyway.' Scrivener laughed wheezily. 'That's your first job in the chair. I've got the documents prepared.'

He was in! Philips' heart thumped; his head felt as though it was inflating with excitement. He was *in*! He laughed. 'Of course.'

'In fact,' Scrivener said, 'it might save time if you'd sign it now. Today's date.'

Philips said, 'It hasn't any validity unless—'

'No, no. But you'll be elected, Philips. You'll be elected.'

Philips took out his pen, unscrewed the cap carefully and signed on a line beside which was the word: Chairman.

'Right,' Scrivener said. 'We'll get 'em here for lunch.'

Jane Roper

TEMPLETON held a sheaf of papers in his hand. He said, 'Here, a quickie before the woe begins. There's two little girls talking and one says to the other, "After mummy and daddy's party at the week-end, I found a contraceptive on the patio.' And the other little girl said, "What's a patio?"' ' Templeton laughed cheerfully. 'I have a theory that if we could unearth them, there'd be more accurate history in jokes than in the mutually agreed fiction we all disbelieve.'

Jane listened to the laugh, smiling herself, knowing she was being watched by people who wondered if she would laugh. Curious how women weren't supposed to understand! To laugh was to be a scarlet woman because women weren't supposed to realize sex was funny, or to know the words that were the common coinage of a great deal of masculine conversation.

'Now we come to the gruesome bit,' Templeton said. 'You'll all remember completing those personality test papers the other day? Well I've scored them now and a weird and wonderful lot you are!' He looked round. 'No smiles? Well wait till you see 'em. The thing to remember is that this one test would never settle anything. It gives indications of personality, but one would always use it in conjunction with other tests, I.Q. and so on. Before I give you these papers I'd better tell you that there are loaded pistols in the next room in case any of you want to shoot yourselves. Or me – which is more likely! Now, listen – you'll see that you are scored between one and nine on a number of scales. For example, submissive is at the one end and aggressive at nine. Normality is taken to be five, half-way between. So do try to remember that the idea isn't high scores. Okay?' He walked round the table handing out papers.

'Thank you.' Jane took hers and looked at the scales. A seven on considerate, a two indicated low leadership potential. Six put her at the creative end of the scale; four for patience on a scale that gave nine to impatience.

305

'Now,' Templeton said, 'just look and see whether you recognize yourselves. As I said, it's not expected to be a perfect picture. But if it's reasonably true, it's an effective test.'

Beside her, Steele said, 'It's bloody nonsense.'

'You don't like something?' Templeton grinned widely. 'What's the problem?'

'It may be a picture of Whistler's mother, but it's not a picture of me.'

'Go on.'

'Would you call me submissive?' Steele demanded.

'Personally, no. But I don't know you in your lighter moments.'

Jane winced on Steele's behalf.

'You objectionable little bastard!' Steele shouted. 'You go fiddling about in people's personalities and psyches with no right and less scruple and then try to make fools of them.'

Templeton said, 'Who am I to seek to improve on the work of the Lord?'

'Right. *Viewpoint* is going to examine the whole question of industrial psychologists. Starting with you, by name.'

'There's a law of libel.'

'With which I am totally familiar,' Steele said. 'And you'd be sensible to learn what slander is.'

'Okay, okay. Anybody else?' Not surprisingly, there was nobody. 'I take it, then, that you all agree it's a roughly accurate picture?'

Jane again ran her eyes down the markings. It was, more or less, a picture of her. Not a flattering one, but then it was not intended to be. She looked at the others, busily studying their own reflections, scowling, frowning, smiling according to whether they liked what they saw, then looked at her own again. Seven there meant purposeful? She smiled grimly: it should have been nine, it really should. Patient and purposeful wasn't a bad description. That . . . and disgraceful, unscrupulous, immoral. But she could live with that knowledge provided she was successful. She was, after all, hurting only one man; no, two. And with both there was justice in what she was doing. In any case, a day or two and it could all be over, then she would, with luck, be able to concentrate on living, rather than retribution. There would be no more Philipses, no more Scriveners; not, at least, in her life.

It was difficult to imagine a man more loathsome than Scrivener. Her skin crawled as she remembered. But he was useful, a part of her purpose; until it was achieved, she'd face anything. And the evening before had brought it nearer.

It hadn't been so bad on Tuesday evening, when there had been dozens of people nearby and escape would have been easy. She'd flattered him a little and threatened a little and enjoyed the morsel of revenge. His lust had been part of her calculations, but she had made no allowance for the creation of his obsession and that, it seemed, was what she had awakened in him. Half the evening she'd been afraid he'd have a seizure, the other half . . .

Scrivener's law firm had offices in the City; what she had not bargained for was that he, as senior partner, had a suite there. She had, with justice, been confident: though there were glaring gaps in her information, she still knew enough to worry him.

Scrivener said, 'Sherry?'

She shook her head. 'Gin and French.'

'Very well.' He poured the drink while she looked around her at the opulent office with its dark carpeting and hand-tooled leather. Behind her she heard him say, 'I imagine you detest me.'

Jane frowned briefly, puzzled, then took the proffered drink.

'Do you?' Scrivener asked.

'Why?'

'I don't imagine you enjoyed the . . . the other night.'

What was he up to? Jane felt the ground shifting beneath her feet and was afraid: Scrivener was clever and subtle. Had he worked out a way to put her off?

She said, 'It was my . . . suggestion, you'll remember.'

'Oh, yes. I remember. But you were under pressure.'

'Choosing you rather than the police?'

'Precisely.'

Jane took a mouthful of her drink, feeling it concentrate her mind. His eyes were all over her, prying at mind and body. What *was* he up to?

'It wasn't that.'

'As I recall,' Scrivener said, 'I made no move.'

She almost laughed. Surely the man wasn't conscience stricken! The pirate king nervous because . . .

'None at all. I wanted to keep my job.'

'You could have gone to gaol.'

She shrugged.

'How much do you earn?'

'Five thousand. A little more.'

'Worth keeping I agree. But—' he hesitated.

Jane said, 'The job is worth keeping.'

'Five thousand *is* worth keeping.'

'Are you asking my price as a whore?' Jane asked coldly.

'I wanted to know why you did it.'

'And whether I enjoyed it? The object was your satisfaction, not mine. Quid pro quo. That's apt.'

'It was achieved,' Scrivener said. 'I am wondering how much I should tell you.'

Jane smiled in relief. The territory was familiar again, the fog gone. 'About your island?'

'I'm interested in your attitude to money. And to me.'

'Go on.'

Scrivener sat on the edge of his desk, facing her. 'The question is whether you would . . .' he stopped. 'You see, they could go together.'

'You and money?'

Scrivener nodded.

'You *are* asking my price as a whore.' Heavens, how could she discuss it so calmly!

Scrivener said, 'Whores don't care. They take anyone.'

'What are you proposing?' She took a cigarette and he held the desk lighter for her. The flame shook.

'That is the – er – difficulty.'

Jane looked at him, understanding now: he wanted her, *and* on a permanent basis. But he was worried in case she might hate him and so be dangerous. She said, 'Money's necessary. I'm sure large quantities must be reassuring. But why?'

Scrivener said, 'You know why.' His hand trembled.

'The other night?' She said it, with an effort, coolly.

He nodded.

'And the question is, do I hate you?' Jane said. 'Because you want me again?'

His colour had mounted. Scrivener's face was now almost purple. He nodded again.

Jane was beginning to hate herself, yet the situation held promise to make her go on. Scrivener was clearly desperate. He had the power that money and position confer but at the moment it was defeated by another power, conferred by beauty. If Scrivener were her instrument . . .

'You said you would not be easy to convince. And you weren't. It's not a tender memory.'

'I'm sorry, very – Miss Roper, I'm sorry. I had no intention—'

'I have already said it was my idea,' Jane said.

'*Do* you hate me?' It was as pathetic as it was astonishing to see Scrivener like this: abject, fearful of her whim. Hate? No, it wasn't hate. It was nearer contempt, but not contempt alone because he was too powerful, too tough for that. Hate was what she felt for Philips.

'Hate? No.'

He trembled. Scrivener actually trembled.

'Then will you? I mean—'

'I know what you mean. But you are a rich man, very powerful. Why me?'

'Because you're beautiful. Because I think of you all the . . . all the time.'

'There must be many women you could—'

He interrupted her. 'It's you, don't you understand? You!'

She looked at him steadily, her ears registering the desperation in his voice, her eyes noting the fear in his.

'I'm not a whore.'

'I didn't say it. Please! I didn't! Didn't imply—'

'And I'm not a mistress. Yours or anybody's.'

Scrivener said, 'Christ, I can't marry you! I wish I could, but I'm married now.' He stopped. 'You're saying no?'

Jane crossed her legs slowly, watching his reaction: his eyes followed the movement and he swallowed audibly. 'I didn't say no.'

Relief exploded across Scrivener's face. 'Then you're willing?' She thought for a moment he was going to leap at her. 'Are you, Jane?'

She said, 'There are things I want.'

'Of course. We'll go to Aspreys, anywhere . . .' He moved towards her.

'No.'

Scrivener stopped. 'Jane, what? Please – what?'

'I don't delude myself that you want anything but my body. It's natural, anyway.' Deliberately she stood up, smoothing her dress over her hips, holding her shoulders back a little to emphasize her breasts.

'This is what you want? This and your memory of the night in your office?'

There was a thick sound in Scrivener's throat, and his eyes flickered about her body. Jane said, 'You remember?'

'I remember.' His voice was husky.

'You had me do . . . a lot of things.'

He looked agonized. 'I'm sorry. I didn't mean—'

She said, 'I *could* be just as co-operative again.'

His eyes closed. He was, she knew, projecting pictures on the screen of his mind and, knowing what the pictures were, Jane felt a sudden nauseating flood of deep shame. Angrily she suppressed it. She had always known this might be necessary, always told herself she would do it; this was no time to back out.

'Tell me what you want,' Scrivener breathed.

'A partnership.'

'Jane, I don't understand.'

'Is this office private?'

Scrivener swallowed. 'Of course.'

She met his eyes. 'If you'll tell me about the island, you can go and lock the door.'

He stared at her and his face showed clearly the war going on inside him. She saw anger there and resentment, even self-disgust and despair. But primarily she saw desire.

'It would mean breaking my word,' he said.

Jane smiled. 'We're not here to talk about ethics. Your word to Keyes and Volans?'

He nodded. 'Yes.'

'Would you rather I locked the door? I will, as soon—'

'For God's sake!' Scrivener burst out. 'How can I?'

Jane went for her bag. 'Very well.' She bent, knowing the movement was revealing, then rose and headed for the door. This was it: win or lose in the next few seconds; the distance to the door seemed endless. When she reached it, she turned. 'I shall not come back.'

'Damn it, then! Lock it!' Scrivener said.

'The island?'

It took a moment for him to reply. Then he said, 'Minerals.'

She put her hand to the key. 'What minerals?'

Scrivener stared across the office at her, his face still a battleground of emotions. 'Manganese,' he said finally. 'A mountain of manganese.'

Jane's face stiffened in surprise. What *was* a mountain of manganese? She had no idea of mineral values, but it must be worth a fortune, several fortunes! 'What happens to it? Whose is it?'

Scrivener laughed. 'When Euromob sells us the island, we make a lot of money. You, too, now that you know. There's your partnership!' He came slowly towards her.

'You're going to trick Hodder into selling?'

'Lock the door, Jane.'

'Are you?'

Scrivener nodded. 'We'll all be rich. Lock the door.' He stopped, a few feet away.

Jane looked at him. It had been horrible before; it would be horrible again. Scrivener was breathing heavily, his face suffused with blood. She looked down at the key. Until this moment control had been hers; now it would pass to him. She watched her own hand turn the key, remove it from the brass lock. She said, 'There's one more thing.'

'Well?'

'Philips.'

'What about him?' Scrivener, she thought, looked like a bull about to charge, head down, snorting.

'I want him out. Finished.'

'What's he done?' Scrivener seemed surprised.

Jane held the key. 'You can do it easily.'

It seemed almost like a dream as Scrivener's hand came and took the key from hers. He was grinning and she had not seen him grin before. 'A little persuasion,' he said, 'and you can have Philips' head on a charger.'

She sat, listening to Templeton and trying not to remember, but it was as though every millimetre of her had a memory of its own that recalled each second of its contact with Scrivener and, aware of her compact with him, shrank from tonight's inevitable repeat performance. All the same, she thought, it's going to happen! Philips *will* be ousted. She repeated the words in her mind with satisfaction: *Philips will be ousted!*

She still had not decided what, if anything, to do about Whistler Island and Scrivener's promise that she, too, would become rich out of the vast deposits of manganese. The whole thing was so difficult even to believe that to go farther and think round it was impossible. It was like winning the football pools or something equally miraculous. One thing, though: manganese or no manganese, she would not take her eye off that first target, the ruining of Harry Philips.

Richard Keller returned at coffee time looking pale, his skin almost transparent.

'Richard, you shouldn't have come.'

He smiled a little wearily. 'It's better than hanging round the house.'

'Yes, but – Richard, you should go away somewhere. For a while, anyway.'

'I don't think so. Better back in the nest of vipers. At least things happen.'

Jane thought: if only you knew! As they talked, she was comparing Keller in her mind with Scrivener; one gentle, honest, made to be hurt; the other hard, unyielding, made to hurt. Richard would hesitate a long time before causing upset or hardship to anyone; Scrivener would not hesitate at all, would often enjoy it. She had forgotten, but remembered now, that Richard knew about the expenditure on Philips' house and that he had been agonizing about telling Hodder. Had the greater agony driven it from his mind?

'Mr. Keller?'

They turned. A page had come into the room with papers in his hand.

'Here.'

'Message, sir.' The boy handed it over. 'Do you know Mr. Keyes, sir?'

Jane said, 'Mr. Keyes is, er – over there.'

Richard was reading his own note, smiling a little, shaking his head slowly.

'What is it, Richard?'

Keller said, 'Nothing much.'

'But you're amused.'

'I laugh that I weep not, Jane. They're having another emergency board meeting tonight.'

Tonight! Jane thought. Tonight! Surely even Scrivener couldn't move as quickly as that. But all the same ... She frowned, asked to be excused, went to the telephone in the lobby.

'Ah, my dear.'

'I hear there's a board meeting tonight.'

'Congratulations on your intelligence service,' he said softly.

'You didn't tell me.'

'I didn't know.'

Something told Jane that Scrivener was not alone; necessarily, therefore, he would be even cagier than usual. 'On a charger, you said.'

'Not today. These things take time.'

'Last night,' Jane said. 'You enjoyed last night?'

'Indeed.' Scrivener's voice was so low, and his choice of reply so careful, that she almost laughed.

'Then do your best. And . . .'

Scrivener said quickly, 'And what?'

'You won't regret it.'

313

'I can't promise.'

She said, 'There are bonus marks for trying.'

Jane replaced the receiver and hurried up to her room. There, she sat at the little table, took out a sheet of blank stationery and wrote a brief letter. She sealed it into an envelope with another piece of paper then telephoned her office and asked that a messenger be sent to collect and deliver the letter. Finally she went downstairs, left it with the hall porter and returned to Templeton's lecture on staff selection by job evaluation and testing.

Alex Hodder

IT was two-thirty p.m. and the sun streaming into his office would have made an oven of it if the air conditioning had not kept it cool. The wooden crate stood on the carpet in the middle of the floor, covered in stencils and scraps of coloured paper held in place by staples.

Hodder said, 'All right, Mr. Giesing, I'm looking forward to this. Are there any problems about voltages?'

'Nothing.' Giesing shrugged. 'But your carpet—'

'Will clean quite easily,' Hodder smiled. 'So let's go ahead, eh?'

Giesing and his engineer, who had brought the crate from Germany, levered it open carefully. The machine inside was about two feet square and eighteen inches deep. The engineer opened a small panel, and took out the electrical lead and looked round for a socket.

'Over there,' Hodder said. 'Dreizehn ampères, zwei hundert vierzig volts.'

'Danke.' The engineer connected the lead with deft fingers, slid the plug into the socket, then made an adjustment at the back of the cabinet. He nodded to Giesing. 'Rettig, Herr Direktor.'

'Something to copy?' Giesing asked.

Hodder crossed to his desk, looking for some harmless document with which to test the machine and his eye fell on the letter. Not that, at any rate! He found a copy of a circular from the Pensions Department. Giesing said, 'Thank you. At this time the machine takes a few seconds to be warm. We hope to eliminate that. So all that you do is to slide the document into this aperture . . . wait . . . and here is the copy.' He handed both original and copy to Hodder.

'It's good. It's very good. Tell me again how it's done.'

Giesing said, 'I am not the engineer. It is a magnetic process.

315

The copy powder contains particles of iron, that is really what I know. But it is good, nicht wahr?'

Hodder nodded. 'Reliability?'

'There is little to go wrong.' Giesing smiled. 'Too easy. We build it and it works.'

'And goes on working?'

'Heinz?' Giesing turned to the engineer.

'Jawohl. Is easy. More ink. More paper.'

Hodder said, 'It's too easy, Mr. Giesing. Why haven't 3M and IBM and Xerox Corporation used this principle?'

'Perhaps because nobody thought of it. Like the hover-craft.'

'And the costings?'

'Manufacturing costs are detailed in the folder you have,' Giesing said. 'We have also included a plan for the marketing of the machine and suggested costings for that, too, but of course other means may be used.'

'Who is we?'

'In Germany. Now Mr. Philips has suggested Mr. Verity work with me.'

'And that's all right by you?'

Giesing said. 'All right. I understand him.'

'Fine.' Hodder placed the original in the machine's mouth, watched the perfect copy appear. 'Leave it here, Mr. Giesing will you?'

'It should be covered, sir.'

Hodder laughed. 'Are you worried about spies or dust, Mr. Giesing?

When they had gone he sat for a few minutes, staring at the copier. It was difficult to believe that this box of tricks would produce revenue enough to pull Euromob round. But one bit of manna from Heaven was not, it seemed, enough. Now in that letter also he had a stick with which to beat Philips if Philips was awkward again. Hodder walked to the window and looked out at St. Paul's, so near he sometimes felt he could reach out and touch it. It was like that now, silver-grey and magical against the blue sky, with the City's ghastly egg-boxes spread around it. He looked at the new Stock Exchange build-

316

ing: when it closed in twenty minutes or so, Toller's bid would be made. Not, of course, until then, in deference to the fallacy that the City played fair. There'd be after-hours trading at high speed, Hodder knew. He hoped there would also be burned fingers. Meanwhile there was nothing to be done. The board meeting to discuss Toller's offer had been called; the machine was here. For twenty minutes he could stand and stare. If Toller's bid were successful, of course, he'd have a great deal more time to stand and stare and half of him, Hodder acknowledged wryly, would like that very much.

His tea came and he drank it, looking out over the City, conscious that he might be fiddling while Rome burned. Then, at three thirty-one his telephone rang and his secretary said, 'Mr. Toller is on the line, sir. Mr. Ray Toller.' She sounded frightened.

'Put him on.' Hodder waited, heard the click. 'Hello.'

A voice said, 'Mr. Hodder? Mr. Alex Hodder?'

'Yes.'

'My name is Raymond Toller. I am calling to tell you that I am—'

Hodder couldn't resist it. He said, 'Putting in a bid for Euromob.'

There was a brief silence, then Toller said, 'That was a good guess, Mr. Hodder. I think it a proper courtesy, on these occasions, to inform the chairman of the terms of my offer to shareholders.'

'Thank you, Mr. Toller. I appreciate the courtesy.' Courtesy! Hodder thought. It was a small piece of sadism: a phone call sudden enough to frighten a man to death! 'However, I believe I know the terms. One hundred and five pence a share.'

Another silence and Hodder looked at the phone, smiling. At last Toller said, 'Another good guess. One hundred and four, to be precise.'

'It wasn't a guess.'

'May I ask, then, how you knew?'

'Not in the expectation of a reliable answer, Mr. Toller, I'm afraid.'

'Well, I hardly think it will affect the issue.'

Hodder said, 'The market undervalues us. So do you.'

'We'll see.'

'So we shall. Thank you, Mr. Toller. Good-bye.'

Hodder hung up almost ashamed of his own sense of ease; it was wrong that he should feel relaxed and confident. Could it be because he didn't care any more? No, he cared. Enough, at all events, to fight. He put his finger on the intercom button.

'Yes, Mr. Hodder?'

'Toller's announced a bid for us,' Hodder told his secretary.

'A take-over bid, sir?'

'That's right.'

'Oh, Lor!'

He grinned as her mask slipped. 'Don't worry,' he said. 'Worse things happen at sea.'

She said, 'Yes. Thank you,' but doubtfully.

Hodder wondered idly why she might be afraid. She earned thirty pounds a week and could get another job at the same salary, simply by picking up the telephone to one of the secretarial agencies. Perhaps it was because women liked their lives to be unexciting, preferring the evenness of predictable events to the jagged excitements of adventure. Change was unsettling, so change was resented and resisted. No doubt the whole thing was biological anyway. Though, come to think of it, plenty of men put up equally vigorous resistance to change.

Toller had, he thought, acted with remarkable speed, preparing the bid in the few days since Salt's invitation on television. He wondered suddenly whether Salt knew about the bid and reached for the telephone.

'Yes?' Salt's own voice.

'Hugh? It's Alex.'

'Yes?' Salt's tone was cold and formal.

'I was telephoned a few minutes ago by Ray Toller. He's bidding a hundred and four pence cash for Euromob Ordinaries.'

'Thank you, Mr. Hodder.' There was a brief hesitation before the 'Mr. Hodder' which made it the more chilling.'

318

'I take it you knew.'

'Presumption.'

Hodder listened sadly to the acid tone of Salt's voice. The old man clearly hated him now: blamed him for the coup. The fact that he had always liked Salt made it worse; he had been bound by the rules of procedure and the inevitability of facts. He said, 'Not personal presumption, Hugh. I'd like you to believe it.'

'One cannot complain about ambition, Mr. Hodder. Thank you for the information. Good-bye.'

'Hugh!' Hodder heard the pleading quality as his voice sought to continue the contact.

Salt said, 'It is a matter of choice. If one does not agree one must oppose, Mr. Hodder. One aligns oneself by one's own actions. Good-bye.'

The phone clicked and the good-bye was to thirty years of respect and friendship. Hodder's mouth curved in regret, acknowledging the truth of what Salt had said. He'd been trying to have his cake and eat it and the old man, typically, would have none of that. Whatever else Salt might be and have been, arrogant, capricious, cold, he was of a piece, his character his own. In a world where so many people aped others, that was in itself a tribute.

Was it, Hodder wondered, true of himself?

A little more than two hours later, he said, 'Very well, gentlemen. We'd better begin. I'm not entirely sure whether we have one extraordinary meeting of the board, or two. I have called a meeting to discuss today's take-over offer for stock in this corporation, but I believe the company secretary had received earlier a notification from another quarter?' He looked at Keller, who nodded.

'Since that notification preceded mine we must, according to Standing Orders, presume this extraordinary meeting has been called at the request of Sir Kenelm Scrivener and Sir Ranald Duff. I'm sure they will tell us why.'

Scrivener rose. 'It is my belief that the performance of the chairman on television earlier this week was such that it will be impossible for any shareholder, any director, to have confidence

319

in him as chairman. Accordingly, I propose that he be removed from the chair by direction of the Board.'

Hodder felt his face drain. He stared down the table at Scrivener for a moment; Scrivener had resumed his seat and was looking to his front.

'Very well. I accept the motion, of course, if there is a seconder?'

'Second.' Predictably, Sir Ranald Duff.

Hodder looked round the table at the familiar faces that were now turned away. This was a put-up job, a fix; the same kind of fix that had booted Hugh Salt out a week – was it only a week! – earlier. He said, 'Gentlemen, a vote will be unnecessary. You have my resignation, with immediate effect, as chairman of this corporation.'

Scrivener rose rapidly, 'I propose that Mr. Henry Philips do take the chair.'

'Second,' Duff said.

Hodder rose and shrugged, watching Philips rise from the managing director's place at the table and walk towards him. He slipped quickly into Philips' seat, feeling Scrivener's eyes on him threateningly, like cannon.

'I propose that Mr Henry Philips be elected chairman of the Board of this corporation.'

Duff said, 'Second.'

'You have heard the motion,' Philips' face was blander than ever, though a thin film of perspiration glossed his forehead. 'Those in favour? Those against? The motion is carried. I thank you, gentlemen for your confidence in me and I assure you that I shall do everything in my power to increase the efficiency and the profitability of the corporation, for the benefit of shareholders and staff alike.'

Just like that, Hodder thought. A minute from start to finish. It was unbelievable. Then Scrivener was on his feet again quickly.

'Has the chairman noticed that Mr. Hodder remains at the Board table?'

Hodder said, 'Through you, Mr. Chairman, may I say that I resigned as chairman, not as a director. Sir Kenelm must have forgotten that they are separate appointments.' He smiled across at Scrivener. Curious that he now felt so detached that his mind could be so still and observant.

'Easily remedied,' Scrivener said. 'I propose that he be—'

'No need. I resign.'

'Then get out.'

Hodder said, 'My resignation is with effect from midnight tonight.'

Scrivener flushed. 'In that case—'

'What,' Hodder asked Philips gently, 'is my colleague's hurry?'

Harry Philips

PHILIPS took off his glasses, polished the lenses with his breast pocket handkerchief, then put them on again. Why was Scrivener doing this charging bull act? Damn it, he'd *proposed* Hodder a week ago. 'All right, gentlemen,' he said soothingly. 'Mr. Hodder has tendered his resignation with effect from tonight. He has served the corporation with distinction many years. There seems no reason why he should not remain until the end of this meeting. Is there any other business before this Extraordinary Meeting of the Board? No? Then it is closed. Now, Mr. Hodder . . .'

He watched Alex Hodder with satisfaction. Now there was no alternative for him but to get up and leave. But Hodder did not.

'Mr. Hodder, it *is* the end of the meeting.'

Hodder nodded.

'Then you should withdraw.'

'It is my intention,' Hodder said, 'to report to the Board a conversation I had earlier today with the chairman of Toller Securities.'

Damn! Philips said to himself. He made himself smile. 'There can hardly, in the circumstances, be objections to that.'

Duff muttered, 'When a man's dead he should damn' well lie down.'

'But he's not dead when he still has relevant information.' Hodder's voice was gentle. 'And we haven't reached that point in the agenda yet.'

'All right,' Philips said. 'This extraordinary meeting of the Board was called by the previous chairman to give some initial consideration to the terms of a take-over bid for the corporation from Toller Securities. The Corporation's ordinary shares closed tonight in the London Stock Exchange at sixty-seven pence.' Philips glanced from man to man round the table. 'The

322

offer from Toller Securities is, I understand, one hundred and four pence per share.' He wondered whether any of the others managed to get in and so have a useful each-way bet. With the Chairman's seat beneath him and a profit of eighteen thousand pounds in prospect if Toller's bid were to be accepted, he had some cover, at least. 'What,' he asked, 'is the feeling of the meeting?'

'Bloody man.' Philips looked at the speaker. Peter Cole, chairman of Fabricated and Domestic Products Ltd., sounded almost petulant. 'Euromob's worth more than that and we all know it.'

'Indeed,' Philips said. 'Substantially more.' He knew that what was worrying Cole was a simple fact: if Toller owned Euromob, a Toller-nominated director would sit on Cole's board at F. & D. The tungsten-tipped end of a very nasty wedge.

'You don't approve?'

'At that price? It's just a bloody nuisance, a bid like this.'

Hodder said gently. 'Sixty-two per cent. Not bad.'

'You were going to tell us, Mr. Hodder ...' Philips tried to hurry him.'

'But not yet.'

Philips controlled the frown that momentarily lowered his brows. 'Very well, any other views? John?'

John Hyde-Compton stopped tapping his little finger on his blotter and looked up. 'I'm against. Flatly against. I think this corporation has immense potential and it would be tragic if Toller got his hands on it.'

'Thanks, John.' Philips reflected that the first tragedy would be Hyde-Compton's. Toller would move into EUROMOB's publishing division with a big hatchet and an air of enthusiasm. 'It will be interesting to know where we stand. Mr. Lankester?'

Rylands Lankester said, 'I'm afraid that when I have sixty-five pence and somebody offers me better than a pound for it, he doesn't get an argument.'

'You're for acceptance, then?'

'I'm sorry, Mr. Chairman. One simply has to be.'

'Thank you.'

'Of course,' Lankester said, 'we haven't got the offer documents yet. If it's all in some fancy loan stock redeemable half a century hence, I might change my mind.'

James Thornley said, 'From what I hear he's offering cash. God knows where he's raised that much, but cash.'

'In which case—' Lankester spread his hands expressively.

'You tempted, too, James?' Philips had calculated quickly. Thornley, obedient to the rules of the money game, could be expected to recommend acceptance of the offer. Not that things were yet at so formal a stage.

Thornley gave a slightly embarrassed smile. 'I'm afraid so. After all – cash.'

'Lawrence?' Philips turned to Draper, the Plastics Division's withdrawn, thoughtful chairman. Where Cole and Hyde-Compton had good reason to resist the bid, and Lankester and Thornley were almost as predictably ready to accept, Draper was his own man.

'I'm inclined to think not,' he said. Philips nodded; Draper was as useful an ally in this as he would be in many other matters.

'Why?'

Draper smiled and began filling his pipe. 'Balance of arguments, really. Take too long, now.'

Philips experienced a deep sense of relief. He hadn't really been afraid of the result of the discussion, but it was good to have it out of the way. Dissentients in these affairs usually chattered to the papers and if they did so acrimoniously enough, shareholders were even likelier to suspect directorial incompetence and ignore board recommendations. Almost idly, he wondered about Sir Ranald Duff: would Duff go, as he usually did, with Scrivener, or would he be for acceptance? The latter probably, even certainly. It was, Philips reflected, a bloody good job Scrivener had changed his mind and decided to back him for the chair. Hodder's view, whatever it was, didn't matter now: tonight's exercise was more or less academic, part of the ritual of a bid. By the time the formal decision to recommend or reject came to be made, Hodder wouldn't be there.

324

'How do you feel, Sir Ranald?'

Duff looked at him. 'In one word, richer.'

So he was for accepting Toller's offer, too.

'Sir Kenelm?'

Philips sat suddenly very straight, his scalp crawling, as Scrivener said, 'I'll sell. Like a bloody shot.' He stared at the lawyer whose round, flushed, bad-tempered face now looked down at the rosewood surface of the boardroom table. Had he heard aright?

'I'm sorry?'

Scrivener said, with insulting clarity, 'I-will-sell.'

There was a long pause. Philips' eyes went from man to man as his mind flicked the numbers over and over: four would sell, three wouldn't. Even if he brought his casting vote down on the side of resistance, it wouldn't be enough. But what the hell had got into Scrivener? One moment he was pushing Philips into the chair, the next he was going to sell the whole massive corporation! It was a most extraordinary turnabout. Not to say treacherous. Bloody treacherous, in fact!

'Now isn't that interesting, gentlemen?' It was Hodder.

'At least, it's clear and unequivocal,' Duff said. 'If the offer's what he says it is, we recommend acceptance. Right and proper thing, too.'

Philips pursed his lips. 'Well, after all that, shall we pause for a drink? It's going on seven.'

'The ex-chairman has something to tell us,' Scrivener said. 'Let's hear that first.'

Hodder's brow was clear and smooth. 'You wouldn't deny a thirsty man a whisky, Kenelm?'

Philips noticed that Scrivener avoided him, talking determinedly to Duff and Lankester as they helped themselves to drinks but Cole and Hyde-Compton, whistling to keep their spirits up, assured him the shareholders would never sell out to Toller.

Once all of them had glasses in their hands, Hodder, who had been standing alone by the window, turned. 'By the way, there's something in my—' he hesitated briefly, 'in what *was* – no, still *is* my office, that you should see.'

Philips said, 'What's that?'

'The copying machine.'

They trooped through and stood round it. 'Quite a box of tricks isn't it?' Hodder patted the casing.

Philips watched him uneasily. Hodder should not have been behaving like this; was altogether too ... well, too easy. All right, so he wasn't directly ambitious, or had said often enough that he wasn't, but the kind of smack in the face he'd had tonight should have hurt. Yet apparently it hadn't. He wondered why and cursed the built-in security that turned the question without reason into a presentiment of trouble. He said, 'How does it work?'

Hodder clicked a switch and the machine whirred softly. 'Mr. Giesing showed me this afternoon – he's from EURO-MOB, Germany, if anyone doesn't know him – and it was all very simple. You just—' he fed in a sheet of typescript, waited, picked up the copy when it emerged, and handed it to Cole '—do that.'

'Very good,' Cole said. 'As good as any of the others, I should say. Cost?'

'Roughly half.' Hodder was producing other copies and handing them round to Lankester, to Duff, to Hyde-Compton and Draper.

Chairman last, Philips thought in irritation. 'May I?'

'Oh, sorry,' Hodder turned again to the machine. 'Here you are.'

'Thanks.' Philips glanced down at the paper, noting automatically the density of the markings produced on the surface. 'Very g—' he stopped, aware suddenly what the markings meant. He felt himself go cold and the saliva drained from his mouth. The signature of authorization was missing; he'd forgotten to get Salt to sign! Forgotten ... what a thing to forget! He raised his eyes with an effort and looked at Hodder who, calm and infuriatingly relaxed, was waiting. Philips' eyes flickered at the others. Were they looking at copies of the same document? Had Hodder used his blasted machine to distribute a message of doom for *him*? But Hodder met his eyes and shook his head almost imperceptibly. Almost, Philips thought with astonishment, conspiratorially.

'Interesting, isn't it?' Hodder said. 'When you think of the money Xerox have made. Even in Britain, via Rank. And we can work at half the cost.'

'Toller will do just as well with it.' Duff was unconcerned, a bird-in-the-hand man.

'Pity though.' Hodder didn't argue. 'It will make money all over the world.' Philips, his eyes on the paper in Hodder's hands, watched it being folded neatly and tucked into Hodder's pocket. For me, he thought, it is ticking like a bomb. Hodder *must* be got out, and quickly!

'Right,' he said. 'Let's resume.' When they had all taken their places he turned briskly to Hodder. 'Now. You were going to tell us about your conversation with Ray Toller.'

'So I was,' Hodder said. 'But before I do . . .' he paused and looked at Philips, 'I thought our new chairman might like to know which way I incline. And why.'

Philips said, his tone carefully modulated to exclude the irritation and the fear he felt, 'It is an academic matter since your resignation takes effect tonight. I can see no possible reason—'

'All the same, I'll tell you. I am not in favour of *donating* Euromob to Raymond Toller and his crew of financial brigands.'

'Shut up,' Scrivener said loudly. 'Shut up. And get out.'

Hodder flushed. 'My reason, and I should like what I am saying to be minuted, if you please Mr. Secretary, is that the assets of this corporation are now such, in my view, that to hand them to Toller Securities at this price would be the grossest derelection of our duty as directors. And I do not think, Sir Ranald, that you would wish to be accused of that, either personally or as the representative of your company. Nor, I suspect, would you Peter. I'm certain that Lawrence here would be extremely angry. And rightly so.'

Scrivener said, 'Mr. Chairman, this is wasting the board's time. I propose that Mr. Hodder do now withdraw!'

Philips, the image of the paper in Hodder's pocket clear in his mind, said, 'Is that necessary? I mean—'

'Second,' Duff said.

'I wish,' Hodder said, 'that this had not become necessary.'

'Motion before the Board,' Scrivener snapped.

'Then I move to amend it, Mr. Chairman. 'I move that the words "Mr. Hodder" be deleted from the motion and the words "Sir Kenelm Scrivener" be substituted. And further, that after the word "withdraw", the following words be added: "upon the Board's acceptance of his resignation with immediate effect".'

The contrast between the two of them, Philips thought, almost turned the boardroom into a bullring. Hodder was slim and cool, Scrivener all horns and lashing tail. But what could Hodder be up to? He *must* know that he was bound to be humiliated and defeated, yet he seemed almost unconcerned. Only Scrivener's manner disturbed him.

'All right,' he said, 'We have a motion proposed and seconded that—'

Hodder interrupted. 'Amendment first, please, Mr. Chairman.'

Philips cursed under his breath. Aloud he said, 'Of course. I'm sorry. Is there a seconder? No?'

'Second me, Lawrence,' Hodder pleaded with Draper across the table. 'I must speak.'

The silence hung. Philips looked down the table to where tension seemed visibly stretched between Hodder and Scrivener. Draper was puffing his pipe thoughtfully.

'Please, Lawrence. For the wavy navy's sake.'

Draper nodded. 'All right, Alex. Second, Mr. Chairman.'

Hodder's eyes closed. 'If I may speak to my amendment, Mr. Chairman?'

There was no alternative now. Philips dared not risk the exposure of the document in Hodder's pocket. 'Briefly then, Mr. Hodder.'

'Thank you.' Hodder faced Scrivener across the table, but spoke to the Board as a whole. 'There are three major assets of this corporation which have a bearing upon the bid. All are more or less unknown quantities . . .'

Philips allowed himself to breathe again. The document was *not* Hodder's subject.

'. . . but one of them,' Hodder continued, 'is at least tangible. I have just demonstrated it to you – the copier in my office. The second is the property valuation which, as you all know, Sir

328

Hugh Salt said he had had conducted. We do not know it's result, nor who did it. But it is reasonable to suppose that our property holdings are now worth a great deal more than book value. Accordingly I instructed Mr. Lankester last week to arrange for a full valuation of all the corporation's property assets.'

Duff said, 'We've been patient, Hodder, but all this is irrelevant. Time to stop. Your motion's lost, anyway, before it's put. Let's vote Mr. Chairman.'

'There is one more—' Hodder began. Scrivener and Duff looked imperiously up the table at Philips and Philips hesitated, torn between the unspoken threat of the paper in Hodder's pocket, and the demands of his two principal supporters. Not, he thought wryly, that their support would be much use if the Board recommended Toller's bid to the shareholders.

Hodder dropped two words softly into the silence: 'Whistler Island.'

Philips frowned, trying to remember where he'd heard that name in the last few days. For a moment he couldn't. Whistler, Whistler . . . the name rang an infuriatingly loud bell. Of course, Scrivener! The island Scrivener's master, Lord Mingulay, wanted. The paper he'd signed – Philips found his throat was constricted and he swallowed heavily – only that morning. The postdated document. Scrivener was glaring angrily at Hodder.

Scrivener's voice grated. 'It belongs to Lord Mingulay.'

'I think not.'

Philips sat, a helpless spectator now at the confrontation, unable to intervene because to do so was to risk annihilation.

'I tell you,' Scrivener spoke slowly, with emphasis on each word, 'that the conveyance of that property has been properly completed.'

'Completed, perhaps, but improperly,' Hodder said. 'Disgracefully. Probably illegally.'

'How *dare* you!' Scrivener blazed. 'You damned *nothing*. You sit and accuse me!'

'Question, Mr. Chairman!' Hodder turned from Scrivener and now looked coolly towards the chair.

Philips nodded.

'I wish to ask, through you Mr. Chairman, whether the company secretary had the documents prepared by our legal department?'

Keller said, 'Yes, sir.'

'At whose instructions?'

'Sir Kenelm Scrivener's.'

'I see. You signed them, as company secretary?'

'Yes.'

'And gave them to Sir Kenelm?'

'Yes, sir.'

Philips felt as though he were on a spit over a fire. One side of him was being singed with discussion of the island; the other waited to be turned into the flames of exposure as a fiddler.

Hodder went on: 'And you were aware, Mr. Keller, that under the laws of this company, the signature of the chairman is necessary to the disposal of property up to seventy-five thousand pounds. After that, the approval of the entire board is required.'

'Of course.'

Now Philips knew, with sinking heart, what Hodder would do.

Alex Hodder

ALEX HODDER looked without satisfaction at the men round the boardroom table. 'Then Whistler Island cannot be the property of Lord Mingulay.'

Scrivener's face seemed to look at him, red and angry. 'Why not?'

'Because I did not sign it.'

Triumph spread like sunrise across Scrivener's face. 'The present chairman did.'

'And dated it when?'

'Today.'

Peter Cole said, 'What the hell *is* all this about. What *is* Whistler Island anyway?'

'Thank you for some sense in this, Mr. Cole,' Scrivener said. 'It's a speck of rock, that's all. In North America.'

Hodder added. 'Which we own.'

'Owned!'

'And which, it seems, Lord Mingulay wanted.'

Cole said, 'Why?'

'To moor his yacht,' Scrivener snapped.

Hodder said, 'Is that the reason? I thought there might be another.' He glanced at Philips, giving him this one brief chance of escape and Philips grabbed it, sweating. 'I understood it was simply rock. Without value.'

Hodder waited, looking at Scrivener, watching him realize that Hodder knew and not just that he knew, but that many consequences must flow from that knowledge. Then Hodder said, 'The island is virtually made of manganese.' Scrivener's eyelids came down, and he screwed up his eyes. There was cold, naked fear behind them.

Philips said, 'Manganese! I didn't know about any manganese. Honestly. I'd no idea!'

He was ignored. The bigger drama was Scrivener's and the others were watching his agony.

'A director of this company sought,' Hodder said, 'to transfer the company's assets to his own pocket. The fact that he is a solicitor and therefore more clearly aware of what constitutes conspiracy to defraud, makes the offence worse.'

Hodder noticed the expression on Duff's face. Sir Ranald was leaning back, away from Scrivener, as though Scrivener were diseased. Hodder speculated uncharitably that Duff was thinking Scrivener had committed the worst offence of all and been caught out.

In silence, the men waited, watching Scrivener, who still sat with his eyes closed tightly. At last, however, he opened them and tried once more. 'The document,' he said, his voice low, 'is in order. It is signed by the current chairman and the company secretary. The conveyance was proper. Whistler Island no longer belongs to the Corporation.'

Hodder met his eyes. It was almost too easy now. 'You know that is not so because you heard the company secretary. Only if the value of the property is less than seventy-five thousand pounds could such a conveyance have been agreed. And it is worth more, much more. Perhaps a thousand or ten thousand times more. Mr. Chairman, could my amendment be put?'

Philips was white-faced. 'I hardly think there will be need.'

'I agree. By God I do!' Duff stared angrily at Scrivener.

Hodder said, 'Well?'

'What do you intend?' Scrivener's bombast had gone but the remnant of his nerve stared across the table.

'Speaking personally,' Hodder said, 'nothing. But I am sure that the Board is well aware of all the possibilities, from the Law Society to the Metropolitan Police.' He turned to Philips, his hand moving, in a gesture of reminder he knew was unnecessary, to his pocket.

Philips, for a moment, looked as though he might cry, but then his face moved into its normal, over-calm flat repose. 'Gentlemen, I feel that much of this is my doing and that the fault, or some of it, is therefore mine. Accordingly, and since I cannot retain the confidence you showed in electing me to this chair earlier this evening, I must vacate it. I intend, if he will accept nomination for the post, to propose that Mr. Alex Hodder be re-elected chairman.'

A voice said, 'Hear, hear.' Hodder turned his head to see Thornley nodding vigorous agreement.

'No.'

'But you must take it, man. You must!' Duff said. 'Can't be without a chairman and who else is there?

Hodder said evenly, 'There's the whole City, Sir Ranald. Somewhere in there you should find somebody who'll take thirty thousand a year if you press him hard enough.'

'Not in the time.'

Hodder said, 'If you imagine that I shall set myself up for the kind of jackal operation you and Scrivener have conducted today—'

Duff said, 'No.'

'What do you mean, "No?" '

'Circumstances alter cases', Duff said. 'Things aren't what they were an hour ago. Nobody would attack now.'

Hodder smiled. 'I'm not quite as green as that. Somebody else will appear to represent the Mingulay interest and he'll be like Scrivener – he'll want to sell. You, Duff, want to sell. So do Thornley and Lankester and, I imagine, Philips, who has a nice new block of shares to profit by.'

'Nobody'll sell now.' They all swung round to face Scrivener who sat slumped in his chair, eyes bloodshot, still truculent.

Hodder looked at him in surprise. Even now Scrivener was not defeated. With expulsion from the Law Society, the loss of his partnership in his law firm, of his directorships, staring him in the face, with even prison a possibility, the habit of laying down the law was too strong. Hodder said, 'Why not?'

'Because there's money to be made. That's why not.' He glared at Hodder. 'I want a large whisky and a few words with you.'

Alex Hodder listened to the involuntary exhalation of his own breath, the amused half-laugh that Scrivener's monumental impertinence forced from him. What on earth was Scrivener going to say? 'All right,' he said. 'I'll listen.'

333

They returned to the Boardroom a few minutes later and Hodder said, 'Sir Kenelm Scrivener wishes to address the board.'

As Scrivener rose, there was a knock on the door and Hodder's secretary entered apologetically.

'What is it?'

'This new copy of *Viewpoint* Mr. Hodder. I thought you should see . . . here.' Her finger pointed.

'Thank you.' He waved her away and looked at Scrivener, waiting.

Scrivener said, 'The man who would sell a bloody great deposit of manganese is a fool. In addition there is the property and the copier. In my view – my *amended* view – it is likely we'll be better off not selling. And if we tell the tale to the shareholders properly, they won't sell either. We sell some property for a start and promise 'em a bonus and we keep Toller off. Right?'

Heads were nodding.

Scrivener went on. 'It would in my view be a bloody disaster if, at this moment, the in-fighting on this board became public knowledge.' Then amazingly, Kenelm Scrivener laughed. 'For me it would be the biggest imaginable bloody disaster, as must be apparent. So,' he went on, eyes glittering with savage amusement, 'we must stick with Hodder. All of us. Including me.'

Hodder took a cigar from his waistcoat pocket and lit it, listening closely as the clouds of smoke spread aromatically around him. Scrivener's cheek really did not know any bounds.

The voice rasped on, gaining confidence with every word. 'We have to fight. We can't fight behind anybody else – not now, there isn't time. And Alex Hodder isn't stupid. He won't take risks with a treacherous lot like this tableful, gentlemen.'

Draper said, 'So?'

'So we appoint Alex to be both chairman and managing director for a period of ten years at a salary of forty thousand pounds a year. That's his guarantee.'

Philips said, 'And you?'

'I remain a director. I represent an interest that will stay behind Hodder.'

Duff blew his nose loudly. 'Makes sense.'

'Only way out,' Scrivener said.

Hodder chuckled at the expressions on their faces. Thornley's jaw hung slackly open, Hyde-Compton, smoking a cigarette furiously, looked from one face to the next, seeking guidance. Rylands Lankester was concealing a smile without much success. Cole was calculating the odds, Draper puffing on his pipe imperturbably. Only Philips looked distressed.

Lawrence Draper said, 'The status quo?'

Scrivener said, 'No. Two changes. One is that Philips ceases to be managing director. He stays on the Board though, By God he does.'

'To keep my mouth shut?' Philips said bitterly.

'And,' Scrivener added, 'We'll have to co-opt the Secretary over there. What's his name.'

Keller said, 'Keller.'

'You'll be a director of Euromob.'

'Also to keep my mouth shut?'

Hodder felt Scrivener staring at him. The lawyer's eyes were now so bloodshot it was almost, he thought, like looking at rear lights. The thought brought his mind back into focus: in the last minutes he had been in danger of losing his detachment and surrendering to the sheer hilarity of a situation in which a totally discredited and thoroughly disliked man was dictating to the entire board by sheer force of intellect and personality.

'Well?'

Hodder looked up at Scrivener, then idly round the table. 'I don't know.'

'I don't damn well blame you,' Scrivener shouted. 'Not one bloody bit.' He looked round the others. 'He needs to see who's behind him, so stand up.'

One by one, they rose.

'You see, Hodder!'

Hodder tried to control the grin that was anxious to break out round his lips, but failed.

'Very well.'

Scrivener said, 'Mr. Secretary, the last item on tonight's

335

agenda will be to elect you to the board. In the meantime, destroy what minutes you've got there. Neither meeting took place. This one is happening . . .'

A few minutes later, in his own office, Hodder picked up the telephone. When, finally, he got through, he said: 'Alex Hodder here, Mr. Toller. I am returning your courtesy. My board has considered your offer and decided not to recommend its terms to the shareholders.'

'They'll accept it, all the same.'

'I think not, Mr. Toller. Not when they learn certain matters, particularly about massive mineral deposits on our territory.'

Unexpectedly Toller chuckled.

'You're amused?'

Toller said, 'I'm laughing so I won't cry. You found out?'

'You mean *you* knew?'

'About the pyrolusite. The manganese? Of course I knew.'

Hodder said, 'Remarkable. You'll withdraw the offer, of course.'

'Naturally. I can't find that much money. But there is one thing . . .'

'Yes.'

Toller chuckled again. 'I have a hankering for – well, call it mischief. I want to buy one of your magazines.'

'Which one?'

'*Viewpoint.*'

'I see. You've seen it?'

'I have.'

'Even though it isn't out until tomorrow?'

'Will you sell me *Viewpoint*? At a reasonable price?'

Hodder said virtuously, 'It is a very old paper. A British tradition. You would have to guarantee its existence.'

'Of course. I don't want to kill it. In fact I'll try to put new life into it.'

'Then subject to that, I don't see why not. At the proper price. I imagine we can agree.'

Toller said, 'You're very kind, Mr. Hodder. Good luck.'

'Thank you. Good-bye.'

336

Judy Kernon

'ORTHODOX? No, I'm not. I'm not anything except mixed-up.'

Giesing smiled and it pleased her to see the smile because it had a wholly different quality from the apologetic lip twitch he had normally offered. He said, 'That is not true.'

'It's true, Reinhard. On religion I'm the craziest, mixed-up kook.'

'Why?'

'I'm just great on modern thinking. No Jahweh, no Passover and I'll go to the movies on Saturday. But pork – and I kid you not, because I once ate some by accident – pork makes me sick to my stomach. Also I'm great with the dairy dishes.'

'Two of us,' he said.

'You make blintzes?'

He laughed. 'Mixed-up.'

The change in Giesing in the last two weeks had been extraordinary. It was the old business of confession being good for the soul: certainly from the moment he'd told her, Giesing had been a different man. It was not that he had forgotten about the woman in Poland so long ago, because clearly he had not; but he was no longer obsessed. Gradually the incident, vile though it was, was moving to a position in his mind in which it could be tolerated.

'When a girl gets to know you, Giesing,' she said, 'you're not such a bad guy.'

'No?' His brow clouded and Judy prodded him with her forefinger.

'No moping.'

'Agreed. You know, Judy, I miss you.'

'You do? Already?'

'I will miss you. That is what I mean.'

'Yeah. I'll miss you, too.'

They were sitting in the common-room, late on Thursday

evening, in the seats that had become theirs by right of use: a little detached from the others, private but not secret.

'I suppose—' he stopped.

'Mm?'

'It is nothing. I just—'

Judy grinned. 'Spit it out.'

'I want to marry you.'

She felt the blood drain from her face. 'You *what*?'

'No?' He was hesitant, a little hurt. 'You are offended.'

Judy said, 'I'm not offended. I'm startled. Did I hear you correctly?'

'I believe so.'

'I believe so.' She mocked his voice. 'And you wonder I'm surprised? I mean, why me?'

'Because I love you.'

'Oy, oy, oy!' Her eyes searched his face, not quite sure what they were looking for, but identifying the topography of sincerity, the shapes of tenderness. 'I'll say that again: oy, oy, oy!'

'Why do you joke, Judy? Is it funny?'

She shook her head. 'Not funny. Really not funny.'

'Then be serious. Come with me. We will walk outside and talk.'

Judy hesitated for only a moment, then rose and went to put on a coat. In her room, she stared at herself in the mirror, trying to see herself as he must see her, wondering what it could be that made him want to marry her. The face that looked back at her was a used face that showed the marks of time; behind that face, unmistakably, somebody lived. Judy grinned at herself. 'Or something!' she said out loud. 'So how about that, Babe? Thirty-six and yet this guy—' she corrected herself '—this *goy* wants to marry you. Whatcha got, kid? Whatcha got?'

At that moment, for the first time, the fact sank in. He actually wanted to *marry* her: to live with her, sleep with her, spend his life with her! My God!' She stared at herself again as the thoughts pelted in her mind: she'd have to live in Germany. Germany! Give up her job, meet his friends and leave her own. Submerge her independent existence in his. Even children! She was *still* young enough for children. She blinked rapidly under

338

the sheer weight of realization and the realized something else: she was thinking as though she intended to accept. But did she? Did she love him? Could she, with Poland forever in the background; with his secret becoming hers, too, adding itself to her own?

And if she did, could she face him? When the door closed and there were just the two of them, would she be able to go to him without a return of the dreadful, paralysing fear that had always. ... She buttoned her coat quickly and with determination and went to meet him.

'But Reinhard, you don't *know* me!' They were stolling beneath the trees in the park with the lights of the cars in Park Lane like a moving necklace of light away to their right.

'All I need to know. But I must tell you what I have. Can give. You know?'

'Reinhard, you're a successful man. You must—'

'It is right,' he said. 'I have the apartment in which I live. It has two bedrooms and the living rooms and somebody who comes in and cleans and cooks.'

Judy laughed. 'That's nice.'

'And I have a lodge in the Black Forest. Very quiet, very peaceful.'

'Does anybody come in to clean that?'

He frowned. 'It is for holidays. I do that myself.'

She linked her arm through his. 'I am an idiot. Me and my jokes. Maybe we'd better not.'

'No. I get used to your jokes.'

'I can't quite get used to this.'

'I had to ask. I have not met a woman before who—' he stopped.

'You could *tell* me. Is that it?'

He nodded stiffly. 'I told you and you talk to me still. I am not disgusting, to you. Is that so?'

'No, Reinhard, you are not disgusting.'

'I do not know, Judy, what love is. I have avoided love, always. But you, I—' She looked up at him, saw the glint of moisture on his cheek and was moved by it. 'That is why I wish to marry you. If you can understand *that*.'

'The lady always says she's honoured,' Judy said. 'But this lady's frightened.'

'Of me?'

She laughed, holding tighter to his arm. 'Not of you. Of marriage. Of – well pretty well the works, I guess.'

Giesing stopped and half-turned, looking down at her. 'I will be kind, I promise. I am not rough, not mean. It was once, just once!'

'I know.'

'Will you, Judy? I had to ask you today, tonight, while we are still here. Will you?'

She smiled, looking at his eyes. She had never realized before that they were such soft eyes. 'I don't know. I can look at you and think, this is my friend, but to look and say, this is my man . . .'

'Try, Judy. Please try.'

'C'mon, Romeo.' She turned him and they moved off again, and she looked down, watching their feet strike the asphalt path. After a moment she made a little hitch-kick that brought them into step and smiled with pleasure.

'You see, Judy. It is better.'

'Yes,' she said. 'Yes it is.'

'You will tell me?'

'In the morning, Reinhard. I promise.'

They walked on a little further and he said, 'I told you, I do not know what love is. That was wrong. I do know.'

But do *I*? Judy thought. She lay in bed, sleepless, trying to bring order into the chaos of her mind. She was Jewish enough to believe that marriage was for ever; American enough to realize that divorce was always possible if a marriage failed; realistic enough to know he would be a good husband in all the usual senses: a good provider, kindly, masculine, strong. And she had been on her own for a long time. This, possibly, was her last chance.

Did she love him? No, not yet, anyway. Did she *like* him? Yes, very much. Very, very much. In spite of . . . yes, in spite even of that. She tried to imagine that he was in bed now; that the space beside her was not empty but occupied by somebody large and male, a body with hands that would touch her, a man who would want to make love to her. She tried to imagine her own hands were his but it was no use: she knew they weren't. His hands would be strange, hers were familiar. Her own touch was comfort. Would his be even tolerable? Could she, in the knowledge that he loved her, tolerate *this* man? She remembered the last time she had tried, years earlier, and revulsion had seized her and she had had to get out of bed and run and hide, begging the man to go, because his touch had conjured up the nightmare ... after almost twenty years, could she now forget?

She was seventeen and she had been on an illicit visit to the movies down on Forty-Second Street that afternoon. Her father thought she was at the New York library, nearby. In the early fifties it had not been considered dangerous for a girl to be alone in the middle of the world's most exciting city, though the climate of violence was already burgeoning. She was sitting upstairs and at the back, fascinated by the sharp, sophisticated, savage wit of *All About Eve*, the incomparable way with a line of George Sanders, of Bette Davis. She was enraptured; that was why she didn't notice the movement in the all-but-empty cinema until somebody took the seat beside her.

She turned, startled but not afraid, to see who it was and saw a boy of nineteen or twenty with dark, shining hair, grinning at her. Judy began to get up, still unafraid. At seventeen she knew the basic techniques of the pass: if a man sat beside you in a cinema, you moved. If you stayed, that was acquiescence and only girls who weren't nice did that. But before she had got hold of her topcoat, somebody else had appeared from the other side: another grinning youth with the shiny black hair and white teeth, the air of defiance that identified Puerto Ricans.

She should have screamed then, but in the early fifties screams were unusual. Instead, she said, 'Excuse me.'

'You sit down.'

'*Excuse me! I want to get by.*'

That was when she heard the click and glanced down to see the grey gleam of the knife-blade flicking over.

'Sit down.'

She stared at the knife in disbelief. It happened, sure, but to other people. Even so, if she'd acted then, made enough noise, run away, jumped over the seat in front, or screamed, all might have been well. But foolishly she had been more afraid that her father would discover she'd been to the movies, than of these two youths from Puerto Rico. Her eyes on the knife, she sat, and as she did so, she heard another click and looked quickly to her right, where another knife blade now shone in the half-dark. She opened her mouth to scream, then, but she had left it too late; the tip of a knife blade was touching her throat and a low voice said, 'You are very quiet. Understand?'

Terrified, she nodded, and the tiny movement intensified her fear, increasing the pressure of the blade upon her skin.

'Very, very quiet.'

'I haven't any money . . .'

'Shh! Silence or . . .' Now there were two knife blades in the darkness and two grinning faces that moved in and out of vision because now she dared not move her head. There was also a hand that came from her right while a voice on her left whispered, 'You be nice to my friend, eh?' They made her remove stockings and pants, and ultimately almost everything else, but that was only the beginning for they did things to her, and made her do things to them that she had never imagined that people could ever do. And then, at the end, when she had thought it was finished, one of them had disappeared and returned with three more and it had all begun again, an endless, silent agony of degradation in the darkness as five of them used her in every way they could think of.

It was an hour after they had gone before she recovered enough to dress and drag herself out into the chasm of light on Forty-Second Street. She drank coffee and then, feeling stronger, washed herself and tried to restore herself to some sort of order. She knew already that she could never talk about this thing. There was no way in which, if she told anyone, even her father, she would be able to avoid describing what had happened. And she knew she could never say it in words, not to anyone.

And since then. . . . It was not that she hated men. She didn't. She knew that the behaviour of the gang of youths had been atypical and that the world was full of decent men, men who were kind, loyal, faithful, gentle, loving. But she had stayed away from them, putting them off with good-humour and jokiness, keeping them at arm's length. Most of them, anyway. One or two had got through. Sam Cook had got through.

She was twenty– what? Five or so, probably. Still in New York, at any rate, and Sam was on the old *Trib*, a reporter whose mind was intellectually curious, too; whose talents were for perceptive depth-writing. Sam was good, in every sense: still young, still idealistic, good-looking in a crinkly, ugly kind of way, and a very nice guy indeed. With him she made the first break-out from the shell she had built around herself. Sam was trustworthy and she trusted him and he remained trustworthy, not trying to hustle her direct into the nearest bed; instead, understanding that she was nervous, he set himself to supplant rather than to defeat her fears, and succeeded. There was nothing to fear in Sam and they could have been married, but Sam went to Vietnam in the days when it was still Indo-China, and died in a bullet-riddled jeep in a muddy delta.

It was two years after that, in London, that the incident with Gerald McCabe happened. She met him at somebody else's wedding when she was feeling low and neurotic and was miserably conscious that orange-blossom was always for other people and that she was destined to be an old maid. Gerald was smooth, slick, and experienced and opportunistic. She had wondered often whether he sensed her thoughts or whether it was merely that some male radar bleeped and said try here. He was all charm and champagne glasses and when they left the reception he took her on the river and then out to dinner, and then to bed. Only it didn't work, in spite of her determination that it should. She sat with him, cold inside, forcing herself to be kissed and fondled, while all the time revulsion was building and building until she'd had to stop, to jump away and beg him to go and her mind had raced back to that afternoon on Forty-Second Street.

She lay, remembering. Only one man of all the men she'd known had been – what? Good enough? No, not that. Trustworthy? Maybe. And Giesing, was he trustworthy? She smiled a little in the darkness. Yes, Giesing was trustworthy. She'd trust him with anything. And that, Judy realized suddenly, also had to include herself. She said the words softly into the warm space around her: 'I trust him with myself,' and decided they sounded a little pompous and amended the sentence; 'I trust him with me.' Then she decided he was entitled to know and picked up the telephone.

'Mr. Giesing's room please.'

A man's voice, puzzled and defensive; well, it was hardly surprising. 'It *is* four o'clock in the morning, madam.'

Grinning in the darkness, 'Don't worry. He won't mind.' He'd better not mind!

Then Reinhard, sleepy, puzzled. 'Ja?'

She said, 'That's the right word. I thought you'd like to know.'

'Judy?'

'It had better be.'

He laughed. 'Say it again.'

'Ja!'

'In German, we would say Jawohl!'

'Then Jawohl!'

'Ich liebe dich,' he said softly.

'Me too. I know now. Do you realize that? I know now. I love you.'

Jane Roper

'FOR you again, Jane,' Judy Kernon held out the common-room telephone.

'*Express* City Office, Miss Roper. Any idea where Mr. Hodder is? We'd like to talk to him.'

'Sorry. You and everybody else. He's tired I'm afraid. Not talking tonight, anyway.'

'Well, perhaps you have some comment. I mean, twice in a few days Euromob pulls enormous rabbits out of the hat and nobody has even smelt them before.'

Jane said, 'It must be puzzling for everyone.' Nothing there he could quote.

'Including your chairman.'

'Oh?'

'Well it was pretty clear he didn't know about the copier.'

'Was it?'

'And the minerals. Nobody knew a thing, apparently, until tonight.'

'What makes you think that?' she asked.

'Somebody always gets a whisper. These things never happen entirely in secret. But this time – nothing.'

'It must be good security.'

The *Express* man said, 'Off the record, Miss Roper, when was the discovery made?'

'I don't quite know. Months ago, I believe. It had to be assayed or whatever it is they do.'

'And not one word has leaked out! It's difficult to believe.'

'Ours,' Jane said virtuously, 'is a remarkably loyal and united board. And you can quote me.'

Four times in the next fifteen minutes she was called to the telephone. Ray Toller had not, before, been beaten after he had made a bid; not withdrawn one. For tonight, at least, the fact that he had backed off from Euromob was seen as equivalent to Napoleon's retreat from Moscow. It was extraordinary to think

345

of his being beaten off by anybody as gentlemanly as Alex Hodder.

He telephoned her himself a little later and she hurried to her room to take the call in peace. When they'd spoken briefly, earlier, Hodder had simply told her concisely about the manganese and Toller's withdrawal. Now he said, 'You'll need the new picture, Jane. I'm chairman and managing director. That's one thing. And you can announce that we are doing a revaluation of our properties here and in Europe and America. Let them sniff a bit of money for the shareholders. They'll like that.'

'Okay. The entire Press is after you at the moment.'

'I can imagine. But no. Tonight we'll remain very cagey indeed. I might pick somebody out for an interview in a day or two. *Financial Times,* probably. Any questions?'

Jane said, 'There is *one* thing. If you're chairman *and* managing director, what about Mr. Philips? Somebody's bound to ask if he wanted to sell to Toller, or something?' Her heart was beating: had Scrivener kept his word and finished Philips? Would his head now be delivered, on the promised charger?

'Sorry, I forgot. No, he simply resigned as managing director. He remains on the board.'

Damn! Damn! Damn! She controlled her voice carefully. 'If they want to know why?'

'Just readjustment of work, Jane. You can say he will be undertaking special duties for the chairman.'

Jane's lips had tightened and her skin felt tight with fury all across her face. 'Right,' she said. 'Thank you, sir.' Her voice was taut with fury. That bastard, that slimy swine Scrivener had let her down! She could feel tears pricking in her eyes, despair tugging at the corners of her mouth.

'Two other things I almost forgot,' Hodder said. 'Richard Keller has been appointed to the board. And we're selling *Viewpoint.*'

'Selling it?'

'To Raymond Toller. He's promised he'll keep it going. Good night, Jane.'

She put down the telephone in a daze. Philips had survived. Philips was still on the board. Philips had not been dragged down and humiliated. But *she* had! He was still at the top, probably waiting now for his next chance, while *she* had undergone ordeal by Scrivener. And now Scrivener had let her down.

There was a knock at her door. Judy Kernon had come to fetch her to the common-room where a *Daily Telegraph* reporter was waiting. 'Are you all right, Jane?'

'All right? Yes, thanks.' She hurried down the corridor and talked to the *Telegraph*, confirming, denying, saying 'no comment' or 'I don't know' frequently.

After a minute or two, she realized that she was watching Steele, and trying to listen to him. He was describing to Gaunt how the *Viewpoint* article had scared Toller off. When she'd finished with the *Telegraph* she returned quietly to her own room and asked the hotel switchboard to connect her with the common-room.

'Mr. Steele, please.' She waited.

'Hallo!' He sounded bouncy.

'Gerard. It's Jane Roper. I'd like a word with you.'

'Well I'm here. . . .' he paused. 'I thought I saw you, just now.'

'I'm in my room.'

'Eh?'

'Gerard. I must talk to you.'

He tapped at her door a few moments later and when she opened it, stood grinning at her.

'Come in.'

He followed, closing the door noisily. 'I forecast this, you'll remember?'

'What?'

'That *you*'d ask *me*. Remember?'

Oh God! she thought. Was the whole damned world to be filled, tonight, with farce?

'It's not—'

'And I was right, you see. A little gnawing worm of thought – that's all it is at the beginning. Then you begin to think about it seriously.'

She remembered now: that absurd conversation in the pub when he'd told her she would virtually order him into her bed! 'No. It's something else.'

He came towards her, talking; his arms held out wide before

him, ready to embrace her. 'And when you've thought for a while I stop being small and fat and become rather more cuddly? That's it, eh?'

'No,' Jane said, 'that's not it. I didn't ask you for—' She backed away.

'I know why,' Steele said. 'I know exactly why you asked me.'

Jane stopped. Her back was quite literally to the wall; she could move away no farther. Despairingly she watched him approach. Was the world filled entirely with lecherous men? She said, 'Look, Gerard, this is important.'

He was very close, now, his face mirroring the pleasure and anticipation bubbling inside him. 'There's nothing more important, Jane.'

Steele reached for her, then, and Jane watched his podgy hand moving towards her. It seemed to be happening very slowly, almost in a dream, a thing that was not quite to be believed. But then one hand was holding her arm and pulling her towards him and he was thrusting his face at her and she could face it no longer. She wanted to scream, to writhe away, to find somewhere quiet and soothing.

She hit him. Hard, with the flat of her hand on his cheek.

'Stand still and listen!'

Steele snarled, 'You bitch! What are you? Some kind of teaser? Come to my room and I'll slap you. That's your trick, eh?'

Jane had intended if possible to break the news gently. To have told him in the crowded common-room would have been dreadfully cruel. Now she didn't care. She said coldly and distinctly, 'Euromob has sold *Viewpoint*.'

Instantly he paled, his eyes widened and stared at her at first in anxious speculation, then in fear. 'Sold it?'

There should not have been any pleasure in it. She should have been sorry for him, but she couldn't be now. All the same, she was ashamed of the relish with which she said, 'Yes, sold. To Raymond Toller. Try your charm on him!'

Mike Farmer

'WHAT!'

'Yes, just now,' Wendy said. She was crying.

'On the phone? Just like that?'

'Oh, Mike! How could you? How could you tell anyone?'

Farmer said, 'Can't I see you? Please, Wendy. Anywhere?'

'I told you for *your* sake. You went and told somebody else—'

He cut her off. 'Are you at home? I'm coming out there.'

'No, Mike!'

'Yes I am.'

He could hear the agony in her voice as she said, 'No, Mike. I will not see you. Not now and not ever.'

'Please, Wendy.'

'I thought you were different. Honestly, I did. I thought you were different! Well, I'm sorry, but that's it. It's over. . . .'

He must, somehow, keep her talking, prevent the cut-off, the finish, the pain of a final break. 'Tell me exactly what happened.'

'Mr. Graham, he's the partner in charge of Toller's affairs . . . well he telephoned and said the bid had been called off because Euromob knew in advance it was coming.'

Farmer's heart sank. 'Go on.'

'He'd worked out that only five people could have known enough and only two could, at that second, have guessed the price. He was one.'

'And you were the other? Oh, God, Wendy, I'm sorry.'

She said accusingly, 'I expect you thought you'd make a lot of money. Well, I hope it's cost you—'

'I told one person. Just one.'

'So did I.' He could hear no trace of tears now, only cold bitterness.

'But, Wendy, it was the man who—'

349

'The man who told everybody.'

Farmer said desperately, 'Wendy, the job doesn't matter. I'll give you a job with me. A good one. We'd be together.'

Her voice was flat and distant. 'I would not work with you, now . . . or see you. Or talk to you.'

'Please Wendy!'

But she had gone. He telephoned her back immediately, but the phone just rang endlessly and he imagined her sitting there, watching it.

Blast Philips! Damn and sodding well blast bloody Philips. Judas bloody Philips. He didn't bloody well care about anything, Mr. Judas bloody Philips. Just so long as the business was— Farmer smashed his fist into his palm, wishing the palm were Philips' face; wishing there was *something* he could do, some act that would damage Philips as Philips had damaged him. But there wasn't. It was nearly ten p.m. and there wasn't one single thing in the whole wide bloody world that he could do!

Or was there? He put on his coat quickly and left his room, hurrying down to the lobby and outside, jumping into a taxi without tipping the outraged commissionaire. It pulled up at its destination a few minutes later and he let himself into the building and hurried along the corridor to the air-conditioned suite where the grey-enamelled boxes stood. He had begun, out of habit, to put on his white coat, when he realized there was no longer any point and he slipped his key into the lock and entered the suite. Around him there was silence apart from the tiny hum of the air conditioning; for all their power, the computers made no sound except at print out and they were not working now apart from their automatic control functions.

He crossed the rubber floor quietly to the records centre where the tapes and discs stood in their racks, selected the seventeen he wanted and began the erasing process. He was very calm now and he worked neatly and quickly, though there was no need for speed. After all, the whole night stretched before him, and there was nothing else to do . . .

FINAL REPORT: EUROMOB COURSE TWO.

FROM: John LONGBOTTOM: Malcolm TEMPLETON.
TO: M.U.N.P. MANAGEMENT GROUP.
DATE: CLOSING DAY, WEEK TWO

1. The course has been unsuccessful as a result of outside factors.

2. With the displacement of Philips as M.D. of Euromob, it is unlikely further courses will be held unless strong sales pressure applied.

3. Four course members left the corporation's employ before the end of the course: Keyes and Sinclair, have both joined Toller Securities (suggest M.U.N.P. seek to retain contact with view to future retainer of M.U.N.P. by Toller Securities). Co-incidentally Steele will also go to Toller, but for other reasons and he is unlikely, one imagines, to stay or succeed. Farmer: Situation already described.

Letter from John Longbottom to Herny Staines, senior partner, M.U.N.P. By Hand. Friday.

Dear Henry,
Euromob is in chaos. One course member, Mike Farmer, apparently went berserk last night and erased most of their computer records.
Suggest you offer, urgently, all possible help in straightening out: such help, inevitably accepted, will give us insight into their financial state and make it more likely our advisory and course-running services will be retained.
Yrs.

J.L.